AN INHERITANCE OF ASH AND BLOOD

BOOK ONE OF HEIRS OF WAR

JAMIE EDMUNDSON

The Weapon Takers Saga

Toric's Dagger

Bolivar's Sword

The Jalakh Bow

The Giants' Spear

Me Three

Og-Grim-Dog: The Three-Headed Ogre

Og-Grim-Dog and The Dark Lord

Og-Grim-Dog and The War of the Dead

Og-Grim-Dog: Ogre's End Game

Heirs of War

An Inheritance of Ash and Blood

AN INHERITANCE OF ASH AND BLOOD

Book One of Heirs of War

Rarn
Publishing

Author website jamieedmundson.com

Cover: Bastien Jez

Visit the Heirs of War page which includes downloadable colour maps of key locations:

For Uncle John

AUTHOR'S NOTE

An Inheritance of Ash and Blood is the first book in my new epic fantasy series, *Heirs of War.*

For clarity's sake, I should add that it is set in the same world as my first series, *The Weapon Takers Saga.* It begins 13 years after that one ends.

Reading the first series is not required - the two series can be read in either order. The three protagonists of this novel do not appear in the first series (they were all too young). But, naturally enough, some characters from that series reappear and some reference is made to prior events.

Whether this is your first time in Dalriya or not, I hope you enjoy your time there.

Jamie, Yarm, 2022

DRAMATIS PERSONAE

Morbaine

Bastien, Duke of Morbaine, the king's brother
Lord Russell, Marshall of Morbaine
Esterel, Bastien's oldest son
Peyre, Bastien's second son
Sanc, Bastien's third son
Loysse, Bastien's daughter
Cebelia, Loysse's lady maid
Jesper, a forester in the employ of Bastien
Brancat, weapons master of Arbeost
Umbert, son of Russell, Peyre's friend
Brayda, a maid in Arbeost
Rab, a puppy dog
Tadita, Rab's mother

Guivergne

Nicolas, King of Guivergne
Domard, Duke of Martras
Auberi, Duke of Famiens
Gosse, a border lord

Sul, Gosse's man
Caisin, Lord Chancellor of Guivergne
Girard, Royal Steward
Sacha, friend of Esterel, heir of Courion
Coleta, Sacha's sister
Aizi/Aizivella, Coleta's friend
Miles, Lord of Corbenay, friend of Esterel
Florent, friend of Esterel
Raymon, Lord of Auriac
Robert, Raymon's son
Arnoul, Lord of Saliers
Ernst & Gernot, Caisin's thugs
Jehan, guardsman in The Bastion
Lewen, captain of the city guard in Valennes

EMPIRE OF BRASINGIA

Kelland & Luderia
Leopold, Duke of Kelland
Hannelore, Leopold's mother
Liesel, his sister
Inge, adviser to Leopold
Gervase Salvinus, adviser to Leopold
Lord Kass, a nobleman
Olbrecht & Heinke, young noblemen in Witmar

Barissia
Walter, Duke of Barissia
Farred, Walter's partner
Elger, warrior
Syele, warrior

Atrabia
Gavan, Prince of Atrabia
Bron, Gavan's wife

Tegyn, Gavan's daughter
Idris, Gavan's son
Emlyn, Gavan's half-brother
Meinir, Gavan's sister-in-law
Ilar & Macsen, Gavan's nephews

Elsewhere in Brasingia
Jeremias, Duke of Rotelegen
Katrina, Duchess of Rotelegen, sister of Leopold & Liesel
Hilde & Stefan, their children
Coen, Emperor of Brasingia, Duke of Thesse
Friedrich, son and heir of Coen
Otto, Coen's chamberlain
Emmett, Archbishop of Gotbeck

Magnia
King Edgar
Queen Elfled
Ida, their son and heir
Wilchard, royal steward
Brictwin, Edgar's bodyguard
Morlin, Elfled's bodyguard
Herin, a warrior

Other
Rimmon, a Haskan mage
Darda, a warrior of the Sea Caladri
Ezenachi, Lord of the Avakaba
Vincente, a Cordentine

North Dalriya c.671
N
W
E
S
THE STEPPE
THE JALAKH EMPIRE
SAMIR DURG
TOZONGAT
SAFER
HASKANY
KHAROVIA
MASADA
SIMALEK
HERACTUS
LUMBERCO
BAZERNO
HIGH TOWER
KALINTH
PERSALA
CHALIOS
ALTA

TO HALVIA
LANTINEN SEA
GRENDAL
SWARTEN
EDELENY
GRAND CALADRI
GREAT R
BLOOD CALADRI
BARBARIANS
GRIENNA
VALENNES
ROTELEGEN
GUSLAR
RIVER COUSEL
BEARMEN
GUIVERGNE
BURKHARD CASTLE
WITMAR
PENFRYN
TREGLAN
ATRABIA
ITAINEN SEA
ARBEOST
ESSENBERG
KELLAND
LUDERIA
MORBAINE
MIDDER STEPPE
BARISSIA
BRASINGIAN EMPIRE
CONFEDERACY

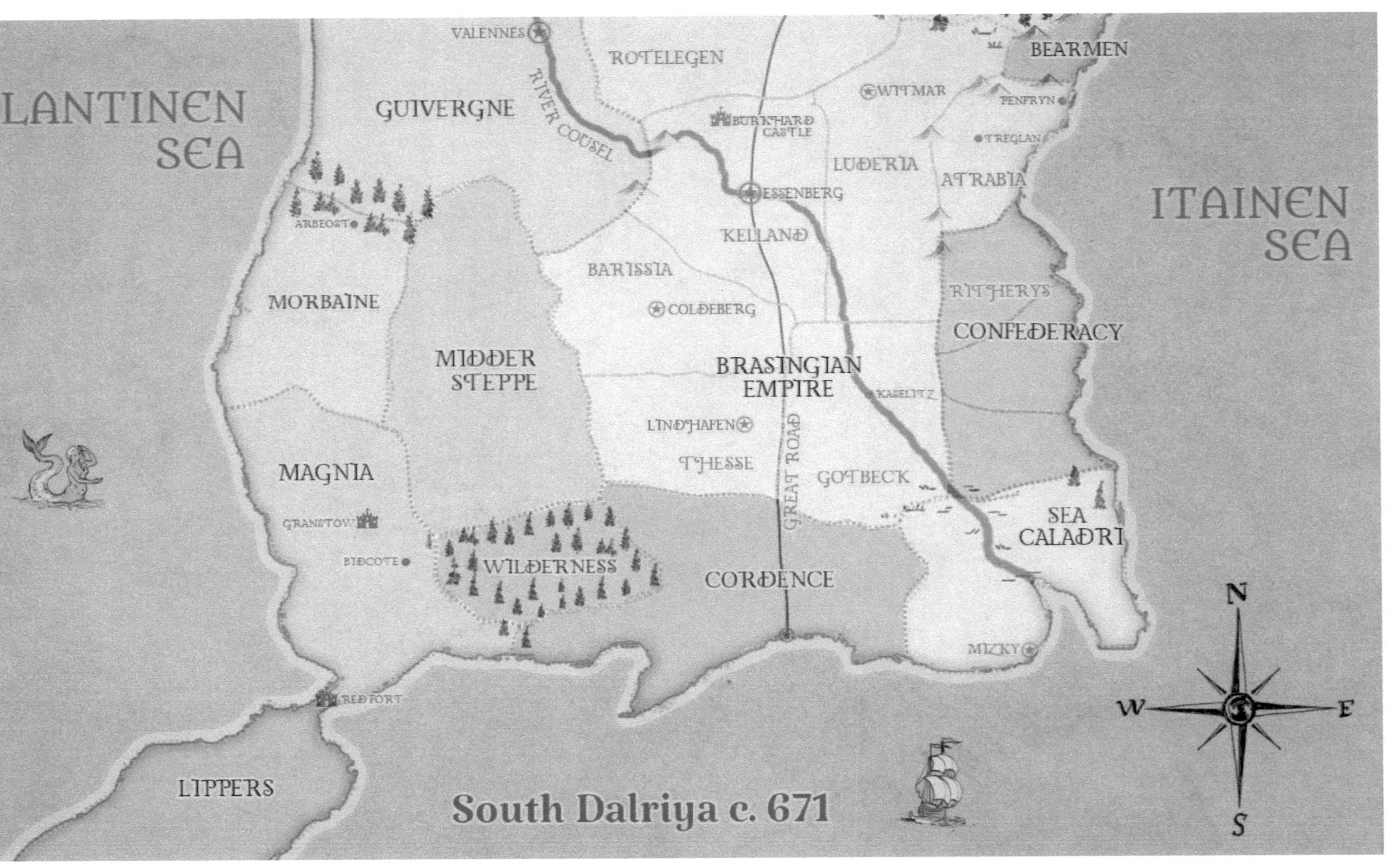

South Dalriya c. 671

PROLOGUE

THE AVAKABA COAST, 671

Darda scratched her claws on the deck as she looked out from the starboard side of the warship.

The coast of Avakaba was alien land to her, though the Caladri crew she sailed with had been plenty of times. It was a simple enough journey, usually. The Avakabi were, so she had always been told, peace-loving and eager to trade. But something had gone wrong. Hence the warship.

Her people had still not recovered from the desolation of their fleet by dragon fire, out in the far Lantinen Sea. They had built new ships since then. But not as many. And the thousands of her people who had burned or drowned could not be so easily replaced. A generation of sailors had been lost. It was only natural that the Caladri should be concerned when four trading vessels that sailed to Avakaba never came home. Hence Darda, a warrior who lived as far from the coast as any Caladri, found herself standing on the deck of a warship. As the captain turned his vessel to the starboard side, Darda looked out with trepidation.

The oarsmen were asked to row hard for a sandy beach where they would make landfall. Looking behind, Darda watched as the three traders, bulkier vessels that sat low in the water, followed the warship.

They were weighed down with timber, metal, and other supplies from their own lands and from other parts of Dalriya. For the Sea Caladri, despite their losses, remained the masters of the Itainen Sea. While they had kept pace well enough to this point, the traders now shrank into the distance, unable to knife through the waves like the warship.

'Everyone off!' the captain called out.

Darda looked around nervously as Caladri sailors vaulted over the side of the ship to land with a splash in the shallows. Surely he didn't mean her as well? But the other soldiers followed the order, too, and she reluctantly gripped the side of the ship. With her other hand, Darda held the scabbard on her belt. She jumped over, her clawed feet sinking into the wet sand as she landed, her hose getting a soaking. Sailors threw ropes down from the deck and she was soon gripping one of them, in a team of four. They moved towards the shore until the rope was taut, then they pulled. All along this side of the ship, and on the other side, too, teams hefted on the ropes, dragging the vessel out of the shallows and then along the dry sand of the beach, until the officers told them they could stop.

Darda was pleased to leave the sailors to it, as the soldiers took up position along the beach. Who knew why those other ships had gone missing? It was more likely they were lost at sea than something had befallen them on land. But soldiers prepared for the worst. She scanned the edges of the beach, where sand gave way to long grass. Out at sea, the first of the traders made its way into the shallows and was pulled up alongside the warship.

'Beware!' came a shout.

Darda swung her neck around sharply to see figures emerging from the grass onto the beach. She made out men and women, carrying boxes and bags with them. Darda drew her sword from its scabbard and the other soldiers did the same. She reckoned twenty, then more came. Maybe thirty now. Tall and well built, their skin was black. The Avakabi.

'It's alright,' said a sailor from behind them in a voice that carried along the beach. 'That's normal. They're bringing their goods to show us.'

Sure enough, stopping at a point still some distance away, the Avakabi unloaded their goods onto the beach. They had wooden boards to lay them on. Darda made out rolls of cloth and clothes and many smaller items, too far away for her to see. Once they were done, the Avakabi stood and waited patiently. When she glanced behind her, she could see that the Caladri merchants from the first trader were lying their goods out in the same way as the next trader was pulled onto the shore.

They waited until the last trader was on the sand.

'Forward!' came the order. Darda and the other soldiers marched over towards the Avakabi, weapons still drawn.

The Avakabi were unperturbed by the armed Caladri approaching them. Indeed, she noticed a dead look in their eyes. They showed no interest in her or the other Caladri at all. Unsettled, she tore her gaze away from them to look at their wares. The small items she could now make out included finely worked gold jewellery. It was strange, she thought, imagining such artistry could be worked by a people who looked like they had no life in them.

The captain of the warship approached with his officers. *No doubt they're used to getting the pick of what's on offer,* Darda supposed.

What's going on here?' the captain demanded, alarm audible in his voice.

Darda looked one way, then another, searching for an enemy. She saw nothing. Turning to the captain, she saw he was pointing at the Avakabi.

'Look at their eyes!' he cried.

They're not supposed to look like that? Darda had time to think.

Then the first blades were drawn. The Avakabi lashed out at the surrounding soldiers. Blood flew as they struck with the element of surprise.

Panic gripped Darda, but she pushed it aside. She launched herself at one assailant, moving in close. Her sword struck the woman's arm, knocking her blade from her grip. The Avakabi threw herself at Darda. Her weight bore Darda down and she landed hard on the sand, breath leaving her chest. The Avakabi gripped Darda's sword hand, trying to take her weapon from her. Darda struggled against the larger woman. She wriggled her body around in the sand, trying to get the upper hand. As she did so, screams surrounded her. Bodies fell to the ground, dark blood wetting the sand. War cries sounded, getting closer. Darda saw feet running. Clawed feet, heading back down the beach to the boats. Followed by many more dark feet as the Avakabi gave chase.

Finally, she could kick out with her legs. Her first kick struck the Avakabi woman in the face, claws drawing long red marks. The woman let go of Darda's sword hand. Her second kick struck her enemy's neck, a wide rent from which her lifeblood spurted out.

For a moment, Darda lay on the ground, expecting an Avakabi blade to end her. She watched as her compatriots sprinted back to the boats, trying to push them into the water. *They're not going to make it,* she realised. The Caladri were forced to let go of ropes; forced to turn and face the Avakabi who came for them. There were so many now. They must have been lying in wait, encouraging the Caladri to let down their guard.

They've not seen me, Darda decided. She summoned the courage to get to her feet and looked around. All the Avakabi were gone, chasing the Caladri towards the boats. Either they hadn't noticed her, or assumed she would be disposed of. But it would only take one of them to see her and call out, and she would be finished. She took a final look at the ships. The Caladri were still fighting, but it was a doomed last stand.

Darda turned and ran the other way, away from the boats. Heart in mouth, she expected more Avakabi to lie in wait for her. But it was clear. She ran through tall grass in a crouch, still grasping her sword, grateful that the terrain might hide her passage. As she ran, her mind raced with plans of escape. She could head north, she decided. Avoid detection. If she kept going, she would reach Magnia. She'd be safe there.

The Caladri have traded with the Avakabi for decades, she told herself. This has never happened before. And what was up with their eyes? She had no answers for the horror she had just witnessed and tried to make herself focus on where she was going.

Then she saw the ships. Four Caladri traders, in a row on the grass up ahead. *So, the Avakabi took them, too. Why?* Her instincts told her to run around them, avoid being seen. But she had unanswered questions, too.

Don't be foolish, Darda told herself, circling around them. She glanced over. There were no Avakabi with the vessels. Then she saw him. A lone man. But not an Avakabi. White-skinned, if bronzed from the sun. He looked Magnian.

Darda made her decision, running towards him. *He's my best chance*, she decided, *of getting out of here. If he's working with them, I'll just strike him down.* She gave her hilt a squeeze.

He looked up, saw her running towards him. He beckoned her to follow him, then moved away, between two of the trading vessels.

Darda followed him, not believing her luck. She got to the end of the two ships and looked for him.

He appeared before she could react, clattering her to the ground. His hands gripped her arms tight, and he placed his weight on her thighs. He was strong, pinning her to the ground. His face appeared above hers. Jet black hair hung down around it.

'No,' Darda said, fear gripping her now. Dead eyes. He was one of them. And she was dead.

Those eyes bored into hers and as he held her down, she sensed a third force enter her.

Not dead, a voice chimed in her mind. *You serve me now.*

Darda tried to speak. She found she couldn't. She found she didn't need to. All she needed to do was obey.

Yes, Master, she told him.

PART I
MORBAINE

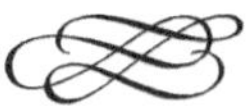

SANC

SANC

ARBEOST, DUCHY OF MORBAINE, 671

'Four more!' Brancat shouted at them.

Sanc lowered his body, arms wobbling with the strain, but he found the strength to push back up.

The boy next to him couldn't, collapsing breathlessly to the ground.

'Three more!' the weapons master demanded.

Sanc stared down at the muddy grass of the training field. He'd landed face first in the dirt more times than he could remember, his body failing him.

Not this time, he told himself. Down and back up, he remembered to breathe as well, something he was prone to forgetting when the pain got too much.

'Two left. Come on Sanc, you can do it.'

Was that encouragement from Brancat? He couldn't recall that happening before.

His entire body shook with the effort now, begging him to stop and let it rest. He nearly gave up, but somehow found himself back in the starting position. Brancat didn't need to tell him he had only one left. He feared that as soon as he bent his arms, he would collapse. He roared with effort as he completed his final press up, then tumbled over onto his back, sucking in air. He felt like he was going to spew up his breakfast. Still, he'd done it. That felt good.

'On your feet, Sanc. Let's see you spar.'

Sanc didn't quite understand. Was this meant to be a reward for finally completing the press-ups challenge? He stood up, limbs protesting at the effort. Brancat handed him one of the wooden sparring swords and took one for himself. The other boys gathered around to watch.

The weapons master towered over him, lean and muscular. Sanc still had the skinny physique of a boy and was a long way off from reaching his adult height. He had watched Peyre shoot up to adult size over the last few years, with a mixture of awe and trepidation. It didn't seem possible that the same thing would happen to him.

'Come on then,' said Brancat. He had the same reluctant tone to his voice that most people had when they spoke to Sanc. He avoided eye contact, and a grimace came to his face, the look one gets when they're about to do an unpleasant chore they've been putting off for a while.

Brancat flicked his sword towards Sanc, forcing him to react. Sanc blocked with his own and stepped to the side. His shoulders protested at having to raise his arms, and he knew they'd stiffen up even worse by this evening.

Brancat followed him, moving left and right, in and out, observing Sanc's footwork. He feinted in, fooling Sanc, who swiped at a weapon that was no longer there. Brancat had withdrawn his sword, redirecting it to smack at Sanc's sword arm. He tsked with disappointment.

Sanc decided that attack was preferable to defence and launched a series of strikes. He went low, high, then wide, aiming for a different target each time. Brancat avoided the assault and smacked him on the leg when he was done, but he murmured 'not bad,' which was about the highest praise Sanc could expect to get. Brancat then launched a flurry of his own, probing Sanc's defences. He tested to see where Sanc was too slow, too eager, not strong enough. Another smack at the end of it made clear that Sanc's defences were breached yet again.

Still, Brancat was nodding to himself, as if he had seen something he liked.

'You're ready for the test,' he decided. 'Maybe tomorrow, if Lord Russell agrees.'

Sanc nodded. 'Thank you,' he said, because some appreciation was expected. In truth, Sanc had no wish to take the test. If he passed, he would move up into the main training class with the older boys, and a longer part of the day would be taken up with exercise and training.

Sanc imagined that when his brothers had been declared ready, a great cheer would have gone up, with plenty of slaps on the back and hands shaken. The boys in his group made little reaction to Sanc's success, save for some sullen looking expressions. Not that Sanc was surprised. Brancat sent them off, his attention already turning to his work with the main class: turning young men into warriors.

If Sanc had little enthusiasm for such things, he now moved with speed and purpose. His free time had begun, and he wanted to make the most of it. The training grounds were on the north-west edge of his father's estate, between the forest and the river, and so he walked across the wet grass back to the Chateau. The other boys talked and laughed and carried on, returning to their homes that clung either side of Arbeost's only road, their voices growing fainter as Sanc pressed on. He had no inclination to return to his room and wash, or change out of his clothes, or any such time wasting. Instead, he made his way to the kitchens. One advantage of being the lord's son was the ability to grab food from the kitchen day or night, and none of the cooks or maids could stop him.

They could tell him off, however.

'Sanc!' Brayda remonstrated as he made his way to the pantry. The young maid looked quite put out. 'You've trailed dirt all along the floor!'

'Sorry!' he said with a smile. He wasn't sure what the fuss was about. Surely it was Brayda's job to keep the floor clean? But he had enough awareness that to say so probably wouldn't go down well.

In the pantry, he discovered another lord's son. Along with his constant companion, Umbert, his brother Peyre was conducting his own raid on the food supplies, shoving much more than Sanc would dream of taking into their carry bags.

'Ah!' Peyre said when Sanc entered. 'I suppose we better leave some for short pants here. How was early morning training?' he asked with a grin.

Since he had turned eighteen last month, Peyre was no longer required to attend training. He no longer seemed to be required to do anything much and so he and Umbert rode off on mysterious expeditions most days, to the gods knew where.

'Brancat says I'm to do the test,' Sanc said. 'Maybe tomorrow.'

'Good work,' said Umbert with a smile, giving him the pat on the back he had missed on the training ground.

'Oh really? I think we should stay to watch that!' said Peyre.

Sanc groaned inwardly. *Why did I feel the need to tell him?* The last thing he wanted was to add to the audience tomorrow.

Peyre and Umbert vacated the pantry, leaving Sanc to it. He remembered a time when they would take him on their adventures, at least sometimes. Someone had once told him that differences in age mattered much less as one got older. But Peyre had now become an adult while he remained a kid. The difference between them had grown wider than ever.

He grabbed bread, cheese, and cooked ham, stuffing them unceremoniously into various pockets. He left the Chateau by the same door he had entered, but rather than heading west back to the training area, he made for the forest that stretched out to the north of the estate. Arbeost had been built close to the treeline, allowing its residents to take full advantage of its resources. The Forest of Morbaine was dense and ancient and none too safe, especially at night. But it supplied the timber for their buildings and the ham Sanc had squashed into his hose pocket. His father spent half his waking life in there—obsessed, in Sanc's opinion, with hunting game.

He walked through the trees that dripped last night's rainfall onto him, the forest moist and earthy smelling. Not far in, he came to the clearing where Jesper had his hut. As he approached, he heard Rab start to bark. The pup seemed to know that Sanc was coming to visit.

He pulled open the door, stepped inside and Rab was on him, his little paws pressed on his thighs and his tongue licking. Tadita came next, an altogether more dignified approach, Rab's mother nuzzling and sniffing. Finally, Jesper looked up from his workbench, where he was making arrows.

'Rab's pleased to see me!' Sanc said.

'Hmm. He can smell your lunch, more like.'

Sanc broke off a piece of cheese and gave it to the pup, then gave Tadita a larger portion.

'Are you alright if Tad and I get going straight away?' Jesper asked him. 'We have traps to inspect, and your father is leading a hunt soon.'

'Of course,' Sanc agreed. He came here to play with Rab almost every day. It gave Jesper and Tadita some time to go out into the forest and get their jobs done. The pup was a bit of a handful: a blur of energy with no common sense.

Jesper gathered his tools, and he and Tadita left the hut. Sanc spent some time with Rab inside, wrestling on the floor in between bites of lunch. They then left and played outside, running around the clearing, in and out of trees, playing chase and fetch. Sanc could feel the stiffness in his chest and arms loosen as he threw sticks for the dog to run down. Rab pelted along, comically fast, his long muzzle and pointed ears giving him a ferocious look. As often as Sanc came to visit, he could still tell how fast the pup was growing. Tadita was long, agile and muscled, and Sanc could see that Rab was going to take after her.

When Jesper returned, Rab was fast asleep after his exertions. He woke, padded over to say hello to his master and mother, before flopping back down next to Sanc on the floor of the hut.

'Did you catch anything?' Sanc asked.

'A fox got caught in a wolf trap. Otherwise, nothing. I think the wolves have moved out of the area, at last. Easier hunting for them elsewhere, now spring has come,' said Jesper. 'How are things with you?'

Sanc thought twice about telling the huntsman. He got butterflies at the thought of all the people he knew watching him. But it was probably rude not to mention it. 'Brancat says I'm to take the test. Tomorrow, if it's agreed.'

'Good. I have no doubts you'll pass it. Brancat wouldn't have put you forward if he thought otherwise. You're not worried about it, are you?'

'Not the test itself.' There wasn't much to be worried about. The test was largely to assess if he had the physical strength to cope with the more intense training that would follow. The weapons element was basic and Sanc knew he had no problems there—he'd been around weapons since he could remember. 'If I pass, they'll make me spend more time training.'

'And what's wrong with that?' Jesper asked as he stoked up his fire and readied a pot of water for cooking. Tadita came over to investigate, knowing that such activity could be a precursor to a meal appearing.

'I don't want to train any more. I just want to stay here and play with Rab.'

'But you're good with weapons, Sanc. You could become a soldier one day.'

'I don't want to be a soldier. And anyway, I'm not that good. Not like Esterel or Peyre.'

'Ha! I know that feeling. I have an older brother, too, remember?'

'Ketil? The one who found Rabigar?' Sanc asked, looking at the pup, now curled into a ball. Sanc loved the stories Jesper told about the heroes of Dalriya. When Jesper allowed Sanc to name the new pup, they had settled on Rab, named after the Krykker hero, Rabigar Din. In fact, Jesper had pulled one of those tricks adults used. He'd told Sanc he could name the dog, and then vetoed all the suggestions he didn't agree with. Still, Rab suited the little fellow so much that Sanc couldn't imagine him being called anything else now.

'Aye. Ketil was older and better than me at everything.'

Sanc turned his attention back to Jesper, a man he found to be so quietly confident in everything he did. He very much doubted the truth of that statement and suspected it was said just to make him feel better. He hated it when adults did that. 'Well, anyway, I already know how to hold a sword and such. I don't want to waste any more of my time training.'

Jesper raised an eyebrow but said nothing for a while, chopping up food with his knife, then placing it into his pot. 'Maybe,' he said at last, 'you'll be something other than a soldier. Your father has two adult sons, after all. What would you choose to be instead?'

Sanc sighed. 'I know you got to choose what you did with your life, Jesper. But most people don't.'

Jesper pursed his lips. 'Maybe you're right. But you're the son of a duke, Sanc. You get more choices than most.'

'Not with these,' Sanc said, pointing with two fingers at his eyes. 'When you have red eyes, everyone else decides what you are. A freak. Because I'm the son of a duke, I'm a freak allowed to live instead of being drowned at birth. That's all I'll ever be.'

'You might find,' said Jesper, 'that those eyes of yours turn out to be a blessing rather than a curse.'

Sanc hated it when adults did that. Pretended it didn't matter, or it was wonderfully unique. As if he was still a stupid child. He got to his feet. 'I'm going now,' he said, heading for the door.

'Good luck tomorrow,' Jesper called after him.

* * *

Quite a few people had turned up to watch Sanc's efforts in the test, commenting that it was an important rite of passage from childhood to becoming an adult. Sanc cared little for such traditions. Nonetheless, a part of him took pleasure from there being people interested enough in him to bother.

Peyre and Umbert had decided to watch. Jesper was there, standing beside Lord Russell, Umbert's father. Umbert had inherited his father's red locks, while many commented that Peyre was the spit of their father; prompting the older folk of Arbeost to say looking at the two young men was like going back in time.

Sanc knew Lord Russell's title of marshall meant he had some sort of responsibility for military affairs, even if he was vague on the details. His father's friend seemed to have a hand in most everything that occurred in the duchy. On the opposite side of the roped-off field, Sanc's sister, Loysse, stood with her maid, Cebelia. Loysse grinned over at him, seemingly oblivious of all the boys gawping at her. Duke Bastien, their father, was absent, though Sanc was hardly surprised at that.

Brancat had him run a circuit of the entire training grounds. He climbed to the top of the rope wall. He threw the hammer—far enough to pass muster, though he heard Peyre's voice ribbing him about the lack of distance.

Finally, it was time to demonstrate some weapon prowess. Brancat had chosen spear and shield. It was hardly Sanc's favourite. He always felt clumsy holding a spear one-handed. Brancat selected one of the older boys for Sanc to fight. He wasn't expected to win, simply give a good account of himself against his superior opponent. At the end of the contest, those gathered about would decide if he had done enough and won promotion to the next class up.

His opponent was Robert. He had a good three years on Sanc and was much bigger. He had arrived at Arbeost from Guivergne a year ago, sent here by his powerful father to be trained as a warrior. Despite the fact he lived in the Chateau and was treated like another of the duke's sons, they'd never had much to do with each other. He looked at Sanc the same as most people did, with a mix of fear and disgust.

The two boys got to it. Confident, Robert came for Sanc, using his spear to go on the attack. Sanc moved his feet, something Brancat had drilled into him so much that it had become second nature. He caught Robert's thrusts on his shield, the impact going all the way up his arm. He struggled, however, to do much with his own spear, concentrating as he was on defence. He would have to show that he could attack as well as defend if he was to impress his audience.

No doubt he telegraphed the effort, forcing himself to lunge forwards; because Robert had gone by the time his blunt spear head reached its target, now empty air. What was more, his opponent had swept his own spear along the ground. Not expecting it, Sanc tripped over the spear and his own feet, landing on the ground rather heavily. He did his best to roll away. But when he got back to his feet, Robert was there. He shoved Sanc with his shield. Still not balanced properly, Sanc fell backwards, landing on his backside.

'Got you,' Robert called out, rather unnecessarily.

Sanc heard more than a few titters of laughter. Not rushing, he moved to get up. Robert offered his spear and Sanc grabbed the shaft, his opponent pulling him back to his feet. Applause greeted this show of chivalry.

'Come on, you little, red-eyed monster,' Robert said quietly, so only Sanc could hear him. 'Everyone's turned out to see a show. Play your part a little. I want your sister to notice me.'

Sanc took his time getting his shield and spear ready. *How glorious it would be if I could send the cocky bastard into the mud,* he thought. *It's a shame I have neither the strength nor skill to make it happen.*

They closed together again. Sanc decided he would try to get some confidence back before he tried another attack. He feinted one way, then quickly moved another, misdirecting his opponent. Robert's spear jabbed into empty space this time. What exactly happened next, Sanc couldn't say for sure. He imagined his opponent stumbling over and falling into the dirt. Not possible, of course. But that's what happened. It was as if a gust of wind came from nowhere and flattened him.

Sanc moved to stand over him. He smacked the butt of his spear into his arse. 'Got you!' he shouted. He looked about the training ground nervously. Maybe it was silly, but for some reason, he felt guilty about Robert's predicament.

No one else seemed to harbour such thoughts, however. Their audience was mainly laughing about it.

'Check to see if there's an arrow sticking out of him, Sanc!' Peyre called out. 'Only a Caladri archer could have felled someone like that!'

More laughter. Not quite the show Robert had wanted. Sanc offered his hand, and the red-faced boy had no choice but to accept the gesture.

Brancat was one of the few who found nothing amusing. With a shake of the head, he declared the contest was over and that Sanc had passed his tests.

Sanc wasn't gloating, however. He mainly felt relief. That the test was over, of course. But more so that whatever had happened to Robert had gone unnoticed.

Then he met eyes with Jesper and Lord Russell and realised that he was sorely mistaken. They were both looking at him as a falcon looks at its prey.

SANC

ARBEOST, DUCHY OF MORBAINE, 671

During the weeks that followed the test, Sanc adjusted to the longer and tougher sessions on the training grounds. There were a score of boys in the group, from Sanc's age up to seventeen; and therefore a range of abilities for Brancat to manage. Sanc wasn't surprised to find himself the smallest and weakest of the group. Neither was he surprised that he remained friendless. But he was the duke's son and his new classmates stopped short of direct insults. Even Robert, who clearly hadn't forgiven him for whatever happened at the end of their fight, restricted himself to the occasional look of cold fury.

The work of the estate followed its familiar cycle. Barley reaping time came. It was usual for Sanc's father to have left the estate by this time of year and begin his tour of the duchy, visiting the places and people he hadn't seen since before winter. It was Loysse who told Sanc why their father had not yet departed. Duke Bastien had agreed to welcome an ambassador from Kelland, in the Empire. Sanc knew all about Kelland, from the stories Jesper told him. Home of the great city of Essenberg, it had been the duchy of the previous emperor, Baldwin, who had fought and died defending Brasingia from the Isharite invasion. If the embassy wasn't of interest in itself, Loysse told him that their oldest sibling, Esterel, had been recalled to Arbeost to coincide with the arrival of the Brasingians.

It was more excitement than Sanc and Loysse were used to, but it became clear their father didn't share their feelings. He chafed at the delay to his routines and became short-tempered. Sanc, who stayed out of the man's way as a matter of course, spent his spare time at Jesper's hut, playing with Rab. Neither the forester, nor Lord Russell for that matter, had spoken to him about Robert's strange fall at the end of their contest. But Sanc did sometimes catch Jesper glancing at him sideways, a look of scrutiny on his face.

Sanc hesitated, therefore, when one day after training, he heard voices from the hut as he approached the door. Jesper and Russell were talking within. Sanc was not under the general impression that people in Arbeost talked much about him, but in these circumstances, he thought it quite possible. He couldn't decide between knocking and letting them know he was there, and scurrying off back the way he had come. Caught between the two options, he somehow found himself taking a third—keeping quiet and listening in to the conversation.

'Essenberg is a nest of vipers,' Jesper was saying, sounding as passionate as Sanc had ever heard him. 'Don't trust anyone from Kelland. You don't need to learn the hard way, like we did.'

'I've had dealings with Lord Kass in the past,' said Russell mildly. 'He was always a trustworthy and reasonable man. It's not like Salvinus is coming to pay us a visit.'

'That was when Baldwin was duke. Many years have passed since then. A lifetime ago, believe me. You expect Kass to have avoided corruption in all that time? I know Bastien doesn't listen to me. But he listens to you.'

Russell sighed. 'Don't overestimate the influence I have these days. But I will speak with him. Warn him of the dangers. It's too late to stop them from coming now. We'll just have to manage the situation as best we can.'

It sounded like the conversation was coming to an end, and Sanc tiptoed away. A visit that had seemed exciting a few moments before suddenly seemed full of menace. Jesper, a man who hunted wolves, and who had fought against Drobax and Dog-men in his younger days, had sounded spooked. Sanc got the distinct impression there was a story from the forester's past that he hadn't shared.

* * *

SANC WAS WORRIED that his sister was a bit too worked up. The return of Esterel, someone universally adored by all who met him, never mind by his little sister; combined with the imminent arrival of a foreign embassy, would have been enough incitement on their own. But when Sanc had confided in her that a sinister plot may—possibly—also be present, it had tipped her a little too far over the edge. She had various plans about how she would spy on the Kellish; how she would excuse herself from the feast hall and keep Sanc up to date with the goings-on.

For, as usual, Sanc would not be in the hall when his father feasted his guests. It was a decision that had been made years ago, when he was a child, and had since become an unquestioned part of life at Arbeost. Sanc did *not* attend feasts. He had a vague memory of being told that it would spare him visitors' graceless questions if he didn't attend. He wasn't sure now if that was something that had really ever been said or was a false memory.

In general, he didn't mind about missing out on boring feasts. Dragging dinner out for longer than was necessary made no sense to him when he could be doing other things. On this occasion, though, he was disappointed. He had wanted to see the Kellish for himself. Also, Loysse getting to do all the espionage work by herself felt a little unfair.

To make up for this, Sanc resolved to catch sight of the Kellish delegation when they arrived. When the day came, he forwent his usual visit to Jesper's hut. Instead, he took up position in the stables where the guest's horses would be kept. He arrived in plenty of time, slipping inside when no one was looking, and found a suitable spot in the hayloft. A small gap in the timber panels allowed him a perfect view of the yard outside. All that remained was to wait. His lunch occupied him for a brief spell. Afterwards, he had to admit that spying wasn't as exciting as he had imagined. During training, he daydreamed about lounging amongst the hay. Doing nothing was more difficult than he had imagined.

Sanc knew he had dozed off, he just wasn't sure for how long. Voices outside encouraged him to use his peephole. They were here! The arrival of the Kellish must have woken him. Half a dozen of them, all on horseback, steam coming off their mounts. Lord Russell appeared, ready to greet them as they dismounted. One of their number approached the Marshall, and they embraced briefly. Sanc heard the man's voice echo around the yard, though he couldn't make out the words. He assumed this must be the leader of the embassy, whom Jesper had named Lord Kass. He had a distinctive look—a great moustache dominating his face. Otherwise, Sanc thought he looked old, large, and pale.

As the stable-hands brought the Kellish horses in for food, drink, and a rub down—the noise carrying up to his hiding place—Sanc studied Kass's companions. They all looked to be of a similar type, younger and leaner than their leader. Dressed in leather armour, they carried weapons, and had the look of warriors. One of them caught his attention. He had a wolfish demeanour and was looking about beyond the yard, as if taking in as much information as he could about Arbeost. *Don't trust anyone from Kelland*, Jesper had said. Sanc didn't like the look of that man. Still, he knew what it was like to be judged on appearance. Also, would a spy look about in such an obvious fashion? *It's often the one you least expect*, Sanc reminded himself.

Russell led Lord Kass out of the yard until they were out of sight. The Chateau was only a short walk away and Loysse had informed him that the ambassador would be given a room upstairs. Sanc watched the Kellish warriors follow behind. The wolf-faced man leaned in to another, as if whispering something. Then they were gone, too.

* * *

LOYSSE TOLD Sanc he should hide in her room. That way, when she excused herself from the feast, she could come up and tell him everything that was going on.

Although she was his sister, Sanc understood why nearly all the boys at Arbeost were infatuated with her. She was very pretty. All the older folk said she got her looks from their mother. Sanc supposed that must be true because she truly looked nothing like their father. When they said such things, it filled him with loss and guilt. He wished he had a memory of what his mother had looked like. But at least he could imagine Loysse grown up.

It wasn't only his sister's beauty, however. She had impeccable manners, was very kind and had a sunny disposition. In short, she behaved in all the ways a young lady was supposed to. He knew it baffled people why she spent any time at all with him. What they didn't realise was that having a younger brother allowed Loysse to act like a total fool from time to time.

The chief obstacle to her plan's success was Cebelia. Decorum would insist that she accompany Loysse to the room and back to the hall, never letting the girl leave her sight.

'Hide under the bed,' Sanc's sister instructed him. 'I will tell Cebelia that I have the squits, and she must leave the room or pass out from the stench.'

Sanc laughed. That was the side of Loysse that only he got to see.

ONCE MORE, Sanc found himself stuck, bored out of his mind. It dawned on him that this spying adventure was a lot more fun for Loysse than it was for him. As time dragged by, with the sounds of music and conversation coming from downstairs, he was increasingly tempted to leave and spend the rest of the evening in Jesper's hut. *Loysse won't mind*, he told himself. *Besides, Rab is probably missing me.*

But then he heard footsteps. He positioned himself right under the centre of the bed, then kept still. Loysse entered, along with Cebelia. There followed a protracted argument, as Loysse encouraged her maid to leave. Cebelia was older than the usual lady's maid. She had been maid to their mother, and it had been decided that she should continue the role with Loysse. The upshot of which was, as Sanc now witnessed, Loysse's maid was wrapped around her little finger. His sister won a victory, and Cebelia left.

Loysse crouched down by the bed and Sanc shifted towards her.

'I'll have to be quick,' she whispered. 'I've learned the reason why both Lord Kass and Esterel are here. The Kellish are sounding father out about a marriage! Between Esterel and Duke Leopold's sister, Liesel.'

Sanc made a face. 'Poor Esterel! Summoned home to be ambushed with a marriage proposal.'

Loysse frowned at him. 'Don't be so childish. Liesel sounds absolutely lovely and beautiful.'

'Well, Kass *would* say that, wouldn't he? He's not going to come all the way here to tell father and Esterel how uniquely ugly and horrible she is, is he? Is this all the information you have?'

Loysse looked offended. 'That wasn't easy to get, you know! I was a considerable distance away from that conversation. I've had to use lip reading and many other stratagems to get it.'

Sanc sighed. 'I'm sorry.' He knew such news was important to her. 'But I am interested in the things Jesper said to Russell. About how Kass may be corrupt. What about the men who came here with him? You remember I had suspicions about the one with a wolfish countenance.'

'How am I supposed to track *their* movements? They're out in the hall somewhere, not sat at the top table.'

Sanc deflated at this comment. This plan of theirs simply hadn't worked. While Kass was spinning everyone along with his talk of a marriage alliance, his agents were roaming about, up to who knew what?

There was a knock at the door. 'Are you done, child?' Cebelia asked.

'Just wiping up!' Loysse called back.

Sanc slapped a hand over his mouth to stop himself from laughing.

The door swung open. 'Good,' came a man's voice.

That wasn't Jesper, was it?

'Because Brancat here is waiting to escort you back to the hall.'

Sanc poked his head out from under the bed. Sure enough, Brancat was waiting, a respectful distance from the door.

'Oh,' said Loysse, taken aback. She stood and moved demurely to stand with her maid, who had a pleased little smirk on her face.

'And if there happens to be anyone else in the room,' Jesper added, with heavy sarcasm, 'I suggest they remain where they are for the rest of the evening.'

The door to the room closed and Sanc heard the disappearing steps of Loysse and her escort. *Alright,* he thought, *I feel a little stupid now. But I wasn't wrong about Kass's men. Why else would Jesper be looking out for us?*

* * *

Lord Kass left Arbeost the next day. No diabolical atrocity had been committed. Quite the reverse, according to Loysse: some tentative sounding out about a marriage alliance appeared to have been the sole reason for the visit. Sanc might well have been tempted to forget about the warning he overheard Jesper giving Lord Russell in his hut. Except for the fact that Jesper, along with Brancat, had stationed themselves outside Loysse's room while the Kellish were here. Why? He wanted to ask Jesper where his fear of the Kellish had come from. But that would inevitably involve admitting to his eavesdropping, and he never quite found the moment or courage to ask.

Meanwhile, daily life returned. His father prepared for his tour of the duchy. Lord Russell and a band of warriors would accompany him. Esterel would return to Guivergne. That meant Peyre would be in charge in Arbeost. *The gods help us,* Sanc prayed.

On the day before Esterel was due to leave, he came to watch Sanc at the training grounds. Sanc had never tried harder to impress than with his brother watching. Esterel shouted advice to Sanc, then to the other boys and, before long, Brancat had invited him to help with the session. Their master told them to listen carefully to what Esterel had to say. He needn't have bothered. Esterel's status as a swordsman was legendary in Arbeost. He'd been gone two years, but reference was still made to his skill with a blade—or indeed, with any weapon. It was known that he could best Brancat before he'd reached adulthood.

Once Esterel had a weapon in hand, Sanc saw him transform. A smile lit his features and never left. And Esterel's smile dazzled. For, just like Loysse, it was acknowledged he had inherited his mother's looks. He was tall, blond-haired, and athletic. Nothing at all like his father, whose hair was jet black where it wasn't grey, and was heavily built and muscular. Peyre was a copy of their father. A great fighter in his own right, Peyre could outlast his opponents with his physicality, or batter them into submission. But Esterel...he did things with a weapon that no one else could. That no one else would think of doing.

He proved it. In each hand he held one of the clumsy wooden swords they used in training so that no one got accidentally sliced. And he took on all twenty of the boys, Sanc included. All at once. They charged him, surrounded him—some of the boys, desperate to get at least a hit in, threw things, before Brancat told them to desist. Through it all Esterel smiled and laughed. He blocked, pivoted, danced around so that the boys hit one another instead of him; threw one sword up into the air, leapt like a cat and caught it, all while deflecting spear and sword thrusts with the other. And then he began to teach. He corrected posture and grip, offered tactical advice to his young opponents. Young, maybe, though some were only three years younger than he was. But he was simply in another league.

Through it all, Sanc knew no one else could have got away with what Esterel did. Anyone else would have been called arrogant, flash, patronising. But the boys who fought him loved it. Loved *him*. And when it was done, Esterel walked off with Sanc by his side. Sanc swelled with pride. He knew nothing else would serve to alter his classmates' perception of him as associating so closely with Esterel. Maybe it still wouldn't change much in the end. But if not, then nothing would.

'You're getting good,' he told Sanc with a surprised tone.

'I'm the worst of the lot.'

'You're the youngest, aren't you?'

'Were you the worst when you were the youngest?'

'Of course I bloody wasn't, Sanc. Did you not just see me in there?' He laughed and Sanc couldn't help but laugh with him.

'What's it like in Valennes?'

Esterel raised an eyebrow and seemed to think about it. 'Very different to Arbeost, of course, as Guivergne is different to Morbaine. So many more people for a start, which makes everything more complicated. It's hard to please everyone in Valennes. Hard to be yourself, maybe I should say.'

Sanc thought about that. 'Why did father send you, exactly?' Esterel had been gone two years. Sanc had been ten when he left. He hadn't fully understood why, and no one really told him anything. He just knew that he was living at their uncle's court now.

'Nicolas is childless, yes?' Esterel said.

'So...when he dies,' Sanc offered, 'you will be his heir?'

'Well, father is next in line, then me. But father grew up in Guivergne, already knows all about it. If I'm destined to be king one day, I need to understand the place. But more than that, I need to spend time with the people there. Make them think I'm one of them. Maybe that's not the best way to put it. But you know what I mean?'

'You need them to think you would be a good king?'

'Yes, that's better. People tend to not like folks they don't know and like folks they do know. Whatever the actual merits of the individual. As unfair as that seems.'

Sanc nodded. He thought Esterel would make an excellent king one day.

ALL THREE OF Esterel's siblings got up to see him off. He had travelled to Morbaine with three of his new friends from Guivergne, and they were all mounted and ready to set off, yawning at one another. It was very early and no one was really awake enough for words. But Sanc could tell that it meant something to Esterel that they had made the effort. There was an emotion on his face he was struggling with; no doubt a part of him didn't want to leave Arbeost.

But he smiled, said a farewell and led his friends north. Sanc, Loysse and Peyre stood watching them disappear for a while.

How lucky I am to have siblings such as these, Sanc mused. *It could be so different.*

'Well I, for one, am getting back into bed,' Peyre declared at last.

Sanc and Loysse grunted their agreement with the sentiment.

Later the same day, their father left Arbeost. Sanc wondered whether Peyre and Loysse stood together to see him off. Did Duke Bastien have a tear in his eye at having to say goodbye? Moments of his family's life he would never see or know.

* * *

Duke Bastien and his eldest son had left Arbeost, but Brancat hadn't. The man was as keen as ever to work his charges. Building fitness, reactions, strength and skill. What a chore. As Sanc left the training grounds behind and headed to the Chateau to grab something to eat, he thought the man must dream about exercising. Maybe he did squats in his sleep?

He made his way to the pantry. No trail of dirt on the floor this time: the grass was dry after a week of fine weather. He had taken to bringing a bag with him, like Peyre and Umbert did. And he put more food in there than he had done a few weeks ago. Brancat's workouts were increasing his appetite.

He left the Chateau for Jesper's hut, looking forward to seeing Rab. Jesper was busy these days. It was birthing season for the deer that lived in the forest. Also, with Sanc's father gone, the daily hunts had stopped. Jesper had to patrol the forest, most of the time with only Tadita for company. After a few words, a grateful Jesper left Sanc with Rab and headed off with Tadita into the trees.

Rab knew that when Sanc arrived it was play time, and he bounded around, found a stick, and delivered it to him expectantly. The pup never seemed to tire of fetch. Sanc didn't mind, since they had such a beautiful place to play in. The forest was green with spring. There were patches of bluebells around the clearing. Jesper had warned Sanc that Rab wasn't allowed to eat them; though getting the puppy to do as he was told wasn't the easiest task.

Suddenly, the game stopped. Rab was stock still, staring into the trees, snarling.

Sanc had never seen him behave like that before—he was such a friendly pup—and he felt instantly on edge. He peered into the trees. Movement. The large bulk of a man, his form partially hidden behind a trunk.

Perhaps seeing he'd been spotted, he revealed himself and walked towards them. He looked vaguely familiar.

Rab began to bark.

Sanc stepped away, into the centre of the clearing. He'd learned enough from Brancat to suspect an ambush. Sure enough, there was a second man, positioned a few yards away from the first. He revealed himself and approached.

'Rab, come back here,' Sanc instructed.

But the dog continued to snarl and bark, as if he was enough to intimidate two grown men.

Something—a crawling sensation on the back of his neck— caused Sanc to spin around. A third man was entering the clearing. The wolf-faced man who had come to Arbeost with Lord Kass. He'd left with him, too, but had evidently returned, along with two others.

Wolf-face held up one hand. 'It's alright, lad. We're no threat. We just got ourselves a bit lost in the woods.'

I'm not stupid enough to fall for that. Even if he hadn't overheard Jesper's warnings about the Kellish, Sanc was sure he would have realised something was deeply wrong with this situation. But what to do? His mind jumped from one option to the next. When Esterel had been surrounded on the training ground, he had fought his way out. But he wasn't Esterel, and he didn't even have a weapon. He could run for it. But could he outrun three grown men? Not likely. Also, he was loath to leave Rab.

'Quiet that dog, will you, Uwe?' Wolf-face said, tension in his voice.

One of the other men moved towards Rab.

'Leave him be!' Sanc shouted. He felt his hands go clammy, his body went stiff and trembled. A pressure was building inside his head.

The second man came too, and Sanc saw a hand go to a knife at his belt.

Sanc unleashed. What he unleashed, and how, he didn't know. But he found both arms outstretched, palms forward, and two bolts of energy left his body and slammed into the two men, knocking them to the ground.

He turned to look at Wolf-face, a wide-eyed stare on the face of the Kellishman.

Sanc felt a wave of exhaustion. His body was shutting down, telling him to lie down and sleep. He staggered. It was all he could do to stay on his feet.

Wolf-face saw his weakness and allowed himself a little smile. 'Nothing personal, lad,' he commiserated, and took a knife from his belt.

As the man approached him, Sanc tried to react but his limbs refused to respond, his mind foggy.

A black blur entered the clearing. Wolf-face was suddenly met with a growling hound, and a full-grown one this time. Tadita. She bared her teeth and barked, a sound so loud it battered Sanc's ears and echoed around the clearing.

Wolf-face made a snarl of his own and lashed out at her with his blade.

'No!' Sanc uttered, a frail sounding cry.

But Tadita was clever. She hadn't gone charging in and now skipped out of the way of the man's swipe, as if she had been expecting it. She moved around him, in and out, deliberately trying to pin him to the spot.

Then Sanc saw Jesper arrive, a bow held close to his body. He was running as fast as he could, no doubt trying to keep up with his hound. He seemed to take in the scene in an instant, fitting an arrow to the string of his weapon, drawing it and aiming at the Kellishman.

'Alright,' said Wolf-face, raising his arms. But it was a bluff. He feinted to go in one direction, then went the other, landing a kick on Tadita. Then he was running at full speed. Straight for Sanc, a murderous look on his face.

This is it, Sanc thought, too spent for anything more.

Jesper's arrow hit its target. The impact, combined with the man's forward momentum, caused him to spin around and crash to the ground, mere feet from Sanc.

The relief that flooded his body finished Sanc off. He was aware of his legs trembling, a falling sensation, then nothing.

* * *

WHEN SANC WOKE, he was in his bedroom in the Chateau. Loysse and Cebelia sat in chairs by his bed. He groaned, his head fuzzy.

Excited, Cebelia left the room to fetch someone.

Loysse took a strange delight in explaining that he had been asleep for two days, while everyone had taken turns caring for him. Piece by piece, his mind recalled that he had been in the clearing outside Jesper's hut when the three Kellishmen had come for him. He pictured the savage expression of the wolf-faced man, intent on killing him. Why? Because he was his father's son? His stomach lurched at that thought. 'Is Peyre safe?'

Loysse raised an eyebrow and frowned, as if unsure whether he was lucid. 'What's Peyre got to do with it?' she asked. 'You took a fall in the forest and banged your head.'

'Took a fall?' he said, his mouth so dry it hurt to speak. He reached out for a cup of water from the table by the bed. Loysse insisted he sit up first before she was willing to hand him the cup. He drank thirstily.

Took a fall? Well, maybe he did fall at the end. But that was hardly the full story.

The door opened and Jesper entered. He gave Sanc a nervous grin that spoke of relief that he was finally awake. 'Thank you, Mistress Loysse,' he said. 'Would you mind if I had a moment with Sanc alone?'

'Of course,' she agreed, getting to her feet. 'Though I'm not sure he's quite clearheaded yet.'

The forester took the empty chair. 'You're feeling alright?'

'I think so,' Sanc answered. He looked at Jesper, troubled by his memories of the encounter.

'Do you remember what happened?' the forester asked.

'You shot that man. Just in time.'

Jesper nodded. 'We can thank Tadita for that. She must have heard Rab's barking. I've never seen her move so fast.' He looked at Sanc. 'Do you remember anything else?'

Did Jesper know, or at least suspect, what he had done to those men? Some dark force had come out of him. He trusted Jesper, to an extent. He had saved his life, after all. But could he trust *anyone* with such knowledge? Would he be cast out, or worse, if people found out about it?

Jesper gave him a sympathetic look, as if he guessed at his thoughts. 'You used magic in the clearing. To defend yourself.'

'Magic?' Sanc thought about it. *Magic?* It couldn't have been. Like the sorcerers in Jesper's stories? The Isharites and the Caladri? A few humans had wielded such powers as well. But it was an incredibly rare thing. 'No,' he insisted. 'I don't have magic.' People in Morbaine saw sorcerers as evildoers, in league with demons and such. That wasn't him.

'I've suspected that you do for a while now. When I saw Robert go flying into the dirt the other day, it all but confirmed it in my mind.'

Sanc recalled the fight. How one moment Robert was lording it over him, the next he was flat on the ground. Sanc hadn't touched him. Afterwards, he'd seen Jesper and Russell staring at him. Did that mean Lord Russell also suspected him? Did his father? That was an unpleasant thought.

Sanc tried to think. Was what happened in that fight so different from what he had done to the two men in the clearing? He had felt so tired afterwards, as if the power he had used was sucked out of him.

He swallowed as thoughts and questions threatened to drown him. 'I don't know what to do, Jesper. I don't know anything about magic. Am I going to be in trouble?'

Jesper grimaced. 'I know nothing of magic, either. But I know someone who does. I will ask him to come see you. I am wary of saying more in case it is the wrong thing to say. Sanc, I need you to do your best to forget about what happened. Try to carry on as normal.'

Carry on as normal? Was he for real? 'But the Kellishmen who came here with Lord Kass—they returned to kill me? Because of my magic? I don't understand. Where are they now? Have you asked them why they were sent to kill me?'

Jesper looked away. 'They're dead.'

'Dead?' His magic had killed them? Did that make him a murderer? Sanc studied Jesper's expression. Or had the forester done it? 'Even the wolf-faced one, who you hit with the arrow?'

'Sanc,' Jesper said, his voice firm. 'They're dead. I buried them out in the forest. You must tell no one what really happened. You fell and banged your head.' He returned his gaze to Sanc, deadly serious. 'Do you understand?'

SANC

ARBEOST, DUCHY OF MORBAINE, 672

Sanc told no one about the three Kellishmen who had attacked him. That didn't mean they left his thoughts for long. During the day, his mind repeated the event over and over. Somewhere out in the forest were the graves of three men. He couldn't escape the guilt that he had killed again. With sorcery. That he had been defending himself didn't change that fact. Each night, his dreams served up a slightly different version of the encounter. Always, though, the nameless, wolf-faced man appeared—closing in on him, intent on murder. He would wake hot and sweaty, sometimes vaguely aware he had been talking in his sleep. It was just as well he had his little room to himself.

For everyone else at Arbeost—except Jesper, of course—nothing had happened. Daily life continued. For Sanc, that meant training with Brancat. The weapons master was pleased to note that Sanc applied himself to his training with more dedication, even if he had no idea why.

Sanc's father and his entourage were away from Arbeost for months, touring each region of Morbaine. It wasn't until the middle of summer that they returned. Not long afterwards, Jesper left for the south, taking Tadita with him. Sanc knew it must be to do with him.

Jesper had spoken of asking an acquaintance to come to Arbeost to help Sanc. But Jesper shared nothing else with him. Sanc suspected Jesper had informed other people about what had happened. Lord Russell, very likely. Maybe his father. Surely, if the Kellish were sending assassins into Morbaine, his father needed to know? But no one spoke with him about it. They wouldn't want to share their thoughts with a red-eyed child who could harness dark magic.

One reason for his suspicions was that his brother Peyre, along with his friend Umbert, started spending more time with him. They helped him look after Rab, who had been left behind by Jesper. The pup slept with Sanc in his room, but during training someone else had to look after him, and often this was Peyre. Sometimes, Peyre and Umbert took Sanc horse riding with them, after Brancat had mentioned that riding a horse was a skill expected of a duke's son. At other times, they would happen to bump into him, as if by coincidence, at odd times and places. Sanc knew full well that Peyre would have done none of these things unless someone had told him to.

It wasn't until the end of Gathering Time that Jesper returned. He was alone. He told Sanc that he had left a message for his acquaintance, but that he couldn't be sure when or even if he would come. It made no sense, the forester maintained, to say more than that. As the weeks went by, no one came to Arbeost, and nothing induced Sanc to call on his powers again. He began, finally, to put the episode to the back of his mind.

A new year began and Sanc turned thirteen in the dead of winter. Loysse presented him with a scarf. She had knitted it herself, and she and Cebelia were very proud of it. Jesper told him that Rab was used to sleeping with him and that it could become a permanent arrangement, if he wanted. That was such good news that Sanc didn't expect anything more.

But that evening, as he was readying himself for bed, there was a knock on his bedroom door. He opened it to find his father standing there. Being in the presence of his father always made Sanc nervous, but that feeling doubled when it was just the two of them. Duke Bastien looked tired, bleary-eyed, the grey hairs on his head and in his beard winning the contest with the black. Sanc could smell the drink on his breath. He tried to imagine his father as a young man, a few years older than Peyre. Happily married.

'You're becoming a man now,' Bastien said, 'leaving childhood behind.' With an iron will, Sanc's father made himself look his son in the eye. It was the look he'd always given him: a look of horror, even if it was dulled by the drink and the thirteen years that had passed. He held out a knife, bone-handled, in a leather sheath. 'You can wear this on your person now, so that people know you are a man.'

So many words competed in Sanc's mind. Things he wanted to say. Most of all, he wanted to say sorry. *I'm sorry I killed mummy. Believe me, no one is sorrier than I am.*

'Thank you, sir,' he said, taking the gift.

Bastien nodded. His lips parted. Were there words he wished to say to Sanc? Words that he'd been unable to utter until now? 'You're welcome,' said Sanc's father. He turned away, uttering a ragged sigh of relief as he left.

* * *

THE FIRST SIGNS of Spring showed, though the training grounds remained as sodden as ever. Sanc wasn't the youngest or the smallest of his group anymore, and he had to admit he found the sessions a bit more bearable than he used to. Not enjoyable, though. That would be going too far.

Having collected his lunch, he marched through the drizzle towards Jesper's hut. Surely, the forester would have his fire going to ward off this pervasive damp? Eating his food by the fire sounded like heaven right now.

When he entered the hut, he was surprised to find a stranger there, who had already taken a spot by the fire. The man stood as Sanc entered, while Rab bounded over to greet him with his usual enthusiasm.

'Play will have to wait awhile today, Rab,' said Jesper good naturedly. 'Sanc, this is Rimmon, the friend I have mentioned to you. Come, we'll all sit by the fire and talk while we eat.'

Oh well, Sanc thought, *at least I'll get dry.* Still, he was nervous of this man. Nervous about the reason he was here. He had allowed himself to put the topic of magic to the back of his mind. For it to reappear without warning was uncomfortable.

Jesper moved Tadita from the fire and put a chair down for Sanc.

He took a seat, glancing at the man Jesper had named Rimmon. He was tall and slim, flame-haired, solemn looking, with chestnut brown eyes that had a pensive intelligence to them. He looked older than Jesper—closer to his father's age. He held out a hand—long, thin fingers—and Sanc shook it.

'It is a pleasure to meet you, Sanc.' He had an accent Sanc had never heard before. 'I have hoped for this day to come. But I understand full well that you are not celebrating. You'd rather not have to deal with it. Trust me, I felt exactly the same once.'

'You're a sorcerer?' Sanc asked.

Rimmon looked at Jesper quizzically.

'I've told him very little about magic. Haven't mentioned you at all. I thought it was best that way.'

Rimmon nodded. 'I don't disagree. I've just never known you to be so discrete, Jesper.'

'Older and wiser,' Jesper replied with a grin.

The exchange between the two men told Sanc they had a shared history—the gentle banter of old friends. It made him relax a little and his curiosity got the better of his caution. 'You were in the wars against Ishari, like Jesper?'

'Oh, he knows all about the war,' Jesper said. 'Doesn't stop asking about it.'

Rimmon gave a smile that turned into a grimace. 'I am Haskan born, Sanc. You know which side Haskany was on?'

Sanc knew alright. 'Arioc became King of Haskany, and the Haskans,' he paused for a breath, worried that saying it out loud might be taken as an insult, 'fought for Ishari.'

'Quite so. My part in those wars was quite different from the usual fireside stories of heroes and villains. As a Haskan, I was recruited to serve Arioc. Then, I fought against him in the army of his wife, Queen

Shira. I was there when she died at the Battle of Simalek. When that rebellion failed, I begged for forgiveness and served Siavash, the new Lord of Ishari. Assigned to the host of a Magnian by the name of Herin, we betrayed Siavash and fought with the Knights of Kalinth at Chalios.' Rimmon paused, studying Sanc's reaction. 'A tale of self-preservation and divided loyalties that contrasts nicely with the usual songs, wouldn't you say?'

Sanc nodded, realised his mouth was open like a bass fish, and closed it. He had to admit, he loved the stories of the heroes of the Isharite Wars: fighting impossible odds such as at the Siege of Chalios in Kalinth or Burkhard Castle in the Empire. He'd never given a thought to the people caught in the middle. When the Haskans were mentioned in the stories, they were the craven tools of the Lords of Ishari. Now, he could see such accounts for the simplistic and dismissive treatment they were.

'You fought with magic?' he asked.

'Yes. It was my magic that saved me. When the other Haskan rebels were getting strung up, I was forgiven. Deemed useful enough to be given a second chance. Our powers aren't always a curse, Sanc. There, that's your first lesson,' he said with a smile.

'Talking of which,' said Jesper, 'Rimmon has agreed to teach you. It will mean spending less time with that dog. Come here after your martial training, as you do anyway, and you will study with Rimmon.'

Sanc didn't like the sound of that. 'No offence and thank you for coming all this way,' he said. 'But I don't want to be a sorcerer. Can't I just not use magic? I haven't used it since those Kellishmen were here.'

'Unfortunately, it doesn't work like that,' said Rimmon. 'If you don't learn how to control your power, you will release it at times of stress and danger, anyway.'

'Like that time you sent Robert flying to the ground,' Jesper added, as if Sanc hadn't already made that link.

'However much you choose to use your magic as an adult, I can guarantee you there will be times you will be glad of it. Let's recreate the last situation you found yourself in,' Rimmon suggested. 'You managed to defend yourself from three armed men, so I've been told, with a little help from Jesper and Tadita. But imagine one of them had a hold of Rab. Or even worse, let's say they had your sister. An indiscriminate blast of magic like you used would have hurt her as well. I can teach you to use your magic with precision; to protect others, as well as yourself.'

There wasn't much Sanc could say to argue with that. 'Alright,' he relented.

THE NEXT DAY, Rimmon told Sanc they would head into the forest, away from prying eyes. He let Sanc lead the way, to a glade where they would have some space. Sanc assumed his father must know that Rimmon was now living in Arbeost. Whether he knew who—what—Rimmon was, he had no idea.

'Every teacher I know of begins the same way,' Rimmon told him. 'Defence. If you can defend against a magical strike, or a weapon strike for that matter, you are infinitely safer. Even if you learn nothing else. Now, don't worry. We don't start with magic. We start with a few of these,' he said, picking up a stick from the forest floor and snapping it into two smaller pieces. 'You are drawing on the same power you used against the men who attacked you. At first, you're probably going to use too much. That's one of the things we're learning here. How to draw the exact amount of power we want.'

Rimmon and Sanc stood facing each other. The Haskan readied a stick.

'Wait,' Sanc said suddenly. 'How do I call the magic?' He held up one hand, palm faced outward. 'Like this?'

Rimmon gave a smile, as if he had been expecting the question. 'Everyone is different. Many people find that using their hands helps them to channel and direct their magic. Others don't use their hands at all. You'll find what works for you.'

'I think I'll use my hands,' Sanc said, finding the idea of using no gesture at all alien.

With no further warning, Rimmon threw a stick. Sanc tried to summon his magic to deflect it. Nothing happened, and as the stick reached him, he caught it instead.

Sanc looked at his new teacher sheepishly. 'I tried.'

'I'd have been surprised if it worked first time. For most people, their magic emerges when it's needed—when they're in danger, or when they're unable to defend themselves by any other means.'

Sanc thought back to the Kellish attackers in the clearing. He'd known that he was outnumbered by stronger men. It made sense that his magic came to the rescue in that situation.

'We're trying to take your magic to the next level—to deploy it in a much more conscious way. We want you to call on it whenever you wish to, not only when you're under duress. It's not easy. Your mind sees no threat from the stick. It knows very well that you can knock it aside or catch it, as you did. Therefore, the magic is not released. This time, it may help you to think about a time when you were scared or felt threatened.'

Sanc thought of the wolf-faced man, running straight for him. That memory had haunted his dreams as well as his waking thoughts. 'Alright, I have one,' he said.

Rimmon threw the stick.

Sanc told himself it wasn't a harmless twig, but the wolf-faced man, come to kill him. He thrust his arm forwards, intending to hurl it far away. Instead of sending the stick spinning away, he obliterated it. While still in mid-air, it shattered into fragments of wood that fell to the forest floor a few feet from where he stood.

'Excellent!' said Rimmon, more enthusiastic than Sanc expected. 'We just need to decrease the power somewhat.'

* * *

OVER THE NEXT FEW DAYS, Sanc worked with Rimmon on his defence. When Sanc had mastered one aspect, Rimmon progressed things: from sticks to stones, thrown with increasing ferocity. Sanc's teacher asked him to do more with the flying objects: drop them to the ground; send them off to the left or right; hold the object in mid-air, then send it back from whence it came. Sanc could feel that this strange power within him was, step by step, coming more firmly under his control. He could decide, with increasing accuracy, exactly how much power was required for what he needed.

The experience was exhausting. Tired out physically from weapons training, he then had to concentrate on his magic. Every time he drew on his power, he could feel it draining energy from him. Rimmon was careful not to push too hard, constantly checking how he felt and stopping the lessons if there was any doubt. Even so, every night Sanc went to his bed feeling depleted, going to sleep as soon as his head hit the pillow.

Elsewhere in Arbeost, Sanc's father remained on the estate, delaying his departure south for the second year in a row. Sanc had little idea why. He knew a messenger had come from Guivergne. Since then, there had been a tension among his father's small group of advisers. Noblemen from Morbaine came to the Chateau and left again, tight-lipped and serious-looking. Something was going on, but everyone knew that Duke Bastien was a cautious man and they would find out only when he decided to let them know.

It was Peyre and Umbert who told Sanc. After morning church, they took him for a ride out east of Arbeost. Past the shepherds' huts, out into the empty and wild country that rolled on for miles until the next settlement. They dismounted on the top of a hillock with a fine view and Peyre laid out a small feast he had gathered from the kitchen, while Umbert saw to their horses.

'There's going to be war,' said his brother, the drama of the statement a little diluted with his mouth full of cheese.

Still, the idea of war sent a shiver of excitement down Sanc's back. He loved Jesper's stories, terrible as they were. There was a part of him that resented the quiet and peaceful part of the world where he lived. Morbaine was one of the few places in Dalriya that had escaped the horrors of the Isharite Wars. He knew it was odd and that he should be grateful for it. Still. How could one have adventures without a bit of danger?

'Tell me everything,' he told his brother.

Peyre grinned. 'Father told me the order has come from Uncle Nicolas. He wants an invasion of the Midder Steppe. The plan is for a royal army from Guivergne to strike from the north, while father leads a force to meet them. They meet and carve out a piece of territory that will link Guivergne and Morbaine more closely. Right now, one has to travel through the forest or the Steppe to get from one to the other.'

An invasion of the Steppe? Sanc knew a bit about the place. Occupied by tribes who travelled about the grassland with their herds. 'But why attack the tribesmen? Have they done something wrong?'

'Exactly,' said Umbert, joining them. 'My pa says Nicolas has some made up excuses for an invasion. But it isn't a just war.'

Peyre frowned. 'It's not like we're taking all their land. They'll still have plenty left. Anyway, I'm more than ready to get my first taste of military action. And Sanc, you're not going to believe this. You're coming as well.'

Peyre was right. That came as a surprise. 'Really?'

'Father told me to tell you. Orders of the king. Says he wants to meet us both.'

That made sense. Sanc wouldn't have believed it was their father's decision. 'I wonder why.'

'I expect it's because Esterel has been talking about us,' said Peyre. 'And anyway, shouldn't an uncle want to meet his nephews? A king his heirs? It's more than a little strange that we've not met him before this. Father has a strained relationship with his brother. That's not hard to see. Maybe this will bring them closer.' He paused, glancing at Umbert. 'What is it?'

'Nothing,' said his friend. 'Well, it's just that my pa has talked of it before.'

'Out with it, you bastard! What do you know about our father that we don't?'

'You swear you won't tell anyone I told you?'

'I swear I'll smash your face in if you don't spit it out right now!'

Umbert looked a little dissatisfied with this oath, but evidently decided to proceed, anyway. 'My pa said King Nicolas and Duke

Bastien were both equally in love with your ma. And that she chose your father over his brother.'

Sanc looked away. He always felt acutely self-conscious when his mother was mentioned in conversation.

Peyre let out a whistle. 'That would explain a lot. And she chose our dad over becoming queen of Guivergne? He must have been a buck when he was younger!'

Sanc and Umbert looked at Peyre with the same, shocked expressions, before all three of them fell about laughing.

LATER, in Jesper's hut, the mood was more sombre.

'I can't believe it,' Rimmon said to Jesper. They, too, had learned of the impending military campaign. Sanc had not known the sorcerer long; but he had certainly never seen him angry before. 'All the work I've been doing, and they decide to fritter away their resources on this nonsense?'

'In fairness,' said Jesper, 'I don't think Duke Bastien is thrilled about it, either. But he can't refuse a direct order from his king. Not without causing even more harm.'

'I understand that,' Rimmon replied. 'I just can't get over the sheer stupidity of it. And now *he's* going to war,' he added, jabbing in Sanc's direction with a thumb.

A bit rude, Sanc thought.

'I don't see a choice but to step up his training in the time we have left,' Rimmon added.

'It's not like they're going to stick him in the front row of the shield wall,' said Jesper.

Rimmon gave his old friend a stare. 'Well, haven't we grown complacent in the last few years? Have you forgotten what can happen when you give an idiot a weapon and an excuse to use it?'

Jesper shrugged. 'Do what you think is right.'

Rimmon looked balefully between Jesper and Sanc. 'I've been thinking about a test involving both of you. Well, no time like the present. Come on. Jesper, you'll need your bow and arrows.' The sorcerer strode outside purposefully.

Sanc and Jesper shared a look—a wordless agreement that this wasn't likely to be good—before they followed him out.

Tadita and Rab came too, the latter with the optimistic expectation that it was play time.

Rimmon led them to the glade where they practised magic. He instructed Sanc to stand at one end and Jesper at the other.

Sanc saw where this was going.

'It's about time you witnessed Sanc's progress,' Rimmon told Jesper. 'Hit him with an arrow.'

'Have you gone mad? First you complain the lad is being sent to war, then you want me to shoot him?'

'He's *going* to war, so he needs to be able to defend himself. You're happy, Sanc?'

Sanc knew he could do it. It had been days since he'd failed to control a stone exactly how he wanted. 'Yes.'

'You're sure?' Jesper asked.

'Ready,' Sanc confirmed calmly.

Jesper shook his head, but went ahead and strung his bow, then nocked an arrow. He aimed high, so that the flight of the arrow would be a fuller arc. It would reduce the force and speed of the missile somewhat, giving Sanc more time to work with.

Sanc focused, knowing that this new threat would require his full attention. The arrow came through the air, almost lazily compared to the stones Rimmon had flung at him. Sanc held one palm out towards the missile, a motion that helped him focus on what he needed to do. The arrow climbed to the apex of its trajectory, then fell towards Sanc with gathering speed. Jesper, Sanc noted, had decided to be deadly accurate. As it fell towards him, Sanc altered its course. Not with too much power, like he had the very first time when he had exploded Rimmon's stick. With the correct amount for what he wanted to do. The arrow bent, its new path making it curve around in mid-air and return in the direction it had come from. Jesper ducked instinctively as his arrow passed safely over his head.

'You cheeky urchin!' Jesper shouted.

Tadita barked in agreement, and Sanc laughed.

'Fetch my arrow,' Jesper instructed his dog. He turned to Rimmon. 'How did he get that good so quickly?'

'You know I have my theories on that,' said Rimmon.

Jesper turned thoughtful, as he and Rimmon strode over to Sanc's position. 'You're going to have to be very careful, Sanc,' Jesper told him, serious now. 'There is nothing more important than the work you are doing with Rimmon. It would be very tempting for a boy of your age to use this magic you have. To show off, or make your life easier, or whatever reason.'

Sanc was a little offended by that. Since when had he been a show off? He was anything but.

'But we can't let people find out what you can do. Such news would spread quickly, to the wrong people. You will have to restrain yourself.'

'I will,' Sanc promised.

Jesper patted him on the shoulder. 'Good lad. Because that was incredible.'

Am I really so good at this? Sanc asked himself, as faithful Tadita returned with the arrow in her mouth. It was difficult to tell. In weapons training, he could compare himself with the other boys. He knew he was nothing special. But with magic? There was only Rimmon, who, of course, was infinitely more experienced. But both men had implied he was a fast learner. *Imagine, a few weeks ago,* he told himself, *if you had been told you could stop an arrow in mid-flight and send it where you wished, all with the power of your mind.*

I am becoming a sorcerer. It was thrilling, disconcerting, and terrifying, all at once.

SANC

ARBEOST, DUCHY OF MORBAINE, 672

As the days passed, the impending invasion of the Midder Steppe began to dominate life in Arbeost. Warriors and wagons of supplies arrived at the settlement. Tents appeared either side of the road as the population swelled. It was all people would talk about. Everyone's jobs were subsumed into the war effort. Brayda and the rest of the kitchen staff were red-faced and short-tempered, having to feed so many new people. Jesper was out in the forest every day, leading a team tasked with logging timber.

For Sanc, it wasn't so bad. Weapons training was suspended, since the training field was full of the warriors who would fight under his father. Many of these men were strangers to one another. When Sanc passed by, there was usually a lot of shouting and jeering and posturing going on as they observed one another's skills, strength or temperament. Peyre was more than often in the centre of things, his voice one of the loudest and most excitable. It wasn't Sanc's scene, so he hadn't minded one bit when Brancat told the members of his class they were forbidden from mixing with the adult warriors. Sometimes he'd see Brancat there, trying to do something more productive. He'd line them up in ranks and get them to practice forming the shield wall, pointing out the gaps or weaknesses. Even then, there was constant chatter and laughter. Sanc realised he knew nothing of war, but what he'd seen so far hadn't been what he'd expected.

Of course, Sanc didn't get to keep all the time he'd saved from weapons training. Rimmon claimed a good portion of it for his lessons in magic, while still being careful not to tire his charge out too much.

'Expending too much energy at once can have serious consequences; even death. Wizards have lost their powers permanently; lost consciousness for days or weeks. That's one reason you're learning how to portion out your power—to use the smallest amount necessary, so that you always have an emergency well to draw on.'

Happy with Sanc's defence against missiles, Rimmon had progressed to melee combat. Again, it was sticks at first, but then he used spear, sword and hammer. He slashed and thrust at Sanc; came from the side, high or low; feinted with the spear blade, then jabbed somewhere else with the butt; came in close with the hammer, using the blunt end and the spike. It was genuinely scary, even though Sanc wasn't particularly impressed with Rimmon's moves. *I suppose if you're a sorcerer, you don't need to learn to fight. Which makes it a little unfair that I have to do both.*

Whatever Rimmon did, Sanc was up to it. For Rimmon had taught him an even stronger defence. Encased in a sphere of magic, it didn't matter where Rimmon's strike hit. Sanc's magic deflected it. The issue with such powerful magic was the amount of energy it took to keep it going. But the more Sanc practised, the easier it got to hold the sphere in place.

They also had a bit more time to talk as well. It was natural for Rimmon to refer to his teachers, the last of whom was Pentas. He was one of the prominent figures from the Isharite Wars. Servant of Madria, he had fooled the Isharites into thinking he worked for them —so much so they had appointed him onto the Council of Seven. Siavash had got his revenge for the sorcerer's betrayal when he had killed Pentas at the Battle on the Pineos in Kalinth.

'So every sorcerer learns the same magic?' Sanc asked his teacher.

'Sort of. We all must learn the basics. But each mage has their own specialities. Either powers that come naturally to them or that they choose to pursue.'

'What do you mean, come naturally?'

'Well,' said Rimmon. 'Take the Magnians: Soren and Belwynn. They could talk to one another in their heads. Telepathy. I have been told it was something that developed between them as children.'

'And the powers people pursue?'

'Pentas worked hard on his powers of teleportation. It was important to him that he could travel about Dalriya at speed.'

'That was how he and Belwynn got to Samir Durg and killed Lord Erkindrix?'

'Quite so.'

'What about you, master?' Sanc asked.

Rimmon made a face. 'Combat magic for the first part of my life. In recent years, you could say I've been working on something similar to teleportation.'

'But you don't want to tell me what it is?' Sanc asked, knowing he was being cheeky.

Rimmon smiled. 'You're a sharp one. I very much want to tell you. When the time is right.'

AT LAST, the tension that had been building for days found some release. Sanc's father ordered his force out of Arbeost. They took the road south: men and women on foot; on horseback; in pulled wagons. They had a few hundred warriors, along with others whose services the duke had decided he needed along the way, or in the Steppe. Among this force was Sanc himself, riding a horse next to his brother, Peyre. He was coming at the request of the king, and despite the sour looks he received, not a single man in this company—not even his father—was going to question a royal order.

Close by were Jesper and Rimmon. Sanc had been a little surprised to hear they were coming as well. But then, there couldn't be many in his father's force more experienced or more useful in war than the forester and the sorcerer. He still didn't know whether anyone but the three of them knew about Rimmon's abilities. If his father, or Lord Russell, knew, they were keeping it to themselves. *Perhaps to protect me.*

Those left behind waved them off, a range of emotions on display. Loysse looked tearful. She was to stay behind, left in charge of Arbeost despite her tender age. Brayda beamed with delight at seeing the back of so many stomachs that would no longer need filling.

'You're probably wondering why our force is currently so small,' Peyre said to him, loud enough for those around them to hear as well.

Sanc hadn't been. Now that Peyre mentioned it, three or four hundred warriors didn't seem so many. But he had no real idea what an appropriate number was. Peyre loved to discuss the details of army management, whereas Sanc found all that rather dull. He liked Jesper's stories, where individual heroes did something brave or spectacular. Jesper didn't dwell so much on food supply chains.

'Father has ordered units to be raised all across Morbaine,' Peyre explained. 'Only now have they been told to move to the border. If we had massed on the border, we would have given the enemy warning of our intentions. You see?'

Sanc responded with what he hoped was the right amount of interest. Not too little to seem rude, but not so much as to encourage his brother to elaborate.

Another aspect of their journey Sanc wasn't prepared for was the slow progress. When he went riding with Peyre and Umbert, they would give their horses their head and speed across the countryside. There were only a handful of horsemen who now rode at a good rate: the scouts. They would investigate the territory ahead, regularly reporting back to Brancat. If the weapons master was told anything of import, he would pass it on Lord Russell. But as far as everyone else was concerned, they travelled at the pace of the slowest: the men who marched on foot and the wagons laden down with timber or other supplies. Put simply, war seemed to be a lot more boring than Sanc had imagined, or Jesper and the storytellers had led him to believe.

They pushed on until evening, when they stopped at a spot with rolling plains around it. A second company of Morbainais, led by a pair of noblemen, had arrived just before them, nearly doubling their numbers. Armed men milled about, greeting their compatriots.

Brancat used his training ground voice to good effect, trying to get the camp organised. 'Come on!' he bellowed, looking about for anyone who might be dawdling so that he could shout at them. 'This is good practice! We'll need to be faster than this in the Steppe!'

Peyre and Sanc weren't spared his exhortations, lending their strength to the preparations. Lengths of timber were unloaded from wagons and driven into the ground, marking out the boundary of their camp and providing some basic defence, even if the wind and rain were to be the only enemies this night. After this was done, the brothers were informed they were on lookout duty. Umbert joined them at their post and the three of them looked out from the barricade at the countryside around their camp, as the sun set and cast long shadows across the unknown terrain.

So used to the familiarity of Arbeost, nestled in the forest, this new vista made Sanc feel both apprehensive and excited, even though he knew they were still in his father's duchy. 'Imagine if the Middians of the Steppe came out of the darkness and attacked our camp,' he whispered, his mind's eye displaying the enemy warriors, creeping through the long grass, dressed in animal skins and holding deadly looking spears.

'I would defend the walls,' said Peyre dismissively, 'then lead a counter-attack to discover the location of their hideout.'

Umbert rolled his eyes behind Peyre's back, and Sanc suppressed a grin.

'I'm wondering about dinner,' said Peyre, evidently done with the game of imagination. 'I'm used to getting what I want from the kitchens, but that's not going to happen on campaign.'

'The hardships of war,' Umbert suggested.

'Indeed, Umbert, indeed,' Peyre agreed. 'I just hope they haven't forgotten about us.'

* * *

THEY WERE UP EARLY the next morning, returning the timber of their portable camp to the wagons, and then heading east. Peyre's analysis was proved correct: more companies of warriors joined theirs until their army had swollen to a few thousand. To Sanc, the grassy plains of eastern Morbaine looked much the same as the grassy plains of the Steppe; nonetheless, there was a border between the two states, and here they stopped for lunch. When they moved on, Bastien left a portion of his force behind with some of the wagons, to begin construction on a wooden fort. Everyone else crossed into the Midder Steppe.

Sanc had imagined that invading the Steppe would have involved a mighty battle on the border, but there was nothing of the sort. Men loosened the weapons in their belts and looked about them a bit more warily, though in this open land surely it would be easy to see the enemy coming. Brancat's scouts still went back and forth. Jesper and Rimmon now rode either side of Sanc and Peyre, an unspoken admission that things had become more dangerous. But otherwise, the Morbainais continued marching at the same pace and in the same direction as before.

After a while, the activity of the scouts became more frenetic. Rumours of Middian activity were passed down from the front of the line. Jesper pointed to the right, where Sanc could just make out the outline of a couple of riders before they turned away. Lord Russell rode down from the front, Umbert and half a dozen other warriors with him. He shouted out a stern warning that the duke's orders were not to attack the Middians and that anyone who disobeyed was to be strung up. They continued on, giving the same warning to the men and women who marched on foot and to those who guarded the lumbering wagons.

'What are we here for, if not to attack the Middians?' Peyre demanded, frustrated. He muttered to himself a while longer before riding ahead to interrogate their father.

'Why does my father want to avoid fighting?' Sanc asked. 'We're going to have to fight them at some point, aren't we?'

'I believe Duke Bastien wishes to avoid unnecessary bloodshed,' said Rimmon. 'I wholeheartedly agree. Perhaps he can even fulfil his objectives without fighting.'

'How can you invade somewhere without a fight?' Sanc asked, confused. Why had his father raised all these warriors if not to attack the enemy?

'It's safe to say your father wasn't in support of this campaign,' said Jesper, keeping his voice quiet so that no one else could overhear. 'He's here because he has to be. He has no real quarrel with the Middians.'

'Then why didn't he argue against it?' Sanc asked, making sure to keep his voice quiet as well.

'I expect he did. But such arguments are best done in private, don't you think?'

Sanc nodded. He understood. It wouldn't do any good to have people know about a disagreement between his father and the king. He felt a little sorry for his father, having to go through with it against his better judgement. He felt a sense of relief that all that burden of politics would fall on the shoulders of Esterel and not him. He thought about what Jesper said some more. 'But the Middians will attack us in the end anyway, won't they? We're taking their lands, after all.'

'I'm sure your father,' Rimmon said, 'is hoping to have such a supe-riority that the Middians won't attack. Remember, your uncle is bringing a force at least this size from the north.'

'But surely the Middians will fight anyway?' Sanc demanded. 'To not fight us would be cowardice.'

'To avoid battle with a superior force isn't cowardice, it's wisdom,' said Jesper. 'What will getting themselves killed do for their families? They may resort to other tactics. Harass us; attack our supplies; look for allies; bide their time. If they have leaders who use their brains instead of their emotions, that's what will happen.'

'But what about the siege of Chalios?' Sanc asked. 'You were both there. You fought against far superior numbers.'

'That was different,' said Rimmon. 'A last stand. We had no alternatives left, other than to concede dominion of Dalriya to the Isharites. Whatever this is,' he said, gesturing at the Morbainais army, 'it's not the end of the world. I hope the Middians decide to live and fight another day.'

A halt was called. A nervous energy spread through the army, as warriors waited for the order to form into battle lines. But time dragged on and no such orders came. Jesper told Sanc to dismount and see to his horse while they waited. They took Rimmon's and led the three animals over to a juicy patch of grass where puddles of water had collected. Sanc sighed.

'What is it, boy?' Jesper demanded, as he picked at the horses' hooves.

'I hadn't thought there would be quite so many boring bits to a war as there seem to be. Your stories aren't like this,' he added, trying to keep an accusatory tone from his voice.

Jesper smiled. 'I shall make sure to include more of the boring parts from now on.' His smile disappeared as he became more serious. 'It's true, most of any war, just like any part of life, is uneventful routine and hard work. Then, occasionally, you get the thrill—or terror—of combat. Most people, when they've experienced that, decide that uneventful routine isn't so bad after all.'

The orders to resume the march came, and Sanc returned to his position in the column. The Morbainais carried on, in the same direction and at the same pace.

Peyre came down the line and returned to his position next to Sanc. 'Only fifty of them at most,' he said. 'Came to complain and argue and demand we leave. No sign of them putting up a fight. Looks like we have a wait on our hands before we actually see some action.'

SANC'S FATHER called an early halt to his army's progress. A huge area was staked out for their camp, so it was no surprise when Sanc, Peyre and Umbert were called upon once more to take their turn at guard duty. Jesper and Rimmon were with them this time, confirming Sanc's suspicions that their father had given the pair the job of ensuring no harm befell his sons. Sanc couldn't understand why such a large area had been claimed until he realised what was happening in the centre of the camp. The foundations for a second fort were being set in place. The carpenters and other craftsmen worked hard until the light faded. It felt suddenly eerie, knowing that the Middians were out there somewhere.

'I wonder if they'll attack?' said Umbert.

'It's possible,' said Jesper, 'if just to make our lives a little uncomfortable. Risky on the first night, though, when we're all sharp-eyed and ready for it.'

'I wish they would,' Peyre declared. 'It's all very well, father building forts and defending our progress. But we need a proper battle, at least to demonstrate that we're the superior force. Hiding behind walls encourages them to think otherwise.'

'Maybe your father would rather see as many men as possible back home safe to their families,' said Rimmon, 'than giving their lives to demonstrate how superior they are.'

Peyre looked Rimmon up and down. 'Who are you again?'

* * *

ON THE NEXT DAY, they left behind around five hundred men to complete work on this second fort. More than sufficient, Sanc assumed, to see off the threat from the local inhabitants.

His father continued his methodical invasion, turning north now for the rendezvous with the Guivergnais. Not long into the afternoon, they stopped and construction began on yet another camp. This, they learned, was the location where the royal army would meet them. First up was a large tent where Bastien would greet his brother.

If the invasion hadn't provided the excitement Sanc had been expecting, at least his thoughts could now turn to meeting the King of Guivergne. Meeting your monarch for the first time was surely a special occasion. That it was his uncle, of course, made it even more so. He did wonder why Nicolas had asked to see him. Peyre thought it was only natural, but Peyre was Peyre and Sanc was Sanc. Few people chose to see *him*. But, he supposed, Nicolas was a king, with all the wisdom and sense of justice that came with such authority.

They were still hauling timber off the wagons when they heard the shouts. The royal army was approaching! He climbed atop a wagon to look. He could see the front ranks quite clearly and behind them a long column of warriors stretching to the horizon. No surprise, he supposed, that the king had more soldiers under his command than his father did. The front ranks stopped and Sanc watched as they broke up and made their own camp, about half a mile away from the Morbainais. A small detachment of riders emerged from the frenetic activity and approached. Trumpets blew as they neared, signalling the royal approach.

'Finished already, Sanc?' Brancat called up.

'No, I—'

'Then let's get on with it. You can gawp in your own time.'

THERE WAS QUITE A WAIT, but eventually, Sanc and Peyre were called for their meeting with the king. They looked at one another as they approached the open entrance to the tent, guarded by half a dozen warriors, sharing in the anticipation.

Upon entering, Sanc was relieved to see it was a small gathering. From Morbaine, there was only his father and Lord Russell. From Guivergne, four men.

One of them was Esterel, his chain mail hauberk framed by a deep red cloak that caught the eye. He came over with a grin, first clasping Peyre in greeting, then Sanc. 'Your Majesty, my brothers, Peyre and Sanc.'

Peyre got down on one knee before one of the men and Sanc quickly followed. When he looked up, he felt a little stupid. Since Nicolas looked so much like their father, he should have known it was the king. An older version, to be sure, but the same dark hair turning grey; the heavy-set build that in the king's case had turned more to fat. His face was jowly, his eyes tired looking. The king gestured that they should stand—Sanc waited for Peyre to get to his feet first, just in case.

'Welcome,' said Nicolas, his voice deep toned and gravelly. He looked them over. 'Neither take after your mother, Esterel, as you do.'

Esterel gave a smile at the odd comment.

He's always been good at smiling, Sanc thought. He glanced at Bastien, who had a face like thunder. *Father, not so much.*

'This is Domard, Duke of Martras,' Esterel said, introducing the older of the other two men, who nodded at Peyre and Sanc with good humour, 'and Auberi, Duke of Famiens.'

The second man was younger, about the same age as Esterel. But where Esterel was all long hair and flamboyance, Auberi had his hair cropped to his scalp and wore a simple soldier's garb. He was staring at Sanc, a frown on his face, as if he couldn't quite believe what he was seeing. Sanc was used to that and ignored it.

'This one has the family look,' Nicolas continued relentlessly, gesturing at Peyre. Then it was Sanc's turn. The King of Guivergne looked into his eyes without fear, unlike most people. 'So, this is the creature that killed my Alienor,' he said—a longing, far away tone to his voice. 'You promised to protect her,' he said to Sanc's father, using a matter-of-fact tone that contrasted with the accusatory words.

Bastien's face went red with anger. He started forward, Russell gripping his arm to keep him in place. Peyre looked shocked; Esterel mortified. Domard looked away; even Auberi tore his gaze from Sanc's eyes and looked elsewhere, uncomfortable.

The king's lips curved slightly, taking pleasure in the reactions. Sanc rarely got angry when people said such things to him, but he felt it now. For his family more than for himself. *Nicolas is a king.* That had made him expect better of him. He was disappointed to find that he was just a man, with weakness and flaws for all to see.

If my own uncle and king talks to me in such a way, what hope is there for me in this world?

· · ·

SHORTLY AFTER SANC and Peyre escaped the tent, Esterel found them. 'I'm sorry about that,' he said. 'I didn't see it coming.'

'It's alright,' said Sanc, embarrassed. 'It's not your fault.'

'He's a lonely, bitter man,' said Esterel. 'He's not all bad. But he has a terrible relationship with father. That's who he was trying to hurt back there. There's a history between them.'

'We know,' said Peyre.

Esterel looked at him quizzically.

'Umbert told us about him and mother.'

'I see.'

Sanc felt most sorry for Esterel now, having to spend his time in the royal court trying to please that man.

'I swear,' said Peyre, holding up finger and thumb, 'I was this close to knocking his block off.'

'Well,' said Esterel, allowing himself a smile. 'That would probably have made things worse.'

Sanc couldn't help but laugh. 'Imagine—' he said, suddenly finding the idea of it hysterical.

Even Peyre was smiling now.

Esterel patted Sanc on the shoulder. 'That's the spirit. If it's any consolation, the invasion has gone remarkably well. We encountered some brief opposition, but otherwise our progress has been almost as smooth as yours. There's not an awful lot the Middians can do about it, at least right now. We hope they'll respond to the suggestion of a treaty.'

'They're just going to give up their land?' Peyre asked, incredulous.

'Nicolas is ready to offer them a reasonable deal. The danger for them is if they don't come to terms now, we take more. As for whether they stick to any agreement, that's less likely. No doubt they'll try to persuade the other tribes of the Steppe to support them. But that's not going to happen any time soon. Anyhow, you'll be alright?'

'I'm fine,' Sanc answered. 'I will go for a walk by myself for a little and clear my head.'

'Good. Well, I'd better get back.'

Esterel returned to the tent to serve the king while Sanc went for his walk. He needed some time to himself—time he was used to getting back home at Arbeost. On campaign, it felt like everyone was in each other's space all the time. He walked over towards the far end of camp, interested in inspecting the Guivergnais camp that was being established next to theirs. The royal army required a larger space to accommodate all their people. But there was no attempt to build anything permanent over there, whereas his father had enough spare materials to begin the construction of yet another fort.

Sanc was so involved in his observations that he didn't notice the four boys approach until they were on him.

'This is him,' said a familiar voice. Robert.

The three boys he was with all looked to be a similar age to Robert, at least two or three years older than Sanc. They wore high quality clothes and armour, identifying them as the sons of high-ranking noblemen.

'He looks like a sorcerer,' one of them said, as if confirming a recent conversation.

Sanc could feel the disgust coming off them as they stared into his eyes. He could sense the violence in the air, but he didn't know what to say to stop it. He had the feeling nothing he could say would help.

'That's how he beat me in combat,' Robert said. 'I couldn't take my revenge in Morbaine, living with his father. But I'm free now.'

'We don't tolerate demon-talkers in Guivergne,' said his friend. 'Come on.'

Two of the boys came for him. Sanc felt his magic stir as they approached. It was only natural to want to defend himself, and he had to concentrate on controlling his powers to allow them to grab his arms without reacting. He knew he couldn't use magic against these boys. They would run and tell their fathers. Even being a duke's son wouldn't be enough to save him.

Robert's fist slammed into his solar plexus. Sanc gasped like a fish, suddenly unable to breathe. He would have collapsed to the ground, but the boys held him up by the arms. His magic screamed to be released—to shoot out at the boys restraining him; to punish Robert. He kept telling himself not to lose control.

He felt a blow to the mouth that rocked his head backwards. He tasted blood. He heard a shout, and then he was released, sagging to the ground. Groggy, he sat up.

Robert was on the ground, blood spurting from his nose. Standing over him was Peyre, eyes blazing with fury. His brother looked about him, mouthing as if trying to speak, but too furious to get any words out.

Behind him, Umbert had a hold of the fourth boy and pushed him away from the encounter.

The two boys who had been holding Sanc backed away from Peyre. He looked more than ready to hit someone else. One of them glanced at Robert. 'What have you done?' he cried. 'Is he dead?'

Sanc looked at Robert, his vision slowly focusing. Apart from the blood dribbling from his nose, he looked like he had fallen asleep.

Oh no, Sanc said to himself. *Please don't be dead.*

To FIND himself back before his king so soon was hardly what Sanc would have wished for. In these circumstances, it was excruciating.

At least Robert is alive, Sanc told himself. He sat on the floor with a cold cloth to his face, looking totally miserable and embarrassed about what was going on around him.

Nicolas had been asked to give justice. It was the fathers of the boys from Guivergne who were pressing the matter, complaining to the king about what Peyre had done. The four noblemen glared at Sanc, even though it was clear as day that he had simply been a victim in the encounter. Duke Bastien glared at Robert, a boy who had lived with him for so long and who he'd treated like one of his sons. Peyre glared at the other three boys, as if he still had some punching to do. King Nicolas glared at the four noblemen, making their protestations. For all the king's faults, Sanc detected a distaste on his uncle's part at making such a meal over a punch up that had got out of hand.

But there was politics going on here. That was obvious to Sanc, even if he was mostly ignorant about who these men were or why they wanted to make trouble for his family.

When the noblemen were done, King Nicolas turned to his brother with an air of reluctance. 'What do you say to the charges, Duke Bastien?'

Sanc's father looked at his brother, stone-faced. 'I admit to my son's part in them,' he said, with a look at Peyre. He looked at Russell who nodded at him. 'As punishment, I banish both Peyre and Umbert from Morbaine. They will leave tomorrow, if Your Majesty agrees to it.'

Peyre's jaw dropped open.

Nicolas was wide-eyed with shock. 'Well. That is ample punishment in my book. I trust my lords feel the same?' he added, with a look to his noblemen that suggested they'd be wise to agree.

Taken aback themselves, Robert's father and his friends had to agree. Everyone was suddenly keen to vacate the tent. Duke Bastien strode for the exit, signalling for his family to come with him. As a group, they strode away some distance, before Bastien stopped, ready to speak.

'Let me make it clear,' he said. 'I find no fault in what you did today, Peyre and Umbert. The decision I took in there was purely to help Esterel with his task in Valennes. Let them think they've bested us; that may not be such a bad thing. I've had it in mind for a while that it is time for you to leave Arbeost, Peyre. Lord Russell will take you to Coldeberg, where you will serve Duke Walter. He is a good man, and it will do you good to experience a new environment. Do you understand?'

'Yes, father.'

'Umbert, I would be very grateful if you would accompany my son. I know it's asking a lot.'

'I am happy to go, Your Grace.'

'Good lads. Do me proud in Barissia. We'll see you again, when the time is right.'

Duke Bastien looked at Sanc. *Does he blame me for what happened?* But as usual, his father walked away with nothing to say, Lord Russell following him.

Peyre, Umbert and Sanc watched them go.

'Well,' said Peyre at last. 'What a bloody day.' He glanced at Sanc.

Sanc wondered if he was being paranoid, but was there something in that look? He thought back to when Robert and his friends attacked him. He had been so busy trying not to use magic. Maybe Peyre felt he should have done more to fight them off? Had he dishonoured his family? Sanc wished he could tell his brother about his magic, but that would be foolish.

'Thanks for getting them off me,' he said, thinking it sounded lame and childish as soon as he'd said it. 'I have to go.'

He walked off. He'd not gone far when Jesper and Rimmon came marching over.

'Duke Bastien's just given me a dirty look,' said Jesper, looking at Sanc with a wary expression. 'Have we missed something?'

'I don't want to talk about it.'

THE REMAINDER of the campaign was a miserable few days for Sanc. Lord Russell left the next morning for the east, taking his two charges with him. Sanc couldn't help but feel responsible for Peyre and Umbert's banishment. Jesper and Rimmon now stuck to him like glue, as if they were at fault for not protecting him. That made him feel even worse.

The day after Peyre left, the leaders of the local Middian tribes came to the camp to discuss terms with the king. As Esterel had suggested, they were ready to accept some loss of land, given the presence of an army thousands strong, and the construction of forts that allowed the invaders to keep what they had won. For the king's part, he was keen for the campaign to be over quickly, at minimal expense. Some warriors were required to stay, to garrison the new forts. These, in turn, would encourage settlers to take a chance in the Steppe, with free land and a new start.

Esterel came to say goodbye before he left, back to Guivergne. Sanc began the return journey to Arbeost with his father's army. Jesper and Rimmon rode with him. Even so, Sanc couldn't shake off the feeling of loneliness that settled on him like a shroud.

PART II
BRASINGIA

PEYRE * LIESEL

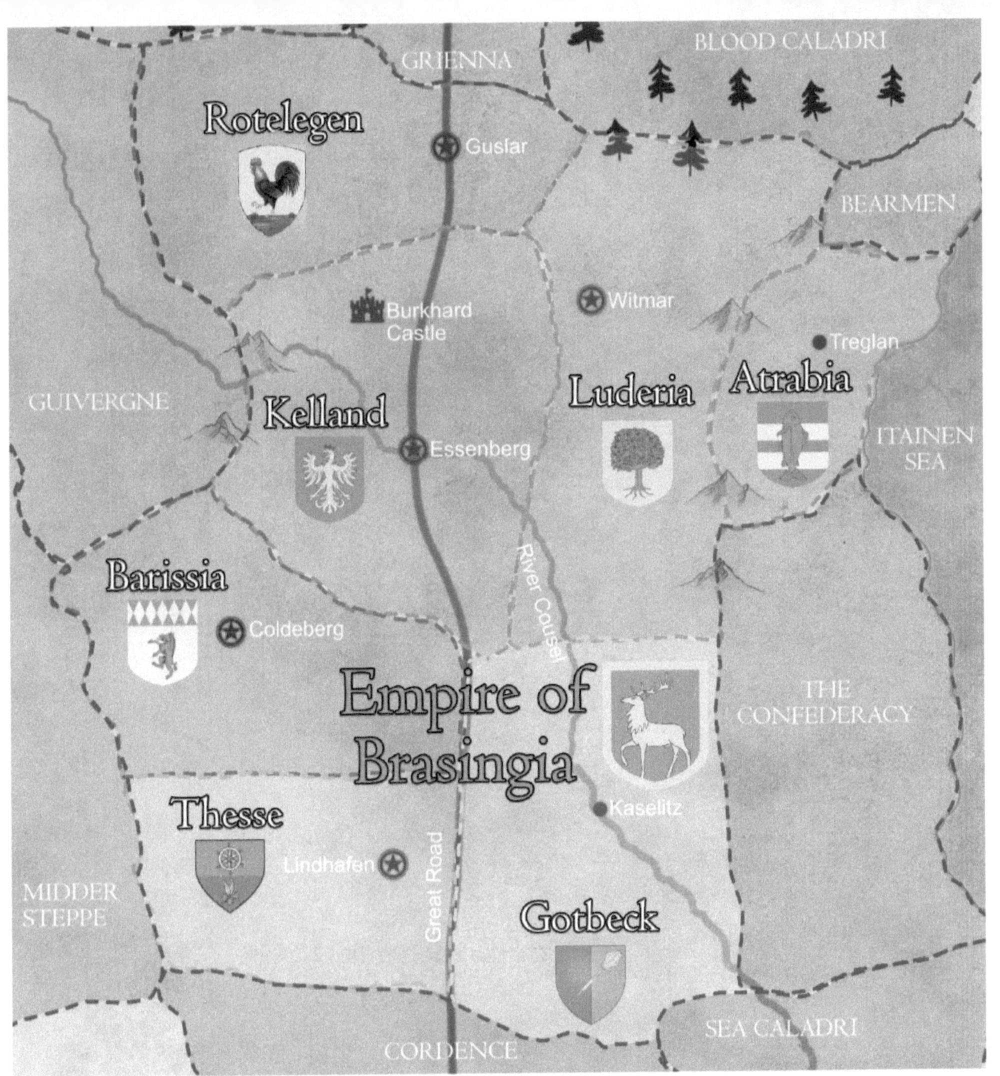
GRIENNA
BLOOD CALADRI
Rotelegen
Guslar
BEARMEN
Burkhard
Castle
Witmar
Treglan
GUIVERGNE
Kelland
Luderia
Atrabia
ITAINEN
SEA
Essenberg
River Causel
Barissia
Coldeberg
Empire of
Brasingia
THE
CONFEDERACY
Kaselitz
Thesse
Lindhafen
Great Road
MIDDER
STEPPE
Gotbeck
SEA CALADRI
CORDENCE

PEYRE

COLDEBERG, DUCHY OF BARISSIA, 672

The barman deposited another tray of drinks onto the table.

Peyre grabbed a pint of beer, taking it to his lips for a swig, before he thought better of it. 'Cheers!' he said, holding the mug up.

'Cheers!' cried his companions, slamming their drinks together.

There is no doubt, Peyre told himself, as he took a few gulps of foamy goodness, *that life in Coldeberg agrees with me. I didn't know what I was missing.* The castle; the shops; so many people, from all walks of life. City life was so busy and exciting, compared with the painfully slow world of Arbeost he had left behind. *I could almost weep for all the lost time.*

The bars. Full of cheap beer and friendly girls. And in many of the bars—such as his current haunt, The Boot and Saddle—the girls loved foreigners.

'So you see, one day,' Umbert was explaining to two new acquaintances, 'Peyre's brother will be King of Guivergne.'

'Oh!' gasped the brunette.

'I think *you* should be the king,' said the blonde, giving Peyre a look.

'Don't be stupid,' said Peyre. 'Esterel will be king.'

'But Peyre will become Duke of Morbaine,' said Umbert, trying to rescue his boasting.

'Duke of Morbaine!' repeated the brunette. 'With everyone bowing to you and calling you "Your Grace!"' she giggled.

'Is Morbaine a large duchy?' asked the blonde, as if she was inspecting the size of a steak in the market.

'Of course it is,' said Peyre irritably. 'At least the size of Barissia.' How could these people not know such basic facts about the outside world? If these two girls weren't quite so attractive he would have moved on by now.

'And I will be *Lord Chief Adviser to the Duke,*' said Umbert.

'Lord Chief Adviser!' repeated the brunette, batting her eyelids at Umbert.

PEYRE WOKE in his bed in his room in Coldeberg Castle. His head was pounding, and he gradually recalled the events of the night before. *Too much drink. Feel like I'm going to be sick.* He looked over to the other side of the bed, where a sprawl of blonde hair covered the pillow next to his. *Oh. It's all coming back to me.* He carefully lifted the blankets, to reveal the curve of a back, the peachy roundness of buttocks. He gently replaced the covers. *Actually, feeling a lot better now.* He thought about waking his bedmate, but something stopped him. *Damn it. Umbert's the one who always remembers names.*

He shifted around in his bed and peered to the other side of the room. Beside the fire, under a pile of blankets, he could make out the red hair of his friend, not much shorter than the brown hair of the girl lying next to him.

Peyre was caught in two minds. He really didn't want to leave the comfort of his bed. With a little sigh, he made himself climb out from his covers into the chill of the room. *The things I do for love.*

He tiptoed towards Umbert, then leaned over to wake him.

A knock at the door. Umbert and his girlfriend both turned at the noise, then both gave little screams when they saw Peyre bending over them.

He quickly put a hand over his bits. 'Sorry,' he said, turning towards the door.

'Ew!'

He put his other hand over his backside. 'Gods! What, you've never seen an arsehole before?'

'I've seen you plenty of times!' said Umbert, making his friend giggle.

Peyre crossed back towards his bed, muttering darkly. *What have I told him about making witticisms at my expense?*

As he grabbed his pillow, his bedmate emerged, propping herself up on one elbow. 'Good morning, Peyre,' she purred.

Shit, she knows my name. 'Hi,' he said grumpily, placing the pillow over his bits. He skirted around the bed to the door as a second knock sounded.

'I'm coming!' he complained, yanking the door open. *Oh no.* 'Hello, Your Grace.'

Duke Walter of Barissia looked Peyre up and down, peered past him into the room, and returned a steely gaze that managed to express both disappointment and disdain. 'I told Farred you wouldn't have forgotten that we were leaving today.'

Peyre's mind raced. 'Wait! It's Lars' Day? I thought that was tomorrow?'

'When we agreed that you *had* forgotten, I said I would come fetch you myself. Because it would hardly be fair to ask a servant to do it, would it?'

'No, I'm sorry—'

'Since every single one of them has already been up for three hours getting everything ready for our departure.'

Peyre sighed. 'No excuses, Your Grace. I'm really sorry.'

Peyre felt a presence by his side. *Oh bloody hellfire no.*

'Sorry for intruding,' said the girl. 'But when I heard it was you, Your Grace, I just had to meet you. I'm such an admirer!'

'An admirer?' said Duke Walter. With polished manners, he took the girl's hand and gave it a kiss.

Gods, please let her be wearing something, Peyre prayed.

There was an awkward silence. Peyre became increasingly concerned that it was because of him.

'Well, Peyre?' asked the girl. 'Aren't you going to introduce me?'

THERE WERE ONLY a dozen in the ducal party that set off from Coldeberg. Umbert hadn't made the cut—it was the first time Peyre had been separated from his friend since Lord Russell had taken them to Barissia. *Not such a bad thing*, Peyre decided. Settling in his new home would have been a lot harder without Umbert. That said, it would be nice not to see his ugly mug for a while.

The road to Essenberg was wide, well maintained and busy. *And this isn't even the Great Road I've heard about. More evidence of just how secluded my life has been.*

Peyre resolved to remain silent unless spoken to on the journey from Coldeberg to Essenberg. It wasn't just the debacle with the departure. Or the fact that all his hosts knew of him was that he had been banished by his own father. It was that he was in the presence of two men whose legends made him feel like a foolish child. Peyre's father was a stern man who demanded respect; but he hadn't done half of what Walter and Farred had done.

Walter was of an age with Peyre's father—iron grey hair had long replaced any colour, while a well-maintained moustache marked him as a Brasingian. Everything about the way he conducted himself said he was a soldier. As Marshall of the Empire under his brother, the Emperor Baldwin, he had masterminded the defence of Burkhard Castle against the hordes of Drobax, who had invaded the empire. Even when the great fortress fell, unable to withstand the assault from a dragon, he'd led the survivors to Coldeberg and outlasted the Isharite attack.

Farred, originally from Magnia, had a past that was, if anything, more intimidating. He was a few years younger, with the brown skin and long black hair of a Middian, tied up in a ponytail. Farred had also fought at Burkhard Castle. He'd been at Essenberg when it had fallen. He had also travelled to other, strange places: visited with the Sea Caladri; even crossed the Lantinen Sea to Halvia.

I'd settle for half the life these two have led, Peyre told himself. *And I'd rather they didn't think me a total ass.*

So, Peyre listened as Duke Walter reminded him who was who in the Brasingian Empire. Many of them were Walter's relatives: the family of his brother, Baldwin, the previous emperor. Baldwin had been killed in the invasion of the empire fourteen years ago. But he had ensured his family survived: his wife, Hannelore, and their three children.

It was the death of Hannelore's father—Arne, Duke of Luderia—that explained the journey they were making today. Her son, Leopold, had inherited Luderia from his grandfather, just as he had inherited Kelland from his father. Of all the things Peyre knew about Leopold, one stood out for him. He was Peyre's age, born within a few months of one another. He was interested in getting his measure.

'Katrina, the eldest sister, is now married to Duke Jeremias of Rotelegen,' Walter was reminding him. 'They'll both be there.'

'And the younger sister may marry Esterel,' Peyre said. *Alright, I told myself to be silent. But no one can remain completely silent, can they?*

'What's that?' Walter asked. He looked quizzically at Farred, who shrugged, giving the impression he cared little about who might marry whom.

'The other sister—' Peyre began.

'Liesel?'

'Yes, that's the one. The Kellish sent someone to Arbeost to discuss a marriage with Esterel. This was last year, so perhaps nothing came of it. It's not like father tells us anything.'

'Sent who?' Walter asked, more interested in Peyre's information than he had expected.

'I don't recall. Huge moustache.'

'Kass?'

'Yes, that's the one. Visited last spring. Esterel came over from Guivergne specially.'

Walter pursed his lips. Clearly, no one had told him of such a plan. 'I would ask that you don't share this story with anyone else.'

'Of course,' said Peyre.

PEYRE HAD ASSUMED they would stop in one of the villages that regularly appeared along the route and was surprised when they simply left the road and began making a simple, makeshift camp. He was sent off to fetch wood for the fire. When he returned, he found Walter and Farred just as busy with the chores as the duke's followers. They seemed to take pleasure in such simple tasks, and he liked the fact they had no airs and graces.

'More opulent surroundings tomorrow night,' Walter commented as they sat by the fire and ate supper, a little apart from his retainers. 'I presume the Duke of Kelland will find room for his uncle in Essenberg Castle.'

'I'm excited to see Essenberg,' Peyre admitted. 'Though I like this as well.'

Walter nodded with a smile. 'Just remember, you're entering the world of politics tomorrow. Not everyone in the empire is as trustworthy as I am.'

'Hmm,' said Peyre. 'Maybe you'd better warn me about who I should be wary of.'

Farred grinned at that. 'He's a sharp one.'

'When he wants to be,' Walter admitted. He seemed to consider what to say. 'Leopold's inheritance of Luderia reframes imperial politics. One man has never held two duchies before. It has implications for the future, too.'

Peyre thought about it. He knew the empire had a strange mechanism whereby the seven rulers of the duchies elected the successor to the emperor. 'You mean he gets two votes when the next election is held?'

Walter nodded. 'You *are* sharp. It puts him not so far away from the number he would need to become the next emperor.'

'Would he not make a good emperor?' Peyre asked.

Walter grimaced. 'That's hard to say. He's a young man now, just entered adulthood.'

'He's the same age as I am.'

'Right. Do you think you would make a good emperor, Peyre?'

Peyre thought about it. He recalled Walter having to fetch him from his room this morning because he had forgotten they were leaving. 'Maybe when I'm older,' he admitted.

'Exactly,' said Walter. 'And very honest of you to say so. Of course, there are people around Leopold who want him to claim his father's title as soon as possible. More power for Leopold means more power for them. Now, it's not as if Emperor Coen is an old man. But imperial politics is always about who will be next.'

It didn't take much reading between the lines for Peyre to speculate that Duke Walter wasn't necessarily in favour of his nephew becoming emperor. It was an interesting admission. 'Can't you speak to Duke Leopold, then?' he asked. 'Everyone in the empire respects you.'

'Ah,' said Walter with a little smile, 'if only that were true. I made a decision, after the Isharite Wars, to live my own life a little,' he said, glancing at Farred. 'I don't interfere in the empire very much and do not see Leopold very often. It's not as if I'm retired—rebuilding Barissia has been a full-time job. And it was natural, I suppose, after the trauma of that time, for the peoples of Brasingia to focus on their own problems. Emperor Coen did a good job in the early years, helping to restore the north. I did my best to support him. But after a while, each duchy became keen to make its own decisions. The Kellish are a proud people. Not so keen to take advice from a Thessian emperor—or even,' he said, putting a hand to his chest, 'the son, brother and uncle of the last three dukes. I'm a Barissian now,' he added, giving another little smile.

Though Peyre could see the bitterness behind the humour.

THEY BROKE camp early and resumed their journey, soon passing from Walter's duchy of Barissia to his nephew's duchy of Kelland. Peyre saw yet more villages, surrounded by cleared land full of crop yielding fields. He was beginning to understand just how populous this region of Dalriya was, something the maps he had studied back home hadn't taught him.

The morning was gone when Peyre got first sight of Essenberg. The city walls blocked his view of the settlement itself, but there was plenty else to take in. If he had thought the road they used was fancy, it looked like a country lane compared to the Great Road that stretched straight and true to the north and south. Caravans of wagons queued for entrance, while others left Essenberg's gates to transport wares elsewhere in Dalriya. The Cousel, the river that cut through Guivergne from the Krykker mountains, also passed through Essenberg on its way to the south coast. Barges came and went, adding to the volume of goods and people drawn to Essenberg. For someone who had thought Coldeberg magnificent in scale, Peyre found it all a bit hard to take in.

Their group approached the west walls of the city, to an entrance that Walter named the Coldeberg Gate. Two of his men rode ahead and arranged a speedy entrance for the duke's party. Some of the guards shouted out a greeting to Walter, who held up a hand in acknowledgement. For all the duke's talk of being classed as a Barissian, it was clear to Peyre that he still had his admirers in the city he had once called home.

As Walter took to the front of their group, Farred fell in beside Peyre and gave him a commentary concise enough to give him a grip on the key locations. 'Essenberg has four districts. This side,' he said, indicating left, 'is the Market Quarter.'

'Makes sense,' said Peyre, observing row upon row of stalls selling goods.

'That side,' Farred pointed right now, 'is the Army Quarter.'

Here the road they used merged with the Great Road and descended to the river. They had to ride in single file across a great bridge that took them to the other side of the city. The citizens of Essenberg crossed both ways: alone, in pairs and groups; men, women and children; in a hurry or a stroll; while traders sold trinkets, jewellery and other small items laid out on white cloth. *There are so many people here, it is dizzying,* Peyre said to himself. *One might live a lifetime in this one place and never get to know half the people who live with you.*

Once over the bridge, Farred pointed out the Cathedral Quarter to the right and finally named their destination, the Castle Quarter. This eastern side of the city seemed a little quieter, the houses bigger. They came to a great square and before them was the castle in question. Much nicer to look at than Coldeberg Castle, Peyre judged, but not half so strong. On the roof, fluttering above the evenly spaced crenellations, was a flag depicting the Eagle of Kelland.

They dismounted at the tidiest looking stables Peyre had ever seen and a steward arrived to see to their needs. When Walter explained Peyre's station, the steward agreed he would do his best to find him a suitable room for the night. He then led them to the main hall of the castle, which Peyre presumed would be where the duke's retainers would have to find a spot to sleep.

'Please, wait here,' said the official. 'His Grace wanted to be informed of your arrival.'

Peyre looked about the place as they waited. It was a grand space, as befit the hall where emperors had often held court. Four pillars rose to support the high roof. Stylised tapestries hung on the walls. Peyre's eyes were drawn to the largest of them all. It depicted a crowned figure standing with his followers atop a mighty fortress. Surrounding them, on the ground below, was a horde of grey-skinned, grotesque monsters.

'Burkhard Castle,' Peyre muttered.

Walter looked up. 'Aye. Each tapestry depicts a Brasingian emperor. They record how they are remembered.'

The image instilled in Peyre a deeper understanding of his hosts. He had heard the storytellers who came to the Chateau in Arbeost tell their tales of the Isharite Wars. Good stories, full of drama and sacrifice. But they had remained stories to Peyre—remote in time and place. But not to these people. Walter and Farred had stood atop that fortress as the Drobax attacked. As a child, Leopold must have come to this hall every day and seen that tapestry and known that the heroic figure was his father.

Peyre's musings were interrupted by the arrival of the ducal family. It was no surprise Leopold had the look of a younger Walter. Peyre judged him to be slightly taller than himself but not as wide. Brown, wavy hair stopped at his shoulders. A handsome enough chap, though Peyre was unconvinced by the wispy moustache.

Leopold was accompanied by three women. The older had to be his mother, the Empress—*former* Empress, Peyre supposed—Hannelore. She looked like an empress—tall, yet curvy, and glamorous. That had to mean the youngest woman was Liesel, her daughter. Soft, honey-coloured hair, hazel eyes and delicate features, she had to be the most attractive woman he had ever seen. *How typical. No doubt that lucky bastard Esterel will end up marrying her.*

That left the woman who stood to one side of the family. She looked quite different. Thin, blonde, average height, her features were child-like. She stood demurely, hands behind her back. It nearly prevented Peyre from working out who she was, but when he did, his stomach churned over. Inge. The witch. Another figure from the stories—everyone who had spoken her name had warned Peyre to be on his guard around her. It was the first time he had been in the presence of someone with magic. Her innocent looks somehow made her seem even more terrifying.

'Hannelore,' Walter said warmly, and greeted his sister-in-law with a kiss on the cheek. 'Duke Leopold,' he said with mock seriousness.

'Duke Walter,' Leopold replied, equally dryly, and they shook hands.

'Lady Liesel.'

'Oh stop it, uncle,' said Liesel, hugging him with affection.

'Inge,' said Farred.

'Farred,' said Inge.

Peyre pretended he hadn't noticed that loaded interaction.

'This is Peyre, son of Duke Bastien of Morbaine,' Walter said, introducing him. 'He is staying with me for a while.'

'Hello,' he said.

Hannelore and Liesel greeted him with friendly smiles.

'Welcome. I know about your family,' said Leopold. 'Your older brother is Esterel. They say he is a very good swordsman.'

Peyre was a little taken aback, not quite able to read the duke. His delivery was deadpan, though presumably he was hoping to impress with such knowledge.

'He's alright,' Peyre said grudgingly. He was relieved when Leopold laughed.

'Uncle?' Leopold asked. 'You will want to rest after your journey?'

'Of course,' said Walter, 'because I'm such an old man.'

'Good,' said Leopold, ignoring or oblivious to the irony. 'I thought I could show Peyre Essenberg.'

Peyre felt a smile creeping over his face. 'I would like to see the city,' he admitted.

Walter made a face. 'You two loose on the town?'

'It's the middle of the afternoon, uncle,' said Leopold, as if taking offence. 'What trouble could we possibly get ourselves into?'

'I'm not sure it's a good idea,' said Hannelore, sounding worried. 'There are all kinds of criminals out there.'

'Perhaps if we sent a bodyguard with the duke?' Inge suggested.

'At the very least,' said Hannelore.

'I'll send one of my men, too,' said Walter.

'There you go, mother,' said Leopold. 'And look at Peyre's sword,' he said, gesturing at the weapon in its scabbard. 'It's not like we can't handle ourselves. Is it Peyre?'

'True,' said Peyre.

'Then it's settled,' said Leopold.

'Oh, darling,' said Inge, looking at Liesel. 'Did you wish to go with them?'

All eyes turned to Liesel. She looked embarrassed—*maybe I have it wrong, but she looks almost frightened,* Peyre thought, seeing no reason for it.

'No, I do not!' she said.

'Damn it, Inge,' said Leopold. 'Of course she doesn't want to come.'

'Apologies, Your Grace,' said the witch demurely. But she was soon smiling.

Is that a smirk on the woman's face? Peyre asked himself. He felt lost in the conversation now, with so many undercurrents at play that he didn't understand. He was glad when Leopold wasted no more time in leading him away.

The two bodyguards kept a respectful distance behind Leopold and Peyre as they passed through the elegant streets about the castle.

'It is very grand here,' Peyre commented.

Leopold wrinkled his nose. 'I suppose so. I prefer the other side of the city, where the commoners live. I feel freer there. Do you understand?'

Peyre thought back to the tapestries in the hall of Essenberg Castle: the great dukes of the past remembered only as heroes. 'Yes, I can see how that could be.'

'I knew you would,' said Leopold. 'There's no one here who understands what my life is like.'

'Well,' said Peyre, 'I didn't grow up anywhere like this,' he gestured. They had reached the Great Road that passed through the city. Here it connected onto the great bridge that crossed the Cousel.

'That's not what I mean,' said Leopold. 'The expectation on one's shoulders; the constantly being watched; measured; judged. I know you are only the second son, Peyre, but you must have some experience of what I am talking about.'

'My father is very stern,' Peyre ventured, looking down at the river swirling beneath them. He wasn't at all sure that he shared the same pressures as Leopold, but he was keen to find some common ground between them. 'He banished me to Brasingia for fighting.'

'There you go,' said Leopold. 'I lost my father, as you know. And since that day, I was expected to fill his shoes. Can you imagine what that is like?'

'Difficult, I am sure.' It seemed to Peyre that Leopold was lonely—keen to share his burdens with a stranger. He needed a friend, and Peyre was flattered that he had seen such potential in him.

They continued along the Great Road for a while, into the part of the city that Farred had named the Army Quarter. Leopold took them off the Road, navigating through side streets that became narrower, smellier and more run down the farther they walked. Peyre had never seen anything like it—so many people squashed into such a small space. Some houses weren't houses at all really, just timber panels crudely lashed together.

'We call these streets the rookery,' Leopold told him.

Two men standing on the other side of the street stared balefully at him, and Peyre looked behind to check that their two bodyguards were still with them. Why Leopold had taken him here, he couldn't fathom.

Leopold stopped outside the grottiest looking drinking hole Peyre had ever seen—the kind of place he avoided in Coldeberg. With a grin, Leopold led them inside. The place was dark, dank, and stank to high heaven. Unsurprisingly, there were only a few customers inside at this hour. They went to the bar and Leopold ordered two drinks, dropping some coins down. The woman serving opened the tap on a barrel and poured a dark ale into their cups.

Dark, so you can't see what's in it, Peyre assumed.

They got themselves seated at a small table, while the two body-guards took up position at the bar, neither electing to order a drink for themselves.

Peyre sipped at the ale—bitter as it went down, with a horrible aftertaste. He looked about. 'What's the attraction?' he had to ask.

'A few coins can get you all sorts here,' said Leopold. He nodded at a couple of women sat against the far wall, looking their way. 'Like them,' he said with a leer. 'Interested?'

'No!' Peyre said quickly. 'You're the Duke of Kelland,' he said to Leopold. 'Not as nice looking as me, of course, but better than most.' That got a grin from Leopold. 'Surely you could have countless girls in this city—nice looking ones, who you don't have to pay or catch something from.'

'Ha! Of course,' Leopold agreed. 'But that's the point. Out there I'm Leopold, Duke of Kelland. I must behave like *him*. In here, I can be *me*.'

Peyre raised an eyebrow. *I guess I should count myself fortunate that there's only one of me.*

'Come now, Peyre. I assume you like girls, not boys.'

Peyre frowned. 'Of course.'

'You know the reason I ask?'

'No, I don't,' said Peyre, confused by the sudden turn in the conversation.

Leopold stared at him. 'You haven't worked out my Uncle Walter yet? Not married?'

'Ah,' said Peyre. 'It hadn't crossed my mind.'

'He and Farred love nothing more than playing with each other's cocks. Disgusting, eh?'

Peyre wasn't about to bad mouth two men he admired to one who'd yet to do anything of note. 'That's their business,' he said, starting to feel irritated with his new acquaintance.

Leopold studied him. He hadn't got the answer he had wanted. He shrugged it off. 'Anyway, my uncle's predilections are good for me.'

'How's that?'

'I'm his heir, of course.'

Peyre took a drink, forcing himself not to shudder as it went down. He wasn't acquiring the taste, that was for sure. 'I see. So you've inherited Luderia. When Walter dies, you get Barissia as well?'

'Exactly. Three duchies under my personal control. You know how the empire works, Peyre?'

'Aye, you need four votes to become emperor.'

'Exactly,' said Leopold, looking pleased. 'But it's not just the title I stand to gain. Look at Coen. Or even my father's reign. My father had the title, but what power did it bring him? He was still only one duke among seven. He still had to cajole and beg the others to fight for him. But I will have the title and three of the duchies. And that will be just the beginning. I'll have the power to rule Brasingia for real—the first man in the empire's history to truly have authority in every corner of Brasingia.'

Leopold's eyes shone with the thought of it. Peyre wondered where this vision had come from—was it this young man's dream or a desire that someone else had planted within him? For to Peyre, it seemed like an ambition all about attaining power for its own sake, rather than benefiting the people he would rule over. Peyre's thoughts turned to Inge—the strangeness of her—a witch openly welcomed at the ducal court.

'You will be the most powerful man in all of Dalriya,' said Peyre, a comment that brought a contented smile to Leopold's face.

'And you will be my friend,' said Leopold. 'And your brother. Why not? Who says Brasingia and Guivergne have to be rivals? That is tired old thinking.'

Talk of relations between Brasingia and Guivergne made Peyre feel uneasy. These were issues Peyre hadn't ever bothered to think about. But Leopold clearly had. How far did his ambitions run?

'When you are so powerful,' said Peyre, 'will you still need that witch Inge at court?'

He regretted it as soon as he said it. It was clumsy and unnecessary.

Leopold looked at him, but he seemed more disappointed than hostile. He shook his head. 'Maybe in Morbaine, sheltered from the Isharite Wars, it is still possible to think like that. But if you'd seen the things I've seen, you'd think differently. You've heard the stories of the siege of Burkhard Castle, surely?'

'Of course,' said Peyre, suddenly feeling like he was being lectured to like a child.

'My father had a powerful sorcerer in his service. Gustav the Hawk. He couldn't stop the loss of Burkhard. Inge was in Essenberg with my family when I was a child. She couldn't stop the loss of the city. We barely got out alive. There are creatures out there far more powerful than you and I can comprehend, Peyre. If I could, I'd have a thousand witches and sorcerers at my court. As it is, all I have is that bitch, Inge. Not much, but infinitely better than nothing, and it helps me sleep a little better at night knowing she's around.'

PEYRE

ESSENBERG, DUCHY OF KELLAND, 672

That evening, Duke Leopold feasted his guests. The hall was busy with servants carrying food, while a five-piece band played music, creating a lively atmosphere. Peyre was honoured to find himself seated at the top table. He was relieved to see that the witch, Inge, didn't have a seat amongst the family—indeed, she was nowhere to be seen.

Leopold's oldest sister, Katrina, and brother-in-law, Jeremias, had arrived from their duchy of Rotelegen. Peyre realised he was observing the members of the most powerful alliance in the empire— between them, they held four of the seven duchies of Brasingia. As Leopold had been keen to tell him, the future of the empire was in their hands. *Why did father send me here?* Peyre asked himself for the first time. It wasn't a haphazard decision, that was for sure. That wasn't how Bastien operated.

Peyre didn't know what the rules might be for seating arrange-ments, but there was clearly a protocol at work. The three dukes and Leopold's mother had central seats. Peyre found himself at one end of the table. Next to him was former Empress Hannelore, and opposite her was Walter. Opposite Peyre was Liesel. She was so exquisite to look at he had to stop himself from staring at her: her luscious hair was plaited and hung over one shoulder; her eyes were flecked with so many colours that they were almost asking to be inspected. The safest thing would be to look elsewhere. But Hannelore and the dukes on the other side of him were busy with their own conversation about the problems of government—he wasn't invited and had nothing to contribute.

So, I must persevere with Liesel, Peyre told himself. *Even though she is far more reticent than her brother.*

'Essenberg is a wonderful city,' he ventured.

Liesel shrugged. 'I suppose so. Do you have many cities in Morbaine?'

'None. I am an utter country bumpkin, I have to admit. You can ride for miles in every direction from Arbeost and not come across another soul. I was bowled over by Coldeberg. But this city is something else.'

'Did Leopold show you the sights?' she asked him archly.

Peyre wasn't about to pretend when she obviously knew very well that he hadn't. 'No, he took me to a horrible dive. My stomach's still protesting after I made myself down my drink.'

Liesel allowed herself a smile at this. It seemed she admired honesty rather than polite chit-chat. Peyre found that he really wanted to make this young lady smile.

'I've known very little except city life,' she admitted. 'Arbeost would be as interesting to me as Essenberg is to you, I am sure.'

Peyre very much doubted that. 'Perhaps you will come to Morbaine soon?' he suggested, remembering the visit of the Kellish to Arbeost and the talk of a marriage with Esterel.

Liesel frowned, confused. 'Why would I be going to Morbaine?'

Peyre felt his face drop. Duke Walter had specifically asked him not to mention the story to anyone. And here he was, close to spilling it to Liesel, when it looked—very much—like she had no idea about it.

'Oh, you never know. You might do.' This was going terribly. Liesel's eyes narrowed with suspicion. 'I'm here in Kelland after all, when I never expected to be,' he added weakly.

'Peyre,' Liesel said lightly. 'Give me your hand.'

Hearing his name on her lips gave Peyre far more pleasure than he would have thought possible. He offered his hand, eager for her touch.

Liesel took his hand. Her sharp nails dug in. 'You are a terrible liar,' she hissed at him.

'That's a good thing, isn't it?' he said. He tried to pull his hand away, but she held on tight. 'Ow!'

Liesel laughed loudly over his complaint. 'Oh Peyre, you are funny!' She waited for her mother and Duke Walter to look away before leaning over. 'Tell me the truth!' she demanded.

'Alright. It's just that there was a delegation from Kelland to Arbeost. Lord Kass was the man in charge. Sounding out my father about a marriage between you and my brother.'

Liesel let go of his hand—Peyre felt both relief and regret. She frowned. 'Doesn't make sense,' she said, as much to herself as to Peyre it seemed. 'They don't let me out of their sight for a moment, and then talk about sending me to Guivergne?' She looked at Peyre, suspicion and curiosity warring on her features. 'What was said?'

'Nothing that I was privy to,' Peyre admitted. 'Who knows what my father or Esterel said in private? Who doesn't let you out of their sight?'

Liesel studied him. 'As if I would trust you!'

'Why wouldn't you?' Peyre asked. 'Haven't I demonstrated my complete inability to deceive you?'

'Yes,' Liesel conceded. 'But also your inability to keep your mouth shut.'

'I swear any secrets are safe with me,' Peyre said, seriously.

Liesel seemed to believe him. She leaned towards him, and he leaned in closer. He could smell her perfume. *Peyre,* he told himself. *You really must concentrate right now.*

'It's got worse since my sister was married,' she whispered to him, glancing to the far end of the table where Katrina was talking with Farred. 'Inge and Salvinus rule in Essenberg. My mother and brother do what they tell them. There's no one to look after me anymore.' Liesel suddenly looked scared and tearful.

Peyre wanted nothing more than to help her. 'Who's Salvinus?' he asked.

Liesel gave him an incredulous look, then shook her head. She leaned in close and Peyre was quick to do the same. Liesel got even closer. He could feel her breath on his ear. 'My mother's lover,' she whispered. 'He's in Witmar now, preparing for Leopold's accession. He's a vile debaucher. Inge thinks it's amusing when he says things to me, and my mother always defends him.' Liesel leaned back in her chair.

Peyre stared back at her, suddenly furious.

'Well, aren't you two getting on?' Hannelore said to Peyre with a knowing smile.

Peyre glanced at Walter, who was looking at him with a stony expression.

'Well, I suppose we are the same age,' Peyre said in response. 'We have a lot in common.'

'We are not!' Liesel said coldly. 'I am two years older than you.'

'Oh Liesel,' Hannelore chided. 'Be nice. She doesn't mean anything by it, Peyre.'

Hannelore and Walter returned to their conversation. Peyre waited, making sure that he wouldn't be overheard. He leaned towards Liesel. 'Why don't you tell Walter about it?'

She shook her head. 'He would intervene,' she whispered. 'Surely you understand? Inge is a witch. She would turn her powers on him. Promise me you won't say anything to him.'

Peyre nodded. 'I promise.'

Liesel smiled. 'Thank you. And Peyre,' she said, looking earnest. 'This is Essenberg, not Arbeost. From now on you must be careful what you say and who you say it to.'

He nodded. 'I understand.'

After the feasting was over, Peyre retired to the small room that had been found for him during his stay in the castle. He found it impossible to stop thinking about Liesel. He put a finger to his hand, rolling it over the impressions left where she had dug her nails in. *Two years older than me? So what!*

. . .

ABOUT A HUNDRED PEOPLE all told left the Witmar Gate of Essenberg. Peyre rode with Walter and his small entourage, while that of Jeremias was a similar size. Then, it seemed, anyone who was anyone in Kelland had managed to get an invitation to Leopold's inauguration as Duke of Luderia.

'Will Emperor Coen be attending?' Peyre asked.

'Not invited,' said Walter. 'Neither is Emmett of Gotbeck or Gavan of Atrabia.' He looked at Peyre and sighed. 'I don't agree with it. Unnecessary; short-sighted; call it what you want. But Leopold and his advisers are determined to turn the screws and let Brasingia know they're in the ascendancy.'

'Which advisers?' Peyre asked him.

'Inge and Salvinus. They're the ones that count. The rest have learned to agree with whatever they say.'

Peyre tried to make sense of Walter's attitude. He had admitted he had taken a step back from imperial politics for his own personal reasons. But by doing so, had he not stored up problems for the future? Then there was Liesel's warning about Inge. She didn't want her uncle ensnared in a conflict with the witch. Peyre had promised her he wouldn't tell Walter about her problems; agreed that he needed to run his mouth off a little less. He resolved to stay quiet. After all, this was Brasingia, not Guivergne. It wasn't his business what happened here.

The numbers involved seemed to make progress slow, reminding Peyre of the sluggish pace of the army of Morbaine during the invasion of the Steppe. They left the road to Witmar for the last part of the day's journey, coming to a country estate owned by the ducal family. It must have had the comfort required by the dowager duchess, for it was quite a detour from the direct route. Duke Walter was offered a room inside the house, but he was content to set up a camp in the grounds. He did accept an invitation inside for supper, however, bringing Peyre with him.

The place reminded Peyre of his family's Chateau back in Arbeost, for the first time making him feel a little homesick. There was a friendly, relaxed atmosphere inside—different from the formalities of the court in Essenberg. The servants had laid out food on tables in the kitchen and everyone helped themselves.

Hannelore had a large barrel of wine opened and insisted it had to be finished. 'To my father,' she toasted, and everyone drank—even Peyre, who had very little idea what kind of man Duke Arne had been.

Peyre looked about for Liesel. Instead, he saw Inge, standing alone with her cup of wine. *Watching me? No, that's paranoia.* Nonetheless, he decided not to go looking for Liesel.

Instead, Leopold found him. The duke was all smiles, playing the role of the gracious host, introducing a series of Brasingians to Peyre. *If Leopold is able to play the part of Leopold, Duke of Kelland, then I can play the part of Peyre, second son of Duke of Bastien. He's a pleasant if rather dull chap, with absolutely no interest in Leopold's beautiful sister.*

He shared some words with Jeremias, Duke of Rotelegen. If he was a little vague on the life of Arne of Luderia, then Jeremias's story had stayed with him. Father and brothers slain by the Haskans, he'd inherited the duchy of Rotelegen at a tender age, facing the worst crisis imaginable. He'd been much younger than Peyre when he'd personally led his troops in the defence of Burkhard Castle, fighting the Drobax. *What a story he could share,* Peyre thought. Instead, they exchanged tedious pleasantries. *He is playing the role of Jeremias, Duke of Rotelegen,* Peyre realised.

Hannelore joined them, cheeks flushed and speaking loudly. At one point she reached out and played with Leopold's hair, before remembering where she was. Peyre found such a display of affection touching. Witnessing such moments always made him wish he could have shared more time with his own mother. The truth was, he couldn't remember her; though he felt sure she had loved him during the brief time they had together.

'I think you will like Witmar, boys,' she told them.

'What is the city like?' Peyre asked her.

'Oh, much smaller than Essenberg. The people are friendlier... more contented with life. It has been such a long time since I returned home. I do wonder if I would be happier staying in Witmar.'

Leopold rolled his eyes. 'That wouldn't have anything to do with my plans to have Salvinus govern Luderia for me, would it mother?'

Hannelore slapped him on the arm. 'Of course not, Leopold!' she said, her eyes twinkling.

'Salvinus will govern Luderia?' Peyre asked.

'Someone has to rule when I am absent,' said Leopold. 'And for all mother makes Witmar sound absolutely lovely, I'll be returning to Essenberg.'

THE NEXT MORNING they re-joined the Witmar Road and resumed their journey north-east. It wasn't long before they had crossed into Luderia. Almost immediately, Peyre noticed how different the duchy was to Kelland and Barissia. Vast swathes of forest lay on either side of the road and the settlements they passed were smaller, their wood buildings blending into the landscape rather than transforming it as the Kellish had done with their huge farms.

'It reminds me of Morbaine,' Peyre commented.

Walter nodded. 'Luderia is a sleeping giant. So much more could be done with it. But Arne was content to leave things be.'

'That's likely to change,' said Peyre.

Walter raised an eyebrow.

'Leopold told me that Salvinus will govern the duchy for him.'

Walter shared a grim look with Farred. 'Leopold is free to appoint whoever he wishes,' Walter said at last.

They rode on in silence.

It was a long day of riding and everyone seemed saddle sore and tired by the time Witmar came into view. The late afternoon sun highlighted parts of the capital and cast others in shadow. Built on a rise overlooking the road, Witmar occupied a large site. Its walls were wooden and flimsy looking compared to Essenberg or Coldeberg. Stony-faced guards wearing the duchy's emblem, the green tree, waved them through.

The streets they rode through were surprisingly quiet. Some citizens came out to get their first look at their new duke. But there was no friendly welcome for Leopold or delight at the return of his mother, Hannelore.

'Rather sombre,' said Walter, frowning.

'Remember Salvinus has been here a while,' said Farred sharply, as if no more needed to be said.

They came upon the castle, which occupied a central position. Peyre could see a stone keep in the centre but everything else was constructed of wood, with huge split logs used to make the external walls. Here, the guards on the walls wore the eagle of Kelland. There were many of them and their presence had the feel of an occupying force. There were gasps ahead of them and when it was the turn of Walter's entourage to ride through the castle gate, they saw why. Four heads had been placed on spikes that extended over the wall. Peyre looked at them with fascinated horror—they had been pecked at by birds, the eyes missing.

'Salvinus,' Farred muttered.

Once inside the walls, the horses were stabled, and the party escorted into the large stone built keep. The castle staff were soon busy identifying the guests and taking them to the rooms allocated for them. Peyre didn't have one, but he was quick to assure an official that he was happy sleeping in the hall. The man gave him a grateful smile and moved on to one of the many people raising their voices and demanding attention.

Peyre looked about the place, wandering through the ground-floor rooms. The smell of food lured him to the heart of the keep, where the kitchens were located next to the duke's hall. *It's a shame I can't help myself, like back home.* Raised voices in the hall grabbed his attention, and he wandered in. He spotted Leopold and Hannelore with their bodyguards. Beside Hannelore was a man he hadn't seen before. He was a middle-aged, soldierly type, with a scar from ear to chin and a sneer on his face. That *has* to be Salvinus. Facing Duke Leopold stood a group of four men. Again, Peyre hadn't seen these individuals before. It didn't take too much working out, once one took in their fine clothes and decorated scabbards, to decide these must be Luderian noblemen.

'Lord Salvinus has abused us and our people,' one of the men was telling Leopold. 'Used gratuitous threats and violence. We ask that you dismiss this minister and give your rule here a fresh start.'

Good luck with that, Peyre thought.

'Whiners who have obstructed my duties here,' Salvinus said dismissively. He jabbed a finger at the man who had spoken. 'I have made every effort to use patience the last few days. You should see what happens when I lose my temper. There'll be violence then, that's for sure.'

'Lord Salvinus has my full confidence,' said Leopold to the men.

Peyre had thought as much. *Is Leopold really so blind to what Salvinus is? Or does he simply not care?*

'I know my grandfather ruled here for a long time, and change is hard to get used to,' Leopold added, in a voice that suggested his words were meant to mollify. 'But I am Arne's lawful heir, and it is your duty to ensure that Luderia respects that.'

'Of course, my liege,' said another man, making a little bow. 'We are all delighted about your accession.' He looked at Hannelore, as if pleading for her to intervene. 'But there are certain laws and liberties in Luderia—'

'—And Lord Salvinus has been invested with my authority,' Leopold interrupted, 'to act as my representative in Luderia. When he speaks to you, it is as if I am speaking to you. Is that understood?'

What else could they do but agree, Peyre wondered, as the four men bobbed their heads in submission. What they said in private, however, would no doubt be another thing. Leopold and Salvinus seemed determined to assert their authority on a people who already respected it. Where would that end, he wondered. But Leopold had made it clear in that drinking hole in Essenberg that he intended to rule Brasingia as it had never been ruled before. That ruthless approach seemed to have begun here in Witmar.

. . .

SUCH UNPLEASANTNESS APPEARED to be forgotten at the evening's feast in honour of Leopold's arrival. The hall was full to bursting as Luderians and Kellish ate, drank and were entertained. It seemed like the feast had been planned by Salvinus days in advance and Peyre, a late arrival to the guest list, hadn't been part of the planning. He didn't mind, however, to find himself some distance from the top table, where Leopold's family and his key advisers dined. Seated next to Farred, with the Barissian soldiers around them, it was possible to relax and enjoy the occasion. Not to mention, from here he could observe all of them: Leopold, Liesel, Salvinus, Inge and the rest—without them noticing.

There was another face in the hall Peyre recognised. He had been placed on a table full of Kellish aristocracy. Peyre was sure, however, that he hadn't travelled with them from Essenberg. He would have recognised that great, wiggly moustache anywhere. Lord Kass had led the delegation to Arbeost, with talk of a marriage between Liesel and Esterel. Talk that neither Liesel nor Walter knew anything about. If he hadn't come to Essenberg with Leopold, he must have come earlier, probably with Salvinus. As Peyre studied him, the diplomat seemed to catch his eye for a moment, then quickly looked away. *He knows who I am*, Peyre decided, *and doesn't want to attract my attention.*

Peyre's focus returned to the goings-on at the top table when he saw Liesel excuse herself. He watched her leave the hall, presumably to visit the garderobe. It suddenly struck him as odd that she didn't have a lady attendant with her. He knew that his sister, Loysse, never seemed to go anywhere without Cebelia at her side.

'You like her?' Farred asked him quietly.

Peyre felt himself turning red at being caught out watching her. 'She's very easy on the eye,' he admitted.

'Oh, sure,' Farred agreed. 'But you like *her*.'

Then something caused the blood to drain from Peyre's face. 'Excuse me Farred, I have to go.'

'Good luck,' Farred offered as Peyre got to his feet and left their table.

But Farred had misread the situation. Peyre had seen Salvinus follow Liesel moments after she left. After what she had told him about the man, ignoring it wasn't an option.

He followed them through an exit from the hall, finding himself in a gallery. He looked one way then the next, seeing no one. *Damn it. I have no idea where I am.*

He walked one way, then stopped, walking back the other. *Stop panicking.* He listened. Voices. *This way,* he told himself, marching to one end of the gallery. Down a short set of stairs, he came to a corner of the castle where a few rooms nestled against the outer wall. Moving quietly now, he could hear Salvinus's voice. Peering around a wall, he saw them both—the man had his arm on Liesel's shoulder, and she was pressed against the wall. Peyre took a few steps back so that he was out of view.

'When your brother leaves, I will have total control of Luderia. Take whatever I want. It's about time you started being nice to me, Liesel.'

'That isn't going to happen.'

'Oh, but it is. Leopold and your mother have already agreed that you should stay here with me. They do what they're told, you see. You're gonna start doing the same.'

There was a fumbling sound. 'Get off,' Liesel said.

Anger ran through Peyre's body. He shook with it. *Control yourself,* he demanded. *And think. You can deal with this without getting yourself killed.*

LIESEL

WITMAR, DUCHY OF LUDERIA, 672

Salvinus pushed her against the wall. He leaned in close so she could smell his foul breath.

'When your brother leaves, I will have total control of Luderia. Take whatever I want. It's about time you started being nice to me, Liesel.'

How she hated this man and what he had done to her family. She wished she had magic, like Inge, and could obliterate him on the spot. But she didn't, and she couldn't.

'That isn't going to happen,' she said, trying to sound confident; trying not to sound scared.

'Oh, but it is. Leopold and your mother have already agreed that you should stay here with me. They do what they're told, you see. You're gonna start doing the same.'

That was the trouble. He was right about her brother and mother. She was alone, and it was hard, at times, not to despair.

With one hand, he kept her shoulder pinned to the wall. The other went to her hip; pulled at her dress.

Liesel grabbed his wrist. 'Get off.'

Salvinus moved his lips to her ear. 'Maybe you can join me and your mother in bed,' he whispered. 'We'll teach you a few things.'

Gods, he repulsed her. He knew it, too; derived a sick pleasure from her reaction. That was one reason she tried—desperately—*not* to react.

The sound of clumsy footsteps came from the gallery. Salvinus pulled away from her. A figure came tottering towards them. Peyre, the boy from Morbaine. *What's he doing here? Praise Alexia he is.*

'The gong's this way, right?' he slurred, as if he was the worse for drink.

Liesel fought to repress a smile. She knew it was a pretence. He must have heard what was happening and decided on this ruse. Clever.

Peyre staggered straight for Salvinus, who grabbed the front of his shirt in a fist. Salvinus was far from amused.

'Hey!' Peyre protested. 'All I'm after is a piss! Actually, I'm not sure this Brasingian wine agrees with me. I feel like I may have to spew. Just a little. Are you going to direct me to the gong, or not?'

'You insolent cur!' Salvinus growled. He pushed Peyre backwards, crashing him against the same wall where he had caught Liesel. 'Do you know who you are speaking to?'

Peyre's eyes went wide. 'I don't give a fig who you are, sir!' he replied loudly. 'You are currently manhandling the son of Duke Bastien of Morbaine! Is this how noble guests are treated in Luderia?' Peyre's volume had risen to a crescendo now.

Salvinus looked towards the gallery with a frown. Then he looked at Liesel.

She nodded. 'This is Peyre, son of Duke Bastien. He accompanied us from Essenberg.'

Liesel watched as Salvinus calculated on the spot. She could tell he would have preferred to give Peyre a good beating. But the more he thought about the consequences of that, the less likely it was he would go through with it. Then, he was laughing—good humour suddenly turned on like a tap.

'Oh my, Lord Peyre! What a comical misunderstanding! I was sure you were some thug, disrespecting Duke Leopold's sister. You'll understand, I'm sure, why I felt the need to defend her honour.'

'Of course. I do apologise, Lady Liesel,' said Peyre. 'But listen, old man, I really do need to find the pisser.'

'Naturally,' said Salvinus. 'This way.' They walked off, arms around each other's shoulder like the best of friends.

'Thank you,' Liesel mouthed to the departing Peyre and wasted no time in returning to the hall.

LIESEL SPENT the night in the company of her sister. Here, in the rooms allocated to Duke Jeremias, she had some security. In the morning, they spoke while they embroidered, an old habit from childhood. Katrina had given Liesel a cushion cover, something even she couldn't mess up. Her sister, meanwhile, was in the middle of some grand project for the cathedral in Guslar. Liesel couldn't help but envy Katrina her sense of purpose. She and her husband were full of plans to restore the battered duchy of Rotelegen to glory. Liesel, meanwhile, lived in limbo—powerless, while she waited for others to decide her fate.

She waited patiently as Katrina shared all her plans and complained about her dragon of a mother-in-law. Then it was her turn. She told her sister about Peyre, and his strange news that Lord Kass had offered her to his brother.

Katrina raised her eyebrows at this. 'I suppose it makes some kind of sense. Nicolas of Guivergne has no children. There's every chance that Esterel will become king one day. Imagine that, Liesel. You would be queen!'

Liesel nodded, not knowing what to think of that. When she thought of such things, there was a numbness inside her that stopped her from feeling anything much.

'What is it?' Katrina asked. 'What's happened?'

Liesel kept her eyes on her work. 'It's getting worse. Salvinus—' She found it hard to say more.

'I'm sorry,' Katrina said. She took Liesel's chin in her hand and raised her face until their eyes met. 'He's not—'

'No, but it's only a matter of time,' said Liesel, feeling herself shaking. 'He's persuaded Leopold and mother that I should stay here.' She watched Katrina search for the right words to say. But her sister wasn't going to pretend everything would be alright and there were no easy answers.

'Maybe I could persuade them to let you visit me,' she said at last.

'Maybe,' said Liesel. It was an idea. Something to cling to.

LEOPOLD'S INAUGURATION took place in Witmar Cathedral. The building was smaller than Essenberg's and allowed a surprising amount of intimacy to the service. The bishop of Witmar seemed to know her grandfather well and spoke of many small acts of kindness from his life, as well as addressing the larger story, that Liesel knew all too well. The marriage of his daughter, Hannelore, to Baldwin of Kelland, a union that had defined the empire. Arne's support of Baldwin at a key moment, leading his troops to Burkhard Castle in defence of Brasingia. Then, the next year, he had sent his only son, Tobias, in his stead.

Tobias had died in the slaughter at Burkhard, burned alive along with his men by dragon fire. As the bishop reminded them of the painful episode, Liesel's mother and grandmother burst into sobs to her right, gripping each other in their shared grief. Liesel couldn't help but wonder how Arne had lived with that decision in the years that followed. Surely, he must have regretted it every day. Fateful in other ways, too, for the death of Liesel's uncle meant that Leopold now inherited the duchy instead. But the service had shown Liesel that there were other parts to her grandfather's life—things to be celebrated—and for that, she was grateful.

Then it was time for Leopold to be confirmed a duke for the second time in his short life. Her brother was seated on a high-backed, beautifully decorated wooden chair. The ceremony was simple and to the point, an approach to life that seemed to be a feature of Luderian life. Leopold agreed to respect the rights of Luderians and fulfil his duties as a duke. Liesel knew, as she watched him, that to her brother, these were nothing more than words that needed to be said.

Then the assembled congregation left their seats and got to their knees. The bishop asked the gods for their blessings and the Luderians agreed to faithfully serve their new duke.

Afterwards, everyone emptied into the cathedral gardens. A crowd surrounded her brother, tripping over one another to congratulate him. All Liesel could hear was Salvinus's brash voice; all she could see were Inge's knowing looks. She retreated, following a path that wound its way through flowerbeds. Footsteps behind made her turn; she was relieved to see Peyre. He walked beside her for a while.

'Thank you for yesterday,' she said at last.

He shrugged. Liesel wasn't sure how to respond to that. It was rude not to acknowledge someone's gratitude.

'Are you alright?' Peyre asked at last. 'He hasn't—'

'I slept in my sister's room last night.'

'Oh. Good. I didn't sleep a wink. We really need to do something about that bastard.'

Liesel smiled. It was nice to have someone on her side. And it was hard not to like him. There was an edge—a confidence to him. But also a decency that few people around her had. 'I've warned you, Peyre,' she reminded him, making a show of looking behind them. No one there. 'You need to take care. But,' she paused, looking into his eyes, 'I thank you for your concern. And your friendship.'

Some unreadable emotion crossed his face for a moment, then it was gone. 'What he said,' Peyre persisted, 'about you staying here in Witmar. We can't let that happen. I was thinking, what if I spoke to Leopold about it? He's your brother, after all. Even if he keeps Salvinus on, for whatever reason, I'm sure he'll agree to you returning to Essenberg with him.'

He made it sound so reasonable, which no doubt it would be in a normal family.

'There's something you need to understand about Leopold,' Liesel said, resuming her walk through the garden as Peyre walked alongside her. 'He was five years old when he lost his father. The Drobax stormed Essenberg—they were everywhere, swarming through the city. Salvinus only just got my family out in time. Leopold was terrified—had no idea why his world had suddenly turned upside down. At least Katrina and I were old enough to understand what was happening. But Leopold…for all his boasting, and titles, and visits to the rookery, inside he's still that terrified five-year-old boy. Mother was just as scared as he was. They've both relied on Salvinus and Inge ever since. Inge is odd; distant. But Salvinus has become father; husband; big brother; adviser; protector. He's taken away their fear because he does everything for them. Standing up to him—saying "no" to him—it all comes back again. They can't do it.'

'I see,' said Peyre. 'Not you or your sister, though?'

'I remember my father,' Liesel said. 'Salvinus is nothing like him.'

Their path opened onto a paved meeting area. Standing there, as if she had been expecting them, was Inge.

'Two little lovebirds,' she said in a silly voice. 'How adorable.'

Liesel was used to the witch's barbs, but she felt Peyre bristle with anger beside her.

'Do you think you're funny?' he demanded.

Please Peyre, don't antagonise her.

'I remember my first love,' Inge continued, ignoring him. 'It was your father, Liesel. I was only your age, and he was a lot older. But who's going to say no to an emperor when he wants you in his bed?'

'That's a lie,' said Liesel, the words leaving her mouth before she'd decided she wanted to say them. Her father wouldn't have shared his bed with a witch. Inge looked nothing like her mother.

Inge had the gall to look offended. 'I don't know why you think I would lie about such a thing. I don't claim he loved me more than your mother. I don't pretend he loved me at all. It was all about the sex with him.'

'Stop it!' Peyre shouted. 'We don't want to hear about your sordid fantasies.'

Inge looked at him coldly. 'Or what?' she asked. Her voice was deathly quiet, her impish manner gone.

'Peyre—' Liesel warned him, putting a hand to his arm.

'Or I'll teach you a lesson!'

Inge's hands shot out. She yelled—an indecipherable noise. Liesel felt the force hit Peyre. One moment she had a hold of his arm, the next he was lying flat on the ground. She crouched down, panicking; she put a hand to his neck, trying to find a pulse.

Inge joined her. 'Here,' she said, taking Liesel's hand, putting her fingers to the right place. 'He'll live.' She stood.

Reassured somewhat, Liesel got to her feet. 'He's just a boy.'

'Be careful then, Liesel. Because this boy will return to Guivergne one day, and we don't want his stories to be full of how terrible the rulers of Brasingia are. Better he never return. Do you understand?'

'I get it.'

'Good,' said Inge. She got closer, her face mere inches away. 'You've lived a charmed life so far, Liesel. Beautiful daughter of an emperor. Never wanted for anything. But such a life has left you soft and spoiled.' Suddenly, the witch's hand was at her chest, her finger and thumb squeezing Liesel's nipple.

Liesel felt her mouth open like a fish, so shocked she had nothing to say.

'But it's time you learned to use your body and your pretty face. That's how you will get what you want from life. Otherwise, you'll forever be a victim.' Her hand slid away. 'And Liesel, darling. Victims are such bores.'

PEYRE

WITMAR, DUCHY OF LUDERIA, 672

Peyre awoke in a bed in an unfamiliar room. As he stirred, still groggy, his memories returned. Inge, in the cathedral gardens— her lewd comments about Liesel's father. He'd wanted nothing more than to shut her up. Then, her outstretched arms. *She used magic on me,* he realised, not quite believing it. He put a hand to his face, his body; checking everything was still there. *Who knows what curses a witch might use?* But he detected nothing untoward.

He got up and looked around the small castle room. There were enough objects in there he recognised for him to work out where he was. Duke Walter's room. He'd obviously been taken there after Inge had cast her spell on him. At least he hadn't been put in some dungeon cell. But he had to find out if Liesel was alright.

Peyre exited the room into a corridor. It took him awhile to get his bearings and then he had to ask a servant for directions. He made for the location he hoped Liesel would be: her sister's rooms. The servant who opened the door asked him to wait. It wasn't long before Jeremias, Liesel's brother-in-law, appeared.

'Can I see Liesel?' Peyre asked him.

'Your manner suggests you won't take no for an answer,' Jeremias observed.

'I apologise,' said Peyre. 'I just need to know she's safe.'

'I understand. Come in, Peyre,' he said.

Jeremias had a suite of rooms for his entourage. He led him into his private room. 'I've told my wife you are here. Take a seat,' he said, gesturing to a chair. The duke fixed them each a drink. 'Ever had arak before?'

'No,' said Peyre, taking the offered cup and giving the amber liquid a sniff. It was strong.

'It'll calm your nerves after what happened,' Jeremias recommended.

Peyre sipped at it. It pickled his tongue, went down smoothly, then spread warmth to his chest. 'Nice. You know what happened?'

'Well. I helped carry you to Walter's room.'

Katrina and Liesel entered the room. Both wore wary expressions.

At least she's safe, Peyre told himself. He looked at them all. 'Do they know what happened to me?' he asked Liesel.

'Yes,' she said. 'You fainted. Maybe the cathedral was too airless for you.' She looked at him, chin in the air, as if challenging him to say differently.

Peyre gritted his teeth. *So that's how she's going to play it? Seems like Inge can do anything she likes and get away with it.* Katrina and Jeremias looked uncomfortable. *So they should.*

'I know it's not what you want to hear,' Jeremias ventured into the silence. 'But you need to take care of yourself, Peyre.'

Peyre got to his feet. The blood rushed to his head, and he swayed a little, whether from his 'fainting' or the arak, he wasn't sure. 'Thanks for the drink,' he said on the way out.

PEYRE STALKED ABOUT WITMAR CASTLE. He'd never been so angry. He realised he missed Umbert, too. His friend had always been someone to talk to. Now he was alone, with no one to confide in, and he was at a loss about what he should do. Liesel was in danger from Salvinus. Too scared to tell people. Those few who did know, like him, were threatened by Inge. Liesel had asked him not to tell her uncle Walter, for fear of what Inge might do. No doubt, after what had just happened in the cathedral gardens, she now feared for Peyre as well.

Peyre's limited options swirled around his mind, each one discounted for one reason or another, then returned to again. The one he knew he wouldn't take was doing nothing. At last, he made a decision. He would find Leopold and confront him.

He found the new Duke of Luderia in the main hall of the castle. He had expected him to be surrounded by hangers on, but there were only three others. One, he knew: Gervase Salvinus, the man who would govern the duchy for him. The other two, both young men, Peyre hadn't seen before.

'Ah! Just the man I wanted to see!' Leopold called out as Peyre approached. He offered his hand and Peyre took it. 'These gentlemen are Olbrecht and Heinke.'

Peyre nodded at the pair, and they nodded back; a little wary, perhaps.

'They're going to show me the sights of Witmar. I assume you're coming, Peyre?'

'Why not?' *This could be my chance*, he realised, *to talk with Leopold on his own.*

'Though perhaps keep young Peyre away from the wine,' Salvinus suggested dryly.

Peyre forced himself to grin at the comment. *Better for this man to think me a fool.*

'He kept down a pint of ale from the rookery,' said Leopold. 'If he can do that, I'll wager he'll have no trouble in Witmar.'

ONCE IT WAS JUST the four of them, Olbrecht and Heinke relaxed a little, keen to show off their knowledge of the taprooms of Witmar. Sons of Luderian nobility, they had the income and leisure to have built up some experience. Olbrecht had a drinker's belly, while Heinke was short and stocky, putting his drinks away like his insides were hollow.

Peyre found he liked the city. Smaller than Coldeberg and not nearly so big as Essenberg, it was easy to get his bearings. Even after they had visited several establishments.

By the time they reached The Black Wheel, they were in high spirits. Leopold introduced himself to the other patrons as their new duke, and, to much cheering, offered them all a drink on the house. When the owner dared to ask him how he was paying for it, Leopold made some vague comment about bringing him the money tomorrow. Peyre couldn't help but find the owner's expression amusing, even if there was a part of him that knew it was wrong.

Even deeper into their cups, Leopold called the man over and pointed out a barmaid they had been admiring. 'She's gorgeous. I want you to set me up with her in one of your rooms.'

'That's my daughter,' said the man.

Peyre could see the man struggling to contain his anger and felt ashamed to be a part of it.

Not Olbrecht and Heinke, though. They didn't hide their amusement: Olbrecht sniggering, Heinke guffawing.

'So?' asked Leopold, an edge to his voice. 'I'm the duke of Luderia, man. If you want my patronage, you'll set it up.'

'Leopold, stop it,' Peyre demanded. 'It's disrespectful.'

'Nonsense,' said Leopold. 'A mistress of a duke is an honourable position. Never mind mistress of the next emperor.'

The fact that Leopold was behaving just like Salvinus served to remind Peyre why he had come along in the first place. 'I need to talk with you. In private.'

Leopold gave him a cold look. 'The only person I want to see in private is that girl.'

'It involves your sister,' Peyre told him. A part of his mind warned Peyre that this was a mistake. It wasn't the right circumstances. But another part pushed him on. Things needed to be said, and if he waited for the perfect opportunity, they never would be.

Leopold looked at him, incredulous. 'You want to speak about my sister?'

'Yes. Liesel.' Peyre was aware of the reactions of those around him. Olbrecht and Heinke had cooled towards him again. He waited while the owner of the inn slunk away, now forgotten by the other three.

'Say your piece here,' Leopold said, giving him a dangerous look.

'First,' said Peyre, 'did you authorise Lord Kass to negotiate with my father about a marriage between Liesel and my brother?'

Leopold's eyes narrowed with suspicion. 'That's a lie.'

'Hardly. I was there. There were plenty of witnesses. Second.' He paused, struggling with the weight of what he had to say next; struggling with how to phrase it. 'Salvinus. He leches after her. Tries to bed her. I witnessed that myself as well.'

Leopold shrugged. 'Liesel is very attractive. I'd try to bed her myself if I wasn't her brother. Wouldn't you?' he asked his two friends, who nodded along. He seemed to think about it. 'Maybe that shouldn't stop me.'

Heinke guffawed with laughter. 'Too much,' he said.

Peyre stared at Leopold. *So, this is who you are*, he thought. *I can't claim that I wasn't warned to keep my mouth shut.* But standing there, looking at Leopold's arrogant face, with Heinke's braying laughter echoing around the inn, he was in no mood to shrug and walk away. 'So, you're too scared of Salvinus to keep him in check?'

It was only there for a moment, then Leopold regained his composure. But Peyre had seen that his barb had hit home. 'Teach this fucker a lesson,' the duke said.

Heinke was only too keen, stepping in to Peyre, fist heading for his midriff. But Peyre had seen it coming. He blocked, then sent his own punch crashing into Heinke's jaw, sending him to the floor of the inn. Pain shot through his hand and wrist and he wondered whether he'd broken something.

Neither Leopold nor Olbrecht looked like they fancied a turn. But then the duke was bellowing. 'Arrest this man!'

Enough Luderians were ready to obey their duke's orders. Enough for Peyre to know it was pointless trying to resist. He was manhandled and forced to his knees, whereupon Heinke delivered the blow to the guts he had been after. The wind was knocked from Peyre's body and he was coughing and spluttering, desperately trying to suck in air.

When he was finally able to breathe and lift his head, Leopold was in front of him. With a knife.

The inn had gone deathly quiet, a nervous quality to the atmosphere.

'You decided to lecture me on how to rule?' Leopold asked him. 'Who do you think you are?' A smile came to Leopold's face then, as if a great idea had come to him. Peyre didn't like the look of it. 'Since you're so obsessed with Salvinus, maybe I should give you a scar just the same as his?' He put the tip of the blade just below Peyre's ear.

Peyre was in little doubt that Leopold would do it. 'I wouldn't,' Peyre stammered. 'My father wouldn't be pleased,' he warned, hating that he was resorting to using his status to stop the bastard from going through with it.

Leopold laughed. 'Am I supposed to fear what the duke of Morbaine might do?' He studied Peyre, thinking. 'Or maybe it isn't Salvinus you're obsessed with. Maybe it's my sister. Yes, that would make more sense. So keen to put your dick in her you're worried Salvinus might get in there first?' He withdrew his knife, only to return it to an even more unpleasant location. 'Maybe I should cut your cock off instead. Protect my sister's virtue.'

Peyre had run out of things to say now. He looked at Leopold, hoping he'd be spared.

'No,' said the duke. 'I like the scar idea best. That way you'll still want to nug all the girls, but none of them will want to.'

Peyre's face burned with agony as Leopold slit his face from ear to chin. Then they let him go and Peyre staggered out of The Black Wheel, only vaguely aware of what he was doing. He felt the cool night air on his wound; it was dripping blood, and he put one hand over it in an attempt to close the wound. He realised he was shaking. A part of him had been sure Leopold wouldn't go through with it— that it was all bluff. That part of him still struggled to believe what had just happened. But another part of him had been sobered up by the assault. That part led him back to Witmar Castle with purpose.

. . .

Walter stood in shock when Peyre burst into his room. 'What happened to you?' the duke asked, peering at Peyre's face, still leaking blood.

'Never mind that,' said Peyre. 'There is something I need to tell you.'

'We *will* have to mind it,' Walter said. 'But if there is something more important, then of course you must tell me.'

At last, Peyre told Walter about what Liesel had confided to him. He carefully relayed the details of Salvinus's assault on her in the castle hall and how he had intervened. Only then did he explain his wound: how he had confronted Leopold about Salvinus. 'I'm sorry I didn't come to you before,' Peyre told Walter when he was done.

'I won't pretend I wish you hadn't spoken to me sooner than this,' Walter said when he was done. 'But at least you've seen sense and done it now. I need to think carefully about how we proceed with this matter. In the meantime, we need to get you cleaned and stitched up.'

Walter dropped Peyre off with the physician of the castle. They'd had to wake him up first. Since the man now worked for Leopold, it was somewhat ironic that he was fixing the damage meted out by the duke. Not that Peyre or Walter told him the truth about how he received the wound. *I'm learning*, Peyre told himself. *Finally.*

When he returned to Walter's room, it was the middle of the night. He found himself in somewhat surprising company. Liesel's sister, Katrina, was seated on her uncle's bed. On a chair sat Lord Kass, the diplomat who had come to Arbeost. Standing over him was Farred, hand not so subtly on the hilt of his sword. Kass looked distinctly uneasy.

'Come in, Peyre,' Walter said tersely. He exuded authority over proceedings and Peyre found himself wondering why exactly he had taken so long to put such a serious matter into Walter's hands.

It is surprising, he marvelled, *how one can be so damned stupid and only realise it afterwards.*

Walter pointed a thick finger at Kass. 'We're getting somewhere. No surprise to learn that Kass was sent into Morbaine on the orders of Salvinus and Inge. More of a surprise is who went with him. Three of Salvinus's killers. I don't know if there was ever any intention of the marriage taking place. It has all the signs of a covert operation—a ruse for these men to gain access to your father's court. Because once Kass set off back for the empire, the three individuals stayed in Morbaine. Can you think of any reason, Peyre? What they might have been up to? Anything stolen, or worse?'

Peyre racked his brain. Nothing was dislodged. He knew nothing of these men Walter talked about. And nothing bad had happened after Kass's visit. Nothing he was privy to, anyway. He shook his head. 'Sorry. Nothing.'

Kass sighed with relief.

Walter looked at Peyre.

I'm not sure he believes me, Peyre realised. *But I suppose I can't complain if he doesn't fully trust me anymore.*

Walter shrugged, reluctantly moving on. He stared at Kass. 'What brought you to agree to such a reckless course of action, I can't understand.'

'I'm sorry,' Kass got out, sounding genuine. 'It's not what I wanted. But things have changed in Essenberg. It's not possible to say no to Salvinus any longer. Not if you don't want to end up at the bottom of the Cousel.'

'You could have warned me,' Walter said. 'Got word out somehow.'

'I know. I'm sorry and ashamed. If I could make it up, I would.'

'You can,' Walter said. 'For a start, this conversation never happened. And from now on, you are my eyes and ears in Essenberg.'

'Of course,' Kass agreed.

'And if I get the faintest whiff of a double cross, you *will* end up in the Cousel. I have killers who work for me, Kass. And they're better than the oafs on Salvinus's payroll.'

'You have my word.'

Walter sighed. 'Get out.'

Kass wasted no time in exiting the room.

'I think we can trust him,' Walter said, as if trying to convince himself. 'At least for a while. But either way, we need to act fast now. News of what happened to Peyre will spread around the castle shortly. It gives us an excuse to leave. Katrina, your role in this will be crucial.'

'She's my sister,' Katrina said. 'I would do anything to see her safe.'

'I know.' Walter moved to the bed and Katrina got to her feet. They embraced. It was hard for Peyre to see Katrina's tears.

'I should have done more to look after you both,' Walter said. 'But there's no point in dwelling on the past. We will all do what's right now. What we do for Liesel will make all our lives more difficult. But it is the right thing to do.' Walter gave his niece a last pat on the back, and they separated.

Katrina headed for the door, stopping as she reached Peyre. 'Thank you for what you've done,' she told him. 'And I apologise for what my brother did. He—he got lost somewhere in all of this.'

When Katrina left, Walter took a long look at Farred, then turned to Peyre. 'Right, young man. You are so upset about what happened tonight that I have decided to return to Coldeberg immediately. That means that if anyone should stop and ask, you will be distraught. Understood?'

'We're leaving?' Peyre asked him. 'With Liesel?'

Walter exchanged a glance with Farred. 'Not quite.'

WALTER'S ENTOURAGE left Witmar when it was still dark. Peyre was grateful when the first rays of sunlight lightened the sky. He'd come close to falling asleep while riding in the darkness. He was exhausted, and the ale he'd quaffed last night had left him with a thumping headache. The daylight, combined with the exercise of riding, gradually improved his condition. His hand constantly strayed to his face, touching the puckered skin. *It could be worse*, he tried telling himself. *Leopold threatened to cut my cock off.*

At times, alone with his thoughts, he contemplated the various ways he might take revenge on Leopold. But more often, he thought about Liesel, hoping she was safe.

They crossed into Kelland before stopping for the night, Walter organising a hasty camp not far from the road.

Peyre was asleep moments after lying down. He had to be woken the next morning. Soon they had re-joined the Witmar Road, heading for Essenberg. But they hadn't gone far when a figure on the road ahead of them caused them to pull up.

Inge stood alone. There was no horse or other form of transport nearby, causing Peyre to wonder how she had got ahead of them. He didn't like to think about such things.

'Where is she?' the witch demanded.

Peyre shuddered. It was as if she had poked into his mind, looking for an answer to her question. But Peyre didn't know where Liesel was.

'She?' Walter asked innocently.

'Don't mess with me, Walter,' Inge fumed. 'I know you're behind it.' She glared at Peyre, who glanced away.

He had never seen Inge come close to losing her temper—hadn't thought it possible. Internally, he revelled in it, but he forced himself to keep a straight face, sensing that a grin might provoke a dangerous reaction.

'Yet you have no proof,' Walter said. 'Just as I have no proof that you've been interfering in other countries.' He glanced in Peyre's direction.

Inge appeared to acknowledge that, and she calmed down. 'In truth, I thought I would find her with you. You've played it well, making me think she was with Katrina all this time. But what you think you stand to achieve by interfering like this, I can't understand. You've made a very big mistake, Walter.' She looked about their group for a moment. Her eyes narrowed. 'Wait. Where is Farred?'

'I sent him ahead, to Coldeberg. He has things to do.'

Inge smiled her mocking smile. Suddenly, she seemed to be feeling better. 'Then I might go to Coldeberg myself. If I find that Farred has abducted Liesel, I'll kill him.' She gave a careless shrug. 'Duke Leopold's orders.'

Walter gave a shrug of his own. '*If* you find him.'

LIESEL

WITMAR, DUCHY OF LUDERIA, 672

Katrina!' Jeremias called. 'Farred is here.'

Liesel looked at Katrina.

Her sister had a nervous expression on her face. She approached Liesel and took her hand, pulling her to her feet. 'Come.'

'Why?' Liesel asked, suspicious. 'What's going on?'

'You need to escape Witmar, Liesel. Come on.'

Liesel shook her head. 'No.' If Farred was here, it meant Walter was a part of this. And the last thing she wanted was her uncle and sister brought into a confrontation with Salvinus and Inge. There would only be one winner in that contest.

Katrina squeezed her hand until it hurt. 'I'm telling you to go. If father was here, he would say the same.'

Katrina's words caught Liesel off guard, hitting her with emotion. 'If father was here, this wouldn't be happening.' But she allowed her sister to lead her into the adjoining room.

Jeremias and Farred were murmuring quietly to one another. Liesel knew very well that both men had fought at Burkhard Castle with her father—distinguished themselves, in their own way. It gave her a sliver of confidence that whatever they had planned might work.

She looked at the three of them. 'I suppose Peyre is responsible for this,' she said.

'Yes,' said Katrina, 'and he did exactly the right thing. Now, let Farred explain things.'

'Katrina and Jeremias will act as if you are still here,' Farred told her. 'Walter will head west, back to Barissia. By the time Salvinus and Inge realise you are not with either of them, you and I will be long gone.'

Liesel hesitated. Cold fear clutched at her insides; but she was sick of that feeling. 'Alright,' she agreed.

'I've brought clothes for you to change into,' said Farred.

THEY HAD to wait until morning, when the North Gate of Witmar was opened. They left on horseback.

'Don't worry,' Farred said to her. 'You make a good man.'

He'd dressed her in warrior gear, a huge cloak covering everything and a hood pulled over her face. Liesel wasn't so sure about the disguise. It didn't look right, and it would only take one observant individual to say something when Salvinus asked questions.

Farred took them north. Liesel glanced across at him, riding his horse like he was born in the saddle. She'd been a little intimidated by Farred as a girl. He didn't talk much, feeling no inclination to put people at ease. His looks had been alien to her—the dark colouring of the Middians, with long hair tied back in a ponytail, had made him seem like a strange savage. Even if she had outgrown such childish judgements, there were other things she had continued to hold against him. Walter's relocation to Coldeberg, in the years after she had lost her father, had been a bitter blow to take. It had been far easier to blame this man than her beloved uncle. Here he was, though, not thinking twice about helping her out of this mess. She knew he was risking his life doing it.

'Are you alright?' he asked, catching her looking at him.

'I'm fine.'

'You ride well,' he offered.

'I loved my riding lessons,' she told him. 'Being outside. I used to complain when Leopold got to go to martial training, and I wasn't allowed, even though he was younger.'

'It's not too late to learn,' he said. 'You're still young.'

I suppose I am, compared to you, she thought. 'Do you intend to go to Rotelegen?' she asked him. That was the obvious destination if they were heading north. In her opinion, a little too obvious, since any pursuers might expect them to head to the duchy of her brother-in-law. The alternative was to the lands of the mysterious Caladri. That was unlikely, though she wouldn't put it past her companion.

Farred turned in his saddle, looking behind them towards Witmar. 'Once I am sure we are out of sight of the city, we will change course to the east.'

Ah, Liesel thought. *I should have expected yet another ruse.* 'East?' she repeated, unable to work out where their final destination might be. East was—well—nowhere.

'To Atrabia,' Farred said.

'Atrabia?' The duchy her grandfather had conquered and added to the empire by force? The Atrabians thought her entire family were devils. Why, by the gods, would they go to Atrabia?

Farred studied her reaction. Was that a smirk on his face? 'No one will expect that,' he said.

* * *

Farred set a gruelling pace. But Liesel was hardly going to complain. The faster they rode, the sooner they would leave Luderia and the less likely they would be caught. She wondered whether her absence had yet been noticed. Were they being hunted already? Salvinus, with a pack of his mercenaries? More terrifying was the thought of Inge, furious at being defied. Liesel knew it was the witch who should be truly feared.

A line of hills marked the border with Atrabia. Farred led them through a pass that wound between two mounds of rock, forcing them to ride single file. He peered upwards. 'Don't be alarmed,' he said, 'but I think we're being trailed.'

'We've only just left Luderia,' Liesel complained. It confirmed everything that was said about the Atrabians in Essenberg. Incorporated into Brasingia by Emperor Bernard; yet they still acted as if they were an independent kingdom. Most damning of all—when her father had called on the Atrabians for aid against the Drobax horde that had invaded the empire, they hadn't come.

The longer they travelled, the closer Liesel came to concluding that Atrabia was simply a wasteland. It made her wonder why her grandfather had put so much effort into subduing the territory in the first place. Everywhere she looked, there were hills and mountains from where the Atrabians could spy on an enemy force. Even the lowlands were covered in woodland and gorse, from where the Atrabians might launch an ambush. She understood enough about war to realise this place would have been hell to take by force.

Liesel let out a sigh of relief when Farred stopped to make camp. The romantic notions she had previously held of adventuring and war had taken a knock after a relentless day of exhausting travel. She was stiff and sore, desiring nothing more than a wash and a hot meal and her bed. She would get none of that. Farred seemed disinterested in providing any sort of comfort for them, tending instead to their horses. He caught her looking over.

'You can rest for a while,' he said.

'Can I not help?' she asked. 'After sitting all day, I'd rather stretch my legs.'

'Of course.' He pointed towards a copse of trees. 'Any dry wood will help with our evening fire. You can do your business in there, too, if you wish.'

Liesel was both shocked and grateful for his plain speaking. 'What about the people following us?' she asked, looking about as if she might spot them. The last thing she wanted was some Atrabian soldier catching her in the middle of her business.

'I'm pretty sure they won't bother us tonight,' Farred assured her.

While Liesel collected fuel, Farred built their camp: two places to sleep and a fire. He prepared their meal. As night fell, they could clearly see a second fire on a rise not far away. So Farred had been right about being followed. She didn't know why, but something about that fire made her feel more reassured than threatened, as if whoever was up there was looking out for them.

'Thank you for doing this,' she said to Farred, realising she hadn't said a word of gratitude yet. She hated the idea that people might think her a spoiled brat. But she'd grown up with people doing things for her on a daily basis; gratitude didn't come as naturally as it should.

'You're welcome,' Farred said. 'You know, Walter and I would have acted sooner, if we'd realised how bad things were.' The Magnian stared into the flames, a brooding expression on his face. 'We got preoccupied with our work in Barissia. The last ten years have flown by, and we didn't take enough notice of the world outside. Didn't want to, I suppose, is the truth of it.'

'No one asked you for help until last night,' Liesel said, feeling sorry for him. Why shouldn't Farred and Walter have been allowed to live their lives? They'd given plenty for the empire already. Farred wasn't even a Brasingian—he didn't owe her anything; much less have to risk his life for her benefit. 'I didn't want to get you involved,' she explained.

'I'm grateful you did—grateful that Peyre told us.' He looked at her. 'I feel like I've been woken from a long sleep.' He grimaced. 'But it's not too late to make amends.'

THEY WOKE early and were soon riding eastwards again. Liesel detected a slight softening in the land about them. The path they took became a mud track, the first piece of evidence that there was any civilisation in Atrabia. Hoof beats caused them to turn around. Three riders cantered behind them, keeping to the pace Farred set, but making no attempt to catch up.

'Our friends from last night,' Farred commented, unconcerned.

Later, they passed through a settlement. A fast-moving stream to the north provided the people with water, and Liesel could see sheep grazing nearby. She reckoned there were about twenty wooden houses in all. She met eyes with a dark featured Atrabian woman. The woman's look wasn't so much suspicious as it was observant. Farred didn't stop and their honour guard passed through the settlement too, still keeping the same distance behind.

As midday approached, they came upon a second settlement, large enough to be called a town. It lay either side of a stream, presumably the same one Liesel had noticed earlier. Rough wooden walls encircled it, defending the crossing point.

Farred called a halt. Looking ahead, Liesel could see the track they followed led to an open gate in the town's wall.

'Best to get permission to enter,' Farred said. He looked behind them at the three riders who had been following them, who finally approached. Two men and a woman, all about Liesel's age, with the same dark eyes and hair of the woman from the previous settlement. All three wore long woollen cloaks and each had a linen bag hanging from their saddle, the length of a short-bow. Their mounts were small and nimble looking.

'We've come looking for Prince Gavan,' Farred said to them.

'He's been told of your arrival,' one of the men answered in a lilting accent. 'We'll take you into Treglan,' he said, nodding at the town ahead of them. 'The prince may be there already. If not, you can wait for him.'

Unlike Essenberg, there were no guards employed at the gate or town walls. Instead, all the folk of Treglan stopped their business to examine the new arrivals as they rode past. Once they realised who the first three riders were, they called out a friendly greeting. Farred and Liesel were treated to a more neutral, silent appraisal. In a land where everyone knew one another, strangers stood out.

Prince Gavan had a house in the centre of the town where Farred and Liesel were taken. Literally, Liesel was amazed to see—a house. No hall or castle or any such grandeur. Their horses were stabled, and they were taken inside. A fire burned brightly in the main room, but no one was there. Liesel and Farred were offered comfy chairs to sit in, and then the three Atrabians left them alone.

Liesel looked around. It was beautiful inside, with blackened wooden frames and whitewashed walls, like the country cottages in Kelland. But it was so small she still found it hard to believe the Prince of Atrabia would choose it as a residence.

Gavan didn't make them wait long. He entered the room alone, wearing simple woollen clothing. He looked relaxed. Liesel reckoned he was the same age as Farred. He had the same warrior's physique, a strong-jawed face with a trimmed beard and brown eyes that had a sparkle to them.

Farred and Liesel went on one knee.

'Please, that is not necessary,' he said quickly, directing them back to their chairs. 'Lady Liesel, be assured I am at your service. You have had some hard travel from what I am told?'

'It was decided we had to leave in a hurry,' Liesel admitted, glancing at Farred.

'Decided by?'

'Duke Walter gave the order for me to take the lady here,' Farred said. 'You can blame him that we've landed on your doorstep.'

Gavan smiled at that. 'It is nothing but an honour to have you both here. I am a little surprised—but pleased—that Walter put so much faith in me.'

'I think it was a case of taking me to the most unlikely location,' Liesel said.

'Ah,' Gavan acknowledged. 'That makes sense. But things really are that serious?'

Liesel didn't know what to say. What ought she tell this prince? What did she *want* to tell him? She knew that while she had come here looking for help, Gavan had never been an ally of her family. 'I wasn't safe at court.'

A slight frown passed over Gavan's face. He seemed to consider his next words. 'It's not a story that I often tell. But I was one of the last people to see your father alive.' He looked at her, checking to see her reaction.

What, Liesel wondered. *He expects me to burst into tears at the mention of my father?*

'I presume you know something of the story.' Gavan continued. 'The Isharite army was loose in the empire. We—the Atrabians—had come west to disrupt their advance. At the same time, your father came east, leading the horde away from Essenberg—well, away from you,' he recalled. 'You were only young, then.'

'I was seven.'

'Baldwin insisted he would face the enemy and that my force should withdraw. My Atrabians should help his soldiers escape— which, of course, we did. It was a very brave thing to witness. Until then, your father had no understanding of me—thought me a coward, I am sure. For my part, I had a healthy hatred of the Kellish, since it was your grandfather who had conquered Atrabia and forced us to join the empire. But in those few shared words, on the day he died, we came to understand each other a little. Too late, it seemed, to change anything between our peoples. But now you are here, Liesel. And I swear I will protect you as if you were my own daughter.'

PART III
GUIVERGNE

SANC * PEYRE

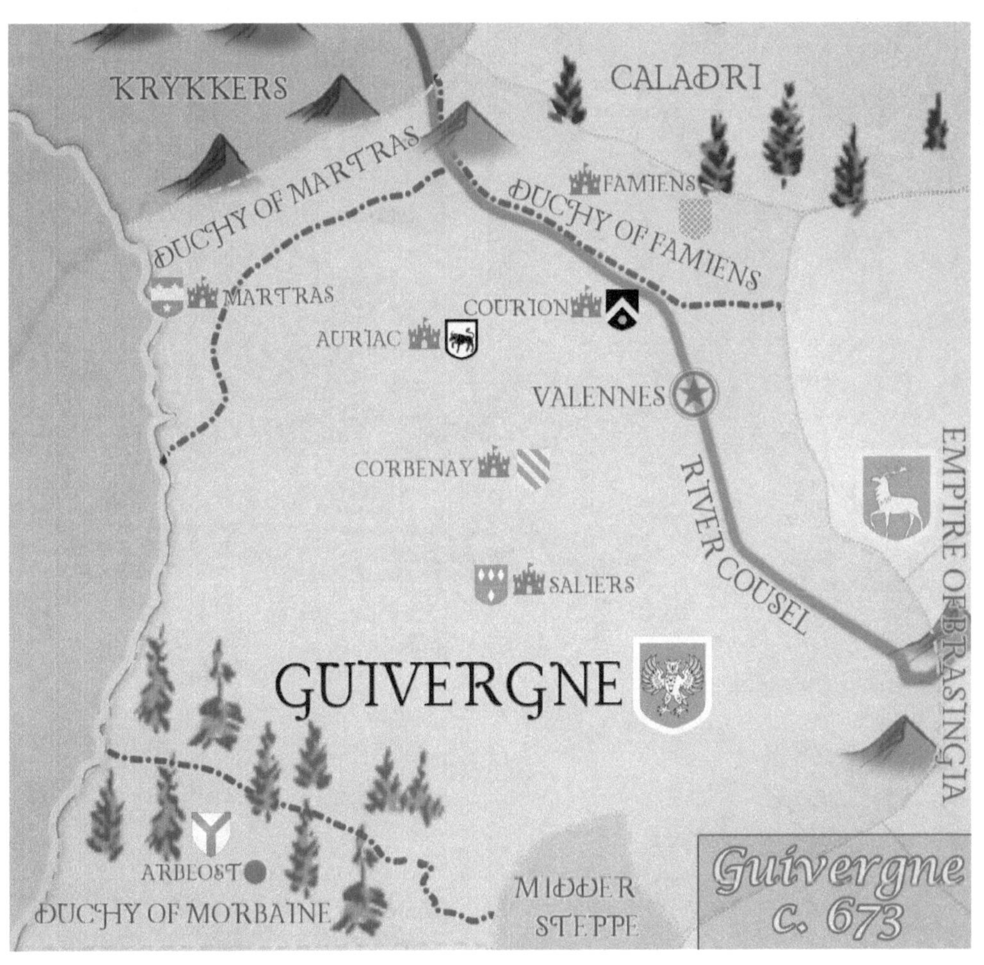

KRYKKERS
CALADRI
DUCHY OF MARTRAS
FAMIENS
DUCHY OF FAMIENS
MARTRAS
COURION
AURIAC
VALENNES
CORBENAY
RIVER COUSEL
SALIERS
EMPIRE OF BRASINGIA
GUIVERGNE
ARBEOST
DUCHY OF MORBAINE
MIDDER STEPPE
Guivergne
c. 673

SANC

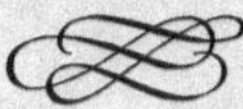

ARBEOST, DUCHY OF MORBAINE, 673

The invasion of the Midder Steppe turned out to be a brief, sour interruption to Sanc's life. Back in Arbeost, the familiar routines returned to fill his days. Weapons training with Brancat; magical training with Rimmon.

Occasionally, Jesper would take him into the Forest of Morbaine. He had decided that both Sanc and Rab were of an age where they could begin to familiarise themselves with the terrain. This largely consisted of extended walks that were enjoyable at first, and then became tests of endurance. Only rarely did they encounter the wildlife of the forest. Jesper explained that the animals needed to get used to his and Rab's scent before they could start approaching them.

As for what happened in the Steppe—the attack by Robert and his friends; Peyre's exile; the attitude of King Nicolas—Sanc had few people to share his feelings with. The only person he told about it was Loysse, and that had been a more palatable version of events. His sister had reassured him their father knew what he was doing regarding Peyre and that their brother would soon return.

It wasn't that Sanc didn't have faith in his father as far as Peyre's future was concerned. It was more the feelings of guilt, shame and rejection that swirled through his mind whenever he stopped to think. So he tried not to think too much. When such feelings surfaced on the training field, they hardened him, something Brancat approved of. With Rimmon, they made him concentrate all the more. *If I'm to be an outcast,* he told himself, *why not embrace the powers I've been given?*

He stopped short of discussing how he felt with Rimmon or Jesper. They had seen real suffering. What would they think of the mewling of a spoiled duke's son?

Summer turned to autumn, and Sanc turned fourteen. His birthday passed largely unnoticed. Loysse had Brayda bake him a cake, which he shared with his sister and Cebelia.

Jesper presented him with a longbow he had made himself. 'You're strong enough to learn how to use one,' the forester told him. 'But you'll need lessons in it,' he warned.

Of course. More lessons. Sanc's age seemed to confirm something in his mind, a feeling that had been brewing unnoticed until now. It was a sense that Arbeost, his home, wasn't really a home at all. Not in the sense of a place where he belonged, at any rate. The feeling told him it would be his last winter in Arbeost. But where he would go—what place he might belong—he had no idea.

RIMMON TOOK him into the forest to go through the last phase of his defence training. He had to learn to protect himself from magical attacks.

'It's not that easy to kill another mage,' Rimmon told him. 'Not one properly trained in magical defence, at any rate. Defending, once you are proficient in it, is less exacting than attacking. Thus, a weaker mage can often hold off a stronger opponent by fighting them to a standstill. Your options are the same as the defences you have learned. Block, redirect, or return a specific attack. If you need to, you can use the same sphere of magic you deploy in melee situations. But that will sap your energy levels much faster.'

Rimmon launched a series of magical missiles at him. Once Sanc got used to it, his teacher varied things. He threw a volley of smaller blasts, then one big one. He changed what they looked like, so that

Sanc got used to their appearance—controlled his fear. A ball of fire felt different to an arc of white lightning or a green pulse, even if they should all be treated the same.

Once Sanc's confidence grew, he was told to walk through the forest. Somewhere out there, Rimmon would be lying in wait. It could be early on or not for hours. The prolonged concentration required was exhausting in itself. It reminded Sanc a little of the boredom he had felt during his father's campaign in the Midder Steppe. Hours of walking or riding, followed by hours on lookout. But at all times, they'd needed to be ready should an attack come.

When Rimmon's attacks came, they could take any form, from any angle. But after weeks of testing, the sorcerer declared Sanc's defence training to be over. They spoke together in the glade where Rimmon had begun his lessons. 'Next, you will learn the attacks I have been using. But that shouldn't take long.'

Sanc was doubtful. 'Are you sure?'

'You've already used magic to attack people, remember. Long before I came to Arbeost.'

Of course, Sanc remembered. He'd blasted two grown men outside Jesper's hut. He shuddered at the recollection. But if he could do that by himself two years ago, then maybe Rimmon was right.

'It's the most instinctive use of magic,' said Rimmon. 'To strike out when threatened. And you've already developed control of how much power to use.'

Sanc nodded. Such words were meant to encourage him but doubts still nagged.

Rimmon sensed his uneasiness. 'What is it, Sanc?'

'I just can't stop asking myself, why me? Why do I have this power and no one else? Is it because of these?' he asked, gesturing at the red eyes that had marked him out as different his entire life.

'Sit,' said Rimmon. 'We need to talk.'

They sat down together on the forest floor. Sanc trailed the nails of one hand through the dirt.

'Every mage asks these questions,' Rimmon told him. 'We are so very different—often feared and reviled because of it—that it's natural to want to understand why we have this power that is part gift, part curse. But as I have got older and wiser, I have learned that people without magic ask the very same questions of themselves. Why am I not healthier; stronger; prettier; more sharp-minded; kinder; more disciplined. All I can say is that life is easier when we accept ourselves for who we are. But finding that acceptance is often a difficult path.'

Sanc nodded politely, even though Rimmon's words sounded like a lot of waffle. 'But what lies behind it?' he pursued. 'Pure chance? The gods? In Arbeost, people say it is the work of demons.'

'Who can say for sure? Gods play a role, but what that is exactly, I don't know. In your case, clearly there is a connection with Pentas.'

'With Pentas? Your teacher?' Sanc asked, intrigued.

'Yes,' Rimmon replied, as if it was obvious. 'You mentioned your eye colour.'

Sanc struggled to grasp what his teacher was saying to him. 'Wait. Do you mean Pentas had red eyes?'

Understanding dawned on Rimmon's features. 'Oh. I'm sorry. I assumed all this time that Jesper would have mentioned that. This conversation is long overdue.'

Pentas had red eyes? The idea that someone else—even someone long dead—had the same condition as Sanc suddenly opened his mind to new possibilities. Perhaps it was silly, but the revelation somehow made him feel less alone. 'But why would Jesper not tell me that?' he wondered.

'That's probably my fault,' Rimmon admitted. 'When Jesper came here to look after you, I warned him to tell you as little as possible about magic. For your protection, as much as for any other reason. Jesper was always someone who stuck close to instructions, and he has probably been more careful than necessary to leave certain details out of his stories.'

'What do you mean, came here to look after me?' Sanc asked, bewildered by the idea. 'You're not telling me that Jesper is in Arbeost because of me?'

'Let me tell you the story,' Rimmon said. 'Then you can ask any questions you might still have. I think you know Pentas was killed at the Battle of the Pineos in Kalinth?'

Sanc nodded, eager that Rimmon reveal whatever information he had.

'Pentas's red eyes were his most distinguishing feature. But there were other things about him that made him an enigmatic figure. He claimed to be a servant of Madria, despite working for Erkindrix as a member of the Lord of Ishari's Council of Seven. Anyway, after his death, the war continued. It was only after its conclusion that Jesper, myself, and a friend of ours got word of a red-eyed babe born in Morbaine. Of course, it was you. When we investigated, it turned out you were born on the same day Pentas was killed.'

A chill ran down Sanc's spine at this. What did it mean? Something told him he wasn't going to get a straight answer.

'We believed this couldn't be mere coincidence. Were your eyes a sign that you were Madria's new servant? Had She passed on some sort of power to you on his death? Did you need to be protected? We wished we could have had answers. But only weeks after the death of Pentas, Belwynn Godslayer killed both Diis and Madria. The goddess of Dalriya was gone; there was no one we could ask about you. It was quite possible that with Her death, your powers—assuming you had any in the first place—had disappeared with her. The only option was to wait for you to get older. We all looked in on you from time to time. But as you approached the age when your powers might be revealed, we agreed that Jesper would stay in Arbeost permanently. There are some out there that might want you dead.'

'Those men who came to kill me?'

'Probably sent from the Kellish court, where Inge the witch holds sway.'

Sanc considered that. He'd spent so much time at Jesper's hut over the years—it had been a refuge. Without letting Sanc know or worry about it, Jesper had been looking out for him. When it had mattered—when assassins had come for Sanc—Jesper and Tadita had saved him. 'So,' he said, his thoughts turning to what Rimmon's story had told him, 'my powers come from the dead servant of a dead goddess?'

Rimmon's eyebrows rose. 'I suppose so. You may think such knowledge unsatisfactory, but it is more explanation than I ever got.'

'What am I supposed to do with it?' Sanc demanded. 'I lost my purpose as soon as I was born.'

'You do what everyone else has to do in life,' Rimmon said. 'Find your own way.'

* * *

ONLY A FEW DAYS after Sanc's conversation with Rimmon, his father received serious news from Valennes. King Nicolas had fallen ill and was bed ridden. Messengers left Arbeost, braving frozen roads across Morbaine, warning Duke Bastien's followers to be on alert.

In Jesper's hut, huddled around his fire on a wintry night, they talked of what might happen. Sanc noticed he was now included in such conversations, when, a few years ago, he would have been left ignorant. Few in Arbeost worried over their king's health. They worried about what might come afterwards.

'Bastien's carefully laid plans could unravel if Nicolas lingers,' Jesper suggested, rubbing his hands together and putting them back to the warmth of the fire.

'Why is that?' Sanc asked him. Rab was laid out on his feet, like a warm blanket.

'Bastien is the heir. Esterel is in Valennes, winning hearts and minds. If the king died today, it would be difficult for your father to be denied the throne. But he has enemies, Sanc. Many see the death of a king as an opportunity for themselves. The king's illness will concentrate minds: encourage those who'd rather not see Bastien on the throne to find an alternative. Conspirators, plotters—they thrive on conditions like this.'

Sanc recalled the noblemen who had made accusations about Peyre to King Nicolas—Robert's father amongst them. They'd been keen to attack his family: forced his father to have Peyre banished, when it was their sons who'd done wrong. He knew they would be among the first to begin the plotting.

'I think it would be better not to get involved,' Sanc decided. 'Leave Guivergne to those curs and stay in Morbaine, where it's safe.'

Jesper and Rimmon shared a look. Sanc knew, before one of them spoke, that he'd said something wrong.

'Sanc,' Rimmon began, gently enough. 'If your father's enemies take the throne of Guivergne, they won't leave your family, the rightful claimants, in peace. They'll come to Morbaine, eventually. Having royal blood is a dangerous business. Duke Bastien knows the best way to protect his children is to become king.'

* * *

SANC'S LESSONS CONTINUED. He hurled magic at Rimmon, trying to break through his teacher's defences with brute force. He learned to use finesse, striking small targets with just the right amount of power Rimmon had asked for. He progressed well enough, but Rimmon had to reprimand him more than once for his lack of focus.

The news from Guivergne was a distraction. Like a rain cloud hovering over Arbeost, everyone underneath it was waiting; knowing that eventually, they were going to get a soaking. A messenger came: a young man Sanc recognised as a friend of Esterel's. He left again after speaking to Sanc's father. The rumour was that the king was making a recovery.

Then, there was Sanc's previous conversation with Rimmon. The sorcerer had revealed why Sanc had been born the way he was. Both his red eyes and his magic had been given to him by Madria, when Her servant Pentas had been killed. She had chosen Sanc, it seemed, to be his replacement. But Madria was dead and Sanc's life was now purposeless. Why bother learning to cast magic when there was no longer any point to his existence?

Beneath such thoughts lay the one that wrenched at him the most. *Why me? Why couldn't you leave me alone? To live a normal, happy life, like Esterel and Peyre?* He raged at a being that no longer existed. *And I know*, he told Her, nonetheless. *That what you did to me killed my mother.*

. . .

'You're ready for your final test,' Rimmon informed him, on a day when bright sunshine heralded the beginning of spring.

Sanc had been practising adding visual and other affects to his magical attacks. When his teacher had explained what was required, it had come naturally. The look, sound and feel of the attack was illusion: adding the glow, crackle and heat of flames made it look like he was casting fire. Combining these illusions with a magical strike was, according to Rimmon, combining two different types of magic.

'It's supposed to be difficult,' the sorcerer said, as if he was complaining about how quickly Sanc had grasped it. 'It took me months to master, not a few weeks.'

Sanc nodded, unsure what to say. A part of him was pleased with his rate of progress; pleased there was something he was good at. Another part was terrified. It occurred to him, based on Rimmon's comments, that there might come a time when he became more powerful than his teacher. Such thoughts only made him feel even more anxious. 'What's next?' he asked.

Rimmon puffed out his cheeks. 'For many mages, that's it. You have learned to control your power; to deploy it when needed, in attack or defence. That is all you need. Some develop other powers.'

'What other powers?'

'We have discussed examples before. Teleportation; illusion; trans-formation; telekinesis. There are others.'

'Which of those ought I to learn?'

'I'm not sure. In magic-rich societies, you would learn the skills of your peers. The Caladri, for example, learn to work together: to tele-port from place to place; to use illusions to confuse those who enter their territories. For individuals such as you and I, you learn what you need, or want to.'

'I don't know what I need to learn,' Sanc said.

'Quite. This is our problem now. You are a fourteen-year-old lad with the power of an advanced mage. Hence, I'm not entirely sure what to do with you. But come. Time for your test.'

They returned to Jesper's hut. Rab wagged his tail, pleased to see them. The dog was even more pleased to learn that he was to be part of their games. They took him outside.

'This is where the Kellishmen attacked you?' Rimmon asked.

'Over there,' said Sanc, pointing. He remembered the forest floor had been full of bluebells then, whereas now it was still in winter's grip.

'Come,' said Rimmon, and they walked over. 'Stand where you stood then.'

Sanc found the spot. It was eerie to be recreating that event.

Rimmon led Rab away until they were about the same distance of the men when they had appeared that day. 'Now. When we first met, I told you why you needed to learn magic from me. Control. You blasted those men that day. But what if one of them had someone you care about?' The sorcerer knelt and put an arm around Rab. 'Can you strike me and avoid your dog?'

'What if I hit him?'

'Exactly. There could be a time when you need to do just this. When the pressure is on, and you have mere moments to execute. Do it now and you'll know you can do it when you have to.'

'I might scare him.'

'Maybe a little. But he's a brave dog, and he's seen you do it before, after all.' Rimmon sighed at Sanc's reluctance. 'This is the test, Sanc. Brancat judges whether you can hold your own in combat, or function as part of a team. I have taught you to do something Brancat couldn't imagine. But can you do it with my arm around your dog? Or does it defeat you?'

I could do it if I had to, Sanc told himself. But he knew that would not wash with Rimmon. He studied his enemy. Rimmon was crouched behind Rab, leaving few parts of his body available to target. One long leg stuck out invitingly. *But if I hit that, he could survive and still hurt Rab. It has to be the face.* Rimmon had his head held higher than Rab. That was the obvious place to target.

Sanc readied himself. *Wait. What if there's an alternative?* He focused instead on the sorcerer's arm, draped around his dog. *I'd have to be quick. No more time to think. Just act.*

He cast his magic. He used his left hand to guide his power, pulling Rimmon's arm away from Rab. Then, quickly, he shoved his right hand forwards, pushing his teacher backwards.

Rimmon toppled over and was then jumped on by an over-enthusiastic dog. He got to his feet, wiping dog lick from his face. He looked over at Sanc with a stern expression. 'Not what I have been teaching you to do,' he said. His face relaxed. 'But it worked.'

* * *

OVER THE NEXT FEW DAYS, Sanc found himself with the unexpected luxury of leisure time. Brancat still wanted him on the training field. The prospect of war sharpened the minds of the boys, even if most were too young to join the duke's army this year. But Brancat's advice on how not to end up with a spear through the guts seemed less theoretical and more urgent than it used to.

But Rimmon no longer needed to see him afterwards. He'd got Sanc to where he needed to be and was content to wait while he pondered what to do with him next. Sanc had even overheard him talking with Jesper about leaving for a while, though he hadn't picked up where exactly his teacher wanted to go. Instead, Sanc and Jesper went for horse rides with Loysse and Cebelia. And, of course, his dog never said no to exercise.

Sanc was playing with Rab outside Jesper's hut when Lord Russell arrived.

'He's a big lad now,' the man commented, sizing Rab up. 'Is Rimmon in?'

'Yep,' Sanc said. 'He's pretending to help Jesper cook dinner.'

'Ah. Always good to show willing. Listen, Sanc, you'd better come in too.'

Sanc followed him into Jesper's hut, where Russell greeted Jesper and Rimmon.

'I have grave news,' Russell said. 'Sanc, your uncle, the king, has died. I'm sorry for your loss.'

Sanc nodded, appreciating that Russell had addressed the news to him. King Nicolas had, after all, been family. But his commiserations sounded hollow, and everyone knew it. What Sanc had seen of his uncle last year meant he had no genuine grief over his passing. 'So, Father will be king now?' he asked.

'I hope so. From everything we hear, it seems more than likely that the succession will be contested. The word is that the duke of Famiens has been persuaded to claim the throne.'

Sanc recalled meeting the man in the king's tent in the Midder Steppe. He'd stared at Sanc and his red eyes. He had seemed young to be a duke, but otherwise ordinary enough.

'What claim does he have?' Jesper asked.

'Most magnates have some family connection to the throne. But he has no real claim, not when Bastien is the king's brother. Nicolas didn't help there, however.'

'The brothers didn't get on?' Rimmon asked.

'Aye. Nicolas was a bitter man. He could have named Bastien his heir. That may have been enough to prevent this from happening. But he liked to use the succession as a tool to control people. A weapon to use against Bastien. Neither was he above implying to others that he might name them his heir instead of his brother.'

'Famiens being one such,' Rimmon suggested.

'I have no doubt. I would say he's young and foolish, but the truth is there are many prepared to side with him.'

'Why?' Sanc asked.

'Politics. They judge they'll be better off with Auberi as king than Bastien. It's a power grab, nothing more. What angers me is not so much the injustice of it, but what a civil war could do to the people of Guivergne. That's what we face if we don't act quickly. Even then, the next year or more are likely to be very difficult.'

A civil war? Would his father have to face his enemies in battle? Sanc had always wished that Morbaine was a bit more exciting. But now that Russell was talking of war, he had a new appreciation for peace.

'Duke Bastien would like to speak with you, Rimmon,' Lord Russell resumed. 'He knows you don't owe him any allegiance. But he plans to lead an army to Valennes, and he would appreciate your help. I thought I should warn you of what he will ask.'

'I had planned to leave Morbaine for a while and return to the South,' Rimmon said. The sorcerer's eyes drifted to Sanc as he considered it. 'If I were to help Duke Bastien, then I would insist Sanc accompany me.'

'Sanc?' Russell asked in surprise, glancing at him. 'It will be very dangerous.'

'He is ready to play his part. He needs something like this to develop his abilities.'

That familiar look of distaste passed over Russell's face, even if he was better than most at hiding it. 'I see. Then you should explain as much to the duke. There are few things he will refuse, if they are a means to becoming king.'

PEYRE

COLDEBERG, DUCHY OF BARISSIA, 673

Peyre stared moodily into his drink while everyone around him at The Boot and Saddle had a whale of a time. Umbert talked with—more accurately, shouted at—three girls at their table. *What stupid things he says,* Peyre observed. *And what nonsense they laugh at.*

The girls excused themselves, asking them to mind their drinks for them.

'What's up?' Umbert asked. 'You've been very quiet. Is it the scar?' he asked, gesturing at the healed wound that Leopold had left on Peyre's face. 'I've told you before. It makes you look rugged. Girls like that.'

Peyre had told his friend all about his exploits in Essenberg and Witmar. Umbert had enjoyed the story immensely, without offering much in the way of sympathy.

'I know it makes me look rugged,' Peyre said with ill-temper. In truth, he was far from confident about his new look, but he wasn't about to admit that. 'It's nothing to do with the scar.'

'Ah. It's Lady Liesel, isn't it? You're still pining for her. Well, just think about what she may be getting up to, wherever she is.'

'Is that supposed to make me feel better?' Peyre demanded, genuinely angry.

'It is Liesel!' Umbert crowed, as if he was eight years old and had won a guessing game.

'Will you shut up?' Peyre asked.

Umbert gave him an offended look and eyed the taproom of the inn, no doubt looking for the return of the three girls.

Peyre supped his drink. He was sure they'd done something to the ale here. It had much less flavour than it used to.

'Isn't that Lord Farred?' Umbert asked him.

Farred had spotted them and was making a beeline for their table. Middians were common enough in Coldeberg, but more than a few heads turned to watch him. Farred was well known in these parts. 'I need to talk with you, Peyre,' he said when he reached them. He looked around. 'Outside, please.'

'Of course,' Peyre said, not disappointed the evening was getting interrupted.

'Should I come too?' Umbert asked. 'It's just that I did promise to look after these drinks.'

Farred gave him an expressionless look. 'You should always keep your word, Master Umbert.'

They left Umbert inside, crossing to the other side of the street, where it was quieter. The evening air was chilly, serving to wake Peyre up and lift him out of his foul mood. He had thought going out would improve his spirits, instead it had the opposite effect.

'I'm sorry to bring bad news,' Farred told him. 'Walter has received word that your uncle has died. Please accept my condolences. He asked me to find you and tell you as soon as possible. Obviously, such an event is more than simply a death in the family.'

Peyre nodded, feeling shaken by the news. It didn't seem real. 'I need to go home. Esterel and my father will need my help. Is Walter still up?'

'He's in his study. He said he'd be available if you wanted to talk tonight.'

'Great. I guess I'm an exile no longer.'

. . .

'I FEEL like I want to contribute something,' Peyre explained to Walter. 'Rather than just turning up with myself and Umbert.'

'You really think it will come to violence?' Walter asked.

Peyre recalled those moments in the royal tent in the Steppe, when Robert's father and his friends had complained about their bully boy sons getting their just desserts. They'd sensed a weakness, attacking Peyre to get at his father. The last year or so of Peyre's life had shaken off much of the naivety he used to have. 'I'm sure of it.'

They were seated in the duke's study, from where he ruled Barissia. His desk was covered in manuscripts, and there was a musty, airless atmosphere. Walter was thinking. 'I couldn't recruit on your behalf or appear to take a side. But maybe I could allow men to fight for your father if they chose to. Your family would have to pay their wages.'

'That would be more than fair,' said Peyre, eager for Walter to agree to it. The idea of arriving in Valennes with warriors at his side had gripped him. Far better than an exile sneaking back with his tail between his legs.

'You're not likely to convince many.'

'That's alright.'

'And I do owe you a favour after what you did for Liesel.'

Neither Walter nor Farred would tell him where Liesel had been taken. They assured him she was safe and that would have to be enough to satisfy him. Though it didn't stop him from daydreaming about meeting her again. 'You don't owe me anything for helping Liesel,' he told the duke.

Walter's mouth twitched. He'd come close to a smile. 'Alright, Peyre. I'll talk it over with Farred. See if we can get you some fellows who aren't the worst kind of criminal.'

'Fantastic!' Peyre was excited about his return now. 'Thank you, Your Grace. Umbert and I will also spread the word in the inns we frequent.'

Walter gave him a look.

'If that's alright with you, of course.'

'I suggest you don't simply sign up any old reprobate,' Walter warned him.

'But it *would* clean up the streets of Coldeberg,' Peyre countered with a grin.

* * *

TWO DAYS LATER, Peyre and Umbert set out from Coldeberg. They travelled north, for Valennes.

In the meantime, a messenger had come to Coldeberg from his father, telling him about the death of the king and asking them to return home. Peyre judged that if he followed these instructions, his father would have left for Guivergne by the time he reached Morbaine. No, better to head for Valennes, where he could help his brother and father secure the throne. Whenever he thought of it, his heart raced. My father, king! Me, a prince! He'd known—all his life, it seemed—that this day might come. But that made it all the more momentous.

With them travelled a score of men and one woman, who represented the sum of their own recruitment efforts and those of Walter and Farred. The woman was named Syele. She grew her blonde hair long, but she wielded a wickedly sharp looking blade and the other Barissians seemed to know her—knew enough to show her proper respect, anyway.

Indeed, Peyre had insisted that all volunteers had to supply their own weapons, a restriction that had ruled out many of the more dubious applicants. Then there was the fact they would not be paid a single coin until they reached Guivergne. Walter warned him that only the desperate would sign up for a promise of money. But Peyre preferred to see the positives. These were individuals ready to grasp an opportunity. For if they helped his father to win the throne, surely he would reward them well.

Walter had refused to pay wages, but he had offered them the use of his horses while in Barissia. The Barissians under his command knew the best route to take and Peyre found himself following their directions. 'Not very leader-like,' he complained to Umbert on the first night. They had made camp outside, and it was too cold to be a pleasant experience.

'That will change when we reach Guivergne,' Umbert reassured him.

'But neither you nor I have been to Guivergne either,' Peyre reminded him.

'There is that,' Umbert admitted.

By the second night, they'd reached the border between the empire and Guivergne. Peyre was surprised how much the landscape had changed. No more neatly laid out villages, over-flowing with crops. The border region was rocky and desolate. Occasionally, they'd pass huge karst rock formations. They looked like they'd been placed upright on the ground by giants.

It reminded Peyre of the stories they'd been told before bed as kids. Oisin, King of the Giants, had sailed over from Halvia, wielding a spear the length of six horses. Oisin Dragon-Killer, they called him, since his spear had been the only weapon capable of slaying the Isharite dragon. It all sounded a little unlikely to Peyre, but these stones made him wonder if it could be true.

The next day they left their horses behind, in the last Barissian outpost, with instructions they be returned to Duke Walter. Before they'd even put a foot on Guivergnais soil, Peyre faced his first mutiny.

'Changed my mind,' said one man, looking at the terrain ahead of them with misgivings. He was one of the older ones and had some influence over his countrymen. 'I don't feel like walking into enemy territory with these numbers.'

'It's not enemy territory,' said Peyre. 'My brother is already in Valennes. Guivergne is loyal to my family.'

'So *you* say,' the man replied, unconvinced.

'You'll all be taken on as soldiers when we get to Valennes,' Peyre reminded them. 'And paid for your service so far. But I only want to take those who are committed to seeing it through. So, if anyone is having second thoughts, by all means, stay behind.'

In the end, four others also decided they'd changed their minds. That made eighteen, including Peyre and Umbert, who began the march due north. It was tough going. But, Peyre recognised, the farther they got, the less chance of his more unreliable recruits deciding to turn around and go back home.

At first, it seemed like no one lived in these parts, but that wasn't true. It didn't take long for them to spot figures watching them. They kept their distance for the time being.

'Eighteen's a big enough number for 'em to be wary,' said Elger, a man who Walter had recommended as a veteran of the Isharite Wars. 'But it's not like we're an army.'

'We've nothing to be afraid of,' said Peyre, trying to sound confident.

The locals let them be on the first day, but early on the second they found themselves shadowed by a group of indeterminate number, walking parallel to them on the high ground. After a while, they disappeared. Peyre encouraged his troop to keep going. Then they spotted the Guivergnais ahead, waiting for them. They'd brought twice the numbers Peyre had, making sure of their superiority.

'Umbert and I will go talk with them,' Peyre decided.

Umbert didn't look too keen on the idea, but he didn't argue.

As they approached the war-band, Peyre got a good look. They were rough looking, wearing fur and leather. Most held spears. *All in all, more than a match for us,* he decided.

Peyre and Umbert stopped and waited. What seemed like an age went past as the Guivergnais stared at them. *They're going to kill us,* Peyre decided. *I could have gone home to Morbaine. But no. I decided to get myself butchered in a meaningless encounter in the middle of nowhere.*

At last, two men left the group and made their way over. One—a huge, bearded fellow, swaggered towards them, suggesting he was the leader. A sword hung on his belt. The other, tall and lanky, carried a spear.

'Who are you?' the leader asked gruffly.

'I am Peyre, son of Duke Bastien of Morbaine. Your name?'

'Gosse,' he offered, then spat on the ground. 'What are you doing here?'

'Greetings, Gosse. I've—'

'Lord Gosse,' corrected the spearman.

'Lord Gosse. King Nicolas has died. I have come to support my father in his rightful claim to the throne.'

'Nicolas dead?' Gosse said suspiciously. 'Can't be. I'd have heard the news. I broke bread with him only last year.' This was said as a boast, as if to emphasise his importance.

'Two years back,' the spearman corrected.

'Alright, Sul, two years back. Point is, he was strong as a boar.'

'I met my uncle last year,' said Peyre. 'And he looked healthy then. But I got a message from my father, and Duke Walter of Barissia received a separate message from Valennes. So it sounds as if it's true.'

Gosse considered these facts before spitting on the ground. He looked over to Peyre's troop behind him. 'Those aren't warriors of Morbaine.'

There was no point in denying it. Brasingians insisted on being clean-shaved, save for their top lip. It marked them out. 'We've come from Coldeberg. These warriors have agreed to serve my father and brother.'

'Brother?'

'Esterel. He's already in Valennes.'

'Esterel,' Gosse repeated with suspicion. 'I'm supposed to believe you're Duke Bastien's boy?'

'You've met King Nicolas,' Peyre said. 'People always tell me I have a likeness to my father and uncle.'

Gosse studied Peyre's features. 'Maybe. But that's hardly proof. I'm not about to let you march foreigners through my lands just 'cos you have the likeness of the king.'

'Then I would ask you to accompany us to Valennes. There you can settle that I am who I say I am, and that my news about the king is the truth.'

'Hmm. Well, Sul?'

'Sounds reasonable. I could accompany them if you wish.'

'You?' Gosse boomed with disgust. 'If anyone is to meet with the king, it should be me. You'll have to stay here and mind the border.'

'Very well,' the spearman conceded.

'Yes, it *is* very well. Why would the king want to break bread with *you?*'

The spearman had no answer to that.

Gosse appeared to consider the idea some more. Then he spat on the ground.

GOSSE ACCOMPANIED them on their journey north. When Peyre counted them, he found the border lord had brought exactly eighteen warriors, including himself. Whether this was a coincidence or not, Peyre didn't know. But the doubling of their number with locals had the effect of making everyone feel much safer. They marched for the rest of the day and the next. Gosse and his followers knew the best routes, and the farther they got, the easier the terrain became.

By the fourth day, they were walking along a decent road. Guivergnais settlements came thick and fast as they approached the more densely populated part of the kingdom. As evening approached, Peyre heard the rushing sound of a great river.

'The Cousel?' he asked Gosse.

'Aye. With a bit of luck, we'll get passage up the river to Valennes.'

'Tomorrow?'

'Now, with some luck. There's plenty o' bargemen travel at night.'

Gosse led them to a way station by the side of the river. A dozen wooden buildings stood near the bank, where there was a long pier for river barges to dock. A score of workers were busy seeing to their craft or loading up goods.

'Come,' Gosse said to Peyre, and the two of them approached a group of men who looked like they were readying to travel upstream.

One of them saw them coming and stood as they approached, giving his back a stretch. 'You're wanting passage?' he asked.

'Aye, to Valennes,' Gosse answered. 'We can pay for it. Will you be going through the night?'

'That's right. But we've not room for all of you. Ten, at most.'

Gosse shrugged. 'The rest of us can wait. We're keen to get there fast, having heard a rumour that the king be dead.'

'Ain't no rumour,' the bargeman said. 'He was dead when we left Valennes, so he's more'n likely to still be dead when we return.'

'Well,' Gosse said, amazed. 'I only broke bread with him last year.'

Peyre decided not to remind him it was two years ago. 'Do you know who holds the capital?' Peyre asked the man.

'Who holds it?' he repeated, confused by the question.

'I mean, who's in charge? I'm hoping it's my brother, Esterel. Unless my father Bastien is already there.'

The bargeman looked Peyre over. 'I honestly don't know, my lord. When we left, all the talk was of the funeral, not the coronation. Likes of us just get told who's in charge. Too busy to pay attention to much more'n that.'

Peyre boarded the departing barges with four of his warriors, along with Gosse and four of his. He left Umbert and Elger in charge with some coins. They'd have to follow on as soon as possible.

At first, he planned to stay awake through the night. The moonlight allowed him to see both banks. He rested his back against his pack and enjoyed the view. They kept close to the right side, where a path ran parallel to the river. The bargemen had mules tied to their craft. The beasts walked the path and were asked to pull them along from time to time. Otherwise, they clopped along beside the barges, looking rather sullen. It had been a physically demanding few days, and the ripples of the river and the clop of the mules were simply too soporific. Peyre closed his eyes and drifted off.

He awoke to early morning light and the sound of subdued, early morning chatter. The barges pulled into a new way station and many of the bargemen disembarked, to be replaced by fresh crewmen.

'How long 'til we reach Valennes?' he asked one of the newcomers.

'Should get there by late afternoon, young man,' he replied.

No doubt some would have corrected the man—insisted on being called 'Your Highness', or 'Prince Peyre'. But Peyre didn't mind it. It was good to learn how people behaved if they thought you were an ordinary person. He certainly didn't want to become detached from the real world just because his father was king.

Leopold of Kelland was a cautionary lesson in the pitfalls of power. Peyre put his hand to his cheek, tracing the line of the scar Leopold had given him. The duke of Kelland and Luderia had turned on him so suddenly, when up to that point he'd acted like they were great friends. He was unhinged. Peyre was sure of it. *At least I helped to get Liesel out of that ugly world. But my family are to become rulers of Guivergne. Maybe I could do more? Not revenge exactly... though there's no doubt I owe the bastard something.* He went through the options in his mind, some more grisly than others. *A broken nose at the very least,* he concluded.

Peyre rummaged in his pack, fishing out the last, squashed bits of hard bread he'd carried from Coldeberg. Not much of a breakfast. *Looking forward to acquainting myself with the kitchens in the Bastion.* He'd been told the fortress in Valennes was one of the finest in all Dalriya; and while he understood that people were talking about its defences, surely it had a larder to match?

'Do you have any spare?' one of his recruits asked, watching him chew on his bread. 'I've ran out.'

'A good soldier rations his food out for the length of the campaign,' Peyre informed him.

The man didn't look best pleased but took the advice. 'Aye. I suppose so, Lord Peyre. Then how about a trade?' He rummaged in his sack and withdrew a wooden carving of a fish, leaping from water.

'You made that yourself?' Peyre asked him.

'Aye, lord. I whittle when I have spare time.' He opened his sack, revealing a wading bird and a half-finished otter. Its head and front paws had emerged from a block of wood.

'I consider that a fair trade,' Peyre decided, taking the fish in return for the last of his bread.

PEYRE

VALENNES, KINGDOM OF GUIVERGNE, 673

Peyre's first sight of Valennes came from the barge. An elegant, arched stone bridge connected the two halves of the city, but only the western part of the capital was properly fortified. The bargemen docked their craft on the east bank, where they had plenty of space to unload their goods.

Peyre, Gosse, and their followers disembarked and gave the bargemen their thanks. Gosse led them up the bank and onto the bridge, from where Peyre could look at both parts of Valennes.

First, he took in the east side of the city. It seemed to stretch on forever, which perhaps explained the lack of walled defences. He was surprised by how much green space there was in amongst the warehouses and shops. Despite its size, it lacked the grand buildings he had seen in Essenberg and Coldeberg.

His attention turned to West Valennes, as they crossed the walled bridge towards a grand-looking gate that allowed entry past its high walls. He looked down at the turquoise waters of the Cousel, that flowed at quite a pace here. It seemed strange that he was crossing the very same river he had crossed in Essenberg. *Maybe Leopold is crossing Albert's Bridge at this very moment? If so, I hope he falls in.*

'I will talk with the city guard, Your Highness,' Gosse told him.

It seemed the closer they had got to Valennes, the more the border lord's doubts about Peyre's identity had evaporated. When it was their turn to ask for entry, Gosse explained their business, gesturing towards Peyre. The guards at the gate looked at Peyre with curiosity.

'Your brother, Lord Esterel, is in The Bastion,' one of them informed him.

'My father?'

'I've heard nothing from Morbaine, my lord.'

'Thank you for your service,' Peyre said to the guards. He was mindful that in these uncertain times, such men might be asked to fight for his family. Or, at the very least, not turn on them.

They nodded to him as he passed through the city gates.

A restrained greeting, Peyre decided, as Gosse led their group of ten into West Valennes. *I wonder whether the rest of the city is as noncommittal as its soldiers.*

As Gosse led him towards The Bastion, Peyre studied Valennes. It was different to the Brasingian cities he had visited, even if he couldn't put his finger on what the difference was. *It feels older*, he decided, *like the buildings are the work of generations long gone.*

The street they walked took them into the central square of the city. People from all walks of life mingled here, in a cacophony of colour, noise, and smells. Peyre's stomach rumbled at the smell of cooking food as it recoiled from the sharp tang of human waste. From the square, they went north, into a more affluent part of the city.

In the northeast corner of Valennes, the towers of The Bastion emerged above the roofs of its neighbours. If the other major buildings of Valennes seemed ancient, its fortress looked like it had been constructed by some unknown, alien race. Its walls were not nearly so high as those of Coldeberg Castle. But they looked equally impregnable. Built in the shape of an irregular five-pointed star, with five further star tips projecting out from between the points, it was an extravagance of sharp angles. Surrounding it was a deep, water-filled moat, making the most of the fort's proximity to the river.

As they walked along the path that led to the open drawbridge,

Peyre imagined besieging the place. He struggled to identify the best way to take it.

Security was high. Despite explaining who he was, they had some wait before the guards allowed entrance. Finally, an official by the name of Girard arrived.

'Apologies, Lord Peyre,' he said. 'If we had known you were coming, there would have been someone ready to receive you.'

'It wasn't possible,' Peyre explained. 'I've come direct from Barissia. These men,' he waved a hand at the motley looking group he had brought with him, 'helped me make the journey in safety.'

'My staff will ensure they get good lodging,' Girard said. 'I can take you to see your brother immediately if that is your wish.'

'Of course,' said Peyre, excited about seeing Esterel. 'Lord Gosse will come with us.'

Gosse puffed up with self-importance. Peyre could tell the man was pleased.

'The Grand Foyer,' Girard told them as they entered a stunning room.

A huge, patterned rug covered the centre of the flagstone floor. A wooden staircase led up to the next floor, where a balcony overlooked the space. The balustrades were beautifully worked, while a great carving of the Owl of Guivergne was mounted on the centre of the balcony. The bird stared down with its round eyes, observing anyone who entered the room.

Girard led them up the stairs and then to one of the angular towers in the fort.

'These are your brother's rooms,' Girard said as he knocked.

Before long, Peyre heard sliding bolts.

Esterel opened the door himself. Peyre had expected his brother's face to open in a broad grin at his own sudden appearance, instead he looked confused, looking from one man to the next. His eyes widened in alarm when he took in Gosse. Then Esterel seemed to recover. 'Peyre!' he exclaimed, and they gave one another a rough hug. 'What are you doing here?'

'I came straight from Coldeberg when I heard the news. This is Lord Gosse, who helped me get here.'

'Ah, I see,' said Esterel, sounding relieved. 'Thank you, Lord Girard.'

'You're welcome, Lord Esterel. Your brother has eight other companions with him, and I will see to their lodging in The Bastion for now, if you wish.'

'I would be most grateful. Peyre and Lord Gosse can stay in my rooms.'

'Very well. Is there anything else I can do for you?'

'None of us have eaten well the last few days,' Peyre told him.

'I will ask the kitchens to make you all something up as soon as they can,' Girard said.

'Thank you, much obliged.'

'If there is anything else I can do, just ask,' said Girard. With a nod to Peyre and Esterel, he departed.

Esterel ushered Peyre and Gosse in to his rooms. He shut and bolted the door.

'Is everything alright?' Peyre asked him.

'Not really. Come through.'

They entered a living area with a table and half a dozen chairs spread about it. Two men stood as they entered, and Esterel made all the introductions.

The first man he named Lord Chancellor Caisin. He was average height with straight, iron-grey hair that went to his shoulders. The second, named Sacha, was one of Esterel's friends who had visited Arbeost two years back. He gave Esterel a run for his money in the looks department, Peyre had to admit. Dark where Esterel was blond, he was tall and athletic looking.

Peyre and Gosse were given bread and wine; Peyre drank thirstily.

'Eat up,' said Esterel. 'I'm not sure you should touch the food that Girard brings.'

'Not touch the food? What *is* going on?' Peyre demanded.

Sacha looked Gosse up and down. 'Is your man trustworthy?'

'O' course I am!' Gosse growled. 'I've ever been a loyal servant of the crown, defending our border against the shit-eating Brasingians.'

'Meaning you now owe your allegiance to Duke Bastien?' Caisin asked sharply.

'Course. Who else would I owe allegiance to?'

'Gosse didn't even know uncle was dead when I met him,' Peyre said. 'He's an honest man.'

Esterel nodded, then sighed. 'Two days ago, in the city streets, some bastard threw a knife at me. We never saw who, but clearly someone wants me dead. I haven't left The Bastion since. But now we have worse news. There's an army heading for Valennes, led by Duke Auberi.'

'Auberi?' Peyre repeated. 'The one from the tent?' He recalled a man about the same age as himself, with short-cropped dark hair, who'd attended on their uncle. He hadn't seemed to take either side when the king had been forced to settle the dispute over Peyre's punch up.

'Duke Auberi of Famiens,' Esterel said with some exasperation. 'You must know who he is, Peyre.'

'Of course I do,' Peyre said defensively. *Gods, I don't recall Esterel so short-tempered as this.*

'He has plenty of support for his claim to the throne. It's said his numbers approach five thousand. He'll reach the city well before father's force gets here.'

'I see,' said Peyre, trying to get his head around this news. It was not what he had been expecting. He wanted to express his outrage at this man's gall in claiming their father's throne, but he sensed his brother was past all that. 'Can we hold the city until father's army gets here?'

'That's our other problem. Most allies we have, I've sent out of Valennes to raise their forces. And we simply can't trust those left to fight for us. Lord Girard most of all.' Esterel gestured at Caisin to elaborate for him.

'Girard was Steward of the Royal Household under your uncle, a position that gave him a lot of influence in The Bastion and beyond.

It's no secret to those in the city that Girard and I were rivals in the king's court,' said the Lord Chancellor. 'I've long had a spy close to him. This spy has confirmed that Girard is in contact with Auberi and other rebellious lords. He controls the royal treasury; pays the wages of every soldier in Valennes. I'm afraid that if he's thrown in with Auberi, he could act against Esterel even before the army gets here. It would give Auberi substantial bargaining power to have Bastien's son in captivity. And now you are here as well...'

'Oh,' said Peyre, the seriousness of the situation now clear.

'With all due respect to your person,' Gosse said to Caisin, 'what if your spy lies? Or you do?'

'Of course, you must all consider that possibility,' Caisin replied matter-of-factly. 'All I can say is, I am loyal to Duke Bastien and have formed a close friendship with Esterel. It would do my career no good to have Auberi and his allies take the throne. I would soon find myself replaced. Nor would I get any benefit from misleading you and encouraging you to leave Valennes. But I fear you must consider that precise move. For the option of escape may soon be gone. The other thing I would say is this. If I have gone to the trouble of placing a spy close to Girard, don't be surprised if he is tracking our movements similarly.'

There was a silence for a while as everyone seemed to think about the situation. Gosse glugged down the last of his drink, looked about for a place to spit, then thought better of it.

'You said you brought men with you?' Esterel asked at last.

'Four each,' Peyre said with a nod to Gosse.

Esterel looked at Sacha, who raised an eyebrow.

'You think you'll need them?' Peyre asked him.

'Maybe. If our enemies really don't want us to leave, it might come down to busting our way out.'

'Perhaps,' said Sacha, 'we should give these brothers some time to talk alone. Lord Gosse, maybe I could show you something of Valennes, unless you are too tired?'

'Too tired? You think a four day march takes anything out of this constitution?' he asked, with a slap to his chest.

'Excellent!' said Sacha. 'Let's be on our way.'

'I, alas, have never had a warrior's constitution,' said Caisin. 'Keep in touch.'

With the three men gone, Esterel and Peyre were alone.

'Thank you for coming,' said Esterel. 'I should have said that first. Honestly, when I saw that big brute, I fancied he'd come to kill me.'

'Ha! You get used to his size after a few days.'

'I'll take your word for that. Would you rather talk here or elsewhere?'

'I must admit,' said Peyre, 'I have an interest in this fort.'

'Of course you do!' said Esterel. 'Come, you shall have the tour.'

ESTEREL LED PEYRE around the flat area that surrounded the fort—an area that his brother called the 'kill zone'. With the walls of the fort on their right, the wet moat lay on their left. Peyre got a whiff of an abysmal smell from the water when the wind blew the wrong way.

'The legend is that the Krykkers built it,' Esterel told him, 'or at least a Krykker designed it. It's quite unlike anything else in Guivergne.'

'Or in Brasingia.'

'Of course, forgive me,' said Esterel. 'You've been having your own adventures abroad. I'm guessing there's a story behind that?' he asked, gesturing at Peyre's fresh scar.

'Oh, I've some stories alright,' Peyre agreed. 'But I'd rather tell them when we are at leisure.'

'True, that would be better. Anyway, The Bastion. The core principle is that there is no blind spot around the entire building, such as you can find with other forts and castles. Archers can target every single square inch of the kill zone. The moat makes it very difficult to tunnel under. In short, it's very easy to defend. I just wish I had some men I could trust to man it for me.'

'Don't worry about it,' Peyre reassured him. 'Father will be here soon. He may not be racing, but the man is so methodical there is simply no chance he won't make it, eventually.'

Esterel laughed at that, but his smile didn't linger. 'I just feel like such a failure. Father sent me here to prepare the way for his succession—keep the Guivergnais loyal enough to the family to stop a challenge. I've been here more than two years and achieved precisely nothing.'

Peyre felt sorry for his brother. It seemed he'd been given such a serious task, whereas their father had never asked very much of him. 'Come on, that's not true. There's that Caisin fellow, and you said you had sent people off to raise forces to help. That wouldn't have happened without your efforts. Is that what your friends are doing?'

'Many of them. Miles has inherited his father's estate and has invited everyone to bring their levies there. I sent Florent west, to the duke of Martras, asking him to support father's claim.'

That's right, Peyre thought. *Those rather dull childhood geography lessons are coming back to me now. Apart from Morbaine, there are two other duchies. Martras defends the Krykker border and Famiens the Caladri one. With Morbaine facing off against Famiens, the allegiance of the duke of Martras might decide the outcome.*

'There are many others I considered friends,' Esterel continued, 'who have slunk away, however. Perhaps some to join with the Duke of Famine. Others to hide in their country estates until it's all over.'

'Duke of Famine?' Peyre asked.

'Oh, sorry. It's just a nickname Auberi has been given. After the Drobax invaded his duchy there was a lot of devastation and hunger.' He looked at Peyre's expression. 'Stupid name, really. No one says it to his face,' he added, as if that made it better.

Peyre thought it a cruel joke, but it didn't justify the man's treachery. 'Maybe it's not such a bad thing,' Peyre considered, 'that you've learned who you can really trust.'

'I suppose so,' said Esterel. 'Man, it's good to see you again,' he said, slapping Peyre on the shoulder. 'I've missed you.'

'Same,' said Peyre, suddenly feeling like he might choke up. Esterel had that effortless gift of making people feel special. He wondered how some of the Guivergnais had failed to come under his brother's spell. 'Look, I didn't want to mention it in there, in case the walls have ears, or we can't fully trust everyone. But there are more of us coming —another twenty-six, hopefully. Umbert is going to follow our route to the city up the Cousel.'

'Umbert!' Esterel cried. 'When did my brother and his daft friend start leading bands of warriors across Dalriya?'

Peyre laughed. 'Yeah, I'm not sure how that happened. Anyway, thirteen with Umbert from Barissia, and thirteen more of Gosse's men. In case we really need to do some fighting.'

Esterel nodded. 'And you think we can trust this Gosse?'

'I think,' said Peyre, 'that some men aren't cut out for double-dealing and all that business. And I think Gosse is one of those.'

'Ha! I think you may be right. Then let's ask him to stay on the lookout for these reinforcements in case they get here in time.' Esterel looked across the water of the moat. 'Even if I've done little to help Father, I'd rather he didn't reach Valennes to find both his sons at the bottom of this stinking ditch.'

'Yes,' Peyre agreed. 'Let's try to avoid that.'

* * *

PEYRE SLEPT in Esterel's rooms, along with Gosse and Sacha. After breakfast, Gosse agreed to return to the river bank and look out for the arrival of the rest of their warriors.

Caisin, the Lord Chancellor, returned. With him were two rough looking sorts. 'Ernst and Gernot,' he said. Both, Peyre noted, had fists the size of a small child. 'I use them when the king needs to deliver justice outside the jurisdiction of the courts.'

Peyre took that to mean they battered people who needed a battering.

'I think it might be wise for you to have some permanent protection, Lord Esterel,' Caisin explained. 'At least until we leave the city. At the risk of causing offence, I would urge you once more to consider that course of action. Auberi's army could arrive at any time.'

'I have allies out in the country,' Esterel assured the man. 'They would get word to me.'

Peyre eyed the two men. He didn't trust anyone to protect his brother except himself. He did, however, have a task that needed doing. 'I need to find out where our men have been lodged.'

'I'll help you,' Sacha offered. 'I know my way around The Bastion.'

With that plan agreed, Peyre and Sacha left Esterel's rooms and wandered about the fortress. Sacha seemed to think the various towers were the most likely places for the men to have been accommodated. 'It might be overdoing it, but safest to keep our mission to ourselves,' Sacha suggested. Thus, Esterel's friend made a pretence of showing Peyre about The Bastion, especially when they passed a servant or guardsman. 'Virtually everyone here owes their position to, or receives their income from, Girard,' he explained.

'Royal Steward sounds like a powerful position,' said Peyre.

'Your father doesn't have such an office in Morbaine?'

Peyre thought about it. 'Lord Russell is his marshall. He does everything in Morbaine.'

'Hmm. Then maybe Lord Russell should take the office when your father becomes king.'

'Maybe.' It was a matter he had given no thought to until now—the business of appointing people to positions in government. In truth, he had only a vague understanding of which title was responsible for what. In Morbaine, things just seemed to get done of their own accord. It made him wonder about Sacha. Perhaps it was unfair in his case, but doubtless there would be some people who befriended Esterel for the sake of advancement. 'Did my brother not ask you to raise forces for him?' he asked.

'My father is Lord of Courion. He will bring men to Esterel's banner. And I will fight and die for him if I have to.'

'Why?' Peyre asked.

'Because I believe he will make a great king. Don't you?'

'Of course I do.'

They entered the ground floor room of a tower.

'Stinks like my lot,' Peyre noted.

But the cots were empty, with no sign of occupation. Except for one item.

'What's this?' Sacha asked, retrieving it from a dark corner.

'An otter,' Peyre told him. 'One of my Barissian recruits liked to whittle in his spare time.'

'This doesn't look good,' Sacha said, worried. 'I'm inclined to heed Caisin's warnings and get Esterel out of here before it's too late.'

'What of these men?' Peyre asked him.

'It's no good you and I looking around asking questions. That's a sure way to rouse Girard's suspicions. Maybe Caisin's fixers are better placed to do that.'

Peyre was desperate to find these men. But he had to concede Esterel's security was the most important thing. 'Alright,' he agreed.

* * *

THEY CREPT out of Esterel's rooms—Sacha leading the way, Caisin by his side. Peyre walked beside his brother. Behind them, the hulking figures of Ernst and Gernot brought up the rear.

When the two men had reported back with their grim findings— eight corpses bound in sacks—no one could argue against the Lord Chancellor's urgings to escape. Even if, as Peyre feared, there was a chance Caisin was involved. His hand hovered close to his sword hilt, ready for a betrayal from Esterel's friends as much as his enemies intercepting them.

The darkness of The Bastion's corridors added to Peyre's sense of being watched, as he felt the hairs prickle the back of his neck. All he could do was follow, not yet able to navigate his own way around the fort. He worried Sacha was leading them into a trap; that the two men behind them might knife them in the back. But there was no other option but to have faith that Esterel had chosen his friends wisely.

The impressive defences of The Bastion had the unwelcome effect of making it difficult to escape the fort. Not trusting the guards who manned the drawbridge on the west side—the only way to walk out of the place—Sacha instead led them to the southernmost tower. They hadn't met a single soul—most residents of the fort were surely fast asleep at this time. But it was really no surprise that they were unable to sneak their way in.

'Lord Caisin...Lord Esterel,' came a bewildered voice. It was a young man, spear clutched in one hand, no doubt given the short straw of night watch. He'd caught them as soon as Sacha opened the door to the ground floor room of the tower.

'Yes, it's us, don't worry,' Esterel said in a friendly manner, stepping in before Caisin's thugs got the idea of solving the problem in a different way. 'What's your name, sir?'

'Jehan, my lord.'

'Jehan, I've been warned to escape before Duke Auberi gets here,' Esterel told him, clearly having decided to give the guard a simple version of the truth. 'My life is in danger, you see. We're leaving via this tower without being seen. I understand it's your job to defend the fort, but you haven't been asked to stop people from leaving, I presume?'

'Well, no, not exactly.' He eyed their group, taking in the weapons they carried. 'But I have been told to report anything odd,' he admitted.

'I won't ask you to lie for me or put yourself at risk,' Esterel said.

'But bear in mind,' added Sacha, 'that Lord Esterel's father is Duke Bastien, who will soon become King Bastien. How would you expect him to deal with anyone who put his heir in danger?'

Jehan looked distinctly uncomfortable. 'I wouldn't do that, my lords.'

'Perhaps,' said Esterel, 'at the very least, you'd be able to delay your report?'

Jehan seemed to think about that option. 'I would get the blame if they knew you'd come through here. It might be better if I simply came with you, my lord?' he suggested, a little sheepishly.

'You'd do that?' Esterel asked him.

'Well, you are the rightful heirs to Guivergne,' said the young man, 'so I owe my allegiance to you, not anyone else. That's how I see it, at least.'

'I am in your debt,' Esterel said. 'I will tell my father about your courage.'

Jehan gave a bashful smile.

Peyre shook his head. *How does he do it*, he wondered.

Jehan led them out through the tower into the kill zone. Peyre couldn't stop himself from looking up to the battlements above them. If they were spotted, they'd be sitting ducks.

It was imperative they were silent now. Sacha went first, lowering himself into the wet moat. Here the angular tower jutted out from the rest of the fort. It was, Esterel's friend had assured them, the narrowest crossing point.

Peyre followed him into the water. It was cold, but the stench was worse. *Hold your nerve*, he told himself, *and don't make a sound.* He swam, keeping his arms and legs to gentle movements so as not to make a splash. *It's just as well it's night*, he told himself, *so I can't see what I'm swimming through.*

He reached the far side of the moat at the same time as Sacha. It wasn't easy pulling themselves out of the moat and over the bank that surrounded it. Peyre slipped back in twice. Just as he thought he had a safe grip, the earth bank crumbled away. The third time, he slithered his way over. He and Sacha then began helping the others out, first grabbing Caisin by an arm each and hauling him out. Peyre was relieved to see they could all swim well enough to get across, no doubt a benefit of living so close to the Cousel. Esterel and Jehan came out safely. Ernst and Gernot were not as easy to lift out as Caisin, requiring everyone's help. But they made it.

Cold, wet, and reeking, they knew it wasn't over yet. Sacha led them off, crouch walking away until they were a good distance from The Bastion. Once they reached the first street, they tried walking naturally, aware there was a good chance they'd meet, or at least be seen by, the city's night walkers. *It's not so easy*, Peyre found, *when you're shivering with cold and want to retch at your own smell.*

Sacha took them through the city, heading for the south gate. If they could get out that way and keep going south, they would have a good chance of meeting up with their father and the army of Morbaine. It wasn't until the central square that Peyre saw people. It seemed some of the homeless of the city chose it as a place to sleep, perhaps finding safety in numbers. In one corner a fire had been lit, surrounded by half a dozen figures, lying prone on the floor or hunched over, woollen cloaks pulled about them. Other shapes moved about in the shadows, barely visible. *How many more*, Peyre wondered, *completely hidden from sight?*

He wasn't the only one in their party who sensed something didn't feel quite right. They looked at one another. Then, there was the unmistakable clink of metal armour; the thud of feet moving in unison. Armed soldiers appeared out of the streets around the Square. Peyre's party was their target, and they knew exactly where they were. They must have watched them enter the Square—been waiting for them.

Ernst and Gernot pulled out weapons: wicked-looking hatchets, perfect for close quarter fighting. The others followed: Peyre, Esterel, Sacha and Caisin drew swords; Jehan had his short spear.

'Let's not be stupid,' said one of the soldiers. He approached carefully, one hand gripping his own sword, the other held forward, palm up. With him were at least a score of armed men.

'Lewen,' said Caisin. 'What's the meaning of this?'

'Captain of the city guard,' Sacha murmured to Peyre.

'I have orders to arrest you,' said the captain. 'I'm to take you alive, you hear me? There's no need for bloodshed.'

'Whose orders?' Esterel demanded. 'Who told you to arrest the heir of the new king?'

'Come now, Lord Esterel,' said Lewen. 'There's no king right now, is there? But there is a man who claims to be king, with an army at his back, a day's march from here. It's not my place to get involved in high politics. But me and my men have an order, and it's been made quite clear what'll happen if we don't carry it out. So don't make us resort to force. Drop those weapons.'

A cloaked, hooded figure shuffled towards the standoff. Peyre could just make out long blonde hair. 'So many armed men in the

Square all of a sudden,' she said in a raspy voice. 'I've got a place you can stick those swords.'

'Get lost, whore!' Captain Lewen shouted.

One of his men moved towards her and the woman departed, far quicker than she had arrived.

The captain looked about the Square, betraying some nerves of his own. The darkness, combined with the figures moving about in the shadows, seemed to put everyone on edge.

'You're making a mistake, captain,' Caisin warned him. 'Let us leave Valennes. Say we gave you and your men the slip. It would be far better than choosing sides like this. What if you've backed the wrong one?'

'I'm not choosing sides. I'm keeping myself and my men alive when the army of Famiens occupies the city, probably tomorrow. So, you have my sympathies and all that, but this is the last time I ask. Drop your damned weapons or I give the order to cut you down.' Lewen's guards edged forwards, reinforcing the point.

'We can take them,' Peyre said to Esterel. *Twenty to seven wasn't great odds. At all. But how good were these men compared to him and his brother?*

Esterel didn't answer, but looked in no mood to drop his weapon.

Lewen's eyes widened in disbelief. Just as his lips opened to give his order, the cloaked woman returned, moving faster than ever. Before he got his words out, he found a knife at his throat.

'Drop it!' she shouted. It was Syele.

Then more figures emerged from the shadows, surrounding the captain's guards.

'No one wants bloodshed tonight,' a voice rang out.

Peyre felt himself grinning like a fool. It was Umbert.

'Drop your weapons,' Umbert continued, 'and on my honour, no harm shall befall you.'

'You're overdoing it a little,' Peyre murmured to himself.

'Now!' came a shout that sounded like the roar of a bear. Gosse.

It did the trick. First one, then another, then all the soldiers were laying down their weapons, Lewen included—Syele's blade still alarmingly close to his neck.

'You should be grateful, Captain Lewen, that our allies arrived in time to save the lives of you and your men,' said Esterel. 'Still, you can tell Duke Auberi the truth, that you were outnumbered and surrendered. I doubt the punishment will be severe. He'll be keen to win over Valennes to his new regime. Mark my words, though. It will be short-lived. We will soon return to place my father on the throne. Bear that in mind over the next few days.'

'Take their weapons,' Peyre called out to his men. 'We don't want them following us.'

His Barissians and Gosse's warriors picked up the discarded weapons. Syele withdrew her knife and quickly backed away from the captain. Within moments, they were leaving the guards behind and rushing south through the city, to the gates.

Sacha was soon organising everyone, unbarring the wooden gates and getting them open, before the gatehouse guards knew what was happening.

Peyre gave Umbert a hug as they waited, his stupid grin returning. Then they were all streaming out of Valennes, over thirty men and one woman. It no longer felt like an escape or a retreat. It felt exhilarating. For, just as his brother had said, Peyre felt sure they would soon return.

SANC

KINGDOM OF GUIVERGNE, 673

The army of Duke Bastien was on the march. It was larger than the army Sanc's father had taken to the Midder Steppe last year. He had stripped Morbaine of its fighters. Everything seemed to depend on the success of this force. Either they put Bastien on the throne, or they would fail, and Bastien and his family would be finished.

For a careful planner like my father, Sanc considered, *it must be hard to risk everything on this one campaign.* But that was the situation the duke found himself in, and he didn't shirk from it.

Sanc felt most sorry for Loysse, who had to stay behind in Arbeost yet again. With her father and two—maybe three—of her brothers at war in Guivergne, it would not be an easy time for her, waiting desperately on any news. As for Peyre, he had yet to arrive from Barissia. Their father had left instructions that should Peyre return to Morbaine, he must rule it in his father's absence. Sanc had his doubts that Peyre would keep himself away from the fighting, whatever instructions he was given.

Sanc missed the company of his brother on this expedition. Peyre's overconfidence could be quite reassuring. He rode beside Jesper and Rimmon instead. He couldn't ask for two more capable individuals to travel with. But adults tended to be serious all the time and sometimes one needed a Peyre or an Umbert to lighten the mood. Tadita and Rab had also been left behind, and Sanc knew he would miss them.

'There's more than a little irony,' Rimmon commented, as their winding column of riders crossed into the Steppe lands, 'that the late king's final act, the conquest of these lands, has made a route for his brother's army.'

'I wonder what he would make of it,' Jesper said.

'The impression I get,' said Rimmon, 'is Nicolas didn't really know his own mind.' It looked like he was about to say more, but the sorcerer glanced at Sanc and stopped talking.

Sanc had a fair idea what his teacher was thinking. His uncle had loved their mother, Alienor; and they were Alienor's children. But they were also Bastien's. Nicolas had been torn by love and jealousy. *And how sad*, Sanc thought, *that he'd never been able to move on and find his own happiness.*

The route they were taking was the same as they had taken the year before. Forts, erected by Bastien at regularly spaced intervals to defend the newly acquired territory, now protected his army's passage. They stopped at each one, Sanc's father reallocating men to or from the garrisons as he saw fit.

A couple of forts already had quite a few ancillary buildings that had appeared since last summer—the beginnings of new towns. This gave Lord Russell options to manage the food supplies that were being transported by cart. Feeding everyone, and not running out of food, seemed to be the major preoccupation of Umbert's father. Whenever the man had a faraway look in his eyes, Sanc fancied he was counting cabbages in his head.

The tribes of the Steppe tracked their progress: Sanc caught glimpses of their mounted warriors. But once their destination was clear, they were content to let them be on their way. A week after they left Arbeost, the army crossed into Guivergne proper.

It was strange to think of Guivergne—his father's rightful inheritance—as enemy territory. But that's what it felt like. Brancat took extra care to supervise the scouts, who rode out in all directions, returning to tell the weapons master what they had seen. The land here was generally rough and undeveloped. They passed only a few scattered settlements, linked by well-worn paths rather than solid roads.

Their march was halted early on the first evening, giving everyone more time to set up camp. The carts were driven up onto a hillock and guards posted around its boundary. The army had got used to Duke Bastien's painstaking style of leadership and there was little grumbling: it was wasted energy, after all.

Next morning, they were quick to resume their journey north. Back on his mount, Sanc felt like he had barely woken up when a group of scouts came charging towards the front of the line. The pace of their return was hard to miss. A muttering began up and down the line.

'Looks like they've found something,' said Rimmon.

'Some people, most likely,' said Jesper.

Only a few moments passed before trumpeters blew their buisines in warning. Riders went down the line, galloping past Sanc's position towards the infantry who trailed behind those lucky enough to be on horseback.

'Is it the enemy?' Sanc asked.

'Yes,' said Jesper.

Sanc was fully awake now. He watched as his father, flanked by Lord Russell and Brancat, called on his horsemen to follow him west, in the direction the scouts had come from. Sanc had never been close to his father, but he had a moment of pride as he watched him, in full armour, ordering the men of Morbaine to follow him. He exuded a confidence that Sanc couldn't imagine ever having.

'Come,' said Jesper, encouraging Sanc to keep up. They left the path, guiding their horses across the grass and vegetation that grew beside it. They came upon a sharp dip that led into woodland. It held their progress up, as each rider had to guide their horse down into the trees.

The stomp of feet and clink of armour signalled the arrival of the infantry behind them. The earth churned until Jesper had seen enough. He called on everyone to dismount and lead their horses down. Others agreed, and so Sanc slid from his mount and led him down when it was his turn.

Those ahead had decided to stay on their feet through the woodland, and so Sanc did likewise. They had to climb up a muddy trail, exposed roots threatening to trip the unwary. The trail levelled off and suddenly Sanc was out of the trees and stepping onto a farmer's field.

'Mount up, Sanc,' Jesper called out.

He did as he was told, and then nudged his horse towards Jesper's place in the cavalry line that was forming. His father had stopped at a point that gave them a good view of the land ahead. A few farm buildings lay in the centre of the plain ahead of them. Beyond, on the far side, was the enemy army. Sanc could clearly see lines of infantry facing them, interspersed with cavalry units. He made out crimson banners with four azure diamonds.

'Whose standard is that?' he asked Jesper, unable to take his eyes off the scene in front of him. It seemed unreal that in a matter of moments he had found himself on a battlefield.

Jesper shrugged. 'I don't know.'

'The Lord of Saliers,' said Rimmon, joining them on Sanc's other side.

Jesper gave the sorcerer a questioning look.

'Russell told me,' Rimmon admitted. 'Sanc, our powers may be needed here,' he said, keeping his voice quiet. 'Our priority must be to keep your father safe. If he is killed, or even injured, it puts the entire campaign in jeopardy. Others are not so important. It's harsh,' he said, giving Sanc a look. 'But this is war. Please stay with me at all times.'

'I will be with you both as well,' Jesper said. 'To give you protection when you are concentrating on other things.'

The infantry emerged from the woodland and soon there was a lot of shouting as the army of Morbaine was organised in the way Duke Bastien wanted it. Brancat's voice was the loudest, but neither Lord Russell nor Bastien himself refrained from yelling out their demands.

Nobles yelled at their own retinues, while infantry and cavalry units had to move this way and that until the leaders of the army were happy.

Whenever he could, Sanc would glance across at the enemy, wondering if they were marching towards their position, perhaps to strike before they were ready. But each time, he could see they hadn't moved at all. Looking back and forth, he gradually took in the numbers on each side. Saliers' force was only a third the size of his father's. *We should win,* he told himself, taking some confidence.

Positioned in the same cavalry unit as his father, Sanc saw him nod at his trumpeters. They blared out his order and the Morbaine infantry lines moved towards the enemy. They went slowly, their captains looking across to ensure they didn't move ahead or fall behind the other units. They presented a wall of steel to the enemy and Sanc allowed himself to imagine how the outnumbered enemy might be feeling right now.

More buisines sounded. He saw his father handed a spear by his squire, then the other men in the front line were armed in the same manner. Only the elite were trained to fight from horseback. Months of extra training in the saddle were required to master the skills. Looking at the row of bristling spears ahead of him, Sanc appreciated why they went to all the extra trouble.

His father raised his weapon into the air and the cavalry walked forward. With a nod from Jesper and Rimmon on either side of him, Sanc nudged his mount to follow.

He thought through what he might do when the two sides met. Of course, he would defend his father. Would he and Rimmon be expected to go on the attack? And what would everyone do when they discovered he was a sorcerer? Sanc had been more than content for that to remain a secret.

More shouting, then the buisines were blown again. They came to a halt. Sanc peered through the gaps in the rank ahead until he could see what was happening. The enemy were retreating, marching away from their positions in an organised manoeuvre. He heard his father's voice, giving vent to his anger. 'Wasting our time,' and 'playing with us,' were two phrases he kept returning to, amid more foul language than Sanc had ever heard from him.

Sanc turned to Jesper, who shrugged.

'Saliers probably had no intention of engaging with us,' said the forester. 'Just slowing us down.'

'He doesn't want us to reach Valennes?' Sanc asked him.

Jesper frowned, as if surprised by the question. 'Maybe. Or he just intends to make our lives difficult. If his forces can't beat us, they'll make a nuisance of themselves instead.'

Duke Bastien's voice was getting louder. He was steering his mount towards them, his advisers on either side. Sanc picked up that he was giving Lord Russell command of a section of the army.

'Rimmon!' his father bellowed.

'Here, Your Grace,' said Sanc's teacher.

'You and Sanc will go with Russell. Offer whatever assistance you can.'

'It might be better for at least one of us to stay with you,' Rimmon offered.

Bastien pinned him with an ill-tempered look. 'Must I repeat my order?' he demanded.

'No, Your Grace.'

Then the duke was breezing past, leading his army back to the path they had left.

Sanc caught Jesper giving Rimmon a smirk.

'No, Your Grace,' Jesper mimicked.

'Shut up,' said Rimmon sourly.

* * *

RUSSELL'S UNIT comprised a good majority of the Morbainais cavalry. Able to move more freely without the encumbrance of the infantry units, they tracked well ahead of the main army, looking for further threats. Once Lord Russell was content that the path ahead was safe, he would take them off it, ranging out west, where they knew Saliers' force was operating.

'Two can play at his game,' he told Sanc, riding next to him for a while. 'If the enemy spot us, they'll be forced to come and drive us off.'

'Leaving father's force free to march north,' Sanc said.

'Exactly,' said Russell, pleased that Sanc understood so quickly. 'And if they don't spot us,' he added, allowing himself a savage grin, 'we catch them in a pincer.' He took both hands off his reins and slammed his palms together, indicating what would happen to Saliers' army.

Sanc could tell that Lord Russell was looking forward to such an attack. It seemed, however, that the Lord of Saliers knew his soldiering. More than once, the enemy appeared, cutting them off. Russell would retreat his horsemen towards Duke Bastien and the rest of the army, hoping to draw Saliers into the main force. But before the enemy got too close, they would retreat out of harm's way.

This elaborate game of cat and mouse unfolded over the next two days. Sanc had never done so much riding in his life. But perhaps it was worth it. For his father's army plodded its way ever closer to Valennes.

The next day, Saliers was nowhere to be seen. The path they travelled became a road and the army of Morbaine made better time.

Early next morning, they came upon a village that straddled the road. It had been burned out. Not just the buildings, but the fields surrounding it. Russell posted a mounted watch and led a troop into the settlement on foot.

Sanc followed Russell into the remains, Jesper and Rimmon with him. He had never seen anything like it. People's homes, their church; everything they had known, destroyed. Some shells of buildings still stood, threatening to topple over. The smell of charcoal remained, even though the fires had burned out.

'No bodies,' said Rimmon, sounding relieved.

'No signs of a killing,' Jesper confirmed, scanning the detritus. 'Looks like the villagers were either allowed to leave or taken away.'

'Saliers did this?' Sanc asked.

'Almost certainly,' the forester confirmed. 'Denying our army sustenance. Doesn't seem to know Duke Bastien or Lord Russell very well. We've enough supplies to get us to Valennes without the need to take extra.'

It seemed insane, to Sanc, that Guivergne had descended to this in so short a space of time. A struggle for the throne had caused the destruction of this community—innocent families with no allegiance to either side. From Rimmon's reaction, he gathered things might get much worse, too. They needed to get his father on the throne; needed to stop this madness.

Warning calls came, and Sanc suddenly found they were running. *Was it a trap prepared by Saliers*, he asked himself, as they pounded out of the village, for their horses.

The tethered horses turned, wide-eyed, at their approach. Men barked at one another, desperate to find their mounts. Sanc found his, but he was skittish at the arrival of so many men and their frantic voices. He danced away, refusing to let Sanc get a foot into a stirrup.

Then Jesper was there, already mounted. He reached over, calm-voiced, and patted the beast.

Sanc clambered up, and they rode with Lord Russell to the north of the village.

Sanc soon spotted what appeared to be a standoff between a dozen of their own mounted troops and a force of armed men, maybe thirty strong, on foot. This force had their weapons in their belts. They didn't, Sanc noted, as Russell's force pulled up, look like they had come to fight.

He studied these men. They were a strange looking mix of fur-clad warriors, moustachioed fighters like the men who had come to Arbeost from the empire, a woman as dangerous looking as the rest, and well-dressed Guivergnais. He fixed on three familiar faces from the latter group.

'Sanc!' Peyre burst out as their eyes met. 'By the gods, what are *you* doing here?'

SANC SAT on the ground with his brothers, Lord Russell, and their various advisers. They discussed what their plans should be, while they waited for his father to arrive with the main force. Sanc knew if his father were here, he wouldn't have been invited to such a meeting. It made it all the more exciting.

He had been introduced to three men who had accompanied his brothers and Umbert in their escape from Valennes. Lord Gosse was a huge bear of a man with a great beard. Caisin was older, with the grand title of Lord Chancellor. Sanc recognised Sacha of Courion. He had accompanied Esterel on his visit to Arbeost two years ago. He looked the part. He imagined them both strolling along the streets of Valennes, being handsome, good humoured, gracious, and charming.

Esterel and Peyre told them all about their escape, how it seemed almost certain that Duke Auberi of Famiens had now occupied Valennes.

'On our journey here,' Esterel told them, 'we spotted a sizeable army heading north-west. We thought it was you, at first. Good job we were careful.'

'Must have been Arnoul of Saliers' army,' said Lord Russell. 'He's been harassing us somewhat. But north-west, you say? Not north, straight to Valennes?'

Esterel shook his head. 'Our allies in Guivergne are raising their forces. They've agreed to rendezvous at Corbenay.'

'My father and others are heading to Corbenay,' Sacha confirmed. 'I fear the enemy might head their next.'

Lord Russell seemed to think about it. 'It's what I'd do,' he said at last. 'Garrison Valennes, then take out our allies in Corbenay. Prevent them from joining up with us. That would leave them with most of Guivergne under their control. They'd fancy their chances of seeing Bastien's army off from that position.'

Sombre nods of agreement greeted this assessment. There was little else worth saying before the rest of the army caught up.

THE FIRST THING Lord Bastien did when he reached them was hug his two sons.

Sanc stood aside, ignored, trying not to acknowledge the awkwardness that other people around them felt.

His father then listened to the news from Valennes. 'You did well to get out,' he murmured to Esterel, then thanked Lord Caisin for his advice. He frowned at Peyre. 'Foolish of you to bring a force from Barissia,' he said. 'We don't want the people of Guivergne thinking ours is an army of foreigners. We need to be seen as Guivergnais. That's what your brother has been trying to achieve here.'

'But father,' Peyre said, going red. 'I promised them pay and a place in our forces.'

'Of course, I'll honour whatever promises you've made, boy. Just think next time, will you?'

Sanc felt sorry for Peyre, as he silently nodded his agreement. The amount of affection the duke had for his sons was painfully apparent when all three were together.

Bastien then listened to Lord Russell's summary of their predicament. He didn't take long to agree with his conclusions. 'There's both a strategic and moral imperative to join up with Corbenay's forces,' he declared. 'If Auberi is also taking his forces there, we may bring him to battle. A decisive outcome is just what we need.'

Assuming, Sanc said to himself, *we're the ones who win.*

SANC

CORBENAY, KINGDOM OF GUIVERGNE, 673

They were a united force once more. It didn't take the scouts long to find the trail left by the Lord of Saliers' army. The direction he had taken confirmed what they had already suspected. The destination was Corbenay.

Sanc rode in the vanguard, not far behind his father and brothers. 'Chances are,' Jesper said, next to him, 'Saliers won't realise his force was spotted by Esterel. They'll assume we're still heading for Valennes, which will have been left ready for a siege. They think they can deal with Corbenay and come back for us.'

'Then they've got a surprise coming,' noted Rimmon.

The bullish attitude of Sanc's friends was shared by the entire army. Perhaps it had something to do with the duke and his sons being reunited. Ordered to force march, even the hard worked infantry seemed keen to catch up to the enemy.

When the light faded, they made a basic camp. Duke Bastien banned fires. Sanc had lookout duty with Peyre and Umbert. It was eerie, looking across an unknown territory, knowing the enemy was out there.

'At least we've done this before,' he muttered, recalling the duties they had been given in the Midder Steppe.

Peyre grinned at him.

Sanc couldn't help staring at his brother's scar as he did.

Peyre noticed and put his fingers to it. The grin disappeared.

'I'm sorry you got banished,' Sanc blurted out. 'It was my fault. But I couldn't fight back against Robert. I had reasons that I couldn't tell you.'

'Don't be stupid, Sanc,' Peyre said. 'There were four of them, all bigger and older than you. Anyway,' he said, sharing a look with Umbert, 'it wasn't all bad in Brasingia.'

Sanc raised an eyebrow.

'He fell in love,' said Umbert. 'Princess Liesel herself.'

'Liesel!' Sanc repeated. The princess who had been offered in marriage to Esterel by the Brasingian embassy. Some of whom had tried to kill him. Some of whom Sanc had killed. 'Is she really as beautiful as that ambassador claimed?' he asked doubtfully.

'Oh yes,' said Peyre, his grin returning. 'But she is just as beautiful inside as out.'

'See,' said Umbert. 'Love.'

'And did she fall in love with you?' Sanc asked.

'Well, I was working on that,' Peyre admitted. 'But things got complicated.' He proceeded to tell Sanc a strange and dark story of a family beguiled by a witch and a mercenary leader. He was shocked when Peyre revealed it was Liesel's brother, Leopold, who had given him the scar. 'So, you see,' his brother finished, 'I have no idea where she is now. Except that Farred promised me he left her somewhere safe.'

It was some story. Once their guard duty was over, the three of them wasted no time in finding somewhere to sleep.

Sanc looked up at the stars in the night sky. As he drifted away, he imagined Princess Liesel staring up at the same sky, thinking about his brother Peyre. He smiled to himself. No. Not possible.

THEY WERE ROUSED EARLY, the sun casting a strip of yellow on the horizon; otherwise, the sky was slate grey.

Soon, they were moving. The mounted contingents led the way but stayed close to the mass of infantry behind them.

Sanc's stomach ached. Something was telling him today was the day. Everyone else seemed to sense it, too. There was a tension, broken by occasional laughter—loud barks in response to jokes that were average at best. Sanc wavered from anticipation to trepidation. He didn't really know how he felt.

Then there was a sudden rush of activity. The scouts had found Saliers' army ahead. The news rippled down the line. Sanc's father gathered his mounted force about him, giving out orders. The greater portion of the cavalry would ride ahead and engage. Esterel was the nominal leader, with Lord Russell and Brancat for support. Duke Bastien, a visibly disappointed Peyre, and everyone not named would stay with the infantry. Including Sanc and Rimmon.

'Shouldn't we go with them?' Sanc whispered to his teacher. They had come to use their powers, after all—what was the point in staying put?

'Now's the time to follow orders,' Rimmon replied, his voice equally hushed. 'I reckon we'll get our chances to help.'

Sanc watched the cavalry force, hundreds strong, ride ahead. His father kept the rest of the army going in the same direction, at what seemed like a crawl. Esterel's horsemen soon disappeared. It was horrible, not knowing what was happening ahead of them.

Sanc chafed at their pace. 'Can't we go faster than this?' he mumbled, wary of his father hearing his complaints. He could see Peyre and Umbert, riding at the front, looking as dissatisfied as he felt.

'No point in tiring out the foot soldiers,' Jesper said. 'I suggest you keep your thoughts to yourself, Sanc.'

Reluctantly, he did as he was told.

A path took them downhill through woodland. Through the trees, Sanc caught occasional glimpses of a stone structure in the distance. Once out in the open, he could see it was a tall castle with a settlement around it. Corbenay, he supposed. Esterel's cavalry, and the forces of

Lord Saliers, were still nowhere to be seen. But faint shouts occasionally carried to them on the wind.

'Let's see what the story is,' he heard his father say. The duke ordered them towards the settlement. 'Get the banners up,' he ordered. The red pall on a white background, representing Morbaine, was held aloft. So too was the Owl of Guivergne, though no doubt the other side also carried that flag.

The town had a simple wooden wall around it, from which armed warriors looked their way. But the castle was the only truly defendable structure. Assuming it was already occupied by their allies, it didn't look large enough to hold their numbers as well.

Duke Bastien called a halt. The town gates were opening. A moment of tension came—no one knew, for sure, who would emerge. It was a few riders. Half a dozen banners came with them, no doubt representing the various lords who had gathered at Corbenay. Sanc didn't know them, but others did, and the tension eased as his father and others recognised allies.

Six men pulled up in front of them. Sanc only recognised one face, and he was the one to speak.

'Welcome to Corbenay, Your Grace.' He was one of Esterel's friends. He was broad, with close cropped chestnut hair and a big smile. 'It is a relief to see you.'

'Lord Corbenay,' Bastien nodded, and reeled off the names of the other five. 'I am grateful for your support. A relief, you said?'

'Aye, it seems you've chased off Saliers' army. But perhaps only into the arms of the duke of Famine.'

'Duke Auberi is here?'

'Only a couple miles to the northeast,' Corbenay confirmed. 'When we saw Saliers' approach last evening, we feared the worst. Had a rough night debating our options.'

'What are Famiens' numbers?' Sanc's father demanded.

'At least six thousand, unfortunately. Auriac is with him, along with several other lords.'

Auriac. That was the title of Robert's father. *Robert is surely there as well.*

'And yours?'

'We have five hundred horse and two thousand foot, Your Grace.'

Duke Bastien did a quick calculation in his head. 'Making our forces about even.'

'Ah,' said Corbenay. 'That's when battles are fought.'

'Maybe so,' Sanc's father agreed.

All heads turned to see a lone rider approach from the northeast. It was Sacha, Esterel's friend. Both rider and mount were slick with sweat. He pulled up and spoke in a loud voice, as if he had just been shouting and hadn't yet adjusted his volume.

'Your Grace,' he said to Duke Bastien. 'Father,' he said with a grin to one of the lords with Corbenay. 'Miles,' he nodded to Corbenay himself. He turned his attention back to Sanc's father. 'We went after them, trying to engage,' he explained. 'Saliers saw us coming and was quick to order his forces to move. He had his horsemen come at us, but they retreated and drew us away from his main force. They nearly led us into the army of Famiens. Esterel told me to report back here.'

'And where is Esterel?' Duke Bastien demanded, a note of worry in his voice.

'They are leading the enemy horse on a little chase. He and Lord Russell wanted to give you some time to make a decision.' Sacha looked at the faces of Duke Bastien; his father; Miles of Corbenay. 'To advance or retreat, or whatever.'

'This is our chance to end this. Stop a civil war,' said Sanc's father. 'We advance.'

A shiver ran down Sanc's spine. Surely, it was also a chance for Auberi to seize the crown, to kill Bastien and his heirs.

He remembered the burned-out village they had passed. Maybe it *was* better to have a decisive outcome. One way or the other.

Moving thousands of warriors where you wanted them to go was more difficult than Sanc had imagined. Finally, his father had his forces lined up to his satisfaction. Lord Corbenay led the men from his fief in a division on the left. Sacha and his father, Lord Courion, commanded the remainder on the right. The army of Morbaine, the largest contingent by far, held the centre.

Duke Bastien had dismounted and put himself in the front line. It was as large a statement as one could make that he would put his own life on the line to win this battle. Sanc knew his warriors would fight and die with him. Sanc, Rimmon and Jesper took up position two rows behind his father. The priority, Rimmon had told him before, was to keep Sanc's father safe. That hadn't changed.

By the time they were organised, Esterel and the rest of the Morbainais cavalry had re-joined them. They had come to no harm, though they had been chased by a huge contingent of enemy horse. The enemy pulled up when they spotted the army of Morbaine. They had a clear view of the numbers and disposition of his father's force. They studied for a while, in no hurry to leave, before returning to their camp.

Duke Auberi could retreat back to Valennes, Sanc supposed. But what message would running from a smaller force send out? Sanc was convinced he'd fight. Once Auberi had made the decision to stand against his father, a battle such as this had been almost inevitable.

Bastien gave Esterel charge of the cavalry, positioned behind the infantry. Peyre, Lord Russell and Brancat joined him. Sanc felt better knowing his brothers had experienced heads with them. Perhaps that was his father's thinking.

At last, they marched away from Corbenay. They followed a road, though their force was spread so wide that most of them marched through the terrain on either side. It was mostly grass, but every so often Sanc found himself having to detour around a tree or hedge, and then relocate himself to his correct position in his line.

They heard the enemy before they saw them: shouting; horns blowing; the squeal of horses. When the two sides saw each other, challenges soon rang out. Men from both sides crashed their weapons against shields, creating an almighty racket that disturbed many a mount. Sanc put a hand on the hilt of his sword, still scabbarded at his belt. He had no shield to bang it against—he would need at least one free hand to direct his magic. Rimmon, he observed, had no weapon at all. He felt there was a strange bravery in that.

He studied Auberi's forces, positioned in a wide formation like their own, with standard bearers signifying which noble house was where. In their centre were the two largest banners, the Owl of Guivergne and what must be the device of the dukes of Famiens, a silver lattice on a field of azure. Sanc reckoned Auberi had slightly more men with him. Certainly, they seemed to have more horsemen. They hadn't planned to fight his father here—merely crush his allies. Now it would be as even a contest as war allowed.

The banging of steel on wood died down, and then stopped. For a few moments, it went deathly quiet. The two armies faced one another, close enough to pick out the detail on each individual's shields; to identify whether they held spear or sword or axe. Then Sanc's father raised an arm. The first buisine, carried by a soldier behind him, blew out. Then others, carried by men embedded throughout the army, joined in. The order to march. Sanc heard answering calls from Auberi's force, as if making it clear they were equally keen to fight.

Duke Bastien's front line took a step forward. Then the next line. Then it was Sanc's turn to shuffle forwards, careful to stay in position. 'I thought they might talk first,' Sanc said, eager to break the silence. 'That's what they did in your stories about the Isharite Wars.'

'Sometimes,' Jesper admitted. 'It seems your father has nothing to say.'

'A tactic, you might say,' Rimmon suggested. 'To project confidence to the enemy. I've known soldiers wait for hours facing each other, building up the confidence to fight. Ah, what's this?'

The sorcerer pointed ahead. Instead of sending their infantry to match them, Duke Auberi's cavalry were moving forwards, passing through gaps in the infantry line. They gathered in a line—a solid wall of horse flesh, many of the beasts as well armoured as the knights who rode them. Most of the riders held lances, giving them both a height and reach advantage over the men in his father's front line.

'They intend to charge us?' Jesper said in surprise.

'They're using their strength,' said Rimmon. 'This Duke Auberi seems determined to win.'

Sanc detected a new note of concern in his teacher's voice. He felt the ground rumble as the enemy cavalry picked up speed, the gap between the two armies rapidly closing. He looked behind them. Esterel and their own cavalry force waited in reserve, what now seemed like a long distance behind. An uneasiness grew within him. For the first time, he contemplated what might happen should they lose.

Rimmon was looking at him. 'They don't have mages in their army,' he said.

Jesper had his bow in hand, pulling back the string and firing in a high arc. Other arrows buzzed their way towards the enemy as they came within range. A fast-moving force was a challenge to hit—many missiles missing their target. Few that struck seemed able to penetrate armour. Sanc saw one rider pull up as his horse bucked in pain. But the missiles had made little impact.

The horses were close now. Sanc could see their wild eyes, flared nostrils, and open mouths. He had never realised horses could be so frightening. Sanc heard his father's voice, shouting to be heard above the growing noise of the battlefield.

'Hold!' he demanded, as his front line readied themselves. A wall of overlapping shields was made ready. Spears and other weapons poked out from the wall.

Surely, Sanc told himself, *a horse won't charge into that.*

A few did. Some horses reared up, kicking out at the warriors on the front line. Some refused. Others pulled up, while their riders struck out with lances. Horses were stabbed. Panicking, they ran in all directions, or fell writhing to the ground.

The awful sounds and smells of battle assailed Sanc as he and Rimmon tried to focus on the position occupied by Sanc's father. Duke Auberi's forces bunched here, calling out to one another. Like hounds with a fox, they'd found Duke Bastien and, instinctively, knew his death would end the battle.

Sanc and Rimmon built a magical defence around his father and the warriors by his side. Try as they might, the enemy found themselves unable to break through. Sanc's father—probably the only one in the melee who understood what was happening—encouraged his men to strike out at the enemy. Riders were knocked from horses, then axes hacked at limbs and sword blades found any weak points in their armour. Still, more of the enemy came.

The warriors of Morbaine were drawn to defend their duke, but outside the area of magical protection, many were slain. The Famiens cavalry cut through them, threatening to encircle Bastien and the half dozen soldiers who now stood with him.

Trusting that Rimmon would protect his father, Sanc used his other option. Attack. He sent bolts of magic at the horsemen. He made no attempt to shape how they looked, instead giving all his attention to ensuring accuracy. One rider after another was thrown from their mounts as Sanc cleared the threat around his father. He exulted in the power he had: the ability to change the course of battle. Wielding such power had its costs, however. He felt the drain on his energy. Even more, he felt the hostility in the looks he was given, from both sides—fear and hatred of what he could do.

'We're in trouble,' Jesper shouted.

Sanc, so focused on his father's position on the battlefield, was suddenly drawn to what was going on elsewhere. Jesper stood, sword drawn, as a group of enemy horsemen came for them. *Drawn by me,* Sanc realised.

Elsewhere, the battlefield looked chaotic. The disposition of their army, over which his father had taken so much care and time, had been compromised. The shield wall had been broken in more than one place, allowing groups of cavalry to get through and attack from the rear: disrupting defences, isolating and surrounding groups of warriors.

Jesper took a few paces forward, in a brave attempt to hold off the half dozen riders bearing down on them.

'Rimmon!' Sanc warned.

He threw one bolt, then another. *Not enough.* Then Rimmon was helping, his magic blasting into the enemy, while somehow avoiding

Jesper in front of them. The remaining riders were thrown from their horses.

Sanc looked about. They were in the clear for the moment. But they were dangerously exposed.

'No!' he heard Rimmon shout.

Cold fear grabbed at Sanc. He looked for his father. Couldn't see him.

Sanc, Rimmon and Jesper all ran at the same time. They made for the spot where the last men standing were being pulverised by the Famiens cavalry. Rimmon blasted the enemy—one of the horses lifted into the air and smashed into another with the force of it. Sanc put a protective barrier around the space where two warriors stood side by side amongst a pile of bodies. *That must be where father is.* He held the barrier as best he could while moving across the treacherous battlefield.

Jesper reached them first, slashing at a cavalryman, until he was through his defences—a high blow connected and knocked him from his horse. The beast turned and ran, while Jesper finished off its rider. Then he dropped his weapon and began searching through the bodies. Sanc and Rimmon arrived and did the same. The two warriors swayed on their feet, exhausted and unable to help.

Sanc moved bodies aside with care, unsure who was alive or dead. Blood, innards, and excreta covered everything, and he gagged, only just stopping himself from adding to the filth.

'Here,' said Jesper, clearing a space around a body.

Sanc's father had gone a grey colour. One leg was twisted at an unnatural angle. Sanc thought he could see the white of bone.

Jesper put a hand to his neck. 'There is a pulse,' he said.

'Can you do something?' Sanc asked Rimmon.

The sorcerer pursed his lips. 'Not really. He needs to be carefully carried from the battlefield and treated. But we can't do that now. The best we can do is stand guard over him.'

Sanc looked about. He tried to fend off the sensation of being overwhelmed. With his father unconscious, the army was leaderless. Then, movement caught his eye. 'Over there,' he said, pointing.

'That's a sight for sore eyes,' said Jesper.

Their cavalry, led by Esterel. They had decided to act, manoeuvring around Corbenay's left division, now sweeping in front of the infantry. The duke of Famiens' cavalry might still have the numbers, but they were dispersed all about the battlefield now, busy targeting the vulnerable infantry. None had the numbers to stop Esterel's united force, who went from one group to the next, striking them down, forcing a retreat. Before long, the enemy cavalry saw what was happening, and a disorganised retreat was called, individual horsemen and small groups departing the scene and making their way back to their camp.

The cavalry pulled up where Sanc stood. Esterel was dashing, long blond hair streaming behind him, lance still in hand. There was Peyre, a ferocious grin on his face. Lord Russell and Brancat looked altogether more serious.

'Bastien?' Russell called out.

'Here,' said Jesper. 'We need to evacuate him as soon as possible.'

'Damn it,' said Russell.

Sanc tried not to take offence, feeling responsible for his father's injuries. But it had been desperate amongst the infantry and these new arrivals had enjoyed a much easier time of it.

One of Peyre's new friends arrived on foot with his men. Dressed in furs, they were a barbaric looking group to begin with; their gore splattered armour and weapons only added to the impression. But, quick to understand the situation, the big man in charge sent four of them off to fetch a stretcher.

Sanc saw Esterel and Peyre surveying the scene, as the battered infantry gathered towards them. They were only now realising just how bad it was. Many men carried injuries, some crying out in pain; and while the duke would be escorted off the field, anyone else who couldn't walk would simply have to wait. The blare of buisines from the enemy camp hurried the need for decisions.

'That'll be the infantry coming,' said Brancat, looking towards the enemy. He scanned their own men. 'And they'll be fresh.'

'I'll dismount and stand in the front line,' said Peyre.

It was said as a statement rather than a question, and Sanc admired his brother's guts.

'Not a bad idea,' said Brancat, looking at Esterel and Lord Russell. 'I'll go with him. Give the men a bit of extra steel.'

Lord Russell said nothing, deferring to Esterel.

'Very well,' Esterel said at last. 'But we can't afford to lose any more cavalry.'

'At least give us Umbert,' said Peyre, gesturing at his friend.

Esterel's face twisted into a smile. 'By all means, take him. No offence, Lord Russell.'

'Of course not,' Lord Russell agreed. 'I am sure Umbert will be as much help on his feet as on horseback.'

Grumbling to himself, Umbert dismounted, along with Peyre and Brancat, and the three of them handed over their reins.

'Good luck,' Esterel said. Then he was calling out orders and his cavalry left the field, returning to a position behind the infantry.

'I think you should leave with your father, Sanc,' Rimmon said quietly.

'No,' Sanc said. 'I am tired, but I have enough left to help.'

'We cannot risk you,' Rimmon told him, studying Sanc for signs that he was hiding the truth.

'Honestly,' Sanc insisted, 'I'm fine.'

With Rimmon giving his reluctant assent, the sorcerer, Sanc and Jesper positioned themselves just behind Peyre.

Sanc's older brother frowned. 'I don't think Sanc should be placed so close to the action.'

'Your father's orders,' Jesper said softly, and Peyre didn't argue. He looked instead at their father, sprawled out on the ground.

Sanc was sure it was strange for everyone, seeing the man with such stern authority, looking so vulnerable.

'My man will stay with him until the stretcher comes,' the fur-clad bear man reassured them. 'I'll stay myself if you really want. But I think I'll be more help with this,' he said, waving a huge sword in the air.

'Please, come join us,' Peyre said, and the warrior took up a position between Peyre and Umbert.

'I think we'd be best setting our line forward a bit,' Brancat said to Peyre. 'It would give a bit more protection to your father and the other injured.'

'Of course.'

Brancat shouted out the orders and the buisines blew, just as the enemy's had done. The infantry of Morbaine reformed its shield wall and marched towards the enemy. Peering to either side, Sanc could see that the left and right divisions were still with them, even if he couldn't tell what condition they were in. Brancat called a halt, and then shouted, 'form up', the order passing along the line. Brancat was so used to giving orders every day he had a natural authority amongst the men. Sanc was glad of it, for it was sorely needed.

There was nothing more to do except wait and watch as the enemy infantry marched closer. Sanc could tell the enemy had a slight advantage in numbers—their line of men was longer. It would allow them to overlap at the flanks, where Lords Corbenay and Courion would have to manage the problem. Otherwise, they were evenly matched. Some of the men-at-arms might have mail shirts, capable of withstanding a hack or thrust. Others would be wearing hide or padded cloth. Some, not even that. *Evenly matched,* Sanc told himself, *except for myself and Rimmon.*

Jesper was one of the first to shoot arrows. Soon, missiles were being sent back and forth, as the two lines of infantry came within range of each other. All a warrior could do was hold their shield up and pray that an arrow didn't find its way through.

'I've got this,' Rimmon told Sanc.

Sanc understood the sorcerer had placed an invisible shield around those close to them—including, of course, Peyre and the others in the front line. No one seemed to notice, except Jesper, who took advantage of the protection to fire his arrows until he had none left. Just as before, some missiles struck the unlucky, but neither side had the numbers to inflict appreciable damage.

The infantry of Duke Auberi and his allies were now coming at them at pace, though disciplined enough to maintain their shield wall. The men of Morbaine raised their own shields and moved to meet them. A great crack sounded across the battlefield as shield met shield. Warriors heaved and pushed. Warriors screamed, as sharp steel was rammed forward—face height; ankle height; into guts; over the top, crashing down onto helmets. Luck had equal importance to skill in surviving those first deadly moments. Except for the front line of the Morbaine infantry, immediately in front of Rimmon and Sanc. No blade struck a single one of them, while plenty of their own strikes found a target.

Up and down the line as the two walls met, men fell on both sides, in equal numbers. Here, the opposing shield walls shifted back and forth as new warriors filled the holes left by injured and dead comrades. But in the centre, the Morbainais found their forward momentum unimpeded.

Peyre, Brancat and Gosse struck out with brutal ferocity, battering away any attempt to hold them off. Within moments, they were through. Just as Auberi's cavalry had broken their own lines, they carved a hole in the enemy's defences. Sanc found himself following his brother through the gap, pushed from behind as much as deciding for himself. Brancat's lessons meant he knew it was crucial they rammed home their advantage before the enemy could react.

He moved to the right, while Rimmon followed Brancat left. He could see Jesper struggling amongst the press of bodies, trying to follow him—ever the protector. To his side, Gosse put a meaty arm around a warrior's neck, dragging him to the ground. Ahead, Peyre and Umbert moved around and attacked the enemy's rear lines. Sanc followed them. As the enemy tried to defend themselves, he joined his brother, using his sword in real combat for the first time.

Drilled since childhood, he allowed his training to take over. Holding his sword two-handed, he struck out at a tall warrior, his blade crashing against his opponent's shield. In fractions of time, he saw his opponent sizing him up. Then the man's shield was coming for him, aiming to crack him in the face and deliver a follow up strike with his weapon. But Sanc knew that move. He lunged forward, falling to one knee. As the shield passed overhead, he drove his sword up towards his enemy's midriff. He felt the shock go into his hands and up his arms as the blade found resistance; and he withdrew to the side, regaining his feet.

His opponent was doubled over in pain. Sanc saw he was wearing leather armour and doubted that his blow had pierced it. But he knew he had to act fast, while his opponent was defenceless. He hacked his blade down onto the man's helmet, focusing on speed rather than strength. He was rewarded when the man slumped to the ground.

Gosse appeared, taking in the scene. He stamped down onto the man's head, then took up position next to Sanc.

Then Jesper was there, taking his place next to Gosse.

The enemy shield wall was breaking up now, its warriors forced to leave the formation to defend themselves against the new front that had been opened. This allowed their own shield wall to gain the upper hand over a weaker foe. The inevitable happened, and it happened quickly—those warriors closest to Sanc's position, in a hopeless predicament, turned and fled. The enemy shield wall disintegrated before them—a wave of men turning around and running back the way they had come. It didn't stop until every soldier, right the way through to the end of the line where the men of Courion fought, had retreated.

With no interest in savouring the sight, Peyre demanded they turn around and head for the left wing of the shield wall. Here, Brancat was attempting to achieve the same as they had done and finding more resistance. Peyre was shouting and Sanc ran to keep up with his brother.

'Steady!' Jesper demanded next to him.

Sanc had to force himself to slow down. His fears had gone and all he could feel now was the thrill of the fight. They fell on the nearest enemy, screaming like wild men. Umbert's grin was as savage as Gosse's. Sanc fought alongside Jesper. They slashed and hit, knowing they were winning; knowing they were turning the tide of the battle. The outcome was the same. The enemy infantry turned and fled as before, running for their lives.

A mighty cheer rose up. Sanc couldn't shake off his stupid grin as he watched Peyre waft his sword in triumph at the sky. Someone was singing.

Then Brancat was shouting. 'We haven't won yet, you fools!' He gestured towards the enemy camp.

Sanc could see the enemy cavalry gathering as their infantry streamed towards them. *Oh*, he realised. *Them again.* It seemed his father's rivals had their strength in their cavalry. Rested, they would be just as dangerous as before.

Brancat was manhandling warriors back into position. Jesper did the same. Understanding the danger, Peyre shouted at his men to be ready.

The enemy horse trotted forwards. The sight sobered their army a little. But not completely. Bolder with success, warriors were shouting at the enemy, asking them to come and fight; calling them every name under the sun; cracking weapons on shields. They readied themselves. But the feeling that victory was at hand had not disappeared.

The enemy picked up their pace, a trot becoming a canter. Those in the middle moved ahead until they had formed a wedge shape. Long lances were couched under armpits. Sanc assumed that some-where among them was Duke Auberi himself; the Lords Saliers and Auriac; maybe Robert and his friends. About half way towards Peyre's shield wall, they turned. Swinging away from the centre, they headed towards the far right of the line.

The warriors around Sanc quietened, unsure what to make of it. Peyre looked at Brancat, confused.

'They're isolating their attack on one section at a time, trying to break us,' Sanc heard Brancat say.

'What do we do?' Peyre asked. 'Go and help?'

'Breaking up formation is the worst thing we could do,' Brancat answered. 'It would give all the initiative to them.'

'What then?'

'We hope the Lord of Courion can withstand it.'

They had to watch as the enemy cavalry, packed tightly in their wedge, slammed into the right division. Screams echoed across the battlefield, the crash of lance on shield. Sanc could see the impact was so powerful that men went flying into the air.

Somehow, the warriors of Courion held.

Auberi's cavalry disengaged and returned to their camp.

Like everyone else, Sanc waited, suddenly feeling exposed. It seemed like the enemy cavalry had command of the field, able to strike anywhere at will. Their infantry had regathered, but made no move to re-enter the fray. They could wait and mop up after the cavalry were done.

Auberi and his allies didn't rush themselves. But after a while the cavalry returned, fresh lances ready.

'We can't let this continue,' Rimmon said to Jesper. 'I'm no use stood here.'

The cavalry began the same manoeuvre. They gained pace and moved into their wedge shape.

Sanc spun at a sound behind them. He saw what he thought he had heard. Esterel had decided to act. His cavalry force was on the move, carrying lances of their own.

Auberi's cavalry swayed, targeting Courion on the right flank again.

Sanc doubted they could withstand a second hit. 'Look,' he said to Jesper, pointing to Esterel's manoeuvre.

That was enough for Jesper. 'Master Peyre. Weapons Master Brancat. Esterel is going to meet the enemy. We need to support him.'

'If we move to the right,' said Brancat, 'the enemy infantry will come, hitting us on our flank.'

'If we allow their cavalry to defeat Esterel, we'll be stranded here and cut down to a man,' Jesper responded.

Brancat and Jesper both looked at Peyre. He hesitated.

'I can help,' Rimmon said into the silence.

Peyre frowned at the sorcerer. Sanc did not know whether his brother suspected what Rimmon was. Peyre turned to him. Sanc nodded in encouragement.

'We're going to go for it,' Peyre decided. 'If we can stop their cavalry, we've won.'

Brancat acknowledged the decision. 'Then speed is of the essence,' said the weapons master. 'We run—get there before they know what's happening. Run until our lungs are bursting.'

'Charge!' Peyre shouted, gesturing to the right flank with his sword.

They ran—a disorganised, howling mess. Any sense of formation soon disappeared, as the fastest got to the front and the slowest laboured behind.

Sanc focused on their destination. He watched as the enemy wedge slammed into their right division. The shield wall faltered, then collapsed. The enemy knights, many now wielding swords after discarding their lances, swung about them, striking down the isolated warriors of Courion.

Then, his brother's cavalry was there. Lances struck enemy knights, horses crashed into one another, the great stallions sent kicking and screaming to the ground. Riders got up, staggered, and were struck down with sword or hammer. It was bloody mayhem and Sanc was running straight for it.

A group of enemy horsemen saw them coming and rode their way. The runners at the front would be picked off before Sanc got there. He focused on one of the knights and shot out his left hand, sending an arc of magic. The rider was blasted from his seat. His horse bolted away.

Then Rimmon did the same. Then again.

Those around them gave Sanc and Rimmon fearful looks. Gosse made the sign of the devil. If they hadn't already worked out what they were, they knew now. Sanc was past caring about that. If they had any sense, they would appreciate what his magic could do.

Peyre was one of the first to reach the enemy cavalry. He had discarded his shield in the run and now grabbed a rider around the ankle, pulling him from his mount. The heavily armoured warrior crashed to the ground in a cloud of dust. Before it had settled, Umbert was striking down on his head. His sword clanged down, again and again, not stopping, until the man's helmet came loose. Then his weapon struck skull. The strike seemed to slide off. His next blow came down on neck. Only then did he stop swinging.

Sanc was unable to tear his eyes away from the brutality; the mess that was left. And that nearly cost Umbert his life. Only at the last moment did Sanc see the knight coming, lance aimed directly for his brother's friend.

He acted on instinct, putting up a shield in front of Umbert.

Umbert and Peyre turned, too late, to see the horseman bearing down on them, faces frozen in horror. Then the lance struck the invisible barrier. An instant later, the horse and rider struck it too, rebounding yards away. When they stopped rolling from the impact, neither got up.

Peyre and Umbert both looked about and found Sanc, his hand outstretched, at the same time. Their mouths fell open. And Sanc knew, for sure now, that his secret had been revealed.

Not that they had time to deal with it now. The brutal melee was still in full flow.

Sanc fought with sword now, resorting to magic only when necessary. He could feel a bone tiredness creeping up on him. It was a tiredness that spoke of damage and danger. Rimmon had warned him of it so many times that he couldn't ignore it, even in the middle of a battle.

But for all his exhaustion, Sanc could still read the flow of battle. They were winning. Esterel's attack had broken Auberi's cavalry into smaller groups, and Peyre's charge had them mired in amongst his infantry, unable to use the mobility that had threatened to win them the battle. Of course, if Sanc could see what was happening, the leaders of the enemy force could, too. Their only option was to retreat and soon the knights were responding to the blare of horns and breaking their way free.

Esterel's cavalry gave chase. Sanc saw his brother ride past as he led the harrying. But the rebel lords didn't stop when they reached their infantry or the outskirts of their camp. They kept going. And their infantry, seeing this, ran after them.

Sanc staggered towards the enemy's camp. Others were doing the same, while some had simply collapsed where they stood. Jesper was nearby—Sanc supposed the forester had never been very far away the entire time.

'We won,' Sanc said, his mouth suddenly so dry he could barely get the words out. At times it had felt like they had lost; at other times, that victory was assured. In the end, it had been a bloody, abrasive tussle. He had no idea how long it had gone on for. He thought of the people who had lost their lives: of the maimed and injured he had seen all around him, and a lump came to his throat and tears to his eyes. 'I hope father lives,' he said at last. So tired now, he didn't really know what he was saying.

'I hope so too,' said Jesper. 'Else I fear the sacrifices made today could count for nothing.'

PEYRE

VALENNES, KINGDOM OF GUIVERGNE, 673

Peyre's father lived. For now.

At least that's something, he told himself. But Duke Bastien had not left his convalescing room in the royal tower of The Bastion since he'd been carried there, and that was two weeks ago. Peyre hadn't been allowed in to see him, either.

Count yourself lucky, Esterel had told him. *Maybe I am,* Peyre considered. No one wants to see their loved ones at death's door. But he couldn't help remembering the last words his father had said to him. Foolish, he'd called him. In front of everyone, as well. It wasn't the ideal final communication between father and son, he thought wryly.

He strolled through the corridors of his family's new home, looking for Umbert. He'd been so sure he'd find his friend in the kitchens that he was, for the moment, bereft of ideas.

Calling The Bastion home took a little getting used to. It was so different to life in Arbeost. Different even to Coldeberg Castle, which had become a home to him for the year he'd spent in Barissia. Everything was so serious here, he decided. Maybe it was just that these were serious times. But power, ceremony and politics were all anyone seemed to care about. How about a little fun and amusement from time to time?

He rapped on Umbert's door for the second time. Shouted for him. Nothing. Gave it a good kick, just in case. Then continued his search.

At least, he reflected, they had taken The Bastion without a fight. Though it was a mixed blessing. They had arrived at Valennes, fully expecting a siege. Instead, Duke Auberi and his supporters had pulled all their troops out of the city and retreated south. They'd taken the royal treasury and anything of value with them, too. Auberi must have decided he couldn't hold Valennes or The Bastion. He may have calculated differently had he known how badly wounded Peyre's father was. As it was, a speedy entry into the comforts of the city and access to its doctors probably saved the duke's life.

However, it meant Auberi was still free, roaming about Guivergne somewhere with his forces. What was left of them. There were plenty of dead left on the battlefield, plenty more seriously injured. Arnoul, Lord of Saliers, languished in The Bastion's dungeon. Personally apprehended by Esterel during the enemy's retreat, it was a story his brother seemed unable to stop repeating to everyone, or indeed embellishing. There was no doubt the victory in battle had given them the upper hand. But his father's illness meant the campaign was stalled.

Peyre passed a room, then stopped, taking a couple of paces backwards. He'd heard giggling. It was female giggling—the sort of brainless noise he associated with girls who went for Umbert.

He opened the door and strode in. Sure enough, he'd found Umbert with a girl in a state of undress. One of the maids of The Bastion. She gave a little cry, covering her chest, and going a deep shade of red.

'I've been looking for you all over!' Peyre said, quite cross.

'I'm sorry,' said Umbert.

In truth, he did look miserable, though Peyre suspected that was more because his knavery had been disrupted. 'Well, I'm in need of companionship, and shouldn't have to spend half the day wandering about trying to find you, for every habitant of the fortress to witness.'

'Of course,' Umbert agreed.

Peyre did his friend the courtesy of stepping outside the room so he could say his farewells. Not that Umbert deserved it. But Peyre strove to set an example when it came to manners, rather than descend to the level others set.

Umbert appeared shortly, closing the door behind him. At least he had the good grace to look sheepish about it. They walked together along the corridor.

'What a mess,' Peyre grumbled, unwilling to forgive him yet. 'I shall be embarrassed every time I see the girl now. And no doubt she will, too.'

'I didn't mean it to happen,' Umbert said. 'We just got talking and one thing led to another—'

'I hope you're not trying to blame the girl,' Peyre said. 'That would be ignoble, even for you.'

'No, Peyre, of course not. I take full responsibility.'

Peyre nodded, mollified. 'She did seem sweet, though. Fabulous pair of duckies.'

'Yes,' Umbert agreed wistfully. 'You are in need of companionship?'

'I don't know what to do with myself today.'

'Perhaps you could talk with Sanc? You keep saying you've been meaning to.'

Sanc. He wouldn't have believed it if he hadn't seen it for himself. His little brother casting magic in the middle of the battle: stopping a mounted knight's charge and saving Umbert's life in the process. He'd always had a soft spot for Sanc. Felt sorry for him a lot of the time. Now he wondered if he'd ever known him at all. It felt like he had become a stranger.

'I suppose now is as good a time as any,' he said, knowing full well he had been putting it off for too long. 'Where do you think we might find him?'

'He and the sorcerer often go to the east side of the city.'

The sorcerer. In hindsight, Peyre felt pretty stupid that he hadn't caught on to what was going on under his nose. The foreigner, Rimmon, had arrived unannounced in Arbeost and spent so much time with Sanc. It seemed so obvious now. *If it wasn't for my exile, I would have worked it out*, Peyre assured himself.

The other aspect that now seemed clear as day was that his father must have known all along. It wasn't just that Rimmon had come to live in Arbeost. The sorcerer and Sanc had been placed in the central division under his father's command for the battle. That had struck Peyre as more than strange. The more he went over the events of the battle, the more he came to the unwelcome conclusion that the two of them probably swung the outcome in their favour. 'Why the east side of Valennes?' he asked Umbert.

'More privacy, I expect.'

That made sense. The west side of the capital was busy, populous, walled in—claustrophobic, even. Peyre had not yet explored the east side, but it seemed much more spacious.

They made their way to the front gate of The Bastion. In the Grand Foyer, Peyre spotted a familiar face on guard duty. Jehan, the young man who had escaped with Peyre and Esterel out of The Bastion. Their fortunes had changed since then, but it seemed that Jehan's life had returned to normal. He stood straight and to attention as Peyre approached him.

'How are things?' Peyre asked.

'Very good, Your Highness.'

Peyre nodded, ignoring the inaccurate title. No one knew how to address him these days. Only if his father recovered and was crowned king, would he become a prince. 'How is Brancat treating you?' he asked.

Peyre's old weapons master was now castellan of The Bastion. Their people had taken over most of the important jobs in Valennes. Miles, Esterel's friend, was now captain of the city guard. The previous holder of the title—Lewen, Peyre recalled, picturing the night-time standoff with the captain during their escape from Valennes—had left the city with Auberi's forces.

'Very well, Your Highness. There is more discipline now than there has ever been.'

That sounded about right. 'Well, nice to see you again, Jehan.

Umbert and I are headed to the east side of the city. First time I'll have visited properly.'

Jehan frowned, looking Peyre up and down. 'With the greatest respect, Your Highness, I have to advise against it.'

'For what reason?'

'The city guard doesn't operate on the east side. It is a lawless place. And you and Lord Umbert look—'

'What? What do we look?'

Jehan seemed to consider his words with care. 'You look like you might be targeted by the gangs who operate there. Maybe if you could wait until I am off duty, I could escort you?'

'We're going now, Jehan. Come with us.'

'I couldn't leave my post. Brancat—'

'Never mind Brancat. I am giving you permission. And Brancat serves my family.'

'Yes, but—'

Umbert put an arm around Jehan's shoulder. 'Lord Peyre is being very polite about it,' he said. 'But he has given you an order.'

'Right,' Jehan said. Reluctantly, he left the Grand Foyer and accompanied them to the front gate of The Bastion.

It was manned by soldiers of Morbaine, who gave them a friendly greeting as they left the fortress and turned south down the main road of the city. At the busy central square—the place where Umbert and Gosse had saved them from captain Lewen's ambush—they turned left for the east gate of the walled, old city.

As they approached, Peyre could hear the rush of the Cousel as it sped south. Guivergnais soldiers manned the gate. Some of the city guard had stayed and kept their posts after Auberi's forces left. The rest had been filled by warriors who served Miles de Corbenay, or other local lords. Whoever they served, they gave Peyre due respect as he passed through.

He was the son of the future king, for one. But Peyre knew it was more to do with the battle and his leadership of the infantry in its final stages. Peyre acknowledged he was guilty of being a little full of himself on occasion. As far as the battle was concerned, however, he felt he had little to boast about. Brancat and Rimmon—even Sanc—had done more than he had and got none of the credit. More than once, he'd overheard men whispering complaints to one another about the 'red-eyed sorcerer'. Nothing would stop Peyre from confronting anyone who criticised his brother. Since his exile, however, he'd learned a bit more self-control. He'd stopped short of actually punching anyone.

They crossed the bridge that took them over the river to the other side of the city. Peyre and Umbert shared a look as they took in the foamy water beneath them—remembering their journey from Coldeberg to Valennes. So much had happened in the last few weeks, it felt like a lifetime ago. 'So,' he said to Jehan, 'what makes you such a valuable escort into the east side? Aside from these?' he said, giving the man's biceps an approving squeeze.

'Well. Although I live at The Bastion now, my family still lives this side of the city. I visit them when I can—bring them money.'

'Maybe we'll have time to visit your family home. After I talk with my brother.'

Jehan shook his head. 'I wouldn't take you there, Your Highness. It's not like the houses in the west side.'

Peyre took in the eastern half of the city as they descended the steps, leading them off the bridge. The west half of Valennes—the old city—was the desirable half to live in. The east side seemed to have sprung up by itself, with no planning—a jumble of different buildings put up wherever their owners desired. 'Remember, I didn't grow up in The Bastion, Jehan. Arbeost is a very simple place. Umbert and I aren't as soft and pampered as you might think.'

Jehan gave a little smile but shook his head, quite firm. 'I couldn't take you.'

He's ashamed, Peyre realised. He remembered his time in Essenberg. Leopold had taken him to the rookery. It had been full of filthy looking hovels—and plenty of unfortunates who couldn't even claim one of those. It was so dangerous, they'd had to walk in with bodyguards trailing behind the duke who theoretically ran the city. Perhaps every great city has such a place, he considered. He understood, now, Jehan's reluctance to let them wander around without a guide.

Peyre raised a hand as he saw Umbert readying himself to argue with the guard. He'd told his friend about his experiences in Essenberg, but some things one has to see for oneself. 'We'll just see Sanc, then return,' he said.

Peyre and Umbert found they were indeed reliant on Jehan to do the looking for them. He led them to the open, green spaces where his brother was likely to have gone, avoiding the rougher locales. Peyre had to admit he would have got lost by himself.

It was the forester, Jesper, they saw first. He was leaning against a beautiful, old beech tree, a sword at his belt and a bow within easy reach. He had the look of someone encouraging passersby to keep on walking. Once he recognised Peyre, he stood up and called out into a grassy area that stood beside a brook, dotted with other trees. Sanc and Rimmon soon emerged and strolled over. More than likely, they'd been practising their spells together. Peyre pushed away his feelings of distaste and fear.

'Peyre?' Sanc asked. 'Is everything alright?'

'Yes, just came to see you. I feel like we haven't had time to talk.' Peyre gestured in the direction Sanc had just come from, and they walked off together. Umbert and the two men took the hint and left them to it.

'It's about the magic,' Sanc said. He sounded nervous.

'How long have you known?' Peyre asked him.

'Not so long. It first happened two years ago. You remember the Kellish embassy that came to Arbeost?'

That wasn't likely to slip Peyre's mind. Walter had tried to get to the bottom of that visit. The duke had interrogated Lord Kass about it. Three of Salvinus's men had not returned to Kelland. Surely, they hadn't been sent after Sanc?

'Three of the warriors from the embassy came back. To kill me.'

Peyre looked at his brother, shocked. How had all this been kept secret from him?

'My powers—' Sanc seemed to struggle for the right words. 'I suppose you might say 'emerged' then. I killed two of them. Jesper got the third.' Sanc gave Peyre an inquisitive look. 'Do you believe me?'

'I have to admit, I might not have done at the time,' Peyre conceded. 'But having been to Essenberg, I know all about Duke Leopold and his advisers.' He gestured to the scar that ran across his cheek. 'But if that's when your powers emerged, why did they send people to kill you?'

'These,' Sanc replied, gesturing to his red eyes.

'Oh.' It was strange. How many times had Peyre defended his brother against people who had called Sanc a devil? And now, it seemed, it was kind of true. 'Then this Rimmon fellow came the next year? To help you?'

Sanc nodded. 'He and Jesper told me to keep it all a secret.'

'But father for one must have known? He knew what Rimmon was and…what you are.'

'I don't see how he couldn't,' said Sanc. 'But no one ever told me so.'

'Huh. How like father. Well, now everyone knows.'

'Yes. I'm more unpopular than ever, if that were possible,' said Sanc.

It was said with a bitterness that made Peyre hurt for him. Not that he could really understand—what it was like to have magic; to have those eyes. 'I wanted to come and say thank you for what you did. For saving Umbert and everything.'

'Umbert has already thanked me. But I appreciate it, Peyre.'

Oh, he has, has he? 'And just to make sure you understand that things haven't changed between us.'

'Thank you, Peyre,' Sanc said, sounding like the little brother he remembered. 'You and Umbert are the only ones who've said that.'

They embraced. 'Of course,' said Peyre. He'd meant what he said. It was just that when he said it, it had felt like a lie.

* * *

THE DAYS PASSED and the feeling of paralysis continued. Peyre's father was too ill to take charge, and it seemed no one was able to make decisions in his absence. Peyre was sure that if his father were well, they would have left the capital and chased after their enemies by now. Instead, the soldiers of Morbaine and of their allies stayed in Valennes. Lords Russell and Caisin seemed to spend all their time sourcing enough food to keep everyone fed. Duke Auberi, meanwhile, had been given the time and space to recover from his defeat.

Esterel invited Peyre to his rooms in The Bastion. The first time Peyre had visited his brother here, Esterel had been fearful for his life. Now, his usual confidence had been restored. His friends Sacha and Miles were also there, and the four of them discussed the situation.

Esterel waved a piece of parchment about. 'Florent has sent word from Martras at last,' he told Peyre. 'He tells me Duke Domard is being perfectly civil, but insists he won't commit his troops to what he considers a fight over the succession. When Florent tries to pin him down, it seems a coronation might be enough to push him into loyalty to our cause.'

'But father is too ill for such a ceremony,' Peyre said.

'Exactly,' said Miles. 'And as long as the throne is empty, there will be trouble in Guivergne.'

'Esterel knows what I think,' said Sacha. 'I say it with no disrespect to your father. But we would be in a much safer position if Esterel were to be made king. I know the nobility of Guivergne would rally around him.'

Peyre was shocked by the idea. Bypass their father while he still lived? But he kept his expression neutral. He realised Esterel had invited him here to sound him out about the idea. Did he want to get Peyre on side? And was he working on persuading others already?

Peyre and Esterel looked at one another for a moment.

'What do you think?' Esterel asked him.

It was said as if all he wanted was Peyre's honest opinion. And perhaps that was the case. But something about the atmosphere in the room gave Peyre pause. He didn't completely trust Sacha, who—like Miles—had now inherited his father's title and lands. Both men had made themselves close allies of his brother and stood to be well rewarded if—when—Esterel became king. Was their advice for the benefit of Guivergne or of themselves?

'That's such a big step,' he said to Esterel. 'What if father made you his regent or some such title, so that you were acting on his authority?'

Esterel nodded. 'I thought of that.'

'The problem,' said Sacha, 'is that Duke Bastien is not king and Esterel would not, therefore, be a formal regent of the throne.' He spread his hands. 'I hope you understand, Peyre. I am speaking openly like this for the good of the kingdom. I pray to the gods that your father recovers. But it seems we're looking at weeks, if not months. The campaigning season will be over. That would prolong this conflict by a year. Enmities would become entrenched. This is how civil wars begin.' He paused, rubbing at his stubble as he looked about the room. 'I've already lost my father and many men of Courion over this dispute. I'm speaking for those who want to see it ended.'

'We understand your position,' said Esterel. 'I'm just unsure what to do for the best.'

'I think you need to speak to father, then,' Peyre said.

Esterel nodded. 'Yes, I think I do. Will you come with me?'

PEYRE'S FATHER sat up in his convalescing bed. Blankets covered his legs. That was where his worst injuries were—a broken leg and a shattered knee—that kept him confined here. There had been complications with the surrounding tissue—Peyre didn't know the details, but he knew it had been touch and go in those first few days. Now, it seemed, Duke Bastien's recovery was more stable. But he looked thin, pale, and tired. Not the man who had always been so strong and proud throughout Peyre's childhood.

'You needed to see me?' he asked, his voice weak and breathy.

Esterel looked nervous. 'It's about the situation, father. Auberi is at large and we've made no progress sat here in Valennes since the battle. We must secure the throne. I'm not blaming you, of course. But Peyre and I were thinking we need to do something.'

Oh great, Peyre thought. *Why am I involved in this?*

'I'm aware of the situation, Esterel,' Bastien said. He'd lost none of his brusque manner, then. 'You think I want to be laid out here, half-dead? What is this 'something' you've come to suggest?'

Esterel looked at Peyre. When Peyre said nothing, he opened his eyes wide.

So, this is why I've been dragged here. 'There has been talk about our options,' Peyre said reluctantly. 'Of making Esterel king—or at least declaring him regent, or some such. Then the country may unite behind him against Auberi.'

'I've worked hard to win the love of the people here, father,' Esterel added. 'That was why you sent me. Why not use it?'

Bastien's face crumpled in pain.

Peyre hoped it might be from his injuries rather than the stupidity of his sons.

'Look, boys. I may not be around much longer, so you two need to learn to think. And by that, I mean long-term: plan towards your goals, consider the consequences of your actions. In other words, think a little further than the end of your nose.

'Esterel will be king. Maybe soon. But what do we gain from making him king now? What would we gain from going after Auberi, fighting and killing our own people in Esterel's name? Losing all that good will he's built up? Resented by so many for the rest of his reign? An earlier victory over Auberi would be a poor trade.

'No. Think about it. I am disliked in Guivergnais. Far better that King Bastien is blamed for the death and destruction. Far better that I am the one accused of seizing the throne and whatever other accusations will be thrown our way. Then, when the time comes, *everyone* will cheer that Bastien is gone; and that sweet, fair, Esterel is on the throne.' He looked at Esterel. 'The undisputed, rightful heir. No crimes attached to your name. Isn't that better?'

Peyre's mouth had dropped open. His father had a plan; he had goals that extended beyond his own life, that involved securing the throne for his son. *Shame on me*, Peyre told himself, *for not giving a single thought to such things. For allowing my sick father to carry all that weight and responsibility, while I swanned about The Bastion, complaining to myself how serious everyone is. I am a man or a child?*

Esterel, too, looked contrite. 'I'm sorry, father. You're right, of course. I just wish I could do something.'

Bastien bared his teeth. 'Soon.' He gestured to the corner of his room, where a walking stick was propped against the wall. 'I am learning to walk with it. I'll not be carried to my coronation. I'll walk in. Then, when I have the crown, you'll have the army.' He patted his leg. 'My fighting days are over.'

* * *

It wasn't a ceremony for the bards to compose songs about, Peyre mused. Or at least, they'd have to use some poetic licence.

Hastily arranged, it suffered from a lack of pageantry. That was hardly King Bastien's forte; or Lord Russell's, or anyone else's, it seemed. *Sometimes our family would benefit from a woman's touch*, Peyre decided. Not to mention, any money they had went on food and wages rather than what his father would have considered a wasteful celebration.

There was little enthusiasm for the coronation beyond the soldiers who had fought for Peyre's father. The citizens of Valennes, Peyre gathered, didn't know his father, or saw him as a foreigner. Strange, when his father had grown up here. According to Esterel, Nicolas's hatred of his brother had, after so many years, poisoned many people against him. Thus, when the carriages had arrived outside the cathedral, the small crowd was in a curious rather than joyous mood.

Bastien had insisted on walking inside unaided. He now waited on the end of Peyre's bench, seated with his three sons, while the Bishop of Valennes delivered his preamble. The cleric had been told, in no uncertain terms, to keep it brief. Even so, Peyre, Esterel and Sanc gave their father concerned, sidelong glances when he wasn't looking. He was drenched in sweat and clutched at his stick with white knuckles.

Whatever he'd taken for the pain hadn't got rid of it. Probably because his priority was staying alert.

On the nearby rows were the noblemen of Guivergne, some of whom had their families with them. Lords Russell, Caisin, Courion, Corbenay. Peyre's friend, Gosse. These were the men who had risked much to put Bastien on the throne. Behind such important men were the citizens of Valennes, the soldiery of Morbaine, and others lucky enough to be found room inside the cathedral for such an occasion.

At last, Bastien was called up for the ceremony. He pushed himself into a standing position and manoeuvred himself, weight bearing down on his stick, into the central aisle of the nave. Everyone around him wished to provide help, but knew they couldn't. He walked, painstakingly, toward the chancel where the bishop waited.

The man had made it clear that it was the gods who would endow Peyre's father with his royal powers and status. *I see no sign of them,* Peyre said to himself, unimpressed with the idea. *Still, if the gods are a king's overlords, it is more convenient if they are usually absent.*

His father approached the steps. A hush had descended on the cathedral so that all Peyre could hear was the click of the walking stick on the flagstone floor, the noise echoing around the large space. Bastien placed his stick on the first step and manoeuvred his injured leg, still in splints, at an angle so that he could get his foot onto it. He then shifted his weight and got the other foot up.

Again, the stick went on the next step, and he levered his leg up. But, this time, Bastien lost his balance. He wobbled, and time seemed to go in slow motion for Peyre. He stared at the hand that held the stick, the whole arm shaking as his father tried to hold his weight up with it. Dread clutched at Peyre's chest. *No,* he thought. *Please, don't let him collapse to the floor.* It wasn't the fear of further injury, or even concern for what others might say. It was his father's pride that he cared about in those precarious seconds, as the man who would rule Guivergne teetered on the steps.

He righted himself. A collective breath of relief escaped from the congregation, and Bastien completed the final, laborious steps of his journey to the chancel. He looked out over the people gathered before him. Stern-faced as ever, but perhaps, Peyre thought, allowing himself a moment to appreciate his moment of elevation.

'I, Bastien, swear to serve the people of Guivergne. I will uphold the commandments of the gods. I forbid all acts of robbery, harm and injustice and will punish all lawbreakers, regardless of their station in life. I will show mercy and strive to remove the burdens on the people. I will bring peace to the land.'

The bishop of Valennes held aloft the crown of Guivergne and then placed it on Bastien's head.

A cry rang out from the Morbainais behind them, and Peyre joined in, the shouts of affirmation filling the cathedral with noise. He looked at Esterel and Sanc. His brothers were shouting too. A grin came to Peyre's face. He was surprised to find it was closely followed by tears.

SANC

VALENNES, KINGDOM OF GUIVERGNE, 674

Sanc strode through the gates of The Bastion, the guards looking uncomfortable in his presence, as they always did. He was used to those reactions.

Out on the streets of Valennes, on a crisp winter's evening, he felt free from the confines of the fortress. Free from Jesper. The man was the closest thing Sanc had to a friend, but he had become a permanent shadow during the last few months. Hard to shake off. Sanc knew, with Rimmon gone, that Jesper felt responsible for his safety. But he needed time alone.

A restlessness had come over Sanc in recent weeks. In Arbeost, his days had been busy. But he was no longer training with Rimmon. The sorcerer had left in the autumn once he was sure the capital would be secure over the winter. All Sanc knew of his destination was 'the South'. Rimmon had given no reason. Sanc could piece together that the Haskan had unfinished business there; business that had been interrupted when he came to Arbeost to train Sanc.

He was no longer required to take part in military training, either. Although no one had said as much, it seemed once his magic powers were revealed, that path was closed to him. Perhaps it was decided he didn't need it.

He would occasionally walk past his old weapons master, Brancat —now castellan of The Bastion. Brancat was civil, but he looked at Sanc like he had betrayed him. Maybe he had, in a way—keeping his powers secret from everyone. Most people now looked at him with either hostility or fear. But he was the king's son, and none dared say anything.

When he was younger, Sanc recalled, he would have revelled in the idea of having day after day to himself, with no commitments. But he had to admit, he was getting bored. He felt a pang of homesickness, too. There were two people he really missed: his sister, Loysse, and Rab. He'd found more love and acceptance from them than anyone else.

He walked the streets of Valennes, through the city centre. It was dark, and the evening had a bite to it. The citizens who were out and about were hurrying, trying to get somewhere: their homes, or the city's inns, warm and inviting on a chilly night. Sanc, though, headed east.

'I have business on the east side of the city,' he told the guards at the gate.

They looked at him uncertainly, weighing up the pros and cons of letting the young son of the king through. He'd regularly gone to the east side of Valennes in the company of Rimmon and Jesper. Sanc could see in their faces they knew he had no legitimate business out there at this hour. But his reputation had grown since the battle at Corbenay. The young prince who had blasted mounted knights to the ground with his dark powers. Not someone it was wise to upset. They let him through.

Sanc crossed the Cousel, the river that separated two very different places, even if they shared the same name. For while his father's laws ran unobstructed in the west, the east was a lawless place. That suited tonight's purpose just fine.

The streets here were really just mud, mixed with the excrement of man and beast. Sanc made no effort to be silent as he squelched along, no particular destination in mind. It didn't take long, on a night like this, for a young man on his own, dressed well, to attract attention. There were four of them he could see; maybe more he couldn't.

He moved without warning, cutting between two houses.

He heard them running after him. They shouted and hollered, the voices of young men about his own age, excited for the chase.

Sanc moved to the back of a house and stopped, pressing himself against the wattle and daub wall. He concentrated on magic more complicated than anything Rimmon had taught him.

Though Rimmon's lessons had led him in this direction. It was the attack spells. Rimmon had got him to change their appearance, from the orange-red of flames to the blue-white of lightning. An illusion. And if Sanc could affect what people could see in this way, what else might he be able to do?

The four boys gathered about, searching for him. Two had knives in their hands. One of these called out with a grin, 'Where are you, friend?'

Sanc's magic told them he wasn't there. It pulled shadows around his body. Would it work? Could he really make himself invisible?

One of them approached, mere feet away.

If it doesn't work, I'll just blast him, Sanc told himself.

The youth looked right through him. He walked over, mere inches from Sanc now.

Sanc held his breath, nervous sweat pouring down his back and sides. Surely the boy could smell him? Hear him? No. He went past, still searching.

Sanc watched them wander about. What would they have done had they caught him? Those knives were surely a clue. Who else had they cornered or chased down on these streets? *Wouldn't it be better,* Sanc asked himself, *to remove these thugs from the city?* He could feel his magic surging. His veins flowed with it; his palms itched, eager to release it.

They'd find the bodies, he reasoned. *And who else would get the blame but me?*

Sanc waited until they had gone. He stopped the illusion. Instantly, he realised how tired he was. That magic had been surprisingly draining. He felt hollowed out. But the restlessness he had felt earlier this evening had dissipated. Was it the magic, he wondered, demanding release? Rimmon had never told him that might happen. Though Rimmon, he was sure, didn't have the same power contained within him as Sanc did.

He moved, making his way back to The Bastion. The magic had worked, yet he still felt dissatisfied. *I answer one question and more come to replace it.*

* * *

SPRING CAME to Valennes and Sanc's days remained empty. Unlike his brothers, he was not invited to play a role in his father's government. They sat on the Council and were privy to decision making. Sanc heard about things later, usually from Peyre. *No*, Sanc told himself. *I'm not consulted on anything, but I'll be expected to jump to it if they have need of my magic again.*

This time, Peyre had a small audience in his room. Umbert and Jesper sat either side of Sanc, for Peyre had promised some juicy gossip.

'Auberi has crossed the Cousel,' Peyre told them. 'Reports say his army's been raiding the lands of his enemies. Including Lord Courion's, apparently,' he said, with little attempt to hide his pleasure at that.

Sacha, Lord Courion, was one of Esterel's friends. He'd travelled to Famiens in the autumn, along with Lord Chancellor Caisin, to negotiate with Auberi. They'd come back empty-handed. Auberi still claimed the throne, and there was nothing they could offer to get round that sticking point.

'How many?' Jesper asked.

'Sizeable,' said Peyre. 'As many as last year, they reckon. The Lord of Auriac has joined him.'

Raymon of Auriac was Robert's father. He'd used a punch up with Robert to turn King Nicolas on their family, getting Peyre exiled in the process. Perhaps he thought he'd burned his bridges and had nothing to lose. But so long as these mighty lords supported Auberi over Sanc's family, there would be no peace in Guivergne.

'We'll have to see if Saliers joins them,' Peyre added darkly.

In his wisdom, the king had released their captive from the Battle of Corbenay at the end of the summer. Not everyone, Peyre included, had agreed with that decision. But Sanc's father had promised peace for Guivergne in his coronation speech. Surely that meant giving people a second chance?

'If he does, the king will have no choice but to take his head,' said Umbert.

'That's true,' said Peyre, sounding brighter.

'Presumably the king is raising an army,' Sanc said. 'Do we know who's leading it?'

'All that's been said for certain,' said Peyre, 'is that Esterel will be given command of the army and father will stay here. But there's no way I'm not going.'

It had been easy, in the last few months, to imagine that the conflict was over, and that King Bastien ruled the country from the Bastion. His father had made his appointments in government—Caisin retained the Lord Chancellery; Lord Russell had been made Royal Steward. There had been a big ceremony—much grander than his father's own coronation—in which Esterel had been confirmed as his heir and given the Duchy of Morbaine, just as Bastien had held that title under Nicolas. The people of Valennes had cheered, and the future seemed secure.

But of course, that wasn't true at all. Only half the kingdom recognised the royal writ. Many still gave their loyalty to Auberi. For all his father's efforts at peace, it seemed only war would settle things for good.

* * *

THE ARMY WAS SEEN off from the capital in a display of support. King Bastien made a rare public appearance to lead the ceremonies. Sanc wondered what he thought, sending all three of his sons off to war while he stayed at home, still too weak to lead his men. But his father wore his mask of strength and certainly didn't confide his feelings to Sanc.

The king charged his son and heir, Esterel, with protecting the kingdom from Duke Auberi. Sanc's father divided his personnel and forces between those who were to fight with Esterel and those who were to stay to defend the capital. As well as his sons, Bastien sent his steward and closest confidant, Lord Russell, with the army. But he kept with him Brancat, whose guards defended the Bastion, and Corbenay, whose soldiers defended the city. Lord Caisin also stayed in the capital; his experience vital to keep the royal administration going.

Esterel took the army north west. The pace was reasonable; most of the soldiers didn't have the luxury of riding on horseback. Sacha, Lord Courion, who knew this region, directed the scouts. Auberi's forces were operating in the region south of the Cousel, but their precise location needed to be pinned down.

By the time they stopped for lunch, the local population had given Sacha's scouts enough information for a decision to be taken. Sanc was invited to Esterel's war council, something that wouldn't have happened if their father was in charge. With them were Peyre, Lord Russell and Sacha.

Sacha summarised what he'd learned. 'The main force is due north. They've been going for easy targets, clearing out food stores, taking livestock, putting buildings to the torch. They've ignored any place with solid walls and a garrison.'

'The duke of Famine's living up to his nickname,' Peyre sneered.

'There's a crossing point where they are?' asked Lord Russell.

'There's a ford nearby,' said Sacha.

'So, if they see us coming they can withdraw into Famiens,' said Russell. 'Make us cross the river and fight them there.'

'That's what they want,' said Peyre. 'I've a better idea. Head west into the lordship of Auriac. Put his lands to the torch, see how he likes it.'

'Hold on,' said Sacha. 'That's all very well. And I understand you have a personal quarrel with that family. But they're attacking my people. We can't just walk away and leave them defenceless.'

Heads turned to Esterel. He had the final say.

'The king's orders are to win the war, not an individual battle,' Esterel said. 'On that basis, chasing them into Famiens gains us little and is the more dangerous option. Raiding in Auriac has a certain symmetry to it and will keep us fed. It might even do more—drive a wedge between Auberi and his principal supporter. At the least, it will be uncomfortable for Raymon of Auriac to see his lands pillaged. Might make him and the other false lords think twice about where their allegiance should lie.'

It seemed to make sense. Sanc wouldn't have known what to do for the best. Russell and Peyre nodded in agreement with Esterel. Sacha, he could tell, still wasn't happy. But he knew better than to argue the point further.

At first, Sanc experienced a thrill of excitement at entering the lands of Raymon of Auriac. The man had a lot to answer for. It wasn't just the business of Peyre's exile and subsequent maiming. If they'd lost the Battle of Corbenay, Sanc knew Auriac wouldn't have hesitated in having Sanc's whole family put to the sword before placing Auberi on the throne.

After a couple of days, however, he realised Esterel's plans for him were limited. His brother had set up a base camp from which small sorties left with specific, scouted targets. Sanc was never included in these. Esterel told him the defence of their position from attack was the priority, and that Sanc's magic would be needed in those circumstances. Maybe that was the truth, rather than treating his younger brother like a child. They hardly needed him to help rob farmers, after all. And Esterel, though he had never really talked about it with him as a brother, seemed to have no problem with discussing Sanc's magic from a strategic point of view.

Then there were the raids themselves. Sanc didn't know what to think. The victims were mostly peasants—men, women and children who hadn't chosen to be part of this conflict. Hells, they hadn't even chosen Raymon as a lord. But they were the ones being punished. Any food they had left at this time of the year had been carefully rationed over the winter, and harvesting was a long time away. *They'll starve. Maybe it does make strategic sense*, Sanc tried to persuade himself. *And maybe—almost certainly—I'm naïve. But it still doesn't seem right.*

On the third day, with both his brothers leading their own raids, Sanc found himself in the company of Lord Russell. He was more comfortable with the man than most people. He'd always taken on the rather odd role of intermediary between Sanc and his own father. Maybe it was boredom, but today he seemed more willing to talk than ever before.

'Jesper warned us, a long time ago, that you might have magic. Your father's status has protected you all this time.'

'I know,' Sanc said.

'But at the same time, he needs to be protected from you. He can't be seen to be too close. Do you understand?'

'I suppose that makes sense. But come on. I revolt him. Always have.'

Russell sighed. 'Your father was infatuated with Alienor. Perhaps you can love someone too much? I always admired everything about your father, but when he lost her, I discovered a weakness in him that wasn't attractive. He's never got over it. And you, of course, remind him of it every day. I'm afraid there was nothing you could do. It's not about you as a person, Sanc.'

No one had ever been as candid with Sanc as this, even if he had worked out most of the story himself over the years. Part of him wanted to know more. Another part wanted to bury it. 'Why didn't he get rid of me?' he asked. It was the one thing about the whole situation he hadn't worked out.

'He did. Sent you to a wet nurse out in the sticks in Morbaine. The plan was to keep paying the family to raise you as their son. But it was your eyes. All the devil nonsense. The locals said they'd kill you; the family said they couldn't guarantee your safety. Arbeost was really the only place where you'd be safe. So, you were brought back.

'Bastien saw himself as a great martyr for allowing the child who'd killed his wife back into the family home. He considered that enough of a concession. I told him you needed a parent. He said he couldn't do that. When Jesper approached us about you, I saw a solution. That man could be a father to you.'

Sanc fought back tears. Jesper, his father? 'I suppose he was. A father to me, I mean.' Hadn't Jesper's hut always been the place where he'd felt happy? Secure? He didn't recall ever offering the man a word of thanks.

Russell gave him an awkward pat on the shoulder. 'Life hasn't been kind to you, Sanc. But it's not been so harsh. You've had good people around you.'

Sanc nodded. It wasn't that he disagreed. It was just that, sometimes, it didn't feel enough.

SANC

AURIAC, KINGDOM OF GUIVERGNE, 674

It was midday, but you wouldn't know it. Grey clouds hung above, and the camp was drenched by a persistent rain. Sanc and Jesper sheltered inside their tent in amiable silence. Jesper cared for their weapons, always content when working with his hands. Sanc listened to the rain, breathed in the smell of it, and watched the drops falling about the camp, where human sized shapes huddled under blankets.

Activity caught his attention as one raiding party entered the camp and another left. Before long, the tent flap was pulled open and Peyre and Umbert entered, dripping water onto the floor. They looked soaked through—a mixture of rain and, by the reek of them, sweat.

'Miserable out there,' Peyre commented, as Sanc and Jesper helped them by unbuckling straps and pulling their hauberks over their heads.

'How did it go?' Sanc asked them.

'Same,' said Peyre, who had led the morning's raid. 'Auriac is laid waste. There are few places left worth plundering.'

'Any resistance?' Jesper asked.

'Nope. We passed a castle. A handful of faces peering over the battlements. I honestly believe Lord Raymon has taken every soldier with him. If we were minded to lay a siege, it wouldn't take long to reduce his strongholds.'

From what Sanc had gathered, the town of Auriac itself had thick walls. There were half a dozen stone built castles at strategic points. Otherwise, they'd run free across the region, with no retaliations. It certainly suggested Lord Raymon had left his lands poorly defended, not anticipating Esterel's tactics.

It was at the precise moment when Peyre and Umbert had stripped off their last items of wet clothing that Sacha paid them a visit. 'Gods have mercy, there's a sight I wish my eyes could unsee.'

'What do you want, Courion?' Peyre growled.

'Come to your brother's tent as soon as you are dressed. The duke of Famine approaches.'

Sanc and Jesper waited for Peyre and Umbert to dress and the four of them crossed the muddy camp to meet with Esterel and Sacha.

'Scouts say they came across the enemy's scouts to the northeast,' Sacha told them once they were inside Esterel's tent. 'The main force is probably four miles away.'

'The pillaging drew them here?' Sanc asked.

'Looks like Auriac is in charge,' Esterel said in answer. 'Famien's play was to lure us into his duchy. No reason for him to come after us here.'

Peyre seemed to make a calculation in his head. 'If we get through the village north of here, we can position ourselves across the fields. They slope down to the east.'

Esterel nodded. 'Lord Russell?'

'He's just set out west,' said Peyre. 'Only about four hundred with him.'

'I'll send a man after them,' Sacha offered.

'Alright,' said Esterel, 'but we can't afford to wait for him. Peyre, you'll take the van. Umbert, with him. Gather up the men you used this morning. I'll take the middle. Sanc and Jesper with me. Sacha, your five hundred will be rearguard. Lord Russell, should he arrive, will be our reserves. Any questions?'

. . .

THEY ACTED QUICKLY, rousing their sodden soldiers, barking out instructions.

Peyre was shouting at the top of his lungs, cajoling his crew into moving again after they had just returned from their morning's efforts. He led them north out of the camp, towards the village. A handful of mounted scouts accompanied his five hundred soldiers. But most of the horses were with Lord Russell, meaning everyone else had to go by foot.

Even Esterel. He led the bulk of their force, almost three thousand warriors. Most of these were the recruits from his new duchy of Morbaine, still not returned home after they left last year. They'd fought to put Bastien on the throne, and they would fight to keep him there. But also, Sanc knew, many wanted this conflict in Guivergne settled, so that they might see their families again.

The path they took was all churned earth, their boots squelching as the ground rose slightly towards the village. Sanc and Jesper walked behind Esterel. Either side of him were some of the best warriors they had, there to protect the heir to the throne.

When they got to the village, the people had already disappeared inside their buildings. *Buildings that might be useful in the event of a retreat,* Sanc noted. Esterel had given the settlement his protection, making it safe from the raids that afflicted the rest of Auriac. It had been a wise decision, giving them access to the resources and skills of the villagers in exchange for any unwanted loot. *Even if they've profited so far,* Sanc thought, *no doubt they'd like us gone. They probably wouldn't object to a battlefield full of the dead to scavenge over, mind.*

It was a one road village, and they were soon following Peyre's vanguard into the fields on the east side. The fields had only recently been ploughed and sown, the furrels waterlogged after so much rain. Fighting here would be a muddy mess.

It reminded Sanc of his days on the training field in Arbeost. A moment of nostalgia came upon him, even though he knew it was ridiculous. He'd hated weapons training. But a part of him wished he were just required to slog away with sword and shield in the dirt, an anonymous warrior, rather than the responsibility and attention his magic powers brought him.

Esterel peeled the middle guard away from the van. Now, with a clear view ahead, they got their first sight of the enemy. Horsemen ranged ahead of a long column of soldiers marching towards them. There was no doubt it was Auberi's full army, drawn here by their pillaging of his close ally.

'What a shameful waste,' Jesper murmured.

'What?' Sanc asked him.

'See how similar the two armies are?' the forester said to Sanc, keeping his voice quiet. 'A war between countrymen is surely the most wicked of all.'

Sanc grimaced. He could hardly argue. Most of the men and women on either side didn't really want to be here. He knew exactly where he placed the blame, however. The Duke of Famiens and the Lord of Auriac had forced them into this.

Esterel's middle division formed up. Behind them, Sacha arrived with the rearguard, taking up position on the left. Peyre and Sacha led much smaller units, whose job was to protect the flanks. Ahead of them, Auberi was arranging his army in the same way. He seemed to have similar numbers.

'More cavalry than us,' Sanc muttered.

Esterel turned to him, having overheard the comment. 'Yes. We could do with buying some time for Lord Russell to arrive with our horse. I have an idea,' he said, eyes twinkling.

Sanc studied his brother. He was a ball of energy, as if made for moments such as this.

'A parley. Why not see what Duke Auberi has to say for himself? Jesper, would you be willing to hold the white flag for me?'

'Of course, Your Highness. Should we send someone to invite Lord Sacha and Prince Peyre?'

Esterel pursed his lips. 'I love them both, but neither are the most diplomatic individuals. Sanc is a better choice. Let's keep our numbers small and encourage them to do the same.'

They had to find horses, for apparently going on foot to a parley was dishonourable. Sanc rode between his brother and Jesper, who held aloft a white flag. On Esterel's other side were two of his best warriors, there for security. They wore helmets that covered their heads save for an eye-slit and at their belts were an array of weapons to deploy if the need arose.

Auberi's forces were still being manoeuvred into position, but Esterel didn't have a long wait before his counterparts arrived at their location between the two armies. There was a dozen of them. Along with their own bodyguards and a man carrying the flag of parley, six noblemen accompanied Duke Auberi. Auberi and Lord Raymon, whom Sanc had met briefly in the Midder Steppe two years before, were the only faces he recognised. Raymon ignored him, while some of his peers couldn't stop themselves from staring at Sanc's eyes.

Sanc wondered if these men thought so many of them might seem intimidating. He felt it had the opposite effect—as if Auberi had a committee of noblemen to please, while Esterel was free to make his own decisions.

'Your Grace,' Esterel acknowledged Auberi pleasantly, as if he were meeting an old friend. 'My lords. Thank you for coming to speak.'

'Esterel,' Auberi said, refusing to call him 'prince'. 'You have something to say?'

The duke seemed angry; sullen.

'Our armies met last year,' Esterel said. 'Many died. It seems right, to me, to avoid shedding blood if we can.'

'If that's what you wanted,' said Lord Raymon, 'you wouldn't have ravaged my lands and abused my people in such a provocative manner!'

It didn't take long for him to get involved, Sanc noted.

'Perhaps I need remind you that your forces began the pillaging,' Esterel countered.

'Nothing like you've done here,' Raymon said, his face going red. 'It will take years for Auriac to recover from this.'

'I've given strict orders not to kill a soul unless my forces faced resistance. That's very different from ordering our warriors to kill each other: the best of our kingdom hacking one another to pieces, so that other nations might come and take advantage of our folly. Surely, we can step back from that?'

'I will allow you to retreat and return to Valennes,' Auberi offered. 'My army will not hinder you.'

'Why should it be my force that leaves?'

'What, then?' Auberi cried, his temper suddenly getting the better of him. 'Your family has seized the throne and now you order me to leave, like a servant you have dismissed? Your arrogance is too much, sir!'

The lords muttered their agreement with this.

'My father did not seize the throne.'

'King Nicolas made me his heir! That's the truth of it, whatever lies you spread.'

'Maybe my uncle said as much to you, Your Grace. I wasn't there to witness it. But my father was the heir to Guivergne. Everyone in the kingdom, from highborn to the lowliest, knows the laws of inheritance. Don't pretend you don't.'

'This conversation is over,' said Auberi, turning away.

'Some other trial, then,' said Esterel.

'What do you mean?'

'I will fight you, or whatever champion you put up,' said Esterel. 'The loser must retreat his army. That way, we save the lives of hundreds of our best fighters.'

Auberi's draw dropped open. 'Is this all a game to you?'

'Really, Esterel,' said Lord Raymon. 'Your prowess with a blade is well known. But this is war, not another competition amongst your friends, where you can win and parade your prize around to your adoring supporters. If I ever had doubts about who should rule our country, they are gone now.'

'Two to one,' said Esterel. 'Your two best warriors against me.'

Auberi shook his head. 'We're done here.' He turned his horse about, his supporters following his lead.

'Three!' Esterel called out to their backs. 'Any three!'

Auberi stopped. Sanc saw him share a glance with Raymon. The two men turned back about.

'You will swear,' said Raymon, 'that if you lose a trial by combat, three swordsmen against yourself, that your army will abandon Auriac and not return?'

'I will so swear.'

Raymon was tempted to take the bait. He looked suspiciously at Sanc and the others.

Sanc knew he should say something. 'Esterel, don't do this,' he said in a worried voice. 'They may injure you.' He gave Raymon a glare. 'Or worse.'

Esterel held up one hand. 'I've not asked for your advice, brother.'

'It seems to me, Your Grace,' Raymon addressed Duke Auberi, 'that this man needs a lesson in humility. Not that I care about him in the slightest. But my people would be grateful if these marauders left. It might avoid a famine in these parts.'

'If the lives of your people are at stake,' Auberi said, 'then I am honour bound to agree.' He looked at Esterel, a slightly puzzled expression on his face. 'We will find you three champions to fight.' He turned his gaze to Sanc. 'I will tell them that if your brother is killed, they will also die. Would that ease your concerns?'

Sanc looked back, surprised. 'Yes. Thank you, Your Grace.'

Auberi nodded. 'Then let's get this done.'

THE SPACE CREATED for the contest came close to looking like a circle, except the warriors of each army were not allowed to get too close to one another. It left a gap through which Sanc could walk.

No one saw him, because he was invisible. No one heard him. On one side stood Auberi, his noble supporters, and a select group of warriors. On the other, Peyre and Sacha had brought similar numbers. Lord Russell had joined them, looking perplexed, as if he had not yet taken in what had unfolded since he had left the camp at midday. Jesper stood next to him, an anxious look on his face as he studied the four fighters.

It had been agreed that each would fight with sword only. Esterel had been keen to get agreement on this—shields would have given his opponents too great an advantage, negating his skill with a weapon. All four were dressed the same: knee-length mail shirts worn over padded gambesons. For all Duke Auberi's dubious promises about Esterel's safety, everyone knew the contestants were putting their lives on the line. At the same time, in a fight of skill such as this, none wanted to be weighed down by excess armour. Neither Esterel nor his three opponents wore helmets, which restricted movement and vision.

The three men chosen by Auberi were all about the same age as Esterel, skilled younger warriors keen to make a name for themselves. There would be some glory in defeating a king's son and a great swordsman such as Esterel. That said, the best fighters and great lords would refuse to take part in such an uneven contest as this.

The conversation died down as Esterel said some final words to his opponents and strode away, stopping when he came to his line of supporters and turning around to face them.

From where Sanc sat on the ground, he could see a small smile of pleasure on his brother's face. Some might have seen it as a show of confidence, but Sanc knew his brother loved the melee more than anything.

Sanc recalled the first time he had used magic: the fight with Robert, on the training field in Arbeost. Brancat had chosen spear and shield. The magic had come unbidden, perhaps prompted by anger. Now, he calmed his breathing and held his hands out before him, concentrating on the magic he would bring forth. Rimmon had taught him to control his power, not to rely on his emotions. It was the most complicated thing he had ever done. For he had to concentrate on keeping himself invisible while intervening in his brother's fight with such subtlety that no one would suspect him.

Warriors on both sides roared as Esterel and his three opponents closed on one another, meeting in the middle of the space. Few, Sanc thought, could be surprised at the tactics of his brother's opponents. As Esterel approached, the middle warrior moved to engage him, before retreating backwards. The other two moved to the side, ready to surround him if he took the bait.

It looked like Esterel would, moving quickly towards his opponent. But when his two allies closed in, Esterel skipped to his right, isolating one of his opponents. His swing was fast and hard. It still looked like his opponent would block it, but Sanc tugged at his arms with his magic, meaning he got into position too late. Esterel's sword sailed over the block, landing a blow on the shoulder. The armour prevented a cut, but the force of the strike would still have done some damage. Before he had a chance to do more, Esterel was forced to dance away as the other two warriors closed in on him.

This was Esterel's problem: finding the time and space for an attack before an opponent came in from the side or rear. He moved in and out, trying to find a gap to attack, but his opponents were even more careful now, working together to see him off. Esterel was fast, no doubt; but he was expending far more energy than his three opponents, moving across the muddy ground. The three warriors shuffled warily about the space, content to wear him down.

Sanc grew nervous. This wasn't a lesson to a bunch of kids, like the one Esterel had delivered on his visit to Arbeost. Two on one would have been manageable, Sanc felt. Three seemed too much, even for his brother. That meant Sanc would have to intervene more directly. But if sorcery were suspected, it would ruin Esterel's reputation.

Then Esterel gambled. He came against one of the warriors, trying to get through his defences. It all happened so fast, Sanc didn't know what to do. Should he help his brother get in a strike, or defend him from the two warriors who rushed him? Before he did either, Esterel took a blow to the side, which sent him slumping to the ground, landing heavily on his knees. All three warriors came in to finish him.

All Sanc could think of was to place a protective shield around his brother. It would save him, but would be far too obvious to every witness of the fight. He hesitated.

Esterel suddenly twisted away, rolling as the blades came down, before getting to his feet and driving upwards. His hilt smashed into the unprotected face of his victim, who keeled over as if all his senses had been taken.

Meanwhile, Sanc ensured that the blows of the other two warriors missed their mark, allowing Esterel to get away.

It was two against one now and the momentum was all with Esterel. While his opponents had looked in control before, the two remaining fighters suddenly looked ragged. Esterel bated them, moving in and out of range. They didn't seem to know if they should defend or attack.

Esterel chopped overhead at one, forcing a high block; he swung a leg, hooking his opponent's, before twisting his body into him with a shoulder barge. Completely off balance, the warrior tumbled over onto the ground. As the second warrior launched a swing at Esterel's lower leg, Sanc pulled at Esterel's blade so that it met the strike. To the onlookers, it looked like Esterel had produced a magnificent block, anticipating exactly where his opponent would strike. But it was Sanc who held the warrior's blade in place, stopping it from smashing into his brother's leg.

Bent over, the warrior frowned, unable to shift his sword. As he opened his mouth to complain, Esterel's knee came up on his chin, snapping his head backwards. Almost dismissively, Esterel slapped the flat of his blade across the side of his head, and the last of his opponents was grounded.

'Watch out!' Sanc heard Peyre shout out as the second man threatened to get to his feet.

Esterel was quickly onto him, the point of his blade levelled at his throat, so that he had no option but to drop his weapon.

The warriors of Morbaine cheered and howled at their duke's victory.

Looking at the other side, Sanc could see a look of sheer hatred spread across Lord Raymon's face. Some of his noble allies applauded Esterel, which must have galled him all the more.

Duke Auberi kept an even expression, though Sanc thought he caught a bewildered look in his eyes. Perhaps, in different circumstances, Sanc would have felt a measure of guilt at his role in the contest. But he and Esterel had just saved hundreds of lives, including those of Auberi's followers, and he had no doubts that his actions were justified.

Auberi's first act was to check on his defeated warriors. Only one looked badly hurt and even he was conscious, even if his nose was sheeting blood. Satisfied he would be alright, the duke approached Esterel and held out his hand, which Esterel took in the warrior's grip.

'Well fought,' Sanc thought he saw Auberi say, having to lipread because of the shouts ringing out around him.

The two shared a few more words, which Sanc couldn't make out. But it appeared that Auberi was sticking to his word and would withdraw his army from Auriac.

The Duke of Famiens still had his army at his disposal; he still claimed their father's throne. By most measurements, Esterel's victory had achieved precisely nothing. But when Sanc studied the faces of Auberi and Raymon, he wondered if the encounter had caused an indefinable shift in the balance of power.

* * *

'THE IRONY IS after Esterel's heroics,' Sacha said, 'that we need to leave Auriac.'

That got a few smiles. Two days after Auberi's army departed, they were meeting in Esterel's tent.

'There's not much left to take in this area,' Lord Russell agreed. 'And I presume we don't actually want to create a disaster here. We still have enough supplies of our own to go where we wish.'

'That's all very well,' said Esterel, 'but I need suggestions about *where* to go.' Sanc's brother lounged on a chair, a cup of wine in hand. He seemed bored now that his fight was done. 'We don't want to live off the land of our allies. We don't want to upset our enemies because we're trying to win them over. We don't want to risk an invasion of Famiens. It doesn't give us many options.'

Everyone looked at one another, but no one had a ready suggestion.

Sanc certainly didn't know what was for the best. It did seem they had reached something of a stalemate in their campaign. But every day they did nothing, they still had thousands of mouths to keep fed. They could, of course, return to Valennes. But Sanc knew his brothers were loath to end things, having achieved so little.

'Permission to enter?'

'Elger,' said Peyre, recognising the voice of one of his soldiers. 'Come in.'

A moustachioed Barissian entered the tent, one of the recruits Peyre had raised in Coldeberg. 'Your highnesses; lords,' he said, nodding at everyone. 'We've encountered riders from the west. Say they serve the Duke of Martras. He's arriving with a force and wants to talk with you, so they say.'

'Domard?' Russell said. 'He's playing his hand at last. Wonder what he wants?'

'I pray Florent has finally convinced him to support our claim,' Esterel said.

'Let's hope for the best,' Sacha said, 'but prepare for the worst. If he's bringing a force, we need to make ready.'

Esterel drained his cup. 'Aye, we'll ready our force, just in case. Lord Russell, could I ask you to meet them and offer to escort his grace here?'

'Of course.'

THERE WAS ONLY a brief wait before Russell returned to the camp with their guest.

Sanc stood with his brothers, watching the approach of Domard, Duke of Martras. He remembered him from their one previous meeting, when the lords of Guivergne had led their forces in the invasion of the Midder Steppe. He was closer in age to Sanc's father than the likes of Esterel and Auberi. Perhaps that explained the caution with which he had responded to the contest for the throne, electing to stay out of it and hole up in Martras.

Only a few armed men had accompanied him into their camp. One of them was Esterel's friend, Florent. The young man grinned over at Esterel and Sacha. That, at least, was a promising sign.

The duke dismounted and gave Esterel a perfunctory smile as he approached.

'Would introductions be in order?' Florent asked him.

Domard waved an impatient hand. 'I know who everyone is.' Telling his warriors to wait for him, he took Esterel's hand in the warrior grip before allowing the prince to lead him into the tent.

Esterel put the duke into a chair and took one for himself. Everyone else had to find a place on the floor. Goblets were filled with wine and after the pleasantries were done, the real talk began.

'Florent here has been bending my ear every day to throw myself behind your father,' Domard said. 'In case you'd come to the conclusion he wasn't trying very hard.'

Esterel smiled in his easy way. 'Glad to hear it. I'd always thought of him as conscientious, but I was beginning to have my doubts.'

Domard smiled back. 'I won't hide the truth from my peers,' he said, acknowledging everyone in the room. 'Of course, both Bastien and Auberi wanted my support. But I wasn't about to risk my position by getting drawn into it. They want the throne; they can bleed for it. But when I do give my oath, I keep it.' He scanned the room once more. 'Everyone knows that.'

'I admire your candour, Your Grace. And does your presence here indicate you are closer to making such an oath?'

Domard grimaced. 'Not quite. But we are in the end game, don't you think? I heard a rumour that you and Auberi avoided another bloodbath. That is progress, no?'

Esterel pursed his lips. 'Maybe. Doesn't feel like we've got much further, in all honesty. A decisive intervention from you might persuade Auberi that enough is enough, however.'

'I hope to intervene, though not in the way you would wish. I would like to think we can bring peace to Guivergne. To that end, I would like to offer myself as honest broker. I believe the time has come when Bastien and Auberi might sit down together and thrash out a deal.'

'We tried that over the winter,' Peyre intervened. 'It got nowhere and Famiens began raiding again this year.'

Domard sipped at his drink. 'I understand, Your Highness. Those negotiations did not go well?'

'Lord Courion?' Esterel asked.

'Lord Caisin and I visited with the duke and his allies in Famiens. It was an utter failure,' said Sacha. 'Our presence there was interpreted as a sign of weakness and only encouraged them to continue their efforts this year. I would like nothing more than for your initiative to work, Your Grace. So long as you understand, it was tough going the last time.'

'I understand,' said the duke. 'Keeping this between ourselves,' he said conspiratorially, 'I may offer Auberi an ultimatum. Something along the lines of we need to stop this and if he doesn't, I may be forced to choose a side. You catch my meaning?'

'That could work,' Esterel acknowledged. 'What do you need from me?'

'I will visit with Auberi. If you could return to your father and persuade him to meet with Famiens? He may feel he has the throne already and needn't stoop to it, I don't know. But I believe it would be in his interests.'

'I don't think that will take much persuasion,' Esterel said. 'But the king won't want to travel far.'

Esterel stopped short of saying their father was still not recovered. Showing weakness wouldn't help them any.

But Domard seemed to understand. 'I'm sure we can agree on a location. Take Florent with you and send him back with instructions on where we can meet with the king.'

Sanc caught eyes with Peyre, who gave him a wink. Sanc allowed himself a smile. It felt like Guivergne might be starting to heal.

PART IV
THE SOUTH

SANC * LIESEL

SANC

VALENNES, KINGDOM OF GUIVERGNE, 675

King Bastien feasted them in the Great Hall of The Bastion. The servants brought them the richest of foods and carried their old platters away. Musicians played for them. Wine and ale flowed, as much as anyone wanted to drink.

Sanc sat at the second table, between Florent, Esterel's friend, and Umbert. In Arbeost, he hadn't attended evening meals. In Valennes, he did. No one had told him why that was. He assumed it was down to the influence of his brothers.

Still, like everything when it came to their father, he'd driven a hard bargain. While Esterel and Peyre sat at the top table with the king and chosen officials like Lords Russell and Caisin, Sanc did not. It was just as humiliating as not being there at all. Everyone in Guivergne knew their place and everyone now learned where Sanc, cursed son of the king, belonged.

Florent and Umbert were as pleasant company as one could find. Florent was modest, friendly and charming. Umbert, down to earth and amusing. But Sanc couldn't help learning how the world worked —he was no longer a child. And he couldn't help dwelling on the fact that he was undervalued.

He smiled at Florent and Umbert, while staring balefully at the top table. Had he not, with Rimmon, won the Battle of Corbenay for these people? In doing so, saved his father's life and gained him the capital? *The throne?* Had he not helped Esterel to defeat Auberi's three champions and end the civil war? Neither of them had publicly acknowledged his contribution. While they accrued the plaudits and the power, top of the Guivergne pile, what had Sanc been given? A place at second table.

Anyone else with my powers would have left, insulted, he told himself. Gone where he was appreciated. *The only reason I stay is family loyalty. But what has this family done for me? How long must I remain grateful that I wasn't drowned at birth?*

'Excuse me,' he said, standing, not really listening to the replies of those around him. He stalked out of the hall. He needed fresh air and time alone. His passions stirred the magic within him. He had learned to control it. One way to do that was to walk away from the things that riled him.

Without really thinking about it, he walked through the corridors of The Bastion towards one of the outside gardens.

'Sanc!' a voice called.

Jesper. *My father figure. Though sometimes he feels more like a nursemaid. Can I not have a moment to myself?*

Jesper was hurrying after him, a broad grin on his face. A second figure was by his side. Sanc checked, his mind not registering who it was at first. 'Rimmon?' he said, surprised.

The sorcerer looked tired; older. He gave Sanc a wry smile.

They clutched one another. A wave of emotion swept over Sanc. He hadn't realised how much he had missed his teacher until he was here, standing in front of him.

'Off somewhere?' Rimmon asked.

'I was just going to get some air.'

'We'll join you.'

Sanc led them out to the small garden. It was an irregular space, enclosed by the walls of The Bastion. They found it empty since everyone else in the fortress was either getting fed or feeding others.

Rimmon sat, puffing with aches and pains as he did.

Sanc stood, appreciating the cool air on his body.

'It's hard to believe how much you've changed,' Rimmon said, eyeing Sanc. 'It's been longer than I'd planned. A year and a half. But when I left, you were a boy. I return and you're a man.'

Sanc gave a small smile of acknowledgement. But his mood still wasn't good, and Rimmon's words only seemed to niggle him.

'I have much to talk about,' said the sorcerer. 'But please tell me what I've missed since leaving. It seems King Bastien's position is now secure?'

Sanc let Jesper do most of the talking. The forester described last year's campaign against Auberi, the pillaging of Auriac and Esterel's victory in the contest with the duke's three champions. How, afterwards, Domard of Martras had acted as a neutral third party in the negotiations between Auberi and Sanc's father.

'Virtually everyone received a royal pardon for their role in the rebellion,' Jesper said. King Bastien's willingness to forgive his enemies their crimes was still a source of debate in the capital. 'Lord Girard was the only one given up by Auberi. Bastien insisted on his execution, for his attempt on the life of Esterel. Everyone else has kept their titles and estates in return for their oaths of allegiance.'

'Well, sounds like it couldn't have gone much better,' said Rimmon. 'We badly need a strong and united Guivergne.'

His teacher's words roused Sanc's interest. Who was 'we'? And why did they need Guivergne to be strong?

'I need to tell you both about developments in the South. While I have done my best to warn the rulers of Dalriya about this threat, news has not spread as wide as I had hoped. Now, things will change.' He paused, looking from Sanc to Jesper. 'I feel like I should start at the very beginning. Ten years ago.'

Jesper nodded his consent.

'Jesper has told you plenty of the stories from the Isharite Wars. He's mentioned a man named Herin?'

'Brother of Clarin,' Sanc said, recalling the stories that had thrilled him as a child. Clarin had carried the Shield of Persala and was one of the heroes who helped Belwynn to destroy Diis. 'Herin fought for the Isharites, rising high in their ranks. He turned at the last, bringing his army against them during the Siege of Chalios.' He looked at Rimmon. 'You were in that army,' he said to the sorcerer. 'And you fought with them outside Chalios,' he said to Jesper.

He had forgotten that sense of awe he had first felt, knowing that Rimmon and Jesper had taken part in such great events. The war in Guivergne seemed to have sucked the childish delight in such stories from him. The reality was so much worse that it was unrecognisable compared to the heroics he had imagined.

'Seven years later,' Jesper said, 'and Rimmon and I still rode with Herin.' He looked at Rimmon.

'You tell it,' Rimmon said to him.

Sanc studied the sorcerer properly for the first time. Tired and worn looking, he looked so much older than before he'd left.

'The three of us were asked to do a service for King Edgar of Magnia,' Jesper began. 'He wanted us to kill Gervase Salvinus.'

'Salvinus?' Sanc gasped. The man who Peyre had told him about with such hatred. Evidently, they'd failed their assignment. 'Wait.' He looked at them both. 'You used to kill people?'

'Yes—no,' said Jesper. 'We'd never done such a thing before. But for Salvinus, we made an exception. We went to Essenberg, got close to carrying out the mission. We found ourselves in the crypt of the dukes of Kelland. Salvinus and Inge, the witch who now serves Duke Leopold, were meeting someone there. Or something.'

'Something?' Sanc asked.

'Ezenachi. Lord of the Avakaba, he called himself. Of the Lippers. At the time, we suspected he was more than mortal. Now we know he is. He implied he ruled the Lippers through mind control. He was about to demonstrate this power on me when Rimmon and Herin intervened. They stopped him just in time. Rimmon and I managed to escape Essenberg. Herin never did.'

Sanc could see the pain on Jesper's face. It looked as fresh as if it had happened yesterday, not ten years ago. 'Mind control?' he asked.

'His victims become puppets,' Rimmon explained. 'Unable to think for themselves, they simply follow orders.' He shook his head. 'You would have to call it luck, terrible or otherwise, that we stumbled onto Ezenachi that day. We would never have known about him if not for that. He has gone out of his way to keep his powers secret.

'His Lipper army has, several times, tried to invade the lands of Magnia. King Edgar has a line of defences to stop them. I have helped the Magnians repulse them. As far as the rest of Dalriya is concerned, if the Magnians can hold them off without help, what threat can they be? Unbeknown to me, however, Ezenachi had made inroads elsewhere. The Sea Caladri—an isolationist people, have been completely turned to his control. It must have taken him years to infiltrate them, building up his numbers before they realised, too late, what was happening. They bring him the greatest fleet in Dalriya. Nowhere is safe any longer.

'More recently, they stepped up pressure on Magnia. That is where I have been all this time, helping Edgar hold them off. The last attack proved to be a diversion. Cordence was invaded. They came from the sea and over the eastern border. King Glanna didn't know what had hit him. Witnesses say he has been captured and turned, like so many of his people. The numbers under Ezenachi's control are growing. The more places he takes, the larger his army becomes. Soon, the balance will shift to him, and he will become unstoppable.'

'Soon?' Sanc asked with a frown. 'He has the Avakabi, the Sea Caladri, and the Cordentines. Surely those numbers aren't enough to threaten the rest of Dalriya?'

'When Ezenachi came to Essenberg all those years before, it was to confirm Inge's submission to him,' Rimmon said. 'We can assume she is still in league with him; that Leopold's duchies won't raise a force against him. The empire is compromised. Magnia is now dangerously outnumbered. Before we know it, this threat could be at the borders of Morbaine and Guivergne. This is why I say the unity of Guivergne is paramount.'

Sanc shook his head. 'It can't be. It doesn't seem real.'

'This is the greatest threat to Dalriya since the Isharite Wars,' Rimmon insisted. 'More of a threat, because who is there with any magic to stand against the power of Ezenachi? Only me.' Rimmon's eyes held Sanc's. 'And you.'

'Me?' Sanc yelped. If Rimmon and Jesper weren't looking at him in deadly earnest, he would have thought they were joking. 'And you only mention this now because—'

'Because last time we spoke, you were still a boy, learning your way. What affect might all this have had on you then? Even now, it is a lot for me to ask of you. But I need your help, Sanc. I will speak with your father as soon as I can. Among other things, I will ask him to let you come south with me. As soon as possible. You need to see things for yourself.'

What did Rimmon expect Sanc could do? The man sounded hysterical; he needed to calm down. 'There may not be any other sorcerers left in the human lands,' Sanc admitted. Inge and Rimmon were the only ones he had heard of. 'But what of others? The Caladri? They have many.'

'The Blood Caladri do,' Rimmon acknowledged, 'and we must warn them. But the Sea Caladri had magi, and they didn't stop him. I know it's a lot to ask, Sanc. You would be leaving your family—'

'It's not that,' Sanc said roughly. Gods, he'd had enough of his father and his place here in Guivergne. 'What if I don't have the power to stop this Ezenachi?'

'You don't,' Rimmon said simply. 'No one in Dalriya does. He is a god, not a mortal. But you're all we have right now, Sanc.'

* * *

SANC STOOD with his brother and Umbert, giving his room in The Bastion one last look, in case he had forgotten to pack anything important.

'Will you be coming back?' Peyre asked him.

Peyre and Umbert were the only people who Sanc would miss. It kept his farewells short. 'I'm not sure,' he admitted.

'It's this business with Cordence?' said Peyre.

Their father had allowed Rimmon to speak his mind to the Council. The sorcerer had left dissatisfied. Sanc wasn't surprised. Talk of dark magic and turning people into puppets would have drawn blank looks, he was sure. These weren't things his family concerned themselves with. Until they saw a threat to their own interests, they would ignore it.

'Rimmon wants me to travel south with him,' Sanc said. 'I don't know. For now, I'm just looking forward to seeing Loysse and Rab.'

That brought a smile to his brother's face. Things he understood. 'Aye, spend some time back in Arbeost and see how you feel. I wish I was coming with you now.' Peyre looked around the room, as if he expected Rimmon to pop up from behind a piece of furniture. 'Don't let that sorcerer pressure you into going if you don't want to. Just tell Esterel. He'll protect you.'

SANC, Rimmon and Jesper left Valennes for Arbeost in the company of a huge army, led by Esterel. They were the men and women of Morbaine who, now that peace had been restored to Guivergne, were finally returning to their homes and old lives. Lord Russell had raised the cash to pay off their outstanding wages, and they were in high spirits, keen to bring their coin back to their families, and tell them the stories of their exploits.

Esterel rode at the head of the column, deep in conversation with his friend Florent. He had his own duties in Morbaine. He would have to tour his new duchy, show his face in each district, and take the oaths of his new subjects. Once he was done, he was to escort his sister back to Valennes, so she could at last take her place at court. Loysse had waited behind for two years. Sanc smiled to himself. He imagined she was quite cross by now.

The army travelled the same way it had come two years ago, following the roads south. They passed through the same places. One was the village, outside of which they had met with Esterel and Peyre after their escape from Valennes. New homes had already been constructed on the site, as sure a sign as any that peace had returned to the kingdom. Sanc was surprised to see no signs of the damage done. *How quickly the villagers are able to return to normality if left alone.*

Further on, Jesper pointed out the location where they had left the road and gone to meet the army of Arnoul, Lord of Saliers. Sanc remembered the moment he had seen the enemy lined up, only a field separating them. Saliers had thought better of a fight that day, withdrawing his forces.

'Whatever happened to Saliers?' Rimmon asked. 'Esterel captured him after the battle at Corbenay?'

'My father released him.'

'Very magnanimous,' Rimmon commented.

'He never took up arms against us afterwards,' Sanc said.

Rimmon nodded. 'Your father played his hand well. I had feared the war might drag on much longer.'

'Maybe,' said Sanc. 'Though almost all our enemies have held on to their lands and titles.'

'You would have fought on for a fuller victory?' the sorcerer asked him. 'Clipped their wings? Removed them?'

Sanc shrugged. 'I don't know. You said yourself you needed Guivergne to be strong. How strong can my father be if his rival still holds Famiens?'

'A king always has enemies,' Jesper said. 'But your family now holds the throne of Guivergne, as well as Morbaine. If Auberi were to rebel again, he would get no second chances, I am sure.'

Next, they passed through the newly won lands of the Steppe. Steppe land no longer, for change had come here, too. Settlements, not any different to those found in Guivergne and Morbaine, were now established. These settlers grew crops as well as herding animals.

Esterel stopped to talk with the warriors who manned the forts that their father had built. The local tribes had tried to take advantage of the conflict in Guivergne to regain their lost lands, and Esterel was full of praise for the small garrisons who had seen them off. They all gazed at Sanc's brother with adoration, as he listened to their war stories and shared his own. Sanc was largely ignored, though some folk glowered at him, while mothers stopped their children from getting too close.

Finally, they found themselves on the last leg of the journey. They closed in on their destination of Arbeost, the dense Forest of Morbaine on their right. Morbaine seemed to be the one place that hadn't changed. As they travelled, more and more people said their farewells and left the column, heading to whichever corner of the duchy they called home.

Only a few hundred of them reached Arbeost. They passed the fields on either side of the dirt path. By the time they reached the village itself, everyone was out, waiting to greet them. They lined both sides of the path, in front of the houses, cheering and waving. Some held aloft flags and banners; some held out flowers and other gifts. They passed the church on their right, the barns on the left, behind them the mill by the river. It was so strange to see everything, just the same as when he had left after so long.

A crowd stood waiting for them in front of the Chateau, where they dismounted. Before he knew what was happening, a dog bounded up to him, barking like a mad thing.

'Rab?'

The dog ran to Jesper, barked. Barked at a group of warriors. Ran back to Sanc and licked him, before rushing back to Jesper again. Sanc smiled. The poor boy didn't know what to do.

'Stop!' said Jesper gruffly, and Rab did what he was told, though his tail wagged back and forth in barely contained excitement.

Esterel, ignoring the nonsense, had already moved ahead to greet Loysse, who stood flanked by the officials who had helped her to run the duchy in their absence.

'You go on,' Jesper told him. 'You know where we'll be.'

'Oh my goodness,' Loysse said when Sanc approached. 'Someone's changed. And grown rather tall.'

She held out her arms and Sanc embraced her, only letting go because so many people were watching.

He could tell Loysse had changed, too. Not in her looks, but in the way she carried herself. She'd been Sanc's age when they'd left. The old Loysse would have screamed and cried and possibly punched one of her brothers for taking so long to come for her. But this Loysse was the model of decorum, bringing her officials into the conversation and quietly praising their work to Esterel, as they praised her. *She's had to grow up*, Sanc realised. *She's had a duchy to govern. A young woman who no doubt has had to fight to be taken seriously by those around her.*

Loysse made sure her officials had found everyone a place to stay for the night before she led Esterel and Sanc into the Chateau. 'You can replace me and start changing everything tomorrow, Duke Ester-el,' she said archly. 'But I want to hear about everything that happened while I was away.'

Esterel and Sanc shared an uneasy look. Loysse had known nothing about his powers before he'd left. He had forgotten and now wasn't prepared for the subject to come up. *I want my sister to look at me like she used to*, he complained to himself, *not the way everyone else does. She was one of the few who never treated me like an outcast.*

'All I've had to go on,' she continued, taking them upstairs, 'is the letters people sent. And there haven't been as many of those as I had hoped.'

'Well, we've been in the field much of the time,' said Esterel.

'I know. Here,' she said, entering their father's solar. She sat them down by the window, drinks already prepared for their arrival.

'You've been living here?' Sanc asked her.

'Well, of course. Father's not likely to come back, is he? Now I'll move out and Esterel can have it.'

'I wouldn't bother,' Esterel said. 'I'll soon be touring Morbaine. When I'm done, I'm taking you to Valennes.'

'Who will run things here?' Loysse asked. 'Sanc?' she asked, glancing at him.

Sanc shared another awkward look with Esterel.

'No, I think Sanc has other duties,' Esterel said. 'I was thinking about Florent. I've brought him with me, anyway. See what he makes of the place. I trust him to do a good job and keep me informed.'

'I see. Well, tell me everything. Don't spare my sensibilities because I'm a woman. That would be most irritating.'

Esterel began with the death of Nicolas and the agitation in the capital when Duke Auberi had claimed the throne. He told Loysse of his surprise at finding Peyre knocking on the door of his rooms at The Bastion, a huge bear of a man with him, who Esterel thought had come to kill him. Loysse gasped and smiled along at his stories.

Sanc grew nervous. How would Esterel tell the story of the battle at Corbenay? Would he describe what Sanc and Rimmon did, or leave it out? He didn't even know which he would prefer.

'Are you alright?' Loysse asked him.

Sanc smiled. She was good at noticing when he was upset about something. 'You know,' he said, 'I've been desperate to see Rab. Would you mind if Esterel told you what happened in Guivergne? Then maybe I can talk to you tomorrow?'

'Good idea,' said Esterel, sounding relieved.

'Well, alright. I *have* looked after the dog, though, you know?'

'I know you will have,' Sanc said, standing.

Loysse stood and gave him a second hug. This time, Sanc didn't rush it. 'I've missed you,' he said.

'Me too. There's been no one to play foolish games with.'

Sanc left, a melancholy feeling about him. They both knew their days of playing games were long gone.

He made the short, familiar walk from the Chateau to Jesper's hut.

As soon as he was through the door, Rab was all over him, licking and mouthing and barking. Sanc petted him until the dog rolled over onto his back, ready for a belly rub.

'He's been whining for you,' Jesper said, pottering about his old home. It had a cold, unlived in feel to it. The forester had got the fire going in the grate, and he had sourced some food from the kitchen.

Rimmon sat by the fire, leaving the chores to Jesper as he always did. He looked tired, though. He still hadn't fully recovered from his efforts in Magnia.

Next to him was Tadita. Having quietened Rab, Sanc went over to greet her and was shocked as she gingerly got to her feet, shaking as she did. She nuzzled into him. 'She's ill?'

'She's old,' Jesper said. 'Poor girl. Two years is a long time for a dog.'

'Feels like two years has been a long time for everyone,' said Sanc.

LIESEL

ATRABIA, 675

'There goes the nanny,' Idris commented, as Liesel overtook him and his sister.

She was desperate to be the first over the rise for once. Idris hadn't always called her nanny, an odd term the Atrabians used for a female goat. This was the first winter she'd been able to match the pair. Cow had been his favourite name at first. Liesel just hadn't been used to walking in such steep terrain, where the air was so thin. She remembered having to stop, her lungs burning and her legs aching, while Tegyn and Idris would stand waiting, sharing looks of pity and mirth.

'Poor cow,' Idris would say, before Tegyn slapped him. 'Sorry. Poor Princess Cow.'

She got to the viewing point first and looked down. The sparkling blue of the Itainen Sea stretched out before her. Down in the valley, she identified the thin blue strip of river that hurled itself from the mountains to the ocean. She would have called it a stream—it was a tiny fraction of the size of the Cousel—but here, they called it a river. She followed its path and found Penfryn, their winter home, tiny and beautiful.

The two years she had lived in Atrabia had been a culture shock for Liesel, and Penfryn, perhaps the most of all. It was a home for

Gavan's immediate family only. The prince had sworn to treat Liesel as his daughter, and so she came to Penfryn every year with them. At first, she found it bizarre that the prince of Atrabia would spend a third of the year in such a remote spot. He would jest with her that the Atrabians governed themselves and didn't need a ruler to interfere.

Except it seemed to be largely true, and the contrast with the city life of her family's seat in Essenberg couldn't have been more extreme. The thought of spending so much time in a tiny hold in the middle of the wilderness had filled the old Liesel with a claustrophobic dread. Now it was her favourite place in the world.

It was a shame they were about to leave. Only the highest mountains kept their snow-topped covering. Spring was around the corner, and it was time to head west and re-join the world.

Idris and Tegyn arrived and looked down, as taken with the familiar sight as she was. Idris leaned an elbow on his sister's shoulder. In physique, they were opposites. Tegyn was small and muscular, with powerful calves and thighs, strong arms and shoulders. Her brother was tall and gangly, with unending, stick-thin limbs. Prince Gavan had told her once he had been the same in his youth, but Liesel couldn't imagine he had ever been as slim as his son. In looks, though, it was obvious the two were siblings. Despite their fair skin, their eyes were as strikingly dark as their hair, and even Idris had lashes that made Liesel jealous.

'What are you staring at, woman?' Tegyn asked her.

'Oh,' said Liesel, a little embarrassed. 'I was just thinking how grateful I am for the last two years. You've become my best friends. I had few in Essenberg. There was Katrina, but she was married when I was sixteen.'

'Soppy cow,' sniffed Idris with a straight face, though he had a sparkle in his eyes.

Tegyn slapped her brother. 'Ignore him. He always acts like that when someone gets emotional. He's afraid of showing his feelings, that's why.'

It was the kind of cruelly accurate criticism that only a sibling could give, and it made Liesel look away. She knew Idris hid behind his sharp tongue. Sometimes, she wished she knew what he really felt.

They made their way back down the mountainside, stopping in a sheltered spot to have their sack lunch. Afterwards, they connected with the river that would lead back to Penfryn. It churned across slate rocks, full with mountain ice melt. As they walked, the cloud cover parted, allowing the sun to warm them. It became surprisingly hot, and they stopped to take off their top layers.

Liesel shrugged off her carrying sack and took off her woollen top, stuffing it into the sack.

'I need to get a drink,' Idris gasped, grabbing his cup from his sack. Beads of sweat dotted his face and the hair around his face was wet.

'Then get me one as well,' said Tegyn. 'And Liesel.'

They handed their cups over and Idris wandered over to the riverbank.

'At least he's good for something,' said Tegyn, tying her sack up.

The comment was more than a little unfair. Idris was one of those people who seemed to be good at most things without trying. Physically fit, he excelled at riding and hunting, and was skilled with weapons.

There was a splash.

Liesel turned her head. Three cups lay on the riverbank. No Idris.

She ran over.

'Idiot,' she heard Tegyn say.

Liesel followed the flow of the river. There, in the middle, getting swept along at some pace, was Idris. Jagged grey rocks loomed at various points along its course. 'He's there,' she shouted over to Tegyn, pointing.

Tegyn stood with her hands on her hips, shaking her head.

'I'll get him, then,' Liesel muttered to herself. She ran along the riverbank, eyes darting into the river to locate Idris, then back to the uneven ground in front of her. She had to navigate her way around the trees that leaned over the stream. For all her efforts, she wasn't gaining on her friend. Then he went round a bend in the river, and she lost sight of him.

A fear gripped her. The river, she knew, was freezing cold. The thought of taking Idris's dead body to his father entered her mind. She cursed Tegyn for not coming to help.

Liesel followed the bank around the bend. There he was! Idris had washed up on a stony section of shallows, his legs still in the water. She ran over. Her foot slipped on a wet rock, and she almost went flying, only just regaining her balance.

She reached him. His eyes were closed, and he wasn't moving. She knelt beside him, unsure what to do. Had he got too cold? Swallowed too much water? She put her hands to his chest, feeling awkward as she did so. He was freezing to the touch. She pressed down a little. She knew she was supposed to breathe into his mouth, but when she looked at his lips, she hesitated. *Think, Liesel!* She told herself. *Is he breathing?* She felt stupid for not checking that first. She leaned over to listen.

Idris's face rose. His lips were on hers, so cold to the touch.

A bolt of desire ran through her body. For a moment, she lost herself to it, returning his kiss. Then she pulled away, gasping for breath.

Idris sat up on his elbows, grinning at her.

The whole thing had been one of his stupid tricks. 'You arse,' she said. She felt stupid; embarrassed. 'There was nothing funny about that.'

Idris lost his grin and his face became more serious. 'I got a kiss out of it, though,' he said. 'I've been wanting that for a long time.'

'You stole it,' Liesel said. 'Tricked me.'

'Don't be like that.'

Liesel got to her feet and stormed away, back to Tegyn.

They walked back to Penfryn in almost total silence.

When Tegyn asked them what was up, neither answered her. 'Idiot,' she said to Idris, assuming it was only his prank that had upset Liesel, and proceeded to glare at him the rest of the way.

He *is* an idiot, Liesel told herself. But her lips refused to agree. They kept reminding her of how they had felt pressed against his.

* * *

THEY LEFT Penfryn two days later, using a trail that took them west through the lowlands of Atrabia. Liesel was pleased that Idris rode next to his father, meaning she could avoid speaking to him. Or avoid not speaking to him. She rode between Tegyn and her mother, Bron, both of whom were very good at talking about little things and at making her laugh.

By evening, they had reached the town of Treglan, close to the principality's western border. No one called Treglan the capital, and it was such a small place that Liesel was glad, for their sake, they didn't. But it was where the prince spent much of his time, a convenient place to meet with people. The family owned a town house, making it easy to settle in. It was a place where other members of the family often stayed, and the other main residents were already there.

Emlyn was Gavan's half-brother, son of their father's second wife. He was married to Meinir, and they had two teenage sons, Ilar and Macsen. All four welcomed them in. The fire filled the main living space with warmth and a pot simmering on the hearth promised mutton stew. They were soon seated, eating, sharing their stories of winter.

Liesel had never warmed to the family as she had to Gavan's. She found Emlyn creepy, Meinir a bore, Ilar and Macsen thick-headed. But four months away from them had helped her to forget some of the things she didn't like, and the reunion was comfortable enough. Once they finished their meal, it became clear that Emlyn and Gavan intended to leave. She overheard Emlyn refer to a 'messenger from the emperor.'

Her ears pricked up at this. She both loved and hated being away from the politics of Brasingia. She felt safe and free from it a lot of the time. But also marginalised and ignorant of what was going on. How was her sister? Her uncle? What new crimes had her brother and his advisers committed? She knew hiding wasn't a long-term solution to her troubles. More than two years had gone by in Atrabia and what had she to show for it?

Gavan looked across at Idris. 'Come, you need to hear this, too.' Idris would be prince himself one day and his father increasingly included him in decisions.

Emlyn looked across at his two boys.

No, Liesel thought, cringing. *He's not going to invite his two young oafs?*

'Ilar, Macsen. You too.'

The boys dutifully got to their feet and followed Idris over. What a sight. Liesel recognised the blank face Gavan wore as the one he used when he was doing his best to be patient, while Idris openly smirked at the situation. But the prince said nothing and all five left the house for their meeting.

'Guess we'll just do all the clearing up, then,' said Tegyn once they had left.

'That is our role, Tegyn,' Meinir chided.

Liesel rolled her eyes inwardly and collected the dishes.

THAT NIGHT, in the bed the three of them shared upstairs, Liesel and Tegyn demanded that Idris tell them about the meeting.

'Emperor Coen is raising an army in Lindhafen,' Idris said. 'He's called on every ruler in the empire to answer his summons.'

'Who is he at war with?' Tegyn asked.

Please, not my brother, Liesel thought, worrying. *Why should I care if it is Leopold?* she asked herself. She was hopelessly conflicted, she knew. Leopold scared her. He didn't deserve to rule Kelland. But if someone saw fit to remove him, where would that leave her? The unmarried older sister of a deposed duke.

'The Lippers,' Idris said. 'They've completely overrun Cordence, so this messenger says. Thousands of refugees have fled into Thesse and Gotbeck. Coen's worried the border's not secure.'

Liesel's brow furrowed. Her tutor in Essenberg had made her study maps and learn about the other powers in Dalriya, but geography didn't stick in her mind. She knew Cordence bordered the south of the Empire and was one of the richest kingdoms in Dalriya.

The Lippers? They spoke a completely alien language to that shared amongst most in Dalriya. Otherwise, she knew, or remembered, nothing.

'Are the Atrabians likely to answer a summons?' she asked them.

The question brought wry faces. It had been a bone of contention between her and the siblings for a while, ever since they were comfortable enough with each other to talk politics. The Atrabians had repeatedly refused to answer her father's summons when the Isharites had invaded the Empire. Idris and Tegyn had given her this and that excuse, but Liesel continued to see it as nothing other than a betrayal.

'They just might,' Idris said. 'Times have changed. It's not the same as being asked to fight for *your* family,' he said to Liesel, unusually serious. 'No offence. And this sounds like a threat to everyone, including the Atrabians. I think father will argue for it. I would. And more importantly,' he said, a mischievous look returning to his face. 'Ilar and Macsen seemed very concerned.'

They laughed together, the talk turning to less serious matters. Eventually, the three of them settled to sleep. Idris's hand slithered towards hers on the mattress. Liesel deliberated for a short while, then took it.

* * *

OVER THE NEXT FEW DAYS, Prince Gavan met with the leaders of Atrabia: the nobility who might provide soldiers; the church leaders who might bless the enterprise and sway their flocks; representatives of the people who might consent to taxes that would pay for a campaign. Liesel observed some of these exchanges, and Idris told her about those she didn't.

Gavan certainly didn't have it all his own way—it was hard to claim the conquest of Cordence, so far away, held any threat to Atrabia. But he argued that honour demanded Atrabia contribute a force, and too small a number would make them look weak. Besides, Liesel could tell the Atrabians liked and respected their prince. If he wanted to cash in some goodwill on such a venture, most people felt obliged to help.

As the Atrabian army slowly took shape, a sense of excitement built in Liesel. It was cut short when the Prince told her she wouldn't be going.

'Safer for you to stay here,' he told her. It was said in an offhand manner. He didn't realise how much she wanted to go. 'Kelland and Luderia have been called up as well as Atrabia. Your hiding place would almost certainly be revealed.'

Liesel had no arguments, except a selfish desire to not be left behind. She understood it wasn't only a risk to herself. The Atrabians might face retribution from her brother if their role in concealing her was revealed.

The day before the Atrabian army was to leave, she was left in the family house, while everyone else was involved in final preparations. Unfortunately, she couldn't escape Emlyn and his family, sitting with them for the evening meal. Gavan's half-brother had been his staunchest supporter in the negotiations and would act as his regent in Atrabia while the prince was away. 'You'll be perfectly safe with us,' he repeated to her during the meal, each time making her feel a little less safe.

He has greedy eyes, Liesel warned herself. *It could just be an older man's attraction to a younger woman*, she reasoned. *Bearable, so long as he doesn't act on it. Or it could be to do with my status as Leopold's sister. Might Emlyn cut a deal with Essenberg in Gavan's absence?* she worried. *Or what if he tries to marry me to one of his dreadful sons?*

Liesel knew the younger, more innocent version of herself wouldn't have picked up on the threat at all. But she'd experienced the unwanted attentions of Gervase Salvinus, and the malice of Inge the witch. Something didn't feel right and after the meal, she escaped the house and wandered around Treglan until she found Idris and Tegyn.

They ended up in one of the town's inns, drinking to their last night together for what could be a long time. Liesel usually revelled in the freedom of frequenting the tap room of an inn, something that would never be allowed in Essenberg. Tonight, though, she found it hard to shake off her anxiety.

Tegyn shook her head as her brother boasted about the enemies he would smite on the battlefield. He wasn't the only young warrior in the inn sharing such sentiments. None seemed to have a clear idea why Emperor Coen might consider war against a people they had barely heard of before the last few days.

'You are quiet tonight,' Tegyn said to Liesel. Sister and brother looked at her.

She supposed she had been dwelling on her own predicament and not joining in as much as usual. She opened her mouth to give some excuse. Then she remembered Witmar. How she hadn't asked for help from anyone. It had taken Peyre, the young Guivergnais boy, to go to her uncle Walter and ask him for help on her behalf. Not before Leopold had taken a knife to the poor lad's face. *Learn your lessons, Liesel*, she scolded herself. 'I have a suspicious feeling about Emlyn.'

'Don't we all,' said Idris. 'What exactly?'

'I can't say. Just the way he looks at me. I don't trust him.' She shrugged, realising how she sounded. 'I'm sure I'm being unfair.'

'Not necessarily,' said Idris. 'I feel the same.'

Liesel and Tegyn looked at him expectantly.

'He's the second son. You don't think he wishes for the crown instead of father? Or instead of me when the time comes? It's only human nature, after all.'

'Oh gods,' said Tegyn, thinking about it. 'Prince Emlyn. With Ilar next in line.' She pretended to be sick. 'Then you must come with us instead of staying here.'

'I can't. Your father asked me to stay.'

'Easily solved,' said Idris. 'We hide you in a wagon and reveal you once it's too late to send you back.'

'I can't go against your father's wishes after he's given me so much. He would be so angry.'

'Hardly,' said Idris. 'I swear to you, once you appear, he'll laugh and say how impressed he is.'

Liesel remained dubious. But once Tegyn took her brother's side, and she'd had another drink, she thought it wasn't such a crazy plan as it first sounded.

* * *

THE ATRABIAN ARMY set off early the next morning. Liesel was secreted in the back of a wagon full of supplies, hemp sacks providing both a comfortable place to sit and a screen that hid her from view.

But she was full of anguish. She worried that people back in Treglan would panic once they found her missing. She dreaded Prince Gavan's reaction to her disobedience; worse still, that it was putting the Atrabians in more danger. With nothing else to do, she closed her eyes and prayed to Sibylla. *I pray for a day when I am more than just a burden on people.*

She felt some relief when she learned what route the Atrabians were taking. Rather than heading directly for Lindhafen, which would have involved cutting through her brother's new duchy of Luderia, Gavan took them due south. Tegyn, who rode next to the wagon for parts of the journey, explained that the King of Ritherys, the northernmost member of the Confederacy, had given permission for Gavan to pass through his lands.

As evening was drawing in, Idris came for her. He took her from the wagon, putting her behind him on his horse. Tegyn joined them. They rode towards the front of the column. Liesel got her first proper look at the countryside of Ritherys, very similar to Atrabia.

Idris found the Prince. Riding beside him was Bron, his wife.

'Father, mother,' Idris said, 'I have something to admit.'

They turned to him and took in Liesel riding with him.

She winced as she waited for their reactions.

Both pairs of eyebrows rose in the air, but it was no worse than that.

'Liesel was worried about being left behind,' said Idris.

'We told her she should come,' added Tegyn, making sure they got the blame for it, not Liesel.

'Then, of course, she should come along,' Bron said. 'Though Liesel, by now you should know you can come to us with such fears.'

'Yes, my lady,' Liesel replied, feeling more than a little ashamed.

'And how have you snuck her away all day?' Prince Gavan demanded.

'Hid her in a wagon,' Idris admitted.

Gavan gave a chuckle. 'An impressive deception,' he declared.

It was exactly the reaction Idris had promised. Idris and Tegyn laughed out loud, and Liesel gave a nervous smile.

'What?' Gavan demanded. 'What's so funny?'

SANC

ARBEOST, DUCHY OF MORBAINE, 675

'How is Jesper?' Loysse asked Sanc as he took a seat next to her on the bed.

He looked around her room, remembering all the games he'd played here. 'He's alright,' he answered.

Tadita had died the day after they'd returned. Jesper was convinced she'd only been waiting for his return before she gave up the fight. Sanc found the idea incredibly sad. 'He took her into the forest, alone. One last time together, I guess.'

'Poor old girl,' Loysse said. 'But it was her time.'

'Yes,' Sanc said. 'I've seen people die before their time in the last couple of years. Tadita had a good life.'

'Esterel told me,' Loysse said. 'About your magic.'

Sanc nodded. He found it was a relief that she knew.

'It doesn't matter at all to me, you know,' Loysse said.

Unlike most people, Sanc actually believed her when she said it.

'I always knew you were special. I'm sorry you couldn't tell me.'

'I'm sorry I didn't,' he admitted. 'Jesper told me not to tell anyone, for my own safety.' He reminded her of the visit of Lord Kass to Arbeost. Then he proceeded to tell her about the attack by the men outside Jesper's hut.

Loysse put a hand to her mouth. 'I'm sorry you've had all this to deal with by yourself, Sanc. It hasn't been easy for you.' She held out a hand, which he took. Then, deciding that wasn't enough, he reached over, and they hugged one another.

'I'm sorry you got left here,' he said. 'I'm sorry—I'm sorry I took your mother from you.'

Loysse pushed him away. 'Don't be so damned stupid,' she said. 'I've never thought that. Not once. Just because father has such stupid ideas, it doesn't mean you should.'

Sanc nodded, allowing himself a little smile. 'Thank you. I wanted to say it, anyway. I'm going to miss you all over again now you're going to Guivergne. Will Cebelia be going with you?'

'Of course!' Loysse said, outraged at the idea that she wouldn't. 'I've also asked Brayda to come with me.'

'Clever. Life's always better when Brayda's baked pastries.'

'Exactly. You're sure you want to leave with Rimmon?'

'I don't *want* to,' Sanc admitted. 'But I know I should. Still, it may not take that long. It wouldn't surprise me if we return to Valennes so that Rimmon can badger father again. I'd quite like to see those two having an argument,' he said with a grin. 'What is it?' he asked, catching a melancholy look on his sister's face.

'I may not be in Valennes when you return, that's all. I'm eighteen now. Ready for marriage.' She tried a smile when she said it, but Sanc could tell Loysse was worried.

'I hadn't thought about that. But Esterel's five years older and he's yet to be married.'

'Oh, don't think for a moment that he'll last much longer. He's the heir to the throne now. He needs to have children of his own. If I know father at all, he's got plans for both of us.'

Sanc could hardly disagree with that. Their father was a planner. Sanc had come to the conclusion that Bastien was made to sit on the throne. For the first time in his life, Sanc saw the advantage of being the black sheep of the family. *At least no one's going to be queueing up to marry their daughter to me.*

· · ·

Sanc rode out from Arbeost in the company of Jesper and Rimmon. Rab padded alongside them, veering off the track for a while, but always returning.

'He's in his prime now,' Jesper said. 'Perfect age to accompany us.'

Sanc didn't know whether losing Tadita had any influence on Jesper's decision to bring Rab with them. But he was grateful. The journey they took now felt so serious. Rimmon's talk of magic, gods and war made him feel like they were taking part in one of Jesper's heroic and momentous stories. Having the dog with them was a welcome distraction.

Although Magnia bordered Morbaine, they first had to travel from one end of the duchy to the next. Sanc hadn't realised just how far it was. They followed tracks that took them through lands still wild and largely untouched. Many of the wooded trails Jesper followed were made by animals. Rab was in his element, sniffing and running off into the undergrowth, alive with spring flowers.

Jesper kept calling him back. 'It's all too new to him still,' the forester explained. 'He doesn't have the sense Tadita had. He'll end up chasing a boar or something. One gash from them and it's over.'

Up and down hills, across streams. It was the first time Sanc had truly explored the duchy beyond the lands around Arbeost. It had a gentle beauty to it. Not so dense as the Forest of Morbaine; more varied than the plains of the Steppe; not so intensively farmed as Guivergne. When they passed through or stopped at the settlements along the way, they seemed to Sanc like sanctuaries amongst the wilderness. In Guivergne, the wilderness had been tamed. Most places had an inn where they could get food and sleep, even if it was just bedding down on the floor of the public room.

While Sanc, Jesper and Rab revelled in their surroundings to varying degrees, Rimmon seemed not to notice them at all. He rode deep in his own thoughts, so that they had to say his name three times before he truly focused on their words. Jesper behaved as if this was nothing out of the ordinary for the sorcerer. Sanc, though, thought the Haskan still looked tired and troubled. Rimmon sighed and grunted to himself when mounting or dismounting and on an evening usually rolled up in his blankets soon after their meal was done.

The south of the duchy was one of the wilder, less populated parts of Morbaine, which meant it wasn't possible to say for sure when they crossed into Magnia. A lack of fortifications on either side was testament to the peaceful relations between the two peoples for as long as anyone could remember.

Rimmon took more of the lead now, for he knew the likely locations of the royal court. They continued due south, keeping up the same pace. The Magnians they met were friendly enough. Sanc certainly felt he received no more stares than he had done in Morbaine. He suspected that Rimmon, with all his coming and going, was a familiar figure to some. A red-eyed companion to a flame-haired sorcerer was, perhaps, less of a surprise in these parts.

As they travelled south, they entered the heartland of Magnia. There were more villages here, and they were larger, often home to a hundred or more families. Their fields and orchards were large and well organised and Sanc could tell from the village centres, with their churches, mills, inns, and craftsmen's buildings, that Magnia was as prosperous as any place in Dalriya.

It was on the seventh day that they came upon a new feature. Castles suddenly dominated the landscape, where before they had been a rarity. Sanc could see several, all built within a few miles of each other.

'The old border between North and South Magnia,' Rimmon explained. 'Both princes garrisoned their side. Now, most of them lie empty. The warriors of Magnia can be found to the south.'

'Because the prince of the North was killed?' Sanc asked, recalling some of the history. The Magnians had led the southern states of Dalriya in support of the Empire against the Isharites.

'That's right. Prince Cerdda was killed in Essenberg. On the orders of Salvinus.'

Gervase Salvinus, Sanc said to himself. *That's a name that just keeps cropping up.*

'Though by that time,' Jesper added, 'Edgar had already married

Cerdda's sister, Queen Elfled. He only took the title king some years after Cerdda's death. It's their marriage—and their children—that have united Magnia.'

'Because they are descended from both families?' Sanc asked.

'Precisely,' Rimmon answered. 'Elfled lost both her brothers in the Isharite Wars. Edgar is an only child. Magnia is blessed, you might say, by having no alternative claimants to the throne.'

'Nicolas had no other claimants, by blood,' Sanc reminded him. 'That didn't stop some people.'

'True,' Rimmon admitted. 'Then you might also say Magnia is blessed by common sense. I suppose a people riven by civil war for so long understood the benefits of peace quicker than the Guivergnais did. I don't think they'd have fended off the Avakaba for as long as they have without such unity.'

Sanc, Jesper and Rab waited outside one of these castles while Rimmon enquired within about the whereabouts of the court. He soon returned.

'Bidcote,' the sorcerer said. 'Another day's ride south of here.'

A nervous sensation gripped Sanc's belly. Perhaps, in part, it was the idea of meeting the king. He thought it was more about what Edgar might ask, or expect, of him.

'The Temple of Toric,' Rimmon said as they rode past the settlement of Ecgworth. 'The old resting place of Toric's Dagger.'

'That's how the Magnians got dragged in to the war,' Jesper commented. 'When the weapon was taken.'

Sanc could just make out the domed roof of the temple poking above the wooden palisade of the complex. 'That's also how Belwynn, Soren and the others got involved,' he said. They had chased Salvinus from Magnia to Brasingia to reclaim the dagger. 'Imagine if it had never been stolen, how different our history would be.'

Rimmon made a face. 'Quite so. The lad knows his history, Jesper. I'll give you that.'

'Where is the dagger now?' Sanc asked. Seven lost weapons of

Madria had been rediscovered to rid Dalriya of the Isharite god, Diis. Of the seven, the dagger was, in his opinion, the most important of all.

'Moneva had it,' Jesper answered. 'Presumably, she still does. It's just that no one knows where she and Gyrmund disappeared to.'

'Couldn't the weapons be used to defeat this Ezenachi?' Sanc asked Rimmon. 'Just like they were used to defeat Diis?'

'It's something I've given thought to,' Rimmon said. 'They were made by Madria to help her champions to defeat Diis and his Isharites. I have no idea whether they would have the same power against Ezenachi. I don't know where half of them are located. The ones I do know aren't exactly easy to get to. All that said, it's surely something we must try.'

The royal estate of Bidcote was only a brief ride from Ecgworth. The village was no different from the others they had passed through, except for the sizeable hall owned by the king. It was obvious, by the numbers of servants around the place, that the royal court was still here.

Their horses were taken for stabling, and they were invited to sit at table by the fire in the hall. Before long, food and drink were brought to them. Shortly afterwards, a small group of ladies entered the hall. A bodyguard came with them, walking to one side but staying close.

'The queen,' Rimmon said.

The three of them got to their feet as Queen Elfled approached. Rab raised his head for a moment, then lay back down. The poor boy had done more walking than he ever had before and was too exhausted to move, even for royalty.

'Rimmon,' Elfled said with a smile, 'it's good to see you again.'

It occurred to Sanc he had never met a queen before. Elfled looked how he had imagined a queen to be. She was elegant and her mixed Magnian and Middian heritage gave her a unique beauty.

'Your Majesty,' Rimmon said with a bow. 'You recall my friend Jesper?'

'Of course. Welcome back to Magnia, Jesper.'

'Thank you, Your Majesty.'

'And this is Sanc. Bastien's boy.'

'Of course,' Elfled said, turning to Sanc. 'Rimmon has told the king and I about you, Prince Sanc. I am most grateful to you for coming here, so soon after the troubles in your own country.'

The queen smiled at him, though Sanc paid little attention to that. In Elfled's eyes, there was no fear or disgust. No pity. Just friendship. That meant more to him than anything else.

'It's a pleasure, Your Majesty,' he said.

'The king is not here?' Rimmon asked.

'Apologies,' Elfled said. 'Edgar and Ida are out hunting. They should be back soon. Our younger three are all in lessons. You will have to make do with me for a while. But you will sit with us for the evening meal. Is there anything else I can do for you?'

'Well,' Rimmon said. 'I did wonder whether the king had brought the prisoners here?'

'Of course,' Elfled said, glancing at Jesper, then back to Rimmon.

Now Sanc could see those emotions he had looked for. Fear, distaste, pity, and more played on her features, though she fought to control them. *What prisoners do the Magnians have here that are so much worse than me?*

'Morlin?' she said to the warrior, who looked on impassively from the side.

He was of an age with Jesper, his blonde beard turning white in places. His scale mail glittered with gold and silver, light enough to wear for long periods, but it looked the part. A sword hung on his belt, and Sanc measured him as a man well capable of using it. 'I will take your guests to see the prisoners, Your Majesty,' he said.

Morlin led them outside. There were several smaller structures out here for storage. The building he took them to was a high-roofed barn that Sanc assumed had once been used to house animals. Morlin opened the door and led them inside. High windows allowed light to filter in past the wooden rafters. 'Over there,' he said, gesturing at two wooden stable doors. 'One in each. They're securely chained. Do you require me to stay, Lord Rimmon?'

'No. I can manage.'

The warrior left them to it.

'What in Dalriya do you have here?' Jesper asked Rimmon with an intrigued smile.

The sorcerer didn't return the smile. 'Prepare yourself, Jesper.'

The forester's smile was replaced with a frown. 'Alright.'

Rimmon reached the doors, looking over each. He opened the one on the left and beckoned Jesper and Sanc towards him.

As Sanc approached, he saw a man seated on the straw strewn floor. His limbs were attached to chains that were riveted to the wooden wall behind him. As Morlin had assured them, he was held securely, but the chains were long enough for him to be comfortable enough. His leather clothing had seen better days but looked high status; along with his lean, powerful physique, he looked like a warrior to Sanc.

The man looked up at them. He was older, somewhere between Rimmon and Sanc's father. Deep lines ran across a face that was tanned brown by the elements. Straight hair, most of it still jet black, fell across one side. But his eyes. *I'm not one to talk, I suppose,* Sanc told himself with grim humour. *But those are unnerving, dead eyes.* It was hard to define what was wrong with them. There was an intelligence there, but no humanity.

'Herin?' Jesper gasped.

The forester reached out a hand as if he might fall. Rimmon gripped his arm, holding him up. In the end, he helped Jesper to lower himself, so that he was seated on the straw in front of the captive.

Herin? Sanc wondered. The *Herin from Jesper's stories. The man they left in Essenberg, ten years ago, to the mercy of Ezenachi?* No wonder Jesper was in shock.

Herin grimaced at Jesper, but there was no sign of recognition in those dead eyes.

'I spotted him last year,' Rimmon told them. 'You can imagine my surprise. He'd been dropped off with half a dozen Avakabi on a remote beach in South Magnia. I suppose you might call it a test run of what they did in Cordence. They ran amok before the locals knew what was happening. Herin acted as their leader.'

'Ran amok?' Jesper asked, still sounding like he was in shock.

'I'm afraid so. A killing spree. And the other thing. Turning.'

'Wait,' Sanc said. 'You mean the Lippers can turn people? Not just Ezenachi?'

'Yes. That is how they've grown in numbers so fast. But only some of them can do it. Amongst this group, it seemed to be only Herin.'

'Herin was turning Magnians?' Jesper said in horror, staring at his old friend. 'Why only him?'

'I can't be sure,' Rimmon answered. 'It seems that only a small fraction of Ezenachi's followers can do it. But Herin's given me a working theory. We know Herin was turned by Ezenachi himself. It's possible that he can pass on his power to certain individuals.'

'Gods,' Jesper said.

'Anyway. I tracked his group down. They tried to escape from me. I kept Herin alive and one other from his party. He's the one next door.'

'With what goal?' Jesper asked. 'Is it possible to undo what that monster has done?'

'I've tried, of course,' Rimmon said. 'Got nowhere. That's one of the reasons I brought Sanc here.'

Sanc stared at his teacher. 'I don't know the first thing about this!'

'You're really piling things onto his shoulders, aren't you?' Jesper said angrily.

Rimmon held up his hands. 'I know, I know. I'll apologise as often as you both damn well want. Yet here we are. I was thinking we could work on it together,' he said to Sanc, as if that was more reassuring. 'Herin was enslaved with magic; maybe magic can undo it. If not, at least we tried. But I feel like we must try.'

Enslaved with magic? For ten years? Sanc didn't know what to think. Didn't know where to start. But he knew this man chained before them had once been a good friend of theirs. 'I can try,' he conceded.

THE EVENING MEAL in the king's hall was a small affair compared to those Sanc had got used to in Valennes.

'Many of our nobles, who would usually be here, are stationed in our fortresses on the southern border,' King Edgar explained.

Edgar was fair-haired like most Magnians, friendly and down to earth for a king. Like his wife, he seemed able to treat Sanc with the kind of courtesy he didn't get back home. Judging by his looks and the ages of his children, Sanc guessed he was five to ten years younger than his own father. But he shared the same tired, haunted look as Rimmon.

Next to him was his son and heir, Ida. The boy had inherited more of his mother's colouring than his father's. Edgar argued with his wife that Ida should sit at the top table and listen to their conversation. 'He's turned sixteen now,' Edgar explained to his guests. 'How old are you, Sanc?'

'Sixteen also. I had my birthday last year.'

'There you go,' Edgar said to Elfled. 'And Sanc has been in battles, not just listened to talk of them.'

'It's no age, for either of them,' Elfled said.

'That's the world we're entering,' Ida said. He spoke calmly but with a firmness that belied his years. 'It's useless to pretend otherwise.'

Elfled gave a little smile. 'Very well. At least I have my other three safely ensconced elsewhere.' She nodded across at Ida's three siblings, seated at a nearby table. Her other guests were also seated at other tables. Leaving them free to speak their minds.

'What are your plans?' Edgar asked Rimmon.

'I took Sanc to see the prisoners.'

'I see,' Edgar said, glancing at Sanc, and then at Ida. Perhaps he regretted his son hearing this?

'I would like to see if Sanc can help me get through to them at all. Starting tomorrow. It would mean staying here a few days if that is convenient?'

'Of course,' Edgar replied. 'How about you, Jesper? If you're at a loose end, you're welcome to come hunting with us. I've just started taking Ida with me. I'm sure he could learn some things from you.'

'It would be an honour,' Jesper said. 'If you would allow it, I'd be grateful to take our hound Rab with us,' he said. Jesper looked about the hall for him.

'Under the table,' said Queen Elfled. 'I may have been smuggling him a treat or two,' she admitted with an embarrassed smile.

Jesper laughed. 'Not to worry. But all the more reason to get him some exercise. His mother was an excellent hunter. I'm afraid his training has been neglected the last couple of years.'

'Then, of course, Rab should come,' Edgar agreed.

'How long do you plan on staying in Bidcote?' Rimmon asked him.

'I hope I can stay away from the border for a while,' Edgar said. 'My steward, Wilchard, is in charge there for now. The Lippers stopped their attacks a few weeks ago. Now we know why, of course: their soldiers were pulled out and sent to Cordence.

'It gives our own forces a much-needed respite. A chance to send men home and reduce our garrisons. But while the lull is beneficial, it raises other fears. If the Lippers now have the Caladri fleet at their disposal, there is nothing to stop them from bypassing our defences and landing large numbers on our southern and western coastlines. I must visit these regions and find the best way to prepare for it.' He shook his head. 'It would be a disaster, just like Cordence. Did you get anywhere with Bastien?'

'No,' Rimmon said bluntly. 'His eyes glazed over at the mention of Ezenachi and magic.'

'I expected as much. Bastien was ever loath to commit men. He used to blame his brother, but—' the king looked at Sanc, as if he had forgotten the connection. 'I'm sorry, Sanc, if those words offended you.'

'They didn't,' Sanc assured him. 'My father is always cautious. The leaders of the recent rebellion against him are still strong. There is a genuine fear of what might happen should they be given an opportunity for mischief.'

'I understand,' Edgar said, though Sanc could tell he was only being polite. 'At least the Empire must now face reality. Coen has an army of two hostile nations on his doorstep. Three, if, as expected, the Cordentine population is being turned to serve Ezenachi. It may sound sore and bitter to hear me say it. But a part of me is glad that someone else must now wrestle with the problems Magnia has faced alone.'

Elfled put a hand on his. 'You have been carrying the weight for a long time, husband,' she said. 'If anyone were to criticise you, they would have me to face.'

Edgar smiled and took her hand in both of his.

Sanc looked at Ida. An irrational burst of jealousy disappeared as quickly as it came. So what if this boy had been blessed with a loving mother and father in his early life while Sanc had not? It only meant he had more that could be taken from him.

LIESEL

DUCHY OF THESSE, 675

When the Atrabian force entered Gotbeck from Ritherys they were delayed, quite rightly, by a force of Gotbeckers. Issuing from the castles that defended the duchy's eastern border, the Gotbeckers took some persuading that they weren't a Confederate army. Prince Gavan had been wise to keep the imperial messenger with him, as well as Coen's written summons itself. Finally relenting, a dozen Gotbeckers agreed to escort them across the duchy, to avoid further misunderstandings.

It took them three more days of travel. On the first night, they stayed outside the city of Kaselitz on the Cousel. By the second night, they reached the border with Thesse. It was late on the third day that they reached the camp of the imperial army, a few miles south of Lindhafen.

A sea of tents stretched out across a meadow, while the whole area was a hive of activity: soldiers, horses, craftsmen, officials, traders, and other hangers on.

The last time Liesel had seen a real army was during the traumatic attack on Essenberg, when she and her family had been forced to flee south to Lindhafen. *It looks more like a fayre than I had expected,* she thought, her eyes trawling across the spectacle from her mounted vantage point, unsure where to stop.

'It makes the Atrabian force look quite small,' she needled Idris.

'It's the quality of warrior you take to war, not the quantity,' he said.

Prince Gavan waited until his force was settled before agreeing to be led off to meet the emperor, as the sun set. Liesel went with him, along with Idris. Her uncle Walter had brought his army and Prince Gavan said it was only right that she should come and greet him after being separated from her family for so long.

The emperor's tent was located to the north of the main camp. When she followed Gavan and Idris inside, Liesel was hit by the smell of food.

'Come,' she heard Emperor Coen say.

'I've brought my son, Idris. And Lady Liesel, too,' said the prince.

As she emerged from behind Gavan, Liesel just caught the emperor's look of surprise before he replaced it with a welcoming smile. He sat at a table with four other men. All were familiar faces to her. 'Of course,' Coen said. 'The food is still hot, please join us.'

They took seats at table, where trenchers already awaited them. The emperor didn't stand on ceremony, tucking in to the food before him. But even in his army camp, he served the finest food to his guests. Wild boar was the centrepiece, but there was also venison, bird pie and vegetables.

Walter and Farred winked at her from across the table but said nothing. They didn't seem to have changed any. Emperor Coen, seated to Walter's right, looked older, but Liesel hadn't seen him for many years. His bald pate made him look older than he was, anyway, she reasoned. Archbishop Emmett of Gotbeck, Coen's closest ally, sat to his right, while on the end of the table, furthest from Liesel, was Coen's son, Friedrich.

He had certainly changed. They had spent much time together in Lindhafen as children. Coen's heir, he was slightly younger than Liesel—the same age as Leopold. She recalled the two had been firm friends as youngsters. But she hadn't seen Friedrich in so long. Now he was a full-grown man, the tallest at table except for Idris. But Liesel thought she could still see the boy she knew in him.

'Try this backstrap,' Coen said to Gavan, handing over a lightly seared, red piece of meat.

'Thank you, Your Majesty,' said the Prince, tasting it immediately. 'Delicious.'

'We caught it today. Friedrich brought him down.'

'Congratulations Friedrich!' said Gavan. 'We Atrabians admire a skilled bowman as much as anything else.'

The conversation continued to dwell on hunting and similar topics while they ate. *Men,* Liesel said to herself. *They have raised an army against some great threat and nary a mention of it. I am sure that if women ruled the empire, they would have agreed a strategy by now.*

At last, when the servants came to clear the main course away, the emperor turned the conversation to the matter at hand. 'I wonder if you have heard anything of these Lippers, Your Highness?'

'Not at all, save for what your messenger has told me.'

'I have received many a warning myself,' Coen said, 'most often from Edgar of Magnia. He has had trouble with them for some time now—asked for the empire's aid more than once. I've sympathised, even sent some subsidies. It would have been a struggle, to put it mildly, to persuade the Brasingians to do more. Felt like I owed Edgar, after all he did for us in the war. But no one in the empire seriously thought the Lippers could amount to a threat. And despite his stark warnings, the Magnians seemed to be holding them off.

'It seems the Lippers have played us for fools. Something sinister has been happening amongst the Sea Caladri, under our noses. Some fell magic has turned their minds to the Lippers' cause. Cordence was invaded from the east, while the Caladri dropped off boatloads of Lippers on the south coast. The Cordentines offered little resistance. Thousands have fled north, crossing into the empire. There are huge camps full of them on my southern border. They bring strange stories.' Coen grimaced. 'They say that just like the Sea Caladri, those Cordentines they've captured are being turned by some dark magic to do the Lippers' bidding. We could face an army tens of thousands strong on our doorstep.'

Liesel stared wide-eyed at her emperor as he told the sort of tale one might hear around the fire on a winter's night. But she knew, all too well, there was no safe division between nightmare and reality. A nightmare had descended on her father and his people once before in her lifetime. Now, it looked like it might happen again.

Idris and Friedrich seemed unaffected. But she studied the faces of the men who had fought against the Isharites: Emmett, Walter, Farred —Gavan, at the end—and there was a weariness there she didn't like the look of.

'With respect,' Walter said, 'there's a bit more to tell. I know Your Majesty, like myself, has been warned about the Lippers from another source. Namely, Rimmon the sorcerer. He has told a tale of a god amongst them by the name of Ezenachi.' His eyes flicked to Liesel. 'How this being came to Essenberg and struck a deal with the witch, Inge. According to this version, the Lippers are the original victims rather than the perpetrators.'

Coen gave an irritated grunt. 'Of course, both Rimmon and Edgar have given me such warnings. But I'll not apologise for dismissing the word of a Haskan sorcerer who served Ishari.'

'Nor should you,' said Walter. 'I've done the same. Worse—I've ignored the caution of friends,' he said with a pained look at Farred. 'But a core strategic principle is *know your enemy*, and I suspect this Ezenachi is the real foe.'

The emperor rubbed his head. 'I take your point, Duke Walter. But in the here and now, it doesn't change our predicament. It is the army of Lippers, Caladri and Cordentines that threatens us. We have gathered the armies of four duchies and for that I give my sincere thanks to each of you. I shouldn't expect any more aid?' he said with a look to Walter.

'Duke Leopold will not put his armies under your command,' Walter said bluntly. 'I am sorry. As for Duke Jeremias, he is a different sort of man. But for him to go against Leopold, and march his smaller force south through Kelland, is too much to ask I am afraid.'

Liesel stared at the floor of the tent. She'd been shamed by her family plenty of times. But this time felt worse than anything else. *I'm glad my father never had to witness it. Or, at least, I hope he can't see what's happened to us.*

'Then it seems to me,' said Coen, 'there is no reason not to march south tomorrow. I suggest we head for the Great Road to deny the enemy use of it. Any objections to that?'

The emperor was met by slow shakes of the head as everyone realised how close they were to being drawn into war.

'You think it likely they will now move against the empire?' Gavan asked.

'I don't know. But we must prepare for it.'

THE THESSIANS PACKED up first and began the march south-east. Prince Gavan's Atrabians followed. While his force was all mounted, the rank and file of the other duchies marched on foot, making their pace much slower than Liesel had got used to. 'One of the laws of warfare,' Gavan told his family. 'The larger the army, the slower it moves.'

Once the day was coming to its close, the emperor stopped his army outside a town called Wohrberg, positioned on the route to the Great Road. While the emperor and the dukes were invited to stay the night at the mayor's house, their children stayed with the army.

Again, Liesel marvelled at how the army turned into a lively fayre on the evening. Friedrich, Coen's son, joined Liesel, Idris and Tegyn as they wandered about, taking in the sights. Groups of warriors sat together gambling. There were fortune tellers, bards and acrobats performing for money. Food and drink carts tempted everyone to part with coin. Liesel saw many women mingling with the men. Some, showing their cleavage with their faces made up, she knew were whores. Peddlers had set up shop, selling everything from the basics, to armour, weaponry, and luxury items.

'How many can afford such things?' Tegyn asked, as she looked at a selection of jewel encrusted rings and other fine things.

'You have your rich nobles' sons, like me,' Friedrich said, self-deprecatingly, 'with more money than sense. Then your professional soldiers, who have a habit of spending their money as soon as they get it. When your job requires you to risk getting hacked to pieces, it doesn't really encourage saving for retirement.'

'I see,' said Tegyn.

Liesel gave Tegyn and Idris a reassuring smile. The Atrabians were different. They were neither rich nor reckless. They'd come out of loyalty to her friends' father. She almost felt embarrassed as their eyes were opened to how Brasingians behaved. *No, I shouldn't be*, she told herself. *These are my people. And there is something joyous as well as frivolous in this atmosphere.*

Idris bought them all cups of mead. It was potent stuff and did a great job of warding off the evening chill. Perhaps it was the drink, but Liesel had to blink several times before her mind processed what —who—her eyes were seeing.

'No, it can't be,' she muttered under her breath.

Inge walked towards them. Her eyes met Liesel's and that smirk that Liesel so detested came to the woman's face.

'Fancy meeting you here, Liesel!' Inge said as she stood before them, her voice dripping with sarcasm. 'A most unexpected delight. And look, accompanied by the new generation of Brasingian leaders. Why, I would say the empire will remain in good hands with such a fine group of young men and women to guide it.'

'Is that the witch?' Idris said from the side of his mouth.

Liesel didn't know whether he meant to, or whether it was the mead, but he said it perfectly loud enough for Inge to hear. Tegyn laughed and Liesel grinned, then fought to remove the smile from her face. She feared they would regret that taunt.

'Oh my,' said Inge, looking up at Idris. 'And a certain brazenness, too. I like that in a man.'

'How is Leopold?' Friedrich asked, apparently completely oblivious to the undercurrents in the conversation. 'Will he be joining us?'

'Is that young Friedrich?' Inge said. 'Well, haven't you grown into a handsome young man? Leopold is just fine. You boys really should meet up some time soon. Unfortunately, Leopold won't be joining us. That is why I am here, really. To stop your father from doing something he might regret.'

'What do you mean?' Friedrich asked, taken aback.

'He mustn't interfere in Cordence.' Inge looked serious now, the sickly smile gone. 'That could have serious repercussions for us all.'

FRIEDRICH MUST HAVE ENJOYED their company because he joined them next morning as the army continued its journey. According to Prince Gavan, the emperor had refused to see Inge when she had asked for an audience and there was an uneasy feeling in the air as they made for the border.

'*Will Leopold be joining us?*' Idris mimicked Friedrich's question from last night. 'Did you really not sense the tension in the air?'

Friedrich grinned. 'I did. I just thought I might defuse it.' He sighed. 'Though a part of me wishes Leopold would come. He was just a normal boy when I knew him. I find it hard to understand how he has changed so much.'

'Friedrich did right,' Prince Gavan said sternly. 'There's nothing to gain by winding the woman up. Remember, Liesel is in a vulnerable situation right now.'

'I don't get it,' said Idris, cross. 'Why must we care what that witch thinks? She wants to drag Liesel back to her mad brother and that bastard, Salvinus.'

'That 'witch' helped defend Brasingia from the Isharite onslaught,' Gavan countered, sounding angry himself. 'She's the only magic user we have left. And Duke Walter is talking of a god loose in Dalriya, turning entire countries to his bidding. None of us have to like her. At the very least, though, we must take heed of the power she wields.'

'Your father's right, Idris,' Liesel said. 'Please don't antagonise her further.'

Idris grimaced but didn't argue. Instead, he dropped behind them in a sulk, not saying a word for the rest of the journey. When Idris was silent, there was little conversation. Shortly, Friedrich said his farewells and rode ahead to the front of the column.

'Who do you think he likes?' Tegyn whispered to Liesel.

'What?'

'Friedrich.' Tegyn raised an eyebrow at Liesel. 'He joined us last night and this morning. Do you think he likes me, or you? I don't mind if you wish to pursue the match, you knew him before I did.'

Nothing of the sort had crossed Liesel's mind. She still doubted that was the reason Friedrich had joined them. 'I don't think of Friedrich in such a way,' she said, preventing herself from glancing behind them at Idris. 'I think of him as a friend of my brother's, that's all.'

'Good,' said Tegyn. 'Because I find him very gentlemanly, and handsome. Duchess of Thesse would be an excellent position for me.'

Liesel gasped at her friend. 'Idris isn't the only brazen member of the family, I see.'

Tegyn made a face. 'We must think of such things, Liesel,' Tegyn told her. 'Neither of us are getting any younger.'

THEY REACHED the Great Road and followed it south. Here the highway served as the border between the duchies of Thesse and Gotbeck. On either side, they came across camps of refugees who had escaped the invasion of Cordence.

Men, women, and children were living in the most basic of circumstances. Local militia patrolled the area, doing their best to control the camps and keep the new arrivals where they were supposed to be. But the further they went, the more Liesel realised just how many people must have crossed the border in the last fortnight, and how managing them all was an impossible task. At some point, if Cordence was lost for good, these people would have to be resettled elsewhere.

They pitched camp close to the border with Cordence, on the

Thessian side of the Road. After a while, Gavan was called for a meeting, and like last time he took Idris and Liesel with him.

In the emperor's tent, regular faces mixed with new. Armed guards stood both inside and out. Liesel immediately sensed the atmosphere was far from the relaxed get together of two days ago.

Friedrich, Walter, and Archbishop Emmet also attended Emperor Coen. Inge was there, her face already a scowl. A Cordentine by the name of Vincente claimed to speak for the refugees. The imperial chamberlain, Otto, spoke first. He brought his master up to date with the news from the region. Cordentines continued to travel back and forth across the border, but in smaller numbers than before. The news they brought was unpleasant. Friends, neighbours, and family now worked for the Lippers. They barely recognised or responded to their loved ones.

'Some Cordentines have been abducting members of their family. Bringing them back into our camps,' he explained. 'We've tried to prevent it, but it's hard to say how common it is. So far, the enemy have respected our border. They operate within a few miles of the empire but get no closer. This must be a strict order they've been given.'

'So what if they respect your border now?' Vincente demanded. 'You think that will last? Look what happened to Cordence. Your Majesty, I urge you to waste no more time and attack the Lippers. Save what's left of our country, before it's too late. I can bring you thousands of Cordentines who will fight for you, pledge their allegiance to you, if you will do it. You could win Cordence, add it to the empire.'

'I have to express my grave doubts,' Otto said, 'that this man speaks on behalf of the people of Cordence. I have argued with him several times about supplies meant for the common folk that his thugs have stolen for themselves.'

'Nonsense!' said Vincente. 'Many families have willingly contributed whatever they have to support our forces. The Cordentines need an army. An army needs supplies.'

'Enough,' Coen said, raising a hand.

'May I speak now?' Inge demanded. Usually so keen to irritate others, the witch now fought to control her own temper.

Liesel could tell Coen disliked Inge. She could see on his face that he was minded to ignore her. But he gestured that she should speak.

'There is a powerful force at work behind these attacks. More dangerous than any other in Dalriya. I urge you, in all sincerity, not to engage with it. We can all commiserate with the Cordentines and do our best to help those who made it out. But under no circumstances should we cross that border and interfere. We would all come to regret it.'

'You bring an army here, and then argue to do nothing?' Vincente asked, incredulous.

Again, Coen held up a hand for his silence.

'Ezenachi,' Walter said. 'This is the force you speak of Inge?'

'Yes.'

'Then tell us what you know of him. Did you have warning of this invasion?'

Inge sighed. 'I knew nothing of it. He is a being of terrible power. Stronger than any mortal—he claims to have arrived in Dalriya from another realm, and I believe it.' She looked at Walter and Coen. 'You probably already know the story, but I'll tell it. He came to Essenberg. I promised the empire would serve him, in exchange for our independence. If you break that promise, he will destroy us.'

'You spoke for *my* empire?' Coen demanded.

'He came to *me*, you understand?' Inge said. 'This is about magic, not constitutional niceties. I gave him the assurances he wanted. Anything else would have been a disaster.'

'So, you've agreed that we are subservient to this creature?' Walter demanded. 'It sounds like you've already given away our independence.'

'Put it how you like, Walter,' Inge retorted. 'Paint me as the villain of the piece, you like that. The truth is I had no choice. *We* have no choice. Whatever freedom Ezenachi chooses to give us—that is how much we will get.'

'Who is this woman?' Vincente demanded. 'You listen to these craven words? What is the Brasingian Empire? Men who hide behind a wench's skirts?'

'Get him out of here!' Coen roared.

His guards were quick to act, grabbing Vincente by the arms. The Cordentine just sneered, allowing them to manhandle him out of the tent.

A silence loomed over those who remained. Liesel understood it. Brasingians liked to think of themselves as the greatest people of Dalriya: the largest empire with the largest army. Inge spoke as if they were dogs who should be grateful it wasn't them getting kicked.

'What else can you tell us about this Ezenachi?' Gavan said into the silence.

Inge turned on him. 'Nothing, Prince of Atrabia! I don't know where he's from, what he wants, or what he will do next. I'm one of the few humans with magic left, and I am nothing compared to him. I have no hope or plan to give you, do you understand? When the emperor of Brasingia orders you to attend him, what do you do Gavan? You come, tail between your legs. So Coen is to Ezenachi as you are to Coen. That's the way things are now, and you'd all better get used to it.'

She turned back to Coen. 'I will leave you to think on what I've said, Your Majesty. You have enough on your plate so I will leave my formal complaint about his—' she pointed back to Prince Gavan, 'abduction of Duke Leopold's sister for another time.'

With that, Inge strode out of the tent.

Liesel felt dizzy. Her whole world teetered on the brink of an abyss, and she knew that if she looked down it would be into a bottomless pit.

SANC

BIDCOTE, KINGDOM OF MAGNIA, 675

I have to warn you,' Rimmon said as they stood before Herin, still chained up in the barn. 'I am taking a risk. Ezenachi has the power to sense other mages when they use magic. He's unlikely to head here while there's a standoff with the Brasingians. But still.'

'How do you know that?' Sanc asked him.

'I learned it the very first time, in Essenberg. He could sense Inge and myself. Not the precise location I was in, fortunately. But he knew I was in the city. Since then, he has come for me twice. When that happened, I got as far away as I could. The last thing we want is Ezenachi turning us and using our powers.'

Sanc frowned. The idea that Ezenachi might control sorcerers hadn't crossed his mind, but it was a terrifying thought. 'How did you know he was coming for you?'

Rimmon gave a grim smile. 'Trust me. Everyone can feel it when he gets near. He travelled to Essenberg in a box. It had some inscriptions on it that perhaps worked to suppress the turbulence he brings. But when they took that lid off in an enclosed space...' Rimmon shook his head. 'The amount of power he has just flows off him in waves.'

Sanc sighed. He understood why Rimmon thought freeing Herin

was so important. It wasn't just their friendship. If they learned how to remove this curse, they could free his other victims, too. But if Ezenachi really was as powerful as Rimmon believed, what was the point? 'We need to find a way to kill him,' Sanc said.

'I know, Sanc. And I know you would like to find the weapons of Madria and use them. But I fear our only hope lies elsewhere.'

'Elsewhere? Elsewhere where?'

'Beyond Dalriya.' Rimmon grinned. 'I'll let you think that one over for a while. Meanwhile, let's see what we can do for Herin. Has your magic developed since I left?'

Sanc hesitated at first, then told his teacher. 'I learned to go invisible. Sort of.'

'What?' Rimmon demanded.

'Not really invisible. Remember, you taught me how to change the appearance of a magical attack? It led me to realise that if I can change the appearance of one thing, I can change the appearance of another. I learned to do it—use my magic to tell people there's nothing there. If I move or make a noise, the spell might break. But otherwise, they don't see me.'

Rimmon frowned. 'I don't see how the two are connected.'

To Sanc, it was perfectly obvious. He shrugged, unable to explain it any better.

'I told you that mages can develop their own unique gifts, didn't I?' Rimmon said. 'I suppose that is one of yours. It just so happens that it is of absolutely no use to us in this situation. Never mind. What I hope we can do is somehow reach Herin. I'm assuming—maybe just hoping —that somewhere in there,' he said, pointing to Herin's head, 'is the real Herin. That he still exists, even after all this time. If we can somehow enter his mind and find him or remove whatever Ezenachi has done to him.' The sorcerer held his hands up. 'Something like that.'

'Have you ever done such a thing?'

'No. I've already devoted days to trying to reach Herin. Nothing. But you might have more success. You're a different mage to me, Sanc. More powerful, certainly. Will you try?'

'I'll try,' Sanc said. He had no idea where to start.

'Thank you. I'll leave you to it for a while. I don't think it's a good idea both of us infiltrating his mind at the same time. I'll be next door. Trying to do the same thing to the Avakabi.'

'Why try with him if you've already tried it with Herin?'

Rimmon looked at him. 'Let's just say I'd try to do things with that one that I wouldn't dare try with Herin.'

Sanc didn't know what Rimmon meant by that, but he nodded his agreement and Rimmon left him alone with Herin. Herin made a lazy attempt to grab at Sanc, the chains preventing him from getting anywhere close. Sanc got the impression that Herin knew very well he couldn't reach him. But if that were to change, he had little doubt Herin would be decisive, fast, and brutally efficient.

Sanc tried to enter Herin's mind. He stared into his eyes. Then tried closing his own and connecting with Herin's consciousness.

This is ridiculous, he soon decided. *I have no idea what to do, nor does Rimmon.* Sanc ground his teeth as he brooded over the stupidity of the task. 'I could have accepted something difficult. A challenge,' he muttered under his breath. 'But this is like being asked to make a suit of armour with no materials, tools, or training.'

Sanc didn't want Rimmon to think he wasn't trying to help his friend. But after a while, even that wasn't enough to keep him there. Frustrated, he got to his feet and left the stable. He stood for a while, stewing, before entering the stable containing the Lipper.

Rimmon sat cross-legged in front of the man, who was chained up, just like Herin. The Lipper was broad and muscular. His skin was darker even than the Middians of the Steppe. For all his differences, he had the same dead eyes as Herin. They looked at Sanc. A snarl came to his face, and he pulled at his chains.

Rimmon turned. 'No progress?'

Sanc shook his head. 'Sorry.'

Rimmon got to his feet, grimacing as he did so. 'I didn't expect immediate success,' he said. 'I don't expect success at all. Come, let's get out of here. Walk with me.'

They walked in silence for a while, no destination in mind. It didn't take long to leave Bidcote for the Magnian countryside. It was lush green and abloom. The insects were out in force. When the sun escaped from behind the clouds, Sanc felt its heat on his skin.

'I've said before,' Rimmon spoke at last, 'that magic comes easiest when it's instinctive. When we're threatened or ready to fight. What we're trying to do is much more difficult. Harness that power within us in a sophisticated way. But such magic can be done. Since encountering Ezenachi, much of my energy has been focused on trying to achieve such a thing. It's a task I've told no one else about. They would probably think me mad. But you might understand, Sanc.'

The sorcerer looked at Sanc for affirmation.

'Maybe,' Sanc said.

Rimmon smiled. 'We have discussed the weapons of Madria recently, and, of course, it's natural to look to them for help again. But there is something you must understand, Sanc. Toric's Dagger and all those weapons were powerful, yes—but, ultimately, just tools. Even those who wielded them—Belwynn, Soren, and the other heroes Jesper has told you about. Tools. It was Madria who wielded her weapons and champions. It was Madria who killed Diis—her divine power, not any mortal or weapon. So you see, when Belwynn made that fateful decision to kill Madria, she left Dalriya godless. In her view, the best outcome for its people. Free of gods. But Ezenachi's appearance has undone her work. There is nothing in Dalriya that can stop him.'

Sanc understood this story well enough. It wasn't new to him. But he was none the wiser about the task Rimmon had set himself.

'We know that Diis and the Isharites came here from another world,' the sorcerer continued. 'Probably not just them. Legends suggest other creatures came here from beyond Dalriya: Lizardmen, Dogmen, Bearmen. Perhaps by sea. Perhaps not. If it is possible to come to Dalriya by magic—'

It hit Sanc. 'It's possible to leave for other worlds?'

'Yes,' said Rimmon. His eyes were alive with the idea of it. 'And I believe I can do it.'

Sanc studied his teacher. *Was* he mad? 'How? It's not possible, surely.'

Rimmon considered his words. 'You told me you came upon your invisibility power through something you learned from magical attacks. Right?'

'Yes.'

'I did the same. Both the Isharites and the Caladri learned to teleport themselves over great distances. It hit me, you see. What if sending someone to another world worked along the exact same principle? You just need to send them further.'

Sanc thought about this. 'But how would you know where to send them?'

'That, young man, is the problem I had to work on. First, you need a location, fixed in your mind, that is safe to travel to. Second, you need the power to do it. I believe I have the first. With your help, the second.'

'If you were to travel to this other world, what would you do? Find another god and bring it back to Dalriya?'

'Something like that,' Rimmon said. He looked at Sanc's expression and deflated. 'Perhaps I am mad.'

'Perhaps,' Sanc said, 'we should keep this idea to ourselves for now.'

THAT NIGHT, Sanc lay awake, too restless for sleep. He thought of travelling to other worlds. He thought of entering people's minds and controlling them. Things no one else would even dream of, Rimmon had asked him to consider as a reality. The burden of magic pressed down on him—part blessing, part curse. Never something he could escape from.

He got up from his bed and left the room that Queen Elfled had provided for him. He passed servants who slept in out of the way spaces along the corridors. Downstairs, greater numbers slept in the main hall. He tiptoed past sprawled bodies. They were used to people going outside to relieve themselves and no one paid him any mind.

The chill in the air and the darkness served to calm Sanc down. The sky was clear, and he looked at the stars above. 'Other worlds?' he asked them. All they returned was a cold silence.

Sanc imagined looking down on Dalriya from such a great height. He closed his eyes and saw a bird's-eye view of Bidcote. The king's hall, where so many slept. The rooms and corridors upstairs, occupied by the lucky few. The houses where the farmers and craftsmen slept with their families. As he looked, small glimmers of light emerged in his vision, each one an individual. In the hall, these glimmers were so indistinct as to be almost invisible. But elsewhere, especially where people slept alone, they were brighter. Two lights shone the brightest of all. Sanc was sure who they were, but he had to check.

When he opened his eyes, his vision disappeared. He walked to the barn where Herin and the Lipper were kept. Outside, he closed his eyes again. He had to fight to regain the vision. But once he did, it was plain. The two dots of light were in the stables. 'Why do you burn so brightly?' he asked them, as he opened the barn door and stepped inside. He brought the vision up once more. The lights were closer now. He could see more details than before: flickers, light and shade, colour. *What am I looking at?* he wondered.

Whatever it was, he needed to get closer. Opening his eyes again, he walked over to Herin's stable and opened the door. As he entered, Herin lurched awake. He growled, tried to jump to his feet, but the chains went taut, and he was pulled back to the floor. He stared at Sanc with his dead eyed antipathy. Ignoring it, Sanc closed his eyes and recaptured his vision. Herin was gone. Next door, the Lipper's light burned just as brightly as before, but Herin's had gone out.

Sanc left Herin's stable and entered the Lipper's, who reacted to him in just the same way. Sanc looked at his vision once more. No lights were in the stable now and yet there were still many others in Bidcote.

He opened his eyes. 'What does that mean?' he asked the Lipper. But the man simply stared back, uninterested in Sanc's questions.

* * *

THE NEXT DAY, as Jesper and Rab set off to join another royal hunt, Sanc and Rimmon returned to the barn. As before, the sorcerer left Sanc with Herin while he went into the Lipper's stable.

'Good morning,' Sanc said.

Herin sneered.

'Was I really wandering around here last night, looking at stars?' Sanc asked him. It seemed more like a half-remembered dream than reality. Something that might be important, but when his mind reached out to understand it, the meaning evaded him. Like trying to catch smoke in one's hand.

With nothing else to pursue, Sanc closed his eyes and tried to recreate his vision from last night. It wouldn't come. He tried to picture Bidcote as he had done before, from a great height. But the image was weak; amorphous.

Not willing to give in, Sanc channelled his magic into the endeavour, forcing structure and clarity into the vision. Finally, he had what he wanted. But no lights glimmered now. Not in the stable or in the hall. It was so frustrating. *Think*, he demanded of himself. *What do they mean?* Desperate, he searched around the estate. There. He'd found a dim light. Nothing like the brightness of Herin and the Lipper last night. Out on the edge of the village, where the farmers' houses were.

He went to see Rimmon.

'I'm going for a walk.'

Rimmon sighed, breaking off his concentration on the Lipper. 'Do you need company?'

'No, it's—' Sanc didn't know where to begin to explain himself to Rimmon. If he tried putting it into words, it would sound foolish. 'I'll tell you later.'

With that, Sanc left the barn and headed toward the lone, glinting light he had discovered. He had to stop every now and again to close his eyes and locate its precise location. He came upon a row of wood and mud houses, set alongside the road to Ecgworth. They seemed deserted—all the farmers would be out in the fields, sowing or ploughing. He closed his eyes once more and identified one of the houses as the place where the light shone. As he approached, Sanc saw a young woman working in the garden outside the house.

She stopped to look at him, a fearful look appearing on her face.

'I mean no harm,' he assured her. 'I am staying with the king. I just need to know something. Is there someone staying in your house?'

The woman looked like she thought she was in trouble. This wasn't going well. 'No one,' she said. 'Just Harry.'

'Harry?'

'My baby.'

'Baby?' Sanc repeated. It dawned on him that was why the woman was in her garden rather than in the fields. Then an idea came. 'Is he asleep?'

'He always naps this time of day,' she said. Fortunately, she now looked more puzzled by him than scared. 'He's quite safe in there,' she added, as if Sanc needed reassurance.

'Yes. Of course.'

Sanc closed his eyes. The baby was close enough for him to see the same details amongst the light he had seen in Herin. The patterns and colours were not as complex. But that made sense if, as he suspected, this was a baby's mind he beheld.

Opening his eyes, he fumbled around in his pockets until he found some coins. 'Here. Get something nice for you and your boy,' he said as he offered the money.

'Thank you, lord,' said the woman, still unsure what to make of him.

Sanc decided it was best to leave before he did anything else odd. He strolled back towards the barn, feeling pleased with himself as what he had learned slotted into place. 'The lights are the minds of each individual,' he muttered to himself. 'They go out when the individual wakes. The lights are brighter in those people who sleep alone. Except the baby, but a baby's mind is different from an adult's. Perhaps those who sleep alone enter a deeper sleep than everyone else. Herin and the Lipper had the brightest lights of all.'

By the time he returned to Rimmon, a plan had formed in his mind.

'I would like to try something tonight,' he told his teacher.

'Tonight?' Rimmon repeated, intrigued. 'Anything you need?'

'Yes. This evening, I would like Herin placed inside a box.'

WHEN NIGHT FELL, Sanc and Rimmon returned to the barn. They moved quietly, since the whole idea was that Herin should stay asleep. Creeping into the stable, they were presented with a wooden box. Inside it, Herin was chained and secured.

Sanc placed one hand onto the box, closer to the captive than he had got before. He closed his eyes. It was so much easier to bring the vision to clarity at night than at day. Sure enough, Herin's bright light was there, pulsing stronger than ever. As soon as he studied the light and shade, he discovered an unmistakable pattern. One part burned brightest. *That's you, Herin,* he said, so sure of it. Circling it—caging it—was a ring of darkness. *And this is the work of Ezenachi.*

Sanc used his magic to attack Ezenachi's prison, trying to free Herin from the enchantment. It resisted him. 'I need help,' he said, and at once, he could feel Rimmon gripping his spare hand. He poured their combined power into Herin's mind until Sanc could feel himself shake. He stopped, gasping for breath. It wasn't working.

What else can I do? he asked himself, desperate for a solution.

This time, he focused his attention on Herin's bright light rather than the surrounding darkness. *Herin?* He called to it. *Break free from your prison. I will help you.* He now sent his magic into the bright light. 'Help me,' he asked Rimmon once more.

They lent Herin their strength; tried to give him courage. All the while, Sanc encouraged the bright force that he believed to be Herin. He refused to dwell on the idea that he was wasting his words. Then the light grew brighter until Sanc could no longer look directly into it. He felt the cage shatter and break around it. When he next looked, the light had dimmed again, but its prison was gone.

Sanc opened his eyes and withdrew his hand from the box. He blinked in the darkness of the stable as he readjusted to the new reality around him. 'I think,' he said to Rimmon, 'we need to check on him.'

Rimmon nodded wordlessly. Sanc could see his desperate hope. The sorcerer grabbed a crowbar and removed the lid from the box.

Inside, they could see Herin, lying on his back, eyes screwed up as he looked at them. 'Rimmon?' he asked.

'Herin!' Rimmon cried, as excited as Sanc had ever seen him. 'You're back!'

'I'm back?' Herin repeated, confused. He looked about before his eyes settled on Rimmon. 'Get me out of this damned box, you fool!'

* * *

NEXT MORNING, Sanc joined a small group who spoke with Herin. They all sat about the fire in Edgar's hall: the king and queen, Rimmon and Jesper. Herin had washed and put on new clothes. He'd wolfed down a full breakfast. He looked more like the man he must have been before his bondage. Yet, a blanket and a place by the fire couldn't stop him from shivering, and he was a long way off the fierce warrior Jesper had described in his stories.

'I thought we'd find you abed, resting,' Elfled told him.

'I've no time to rest,' Herin spat out, no attempt made to address the queen properly. 'Ten years?' he asked, still disbelieving. 'Lost years.'

Sanc couldn't imagine experiencing what Herin was right now. It seemed horrific, to have had such a long piece of one's life taken away.

'I'm sorry,' Rimmon told him. 'I tried to find you. But Ezenachi can sense me when I get near him. When that happens, I have to flee.'

'I'm not blaming you or anyone else, Rimmon,' Herin said. 'I'm grateful you saved me. When Clarin died, I made a vow to be more like my brother. Keep his spirit alive. What would he have done in this situation? Shrugged his shoulders and asked for double breakfast. So that's what I will do.'

'In that case,' said the sorcerer, 'know that it was Sanc here who broke through Ezenachi's enchantment. I had tried and failed.'

Herin studied Sanc. He had a hardness about him: there was no smile or warmth in his look. 'So, this is the red-eyed child we talked of, now become a man? Seems you two were right about him. You have my thanks, Sanc.'

'You're welcome.'

'What do you remember of the last ten years, Herin?' Jesper asked.

Herin grimaced. He looked into the distance. 'I remember our mission to Essenberg. As if it were yesterday.'

'I'm sorry I asked you to go,' Edgar said.

Herin waved his apology away. 'You weren't to know. After Ezenachi caught me, things get vague. Like half-remembered dreams. I was a slave, not even allowed my own thoughts. Images of the people I killed come to my mind. Caladri people. What Ezenachi did to me,' he said, then paused, looking at the floor. 'I did to others,' he whispered.

'You weren't in control of your actions,' Elfled reminded him.

'I know that,' Herin snapped. 'I still feel crap about it. What's the plan with this Ezenachi? I'm hungry to get my revenge on him.'

Sanc shared a look with Rimmon. All they had was the Haskan's talk of visiting other worlds. He didn't think that was the kind of thing Herin wanted to hear.

'We're in no position to get revenge,' Edgar told him. 'The Sea Caladri have been enslaved and his forces have just conquered Cordence. I'm struggling to stop Magnia becoming his next victim.'

'What of the empire and other kingdoms?' Herin demanded. 'Coen is still emperor?'

'He is,' Edgar said. 'There's been no help from Coen, or anyone else for that matter. Now the problem is on his border, things might change.'

'Huh,' Herin said sourly. 'Don't feel quite so bad about sleeping for the last ten years now. Sounds like everyone else has been too.'

For all his talk of revenge and scorn for rest, Herin was forced to go to his bed early that evening, exhaustion getting the better of him. In his absence, Sanc joined Rimmon for a conversation with Edgar, while the queen was busy with their young children.

'I'm glad to see Herin returned to us,' Edgar said. 'Though I'm not sure how much it changes things.'

'I agree,' Rimmon admitted. 'But it gives us some hope. Since Sanc learned how to break Ezenachi's hold over Herin, he might do the same for others.'

The King of Magnia regarded the sorcerer with a dubious expression. 'Even if he can, what do you propose? Catching the Lippers and freeing them one by one? Ezenachi's horde will grow faster than we can reduce it.'

Rimmon held up his hands. 'You are right, Your Majesty. I just mean to say, it is something. Some good news to hang on to. Besides that, I wonder if now is a good time for you or I to meet with the emperor and coordinate a response?'

'Of course, that can be done,' Edgar agreed. 'But Ezenachi?' The king looked at Sanc as he said the god's name.

Rimmon followed his look. 'Sanc doesn't come close to having the power to take him on.'

'No. I know,' Edgar said. 'I just wondered if there was something else we could do. If I can help you at all?'

The man sounded desperate to Sanc's ears. No doubt because he was.

'There is an idea I have,' Rimmon admitted. 'But I will need to have time with Sanc to investigate it. There's no other hope I can offer, Your Majesty.'

'Understood,' Edgar said.

'Would it make sense to try it again, with the Lipper?' Sanc asked. 'See if I can repeat what I did with Herin?'

'Why not?' Rimmon asked. 'Can you get him in the box, just like we did with Herin?' he asked Edgar.

'I'll get it done right away.'

. . .

THAT NIGHT, Sanc and Rimmon returned to the barn once more. In the same wooden box was the Lipper Rimmon had captured. When Sanc studied his mind, it looked no different than Herin's had. The ring of darkness surrounded the bright light of the real man inside. He spoke to the light and poured his magic into it. But something was wrong. He opened his eyes.

'I've hit a problem.'

'What?'

'When I speak to this man, he doesn't respond the same way. I think it might be because he doesn't understand me.'

'Damn. The language barrier,' Rimmon said. 'I hadn't considered that.' He looked at Sanc with a rueful expression. 'You learned how to speak into Herin's mind last night. You broke an enchantment laid on him by a god. Who's to say you can't learn another man's language?'

Sanc smiled. How many people in Dalriya would believe what he and Rimmon were doing? The more he used his magic, the more things that seemed impossible became possible. It was an exhilarating feeling. 'Alright,' he agreed. 'I suppose I can try.'

LIESEL

DUCHY OF THESSE, 675

Liesel walked past the massed tents of the Brasingian camp. It was strange. A place that came alive with energy in the evening, simply stunk like a privy on the morning. She was desperate to breathe in fresh air.

'Hold up!'

Idris. She waited for him to catch up with her.

'Where are you going?' he asked.

'Anywhere I can take a breath that doesn't stink of sweat or—'

'Piss and shit?'

'Exactly.'

'Maybe I'm not the ideal companion then.'

Liesel smirked. 'It's alright. Friend's stink I can handle.'

They passed the last of the tents, navigated their way over the latrine trench, and crossed the grassy plain where the army and the Cordentine refugee camps had made their home.

'Where's Tegyn?' Idris asked.

Liesel debated whether to tell him. But Tegyn hadn't said it was a secret.

'She's gone to see Friedrich.'

'Friedrich? Wait. She has a thing for him?'

'I think so,' said Liesel. She smiled. 'She certainly has a thing for being duchess of Thesse.'

'Ha!' Idris barked. 'Now that I can believe. That poor lad. I should warn him.'

'You'll do no such thing. Tegyn would make an excellent wife.'

Idris raised an eyebrow. 'You must still be drunk from last night's mead.'

They stopped at a rocky outcrop that seemed made to sit on. Liesel pointed into the distance. 'That's south?'

'Yes.'

All she could see was more grass. 'It's scary to think what's going on only a few miles in that direction.'

Idris gave a noncommittal grunt.

'What did you think of the performance in the emperor's tent?' she asked him. 'I find it hard dealing with the idea there is an entity in Dalriya more unpleasant and scary than Inge. It's knocked my frame of reference about the world.'

Idris sighed. 'I find it hard to concentrate on such matters when all I want to do is kiss you. Not by surprise this time.'

Liesel looked at him. Even now, he couldn't keep the mocking smile from his face. His dark hair stood on end. His gangly limbs stuck out all over the place. She didn't know why she liked him. She just knew she did. 'A kiss?' she asked. 'I've just woken up.'

'That's alright. Friend's stink I can handle.'

As she smiled, he leaned over to kiss her, brushing her lower lip. Her mouth opened with his and suddenly every part of Liesel's body was thumping with a beat she'd never felt before. His hand went to her waist. It took willpower to push him away.

They looked at one another.

'Stop it,' she said.

'Stop what?' he asked.

'Smiling.'

His grin grew broader. 'Oh. I can't do that.'

She looked away from him, unsure what to say or do. Turning her gaze to the south once more, she could now see movement in the distance. Screams carried on the wind. 'Did you hear that?'

Idris clambered atop the rock to get a better view. 'Something's happening,' he said finally.

Now there were shouts coming from behind them. A horn blast. From the camp.

A feeling of dread crept up on Liesel. 'It's the Lippers. I know it is.'

THEY RUSHED BACK into the camp, now alive with activity.

Liesel focused on Idris first. She helped him get into his armour and boots. When he was ready, he ran off to join the Atrabian soldiers, forming up under Prince Gavan.

These were the moments when Liesel wished she had been allowed to train and fight like her brother. No doubt, if the enemy were coming, she'd get her chance to contribute. It was the women-folk who were expected to treat the injured, sewing up wounds and all the other gory work created by the butchery of battle.

'Liesel!' came a shout. It was Bron, Gavan's wife. She sounded worried.

Liesel ran over to her.

'Have you seen Tegyn?' Bron asked.

'She went to see Friedrich,' Liesel said. 'Come, I'll take you to that part of the camp.'

Liesel led Bron out from the Atrabian area through a no-man's-land towards the Thessian section of the camp. Closer to the front. 'Have you heard what's happening?'

'No one's told us anything yet,' Bron answered. 'But it must be the Lippers. Invading the empire.'

It certainly seemed like it. As Liesel entered the Thessian sector, she caught a glimpse of Tegyn, heading toward the Atrabian tents. When she called her, Tegyn veered towards them.

'What are you doing?' Liesel's friend demanded.

'Liesel was taking me to find you,' said her mother.

'Oh.'

Liesel was surprised to see Tegyn go red. 'Do you know what's going on?' she asked, changing the subject.

'Yes. Friedrich and I were with the emperor when he was told. He went mad about it. One of the Cordentines led a big force of refugees into their homeland. Apparently, the man has deliberately drawn a force of Lippers back to the border.'

Liesel recalled the irritating man from the last meeting she attended. 'Vincente?'

'Yes, that's the one.'

'But why?' Bron asked.

'He wanted Coen to liberate Cordence,' Liesel explained. 'Coen refused. Now he's trying to force his hand.'

'By starting a war?' Bron said. 'What a little shit!'

Liesel had to stop herself from giggling. She couldn't imagine her own mother talking like Bron.

'Well anyway, there's no more time to waste,' said Tegyn. 'We need to get back and get the archers together.'

'You're going to be fighting?' Liesel asked, shocked. She knew both mother and daughter were highly skilled archers. They had even made Liesel practise so often that she'd become half good herself. But to risk themselves in real combat was something else.

Bron and Tegyn both gave her the same odd look.

'You're not joining us?' Tegyn asked her.

'Me! Wait, you're serious?'

'What, by all the gods, did you think we spent the last two years training you up for?' Tegyn demanded.

They *were* serious. She would get to fight, after all. Liesel felt a big smile split her face. 'Of course, I'd love to!'

Tegyn shook her head at her. 'You're an odd girl, Liesel. Very odd. Come on, we have no more time for your absurdity right now.'

PRINCE GAVAN'S UNIT, Idris included, was mounted. They set off at pace, keen to lend their support to the rest of the Brasingian army.

The hundred or so archers followed on foot. They were a mix

of men and women. Some were specialists. Some had never trained in other weapons or couldn't afford all the equipment needed to fight on horseback or in the shield wall. Others, like Liesel, were amateurs, filling out the numbers. Even so, as she marched beside Tegyn, unstrung bow in hand, she felt insanely proud. For so long she'd felt alone, or nothing but a liability to the people she cared about. Now, here she was, in a unit of warriors. *I think I may have gone insane*, she admitted to herself. *But I like it.*

A mounted bannerman, holding the Leaping Fish of Atrabia, came to lead them into position. He guided the front rank forward until they were where he wanted them, tucked behind Prince Gavan's main force, then held up a hand for them to stop.

To Liesel's right, the sight of the full army, lined up and facing the southern border, was impressive. The numbers of the other three duchies dwarfed those brought by the Atrabians.

Closest was the largest contingent, Emperor Coen's Thessians. The Thessian emblem, a spoked wheel above two crossed ears of corn, had always seemed a little underwhelming to Liesel. But the banner of the empire, the seven antlered stag, also flew here.

Liesel remembered when that flag had flown in Essenberg. When her home had seemed the centre of the world and her father the hero around whom the world spun. Underneath this flag she was sure she could see the emperor himself, and Friedrich close by. They were mounted on their warhorses, the nobility of Thesse with them. Positioned in front of the cavalry, in far greater numbers, were lines of infantry, most armed with shield and spear.

In the distance, Liesel could make out the Mace of Gotbeck flying to the right of Coen's force. On the far side, her uncle's army stood under the Boar of Barissia.

But the sound of fighting wasn't coming from the Brasingian army. It was ahead of them. From Liesel's position, impossible to see. 'What's going on, do you think?'

'You think I can see better than you?' demanded the diminutive Tegyn. She broke from her place in the unit, pulling Liesel with her.

She didn't stop until they were stood between the Atrabians and the Thessians, with a clear view ahead.

Vincente's Cordentines were in full flight. They had lost any sense of shape, if they'd ever had any. The fastest would soon get to the safety of the Brasingian army. The slowest were caught by the fast-approaching enemy. In numbers, the enemy were perhaps the equal of the Brasingians. But Liesel doubted their quality.

Lippers, tall and powerful in piecemeal armour, struck out with long spears. With them were Caladri, their clawed feet giving them a bird-like gait. Then there were Cordentines, the newest additions to Ezenachi's force. They showed no remorse at bringing down their countrymen. Some were killed, others captured. To be turned to Ezenachi's side, by all accounts.

The retreating Cordentines stopped short of the protection offered by the Brasingian army. Many crouched down or hunched over, while others stood by their side, facing the enemy.

'What are they doing?' Liesel asked.

'They have crossbows, see?' said Tegyn, pointing. 'They must wind the mechanism first, before they can shoot.'

As the enemy neared, the crossbowmen stood and took aim. They waited until all were ready. *I was misled*, Liesel told herself. *They were not in full flight, after all.*

The order went out, and the bolts released. Many in the enemy's front row were felled. Shouts of anger rose from the horde as they charged for the crossbowmen.

The Cordentines turned and ran for the safety offered by the Brasingians. A battle now seemed inevitable.

'Bastards!' Tegyn said as the Lippers and their allies got ever closer. 'How many lives will be lost thanks to this dirty trick?'

Horns rang out across the battlefield as the Brasingians readied their forces.

'We ought to get back into position,' Liesel said.

'No!' A single voice cried out over the battlefield. It was louder than any human voice could be. Inge stood in front of the Thessians, arms raised. 'Do not cross the border!'

Liesel looked across to the emperor. She saw him shout, but his voice was drowned out by the noise of the battlefield. Meanwhile, the horns continued to order the advance. Liesel saw the front rank of the Thessians raise their shields, creating an interlocking wall. They marched, placing their left shoulders forward, ready for impact. The rank behind followed, spears held in both hands. No one took heed of the witch's warning.

'Come on!' Liesel insisted. This time she did the pulling, dragging Tegyn back into the unit of Atrabian archers. When they got into position, Liesel took her bowstring from her pocket and began fitting it to the stave. Her hands were shaking, nervous energy coursing through her body. All she could think about was that she was in a battle and that whatever else happened—however small her part was—she had to acquit herself with honour.

Then everything went quiet. No horns or drums, no voices, no clash of wood on iron, not even the snicker of a horse.

Liesel felt a ripple of energy pass through her. It travelled underfoot, making the ground shake. It travelled through her body, echoing deep into her bowels. Ezenachi.

'Brasingia has broken its contract,' a dry voice carried across the battlefield. It sounded like it echoed in unimaginably vast, empty chambers. Liesel's mind crackled with each word.

'No,' a voice dared to contradict. It was Inge. 'It was the Cordentines. They tricked us. We remain faithful.'

'We struck a deal, you and I,' Ezenachi said. 'As allies. You witnessed my power. Have you forgotten?'

'No. We are still allies. I was here, trying to stop this.'

'You tried to stop it. Tried and failed?'

There was a pause. 'Yes. I failed.'

'Then you are no use to me?'

'I am. This is one mistake.'

'But not your first. You won't be forgiven another.'

Ezenachi's voice rose in strength now. Nausea hit Liesel and the people around her. She tried to keep her feet, but like so many others, she sank to her knees. It was as if the entire imperial army knelt to its new master. 'If Brasingia does not listen to you, they must listen to me. This is my final warning. You will serve me, one way or the other.'

Liesel felt the magic as it was released. Her teeth and tongue fizzed with it. She heard gasps and turned her head.

Emperor Coen had been lifted from his horse. He rose higher into the air. He sailed forward, hovering over the lines of his own infantry. He seemed to struggle, but like everyone else—everyone except Inge—he had been struck dumb.

Liesel's ears buzzed as more magic was released. Coen exploded. Fountains of blood gushed out over his soldiers. What was left of his armoured body dropped from the sky.

The unnatural silence continued, as thousands tried to scream in terror and fury and hatred, but couldn't. Slowly, the magic that gripped them dissipated. People moaned, began to move. They got to their feet, uttering the words they had been holding in.

Liesel had no words. She just knew that after this, nothing would be the same.

* * *

The Brasingian army soon dispersed. In a way, Liesel wasn't surprised. It wasn't that Ezenachi had broken their spirits—though she saw plenty of defeated looks. The people who mattered—the dukes—looked as defiant as ever. It was just how the empire worked. No one was in charge any more—no one with the authority to tell the others what to do. Until that position was filled, the seven duchies would operate independently of one another. And if there was one thing they had learned about their new enemy, going it alone wasn't an option.

Who would become the next emperor was a question in everyone's mind, but not on their lips. Liesel hadn't even had a chance to talk about it with her uncle. She and Walter had shared some knowing looks. It didn't need to be said—Leopold was best placed to take the title, yet he would be the worst choice.

As for Friedrich, he had lost his father as well as his emperor. He was operating in a daze. His advisers were keen to get him to Lind-hafen and announce him as the new duke of Thesse. The Thessians had taken Vincente into custody. The Cordentine, who had brought this disaster upon them, was likely to get a quick trial and execution. As for his countrymen who remained on the border, no one seemed to spare them a thought.

The Atrabians were packed and ready to depart. In the end, they hadn't released even one arrow in anger. Liesel's excitement at joining the Atrabian archers felt like a lifetime ago. Uncertain times seemed to be ahead and these people, whom Liesel had come to admire, had always found themselves in a precarious position in imperial politics. She understood their desire to get home.

As they were about to leave, Inge approached. She was like a festering sore that Liesel couldn't get rid of; always there, in the back of her mind.

The witch got straight to the point. 'After what's happened, don't we think it's time for Liesel to return to her legal guardian? Duke Leopold has shown patience. But you have kept his sister for two years now. Enough is enough.'

'Why?' Idris demanded. 'So she can be mistreated all over again? After what's happened, I would have thought the Kellish had other priorities.'

Inge smiled sweetly at Idris. She said nothing, instead turning to Gavan.

'Liesel is under my protection,' he said simply.

Inge sighed. She turned to Liesel now, a mute appeal for her to return to Essenberg.

Liesel thought she should. The last thing she wanted was this adoptive family of hers getting into trouble over her. *But if you do,* she told herself, *you'd just be a beaten dog returning to its owner. And you vowed you wouldn't do that.*

While she hesitated over what she should do, Inge grew bored. 'Have it your way,' she said to them. 'Just don't complain to me.'

· · ·

THEY RETRACED the route they had taken, travelling with the army of Gotbeck into that duchy. When the Gotbeckers dispersed, they continued with a small escort, crossing the Cousel at Kaselitz, before heading on toward Ritherys.

It rained most of the way. As a member of the prince's family, Liesel knew she enjoyed slightly better conditions than most. But after a while, everything—clothes and blankets—became sodden anyway. It seemed apt that the weather was as miserable as everyone felt.

Once through Ritherys, the Atrabians were back on home soil. Their duties to their prince complete, most warriors said their farewells, returning to all corners of the country. Less than a hundred took the road to Treglan.

Before they reached the town, a half dozen riders came toward them. One of them was Gavan's brother, Emlyn.

The prince called a halt. As Emlyn slowed his horse to a walk, Liesel saw a grim expression on the man's face.

'Problems in the empire?' Emlyn asked Gavan.

'You won't believe it,' Gavan said dryly.

'I've heard the gist of it.'

How could he have? Liesel asked herself. An uneasy feeling came over her.

'I'm sorry, Gavan. They got here in large numbers. There was nothing I could do.'

Liesel looked to the side of the road. Warriors emerged from hiding. How was it they hadn't seen them before? She recognised some of them, knew they were Kellish. Then she saw Salvinus, and her heart dropped from her chest.

Gavan and the others drew their weapons, looking around them as the enemy closed in. They were surrounded, but they might push through with a charge. Some of them would get away, surely.

'Don't throw the lives of your people away,' came a voice.

Liesel swung her head to the other side of the road. There, among the Kellish warriors, Inge approached them. Liesel knew that meant escape was impossible.

'Strike me down if you want,' Emlyn said to Gavan. 'But don't get everyone killed.'

No one should die because of me, Liesel decided. 'It's me they want,' she shouted. 'I will go.'

'We just need to take that bitch down,' Tegyn cried. Her bow was drawn, and her missile aimed at the witch.

'Do it, child!' Inge told her.

Tegyn released. The arrow sped towards its target.

With a dismissive hand gesture, Inge sent the arrow into the ground. 'I should kill your daughter for that,' she told Gavan. 'I asked nicely enough. I warned you. Make your decision, prince.' She said the last word with derision. As if he were a prince no longer. 'Tell your people to disarm and not a single one will die. Resist me further, and I will spare only you and Liesel. You will both watch as we kill the rest.'

'Lay your weapons down,' Gavan commanded. He dropped his own sword onto the ground.

No one argued with his order. The clang of metal was like a death knell to Liesel. It told her this episode of her life was over.

'Thank you,' Inge said. 'I'm grateful for that last act of good sense. Duke Leopold instructed us to treat Atrabia with mercy should you cooperate,' she declared, raising her voice for all to hear. 'We will return Liesel to her brother. Prince Gavan and his heir will accompany us, to ensure this good sense continues.'

'No!' Liesel blurted out. 'I will come willingly. There is no need to punish Atrabia for helping me.'

'I gave you that option!' Inge retorted, whip fast. She seemed to struggle to contain her anger. And the worst thing was, she was right. Liesel should have gone with her in Thesse, three days ago. This was her fault.

Inge regained an even temper. 'Emlyn has agreed to take the title of prince until they return.'

The man seemed to shrink under the glares of his countrymen, offering up an apologetic shrug. But Liesel found she didn't blame him. Salvinus and Inge had come. Should he have risked the lives of his family to save Gavan? Surely few would have done that.

'Come,' Salvinus said, one hand raised. 'Let's get this over with.'

Liesel dismounted. She stood with Gavan, who had done the same. Idris stayed on his horse. His eyes blazed with fury.

No, Liesel thought. *Don't do this, Idris.*

'Come, son,' Gavan said quietly, looking up at him. 'Your mother and sister will stay safe in Atrabia.'

'On whose word?' Idris demanded.

Gavan looked over at Emlyn.

'If they harm anyone else,' Emlyn said, 'Atrabia will rise and take vengeance. I swear on the lives of my sons. Bron and Tegyn will be safe.'

The words sounded heartfelt. They worked. Idris dismounted and the three of them walked over to Salvinus and his men. Their arms were pinned behind their backs and their wrists tied with rope.

The Atrabians looked on, emotions raw on every face. Liesel didn't dare meet eyes with Bron or Tegyn. It was a mercy when they were led away.

They were loaded onto a cart. The Kellish would leave immediately, before Atrabia heard what they had done to its prince.

'Idris, Liesel,' Gavan said, as the cart rumbled along, beginning its journey west. 'You must steel yourselves now. If you do, you will survive this and be stronger for it.'

Liesel nodded. She knew he was right. Weakness simply wasn't an option anymore.

PART V
THE TORCH PASSES

PEYRE * LIESEL * SANC

PEYRE

VALENNES, KINGDOM OF GUIVERGNE, 675

Something is afoot, Peyre decided. He was rarely summoned to his father's private chambers. As a member of the King's Council, he saw him often enough, anyway. Not to mention, he knew his sister Loysse had spoken to their father earlier that morning. She had arrived at The Bastion yesterday, escorted to the capital by Esterel. There had been a grand feast in her honour and Peyre had enjoyed catching up with her. Loysse had always been rather sensible; in their time apart, she had become a woman. Since he was three years older than her, it had the unpleasant effect of making him feel old.

When he heard footsteps behind him, he turned and waited. 'So, you're coming as well? I presume you know what this is about?'

'No idea,' said Esterel. Peyre's brother looked like he had not long been out of bed. 'I was rather hoping for a day to myself after travelling non-stop for the last two weeks. If father wanted to see us today, he could have mentioned it.'

'Yes,' Peyre agreed, looking his brother up and down. Esterel looked particularly dishevelled. 'Though it *is* nearing midday. Makes me wonder if you've been *asleep* in bed...or doing something else entirely.'

Esterel seemed in two minds about whether to take offence, but then let slip a grin. 'Yes, well. The heir to the throne must reacquaint himself with his future subjects when he returns.'

'Hmm. The heir to the throne must take care not to sire any bastards, as well.'

Esterel's grin disappeared, and he resumed his progress to their father's chambers, Peyre walking alongside him. 'Let me worry about that. How about you, anyway? Please tell me you've found a lady friend or two in my absence. It's really rather embarrassing, for me, that you are not playing nug-a-nug with the ladies of Guivergne. It's becoming quite rude.'

'I'm not interested,' Peyre said, feeling defensive. He hadn't told Esterel that he still had feelings for Liesel of Kelland. He had more than a suspicion that the ribbing he would receive would be worse than this.

'Find a boy to do it with if that's your desire. People at court are quite open-minded about that.'

'That's *not* my desire. I had plenty of nug-a-nug in Coldeberg. Don't you worry about that.'

'So you say,' Esterel said sceptically. 'Which makes your abstinence in Guivergne even more noticeable. Since you got here, it seems you've only played nug.'

Peyre had to laugh at that. 'Well, if someone takes my fancy, I suppose I should show some generosity to the ladies of Guivergne. In the meantime, I can rely on you to make up for my moderation.'

'Quite so,' said Esterel. He knocked on the door to their father's chambers, and they were called in.

King Bastien was sitting up in bed. Lord Russell stood at his side. Outside these rooms, their father was a man of energy and vigour. Inside lay the truth: he was not fully recovered from his injuries, spending much of his time resting in between public engagements.

Russell murmured a greeting but then left them alone with their father.

'I have news to announce this evening,' Bastien said, 'and thought I should share it with you two first. I informed Loysse this morning.

She is to be married to Duke Auberi as part of the peace agreement concluded last year.'

A stunned silence followed his announcement. Peyre struggled, for a moment, to believe what he had just heard. Had he misunderstood? The treacherous Duke of Famine was to marry his sister?

'Father, you can't be serious,' Esterel finally spluttered. 'Auberi is rewarded for his rebellion by gaining your daughter? You make our family a laughing stock.'

Bastien grimaced, biting down on his anger. 'Our strategy was always to bring Auberi back into the realm. He will become your brother. That is the price we pay, for loyalty from a man who wanted the throne for himself.'

'Then it's not worth it,' Esterel retorted. 'Better to have sacrificed the men and treasure to have finished it. Put his head on a spike! It's not too late to do that.'

'Of course it's too late!' Bastien thundered, spittle flying from his mouth. 'I gave my word! My oath! Witnessed by Martras! I am the king, you insolent boy! Loysse is my only daughter, to marry to whomsoever will strengthen the realm.'

'You kept this plan from me all this time?' Esterel demanded, his anger matching his father's. 'You spring it as a surprise, when the other dukes of the realm have known for months?'

'Because I knew exactly how you would react,' Bastien said. 'Obsessing over your own feelings. Not a thought given to Guivergne and its people. I'm still ruling alone, having to cajole you along the path we must take. Still waiting for you to show me you are ready for the responsibility.'

Esterel's eyes blazed with fury and Peyre thought he might grab their father by the neck. Perhaps he had been invited along to calm his brother. But he was on Esterel's side.

'What about Loysse?' Peyre said, finding his voice. 'She's never even met the man and you give her away to him? Where was her choice? What chance does she have of finding love and happiness like this?'

'Love is an oft overrated reason for marriage,' Bastien said. 'Loysse will become a duchess. If the gods are kind, she will have children and love *them*. It's a fine enough match for her. Gods, Peyre, this is Auberi we are talking about. She'll stay in Guivergne. It's not like I'm marrying her to Leopold of Kelland.'

Peyre fumed. 'Better than Leopold. Hardly a great recommendation, father.' He shook his head. 'For someone who married for love himself, you are acting heartlessly.'

Bastien breathed heavily now, so much so that Peyre worried for his health. 'I loved your mother, boy. I paid for that with years of pain. Loysse is a level-headed young woman. To her credit, she reacted far better than you two. Now leave me, the pair of you. Do what you must to get used to the idea. Because the rest of the court will be told tonight.'

Esterel and Peyre left in sullen silence.

'I will speak with Loysse,' Peyre said.

'Me too.'

Peyre glanced at his brother. He could tell Esterel was fighting to control fierce emotions, too angry to speak.

'I should have taken the throne when I had the chance,' Esterel said at last. 'I allowed you and others to talk me out of it.'

'You're blaming me for this?' Peyre asked. Was his entire family going mad?

'This wouldn't be happening if I were king,' Esterel said. 'That's all I meant.'

'And we'd have had other problems instead,' Peyre countered. He was angry about Loysse just the same as Esterel and was in no mood to take the role of punching bag.

Peyre rapped on the door to Loysse's chambers.

Cebelia, Loysse's lady maid, opened it. She knew why they were there. 'It is your brothers, Your Highness.'

'Let them in.'

They found Loysse with glistening eyes and puffy eyelids, but she looked them straight in the eye and refused to shed fresh tears. 'It's alright,' she said. 'I knew father would have a husband for me when I got here. It took the shock away.' She even allowed herself a little grin. 'You'll be next, Esterel.'

'Huh. The old bastard can try. And you don't have to either, Loysse. I'll stop the marriage.'

'No,' Loysse said. 'I am ready for it. Cebelia and Brayda will go to Famiens with me,' she said.

It still didn't sound real to Peyre. Loysse in Famiens?

'And you two must play your part to make it work. You must welcome Auberi. For my sake, if nothing else.'

Esterel's lips parted, but he seemed unable to get any words out.

'Alright, Loysse,' Peyre agreed. 'For your sake, we'll go along with it.'

* * *

THE DATE for the wedding was set as soon as possible—no doubt, so that all parties involved didn't have the time to back out.

Preparations for the ceremony seemed, from Peyre's remote perspective, horrendously complicated. Loysse threw herself into the organisation, which was just as well, since no one else in the family had the necessary attributes. The court officials, from Lords Russell and Caisin down, were co-opted into the efforts to make it a success. As much as Peyre still didn't like the idea of the wedding, he began to see it was preferable to the previous years, when the royal court had been devoted to the raising and maintenance of armies.

The guest list was an expense as terrifying as war. Of course, the Famiens entourage was large. But every aristocrat across the kingdom demanded to attend the occasion. In some ways, Peyre conceded, it was also a symbol of hope. All their family's enemies had accepted their invitations: Raymon of Auriac and Arnoul of Saliers chief among them. In other ways, it would be a test. Would everyone get through it without locking horns?

Added to the mix would be a few foreign dignitaries, who lived near enough to Guivergne to have been invited on short notice. A messenger had been sent to Magnia, where it was supposed Sanc could still be located, in the company of Jesper and the sorcerer Rimmon. As the days passed, and they heard nothing, Loysse accepted that their younger sibling wouldn't be coming. Of all the inevitable setbacks, this one seemed to weigh her down the most. Peyre hadn't realised how close the two of them were. As near in age as he and Esterel, he supposed it shouldn't have been a surprise to him.

The news beyond Guivergne was bleak. Wild tales had spread up the Cousel. Ezenachi, the Lipper sorcerer Rimmon had warned them about, had killed Emperor Coen of Brasingia in a shocking display of his power. Peyre worried for the people he knew. Walter and Farred, in Coldeberg. Most of all, of course, Liesel. Wherever she was. Of course, her shit of a brother would now plot for the imperial crown. But he had no control over events in the empire, or elsewhere. If his family could make Guivergne a great kingdom, like it had once been in history, then surely they could keep their own people safe.

Loysse's big day came at last. It dawned fair and Peyre found himself in good spirits, like most people, as he joined the grand procession that left The Bastion and made its way into the city. He rode next to Umbert and felt quite magnificent in his new scarlet cloak worn over his linen tunic. His belt, neck chain and buckles were silver, and he had silver rings on his fingers. Many of the noble ladies who joined the royal procession gave him long, approving looks.

If I were a woman, Peyre reflected, *I too would find it hard to turn my eyes away. Maybe I should act on my brother's advice and make an effort with some of these ladies.* For Peyre had to admit, the ladies of the court had never looked lovelier. The tailors of Valennes must have made a small fortune as everyone seemed to have a new, brightly coloured dress, trimmed with rich embroidery. The older women sported elaborate headdresses, while the fashion amongst the younger was to wear their hair uncovered, in plaits, braids, or other shapes, decorated with beads, brooches, flowers and ribbons.

'Who is that?' Peyre asked Umbert, nodding at one group of young women. 'With the long dark hair? I fancy I recognise her, though I can't think where from.'

If Umbert had one use, it was knowing the names of all the women who came in and out of The Bastion. 'That,' he said, 'is Coleta, sister of Sacha of Courion. She is only recently returned to court, after a long absence. She is most comely, is she not?'

'I had thought so before you told me who she is. She must have reminded me of Sacha and now I can't get that from my mind. A shame, really.'

'I do see the resemblance,' Umbert conceded. 'However, that would hardly be enough to put me off, I must admit.'

'You can stop talking now,' Peyre informed his friend. The point seemed moot, anyway. He could see Coleta stealing glances at his brother.

Esterel rode with his friends, Courion and Corbenay. Of course, he stole the show—Peyre was used to that. His brother's blond locks had been styled as carefully as any woman's. His cloak was green, and his accessories were gold. The brothers' outfits contrasted with one another, and this difference seemed to draw even more attention their way.

The procession stopped close to Valennes Cathedral. Hundreds of city folk had gathered to watch the spectacle. They cheered with enthusiasm at their arrival. There was even the odd call of 'Prince Peyre' amongst all the 'Esterel's. His brother had stolen the hearts of the people of the capital. Esterel led them on foot toward the doors of the Cathedral. Waiting for them was the entourage of Duke Auberi.

Like most noble retinues, they had stayed overnight in the city rather than The Bastion. The people of Famiens were a dour looking lot. Auberi himself set the tone, his hair cropped short, wearing a black cloak over a plain tunic. As the group from The Bastion approached him, Peyre could see he looked pale and nervous, as any bridegroom might, he supposed.

'Welcome, Your Grace,' said Esterel, loud and friendly for all to hear.

Auberi allowed himself a smile, and they clasped hands. 'Your Grace,' the duke acknowledged. He looked for Peyre and nodded in his direction. 'Thank you for the hospitality you have shown us,' he said.

Peyre hadn't considered it before, but it must take some balls to enter his former enemy's territory and marry into their family. It was not so long ago that Auberi and Esterel had been on opposite sides of the battlefield; not so long since Auberi had seized Valennes and Esterel and Peyre had been forced to slip away in the night. He thought the man looked lonely, stood by himself. No family had made the journey to Valennes with him. But at least Raymon of Auriac was nowhere to be seen. His absence instantly made the Duke of Famine more likeable.

'Of course,' Esterel said. 'You will soon be a member of the family, after all. Come, let's take our seats inside. Once we do, Loysse will depart The Bastion, and she was quite insistent that I don't mess up the running order.'

Esterel and Auberi led the two groups into the cathedral, taking their seats on either side of the central pew. Peyre sat next to Esterel on the front bench of the bride's side. Opposite them, Auberi sat alone. Peyre turned to watch the space fill up. Duke Domard, architect of this peace, led his entourage from Martras to sit on the groom's side. Lords Caisin, Raymon, Arnoul, came soon after. Duke Walter of Barissia arrived, ostensibly simply representing the Empire. Peyre wondered what help he might request from his father when they met.

A silence settled as they waited for the bride. Lord Russell was the first to appear. With various nods, he got the Bishop of Valennes to ready himself, the musicians to begin, and the congregation to stand.

Then, at last, Loysse appeared, her arm through her father's. The king still walked with that damned stick, and it was far from clear who was supporting whom as they made their way down the aisle. But they arrived without anything going awry, and Bastien settled himself onto his seat next to Esterel, visibly relieved.

Loysse looked beautiful. Her blonde hair had been raised high, and she wore a white gown that glittered whenever she moved. Peyre felt torn between happiness for his sister's moment, and a sadness about who she was marrying. But Loysse had said, clearly enough, that she was content. So Peyre put a smile on his face as the ceremony began.

· · ·

PEYRE'S FATHER had earned himself a miserly reputation compared to the generosity of his predecessor. But no expense had been spared on the wedding breakfast for Auberi and Loysse. Two jellies, with the colours of the two houses: red and white for Morbaine, blue and silver for Famiens, stood on either side of the Owl of Guivergne, delicately crafted from sugar.

The delicacies served at the Great Table just kept coming. Every meat course was stuffed with something or other. There were huge pies full of fish, chicken, or game. The minced veal was named the King's Pie and had a gilt crust formed to look like a crown.

At every other table in the Great Hall, the guests were well fed. Peyre and Umbert made sure, amidst all the indulgence, to save room for Brayda's pastries. Umbert complained to Loysse, at great length, about her decision to take Brayda with her to Famiens, begging her to reconsider. Everyone—even the king himself—laughed at his impassioned speech. When he was done, Peyre warned him he had imbibed far too much wine.

When Bastien got to his feet, everyone at table went quiet, though the hall was still filled with racket everywhere else. 'Everyone knows I'm a man of few words,' he said gruffly, 'though I like to think that when I speak, the words are well chosen. I would like to welcome Auberi to our family. I have given you the most precious gift I have to give. I trust that Loysse and Auberi will support one another, that everyone here will support their union, and that we all remember that we serve the people of Guivergne first and foremost. Now, let's toast this marriage. To Auberi and Loysse.'

Everyone obediently raised their cups and toasted the pair. The musicians were told to play and finally, Peyre could lift his bloated stomach from the table and walk about. He watched Loysse dancing to the frenetic tune with a group of ladies she had somehow befriended in a matter of weeks. He spied Esterel talking with Auberi. His brother then joined in the dancing. They called Auberi over, but he looked terrified at the idea. Peyre saw his chance, moving quickly before anyone else could get in.

'Prince Peyre.'

'Duke Auberi. I'd grab this chance to have a word.'

The man gave a pained look. 'I presume not to congratulate me?'

'To warn you. If I hear you've even looked the wrong way at Loysse, your destruction will be my sole purpose in life.'

'Your brother has just passed on similar sentiments. Whatever else I am, I'm not someone who would punish an innocent girl.'

'Hmm. I would get to you before my brother.'

'I don't doubt that.'

'Very well. We understand one another.' Peyre stalked off, wondering where the hell Umbert had got to.

Looking back to the dancing, he saw an ever-increasing knot of ladies, not far from physically wrestling with each other, to get close to Esterel. A big smile split his brother's face as he pranced about like a buffoon. Then he caught Esterel giving a wink. A brunette, holding the folds of her dress as she danced, smouldered back. *Ah. Sacha's sister, whatever her name is. I'd put money on her being the one causing my brother so many late mornings.*

It was not much longer before Lord Russell got things moving. It was still early for the bedding ceremony. Peyre knew his father must have requested it. A huge crowd took the couple to their room, placing them in the bed, with ribald jokes aplenty. They both looked horribly embarrassed.

'Here,' said a voice from amidst the crowd of bodies that filled the room. Umbert, offering Peyre a cup.

'Thanks,' he said, necking it down. He was relieved when Lord Russell began bellowing for everyone to get out.

Esterel slapped him on the shoulder as they left. 'Just don't think about it,' his brother advised.

Peyre tried not to, looking for someone to talk to. The king said his farewells, but the party would go on for some time yet. Then he spotted Duke Walter on the opposite side of the room. He was talking with Lord Caisin, but when Peyre approached them, the Lord Chancellor soon excused himself.

Peyre and Walter embraced. It had more affection in it than from his own father, and it made Peyre wonder. Walter was a tough man, but had the duke developed some fatherly feelings for Peyre while they lived together?

'It's good to see you, Peyre. Much has changed since the time you spent in Barissia.'

'Aye. In both realms. Farred not here?'

'Looking after the duchy for me.'

'I assume you are here to speak with the king?'

'He has promised me an audience tomorrow. Not that I expect your father to solve the empire's problems. That's up to us.'

'The election is your business,' Peyre agreed. 'But this business with the Lippers. That sounds more like everyone's problem.'

'I'm glad you see it like that, Peyre. I was as guilty as anyone of ignoring what was happening in the south. Hoping it would just go away. But having seen that power at first hand—' He shook his head. 'This is something bigger than any one nation can deal with.'

'What did you see?' Peyre asked, wanting to hear it from someone who was there.

'I saw the Emperor of Brasingia lifted from his horse, held in mid-air, then obliterated. But it wasn't just that. A whole army—thousands of us—just watched. We knelt in the dirt and watched it happen, frozen in place. Then we left and returned to our homes, like good little boys. Even the Isharites didn't do that to us. We fought them, spilt our blood. But this feels like we've already lost.'

Peyre wasn't sure what to say. He thought of Sanc. What was Rimmon doing, dragging his little brother into that kind of fight?

'Anyway, there is other news I need to tell you, Peyre. It's about Liesel.'

He looked serious and Peyre knew it wasn't good news.

'Atrabia. That's where Farred took her. She's been there ever since. But she was with the Atrabian army in Thesse, and Inge found out. She and Salvinus took her—along with Prince Gavan. She's back in Essenberg.'

Back in Essenberg. Peyre felt anger and hatred rise in him. It seemed that nothing in the empire would be right while those bastards lived.

'The politics of the Empire are simply excruciating now,' Walter said. 'I don't have the freedom to get her back, do you understand? It will take all my efforts to stop Brasingia from descending into civil war.'

'You can't let Leopold become emperor,' Peyre said. 'It should be you.'

'It can't be Leopold,' Walter agreed. 'So, it should be anyone else. But if they play games with Liesel—do you understand what I'm saying? The empire matters more than any one life.'

Peyre frowned. Walter was starting to sound like his father. 'So, what? You're asking *me* to help? What can I do?'

Walter gave him a sympathetic smile. 'You saved her last time, didn't you? I have an idea or two, if you're willing to consider them. You don't owe her anything, Peyre. Liesel would be the first to say that. But—'

'Of course, Walter. Of course, I will do what I can.'

* * *

LOYSSE HAD to leave the next day. Peyre found her, surrounded by servants, who were packing up a cart with her possessions.

'I've brought you an extra pair of hands,' he told her. 'This is Syele.'

'Hello,' Loysse said, uncertainly.

Syele bowed gracefully.

Loysse looked Syele up and down. 'To help me pack?'

'Not exactly,' said Peyre. 'Syele is a skilled warrior and has been a valuable retainer of mine. I am putting her into your service. She will be perfectly discreet. But if you ever need someone to carry out those more unusual tasks—the kind that require sharp steel—she will be available.'

Syele heaved her sack onto the cart. 'Don't worry, Your Highness,' she told Loysse. 'My sword is in there. But I always have at least half a dozen knives about my person. Any time you need me to use one, you just say so.'

'Oh,' Loysse said, a little taken aback. Then she smiled. 'Well, I suppose it's always good to have options. Welcome, Syele.' She gestured to the other side of the cart. 'That is my maid, Cebelia. Best not to mention the knives to her.'

Syele shrugged. 'Whatever you think.' She clambered onto the cart, watching the servants complete the packing.

'Thank you, Peyre,' Loysse said.

He saw tears in her eyes and embraced her. 'Don't mention it. I'll see you soon.'

Not trusting himself to hold off his own emotions, Peyre left his sister to it.

THAT EVENING, there was a subdued atmosphere in the hall. Supper was leftovers from last night's feast. Duke Walter, like most of the king's guests, had left for home. But his news about Liesel preyed on Peyre's mind, and he picked at his food.

His father and Esterel still weren't speaking, refusing to look at one another. Even though the marriage was done, it seemed to be driving them further apart.

The celebrations seemed to have tired the king out. He looked paler than he had for weeks, with a sheen of sweat on his face. His shoulders were hunched as if he was in pain, and he rubbed at his chest, complaining of indigestion. If it was anyone but the king, someone would have advised him to stop eating.

Peyre watched as he stood at the table. He swayed on his feet, a look of confusion on his face as he gripped at his chest.

'Father?' Peyre asked. 'Are you alright?'

'I can't breathe.'

LIESEL

ESSENBERG, DUCHY OF KELLAND, 675

While Gavan and Idris languished in the dungeons of Essenberg Castle, Liesel was free to go where she wished. Wherever she went, a cloud hung over her. Feelings of guilt and help-lessness could not be shaken off by new surroundings. *But I will not quail,* she told herself. Gavan had told her to steel herself, and she knew she must. For his sake and for Idris. For herself. *I will play my hand as best I can and put my doubts aside.*

Her brother asked her to attend him. She found him in the Great Hall, with three of the thugs he called friends. She knelt before him while they smirked at her. 'Your Grace,' she said.

Leopold gestured for her to rise. It was done in his usual dismissive way. Her brother revelled in his power, but had no clue how to use it. She was done trying to make him change, done with the persuasions—the begging—of an older sister. It was time to accept who he was.

'I have missed you so much, sister,' he said. His friends were silent, gaping fish that fed on cynicism.

'Not so much as I have missed you, brother,' she said. 'And my home.'

'If you missed us so much, why stay away for two years?'

'It was a mistake to leave for Atrabia. Once there, I couldn't leave.'

'Is that so? Well, not to worry, Liesel. Prince Gavan suffers down in the dungeons for his crimes and insults to us.'

Here is a moment, Liesel. Play the game. Any affection she displayed towards Gavan would only make his ordeal worse. She shrugged, as if disinterested in what befell Gavan.

'His son, too,' Leopold added. He looked hungrily at her. He wanted to see pain and discomfort, wanted to know just how much she cared. He wanted her to beg him not to hurt Idris.

Liesel felt sick with dread at what they might be doing to him. She forced it down. 'I found Atrabia to be very poor and backward,' she said. 'It really shouldn't be called a duchy at all, in my opinion.'

'Hmm.' Leopold studied her, looking for weakness. Finding none. 'I hope I never need go there myself. My friends and I are off into the city. To enjoy the sophistication of what Essenberg offers.'

One of his friends snickered out loud.

Leopold turned on him, a look of cold rage on his face, and the idiot shut his mouth and looked at the floor. 'You should come with us, sister.'

Trying to scare me, now. You'll find all this less easy than it once was, brother. 'I'm sure you will enjoy yourselves,' she said. 'Alas, that ladies such as I must keep ourselves pure.'

'Pure?' Leopold asked with derision. 'What on earth for?'

'I assume you will be marrying me off to some lord or another,' Liesel said. She raised an eyebrow at his blank look. 'To ensure you become emperor, silly. That's what sisters and daughters are for, isn't it? If you want the crown, Leopold, you must use all your pieces. I'm sure your advisers have said as much.'

'I know how to become emperor,' he said, irritated. 'It's already in my grasp. You think you're going to make a difference to that?'

She'd got a reaction from him. That had to be classed as a victory. *Now, what would Inge do at this point?* She walked towards him, slowly, confidently. She looked Leopold in the eye, a light smile on her lips, even though she could still see the gawking faces of his friends. She kissed him on one cheek, then the next, lingering a little longer than was seemly between sister and brother.

'I'm sure you know best, brother. You'll be a great emperor—the greatest Brasingia has ever seen!'

Leopold had nothing. She walked away. *Keep it slow, Liesel,* she told herself, though she really wanted to run away and vomit into a corner. 'Enjoy Essenberg!' she said over her shoulder.

DEALING with Leopold was easy compared to Inge. The witch was the real ruler in Essenberg. After what happened on the border of the empire, she seemed even more powerful. Ezenachi had ignored everyone but her. They had all been sheep and Inge, if not of his species, was the only other carnivore present.

As was her wont, Inge appeared suddenly in the corridor as Liesel walked to morning prayers. She walked with her towards the chapel. 'You're settled back into life in Essenberg, Liesel?' Inge said in the cloying voice she used when at her most sarcastic.

'Oh yes,' Liesel said, in a decent attempt to match the tone. 'How I wish I'd never left.'

Inge's lips twitched, though whether she really derived any humour from it, there was no way of knowing. 'Leopold tells me you two talked of marriage?'

'Indeed. I am not getting any younger,' Liesel said, realising after she said it that she had stolen the phrase from Tegyn. 'And you tried to teach me a lesson once. Do you remember? You said it was about time I used my body and pretty face.'

A lecherous smile appeared on Inge's face. 'I remember it well. And you are asking me to believe you have come over to my way of thinking? What could have prompted such a change?'

'I was in Thesse, remember? I'm sure what happened there had a sobering effect on everyone who witnessed it.'

Inge could hardly argue with that. 'And whom do you suppose your brother should marry you to?' the witch asked.

Here it came. Liesel knew she would prod and probe, try to trap her. She would have to fend her off. 'I was thinking Friedrich would be a good choice. For me and for Leopold.'

Inge pursed her lips. It was far from a stupid suggestion. Liesel had given it careful thought. The Liesel she had to become would choose Friedrich, she was sure.

They entered the castle chapel, a sacred, private space. Inge followed Liesel, and they knelt next to one another. The priest nodded towards them both, attempting nonchalance at the appearance of Inge at prayers. They waited in silence as a few more worshippers entered the small space.

Inge leaned over. 'Because I thought the Atrabian boy was your real fancy.'

Liesel moved her head a little closer, though she kept her eyes on the priest, who had ordered the door closed and now readied himself for the service. 'I didn't say Friedrich was my fancy. But his wife will be duchess of Thesse.' She turned to look Inge in the eye, so close she could feel the witch's breath. 'That is better than princess of Atrabia, wouldn't you agree?'

The priest had begun prayers, but it was mere background noise, as Liesel fixated on the witch's reaction.

Inge raised an eyebrow.

She doubted Liesel. But Liesel had done enough to make her think what she said *might* be true. She returned her gaze to the front of the chapel and tried to focus on the priest's words.

Then Inge was even closer, whispering, her breath in Liesel's ear. The priest continued, trying to pretend he hadn't noticed.

'Often a woman must lie with a man she hasn't chosen. Even me. When I was about your age, a man took a fancy to me. I could hardly say no. Since it was the emperor.'

Liesel's blood ran cold. She wanted to scream out her denials. Her father wouldn't have. She yearned to slap or scratch, to call Inge a dirty liar. But part of her wondered—why say it if it wasn't true?

'I found it hard to understand,' Inge continued, merciless. Her whispering voice sounded so loud in Liesel's ear that she thought the entire chapel must be able to hear. 'What did he see in me? Your mother is so much more of a beauty than I. Maybe it was the differ-ence between us he enjoyed? But whatever it was, what option did I have but to submit and give him what he wanted? And to be fair, I learned to enjoy it.'

Thoughts of her father with Inge infested Liesel's mind, mental images that would stay with her.

Control, Liesel. You can play this game. Steel yourself.

Her heart thudded and her stomach contracted, threatening to vomit. She turned, slowly and deliberately, bringing her mouth to Inge's ear. 'Lucky father,' she whispered.

* * *

LIESEL DID the precise opposite of what she wanted. She sought out Leopold and Inge as if she enjoyed their company. She said things she didn't mean and acted in a way that wasn't her at all. She feared becoming the Liesel she created, that the real Liesel was disappearing. But she had no choice.

Gradually, she found herself included in conversations. As if she was one of them.

Then one evening she arrived for dinner in the hall to find Salvinus seated at the top table. He was in a place of honour next to Leopold. Although he was the junior partner among the terrible trio, he was still the one who scared her the most.

'Lady Liesel,' he said with a broad grin as she seated herself oppo-site him, next to Inge.

'Lord Salvinus. How is mother?'

'I'm keeping her satisfied,' he said with a smirk.

'Mother is truly blessed to have found such a gentleman.'

'Yes, she is. Though if you want a blessing, I'm open to it.' Salvinus glanced at Inge. He looked disappointed that she wasn't joining in.

'Very kind,' said Liesel, unsurprised by the comment. 'But I think you're more suited to the older woman.' She looked around the hall. 'Lady Kass, perhaps?'

Had she hit a nerve? Salvinus glared at her.

'Don't worry about that. I'll still make you scream, princess.'

'Gods!' said Leopold. 'All you've done so far is talk of screwing my family. I had hoped we would be discussing the plan to make me emperor!'

'Apologies, Your Grace,' Salvinus said quickly, though he shot a glare at Liesel that said she would pay for her impudence.

Liesel stole a glance at Leopold. She had never thought to see the day her brother stood up to Salvinus. She had to realise that after two years away, others might have changed as much as she had.

'Perhaps you could tell us of your recent efforts?' Inge asked him, sounding unusually cold towards her ally.

'Emlyn of Atrabia has committed himself to your cause, Your Grace,' Salvinus said to Leopold. 'In exchange for our recognition of his title, of which I assured him. I visited with Duke Jeremias, who said you had the vote of Rotelegen. I also travelled to Trevenza and Grienna. The rulers of both provinces were persuaded that you should be emperor.'

'Trevenza and Grienna?' Leopold said. 'They have no votes. But with Atrabia and Rotelegen, I have four votes. That is a majority, even if Uncle Walter chooses to make mischief.'

'You have two votes,' Inge corrected him. 'Kelland and Luderia. The rest are mere promises. The dukes of Brasingia can change their minds. It's happened in the past. We must do everything in our power to ensure your election and take nothing for granted.'

Leopold gave her a sullen look but didn't argue. 'What else should we do, then?'

'Firstly,' said Inge, 'we act with humility. No suggestion that you already think of yourself as emperor. The changes in Atrabia can work to our advantage regarding the location of the vote.'

'What does that mean?' Leopold asked.

'Imperial protocol says the vote is held in the duchy of the longest serving ruler,' Inge explained. 'That was Gavan. Even if Walter and the others don't formally accept Emlyn as the new prince, they may be persuaded that holding the election there isn't the best idea.'

'But Walter is the next longest serving ruler, is he not?' Salvinus asked. 'I'd rather Emlyn was our host than that weasel.'

'An understandable mistake,' Inge replied. 'But if you cast your mind back, Jeremias inherited the duchy of Rotelegen slightly before Walter was given Barissia. That would make Guslar the host city.'

Salvinus nodded and allowed himself a smile. 'Your brother-in-law would host the election, Leopold!'

'I get it. What else can we do?'

'There's Liesel,' Inge said, and all three looked at her, like a piece of meat in the market. 'A carrot we can dangle in front of the new duke of Thesse.'

'Friedrich?' Leopold asked. 'He's hardly going to cast a vote for me.' He gestured at Liesel. 'However much she pouts at him.'

'True enough,' Inge admitted. 'But we must also look beyond the election. An alliance with Thesse will make ruling the empire more straightforward.'

Leopold didn't look impressed. 'Once I'm emperor, I shall do as I wish. Anyone who stands in my way won't live long.'

There was the old Leopold, Liesel told herself. *Can't say I've missed him.*

'You do recall what I told you about the final moments of the last emperor?' Inge asked him.

Leopold swallowed, nervous looking.

'These are uncertain times,' the witch continued. 'We don't want a civil war. Most of all, we don't want the Thessians bringing Ezenachi into our lands a second time.'

No one said anything to that. It was the shadow at the feast, an inconvenient truth. Their scheming for the imperial throne was like the squabbling of hens before the fox entered the coop.

* * *

LIESEL WOKE WITH A START. She looked about her room, befuddled. It took a few moments for her to realise she was in Kelland, not Atrabia.

A few more to remember the events of the last few weeks. Reality pressed down on her. *I wish I were back in my dreams.*

A knock at the door. That must have been what woke her. Reluctantly, she got out from under her covers and put on her cloak. Pulling ajar the wooden shutter on her window, she could see it was still pitch-black outside. Who would be knocking on her door at this hour? She knew there could only be a few culprits. None of them good. 'Who is it?' she asked.

'Me.' Inge's voice. At least it wasn't Salvinus.

Liesel stared at the bolt on her door as moments passed. She knew she had no choice. She slid it free, then opened the door.

Inge gave her one of her smiles. 'Sorry to wake you at this hour,' she said, making no attempt to sound sorry. She looked Liesel up and down, making her feel self-conscious. 'Liesel, you even look desirable when you've been woken from sleep.'

Liesel swallowed, nervous. She had flirted with Inge, just as the witch flirted with people. But did the woman now want to do more than simply flirt? How would she say no?

Inge studied her face with a sly expression, enjoying her discomfort. 'Your brother wants to see you.'

'At this time?' Liesel demanded.

'He has news that can't wait.'

Several possibilities came to Liesel's mind, each as terrible as the one before. She didn't want to go. But she needed to know.

Inge led her through the castle corridors, not down to the Great Hall, but to Leopold's private rooms. It was eerily quiet. Liesel tried to fight off a sense of dread. She knew nothing good would come from tonight's work, whatever it was.

Leopold was waiting with Salvinus inside his chambers. They were excited about something, their eyes gleaming like predators.

Liesel fortified herself for what was to come. She had to. But being scared all the time was so tiring. 'What is it?' she asked.

'Gavan,' Leopold said, keen to speak first. 'He's dead.'

No. Nausea hit her. She fought it off, making herself stand tall.

They've killed him. *Do you think you're innocent?* she asked herself. *Gavan would be alive if not for your foolishness.*

'Didn't intend to,' Salvinus said without remorse. 'Must have had a weak skull.'

How Liesel wished she could strike out at this thug. Wished she had the power to do to the same to him as he had done to so many others. But she didn't, and she must not lose control. Any words she had to say might come out as sobs, and they would judge her weakness. And weakness wasn't an option. Steel yourselves, Gavan had told them. His last words to her. She would honour them.

'You woke me just to tell me?' she asked, keeping her voice neutral. She still didn't really understand why she was here.

'His son needs to be told,' Inge said.

All three of them looked at her, eager for her to crack. So that was it. A test. She'd claimed that Gavan and Idris meant nothing to her. That she was one of them. Tonight, they would test her claims. Pass this test, and they might decide to trust her. Fail, and they never would again. Her future would be bleak.

'Alright,' she said.

'We also need something from him,' Salvinus added.

'I want to go,' Leopold said, sounding like the little boy he had once been, asking to play a game. 'See how he reacts.'

LIESEL WASN'T PREPARED for what she found in Idris's cell. They hadn't warned her. Idris had a piss pot, but it still stunk to high heaven. Leopold complained about the stench while she tried desperately not to react. *Don't even wrinkle your nose,* she told herself.

Idris sat on a straw pallet in one corner. He was thinner even than usual. Pale, after so many days kept underground. Wherever there was skin to see, there was bruising and cuts. His lips and nose were swollen.

A careless attempt had been made to wipe his blood from the floor of the cell.

What kind of people treat others which such cruelty? Liesel had to wonder. It wasn't even as if they wanted information from him. It was the pleasure of abuse, and she couldn't think of a sin more evil.

Idris gave her a crooked smile. 'Welcome to my humble abode.'

Leopold gave a little laugh at the jest. Liesel glanced at him. *There is something missing from his mind,* she decided.

'Please excuse me not getting to my feet,' Idris continued. 'I'm just not sure I can.'

'That's alright,' said Liesel. 'I'm afraid we come here with grave news. Your father has died. I wanted to tell you myself.'

For a moment he stared at her, disbelieving. When he realised it was the truth, his head sank, his lank black hair covering his face.

'Steel yourself,' she said to Idris, using his father's words. She feared he would lose it—lash out at Leopold and get himself killed.

'I remember when I was told about my father's death,' Leopold piped up. 'It took me a while to get over it. You'll probably be the same.'

Liesel looked at her brother, unable to remove the frown from her face. He was staring at Idris with some grim fascination.

She was convinced it was their father's death that had damaged Leopold beyond repair. She hadn't noticed at the time—she'd been so young herself, and full of grief. Their mother had been no help. She looked from her brother to the man she loved—black and blue, trying to hold himself together. *Gods, please tell me father isn't watching us from above,* she prayed. *He'd be heartbroken to witness this madness that has descended on us.*

Idris lifted his head. He looked at her, devoid of emotion. 'Thank you for informing me,' he said.

'You're welcome. There's one more thing. We think it would be a good idea for you to sign this.' From her bag, Liesel retrieved parchment, ink, and quill. 'It says you recognise your uncle as Prince of Atrabia.'

'Of course,' Idris said, a mocking smile on his face. 'Best man for the job, if you ask me.'

Liesel knelt on the cold stone floor and helped him make his name —his fingers barely able to hold the quill.

'That's it?' Idris asked when she had the parchment back in the bag.

'That is all,' she confirmed.

'Goodbye,' Leopold said, pushing the door of the cell open.

'Don't be strangers,' Idris's voiced carried after them.

The bitterness was lost on Leopold, but it cut Liesel. Her ordeal wasn't done yet, though. Inge and Salvinus were waiting for them.

'Well?' Salvinus asked.

Wordlessly, Liesel handed him the signed parchment.

'I quite liked him,' Leopold admitted. 'Honestly, I think I felt sorrier for him than Liesel did.'

Salvinus studied her.

Liesel ignored him. She looked at Inge instead. A silence stretched between them.

'Thank you for doing that job for us,' the witch said at last.

'He's of little use to us now,' Salvinus suggested.

'I disagree,' Liesel said.

'Why's that?' he asked roughly.

'Emlyn's hardly the most trustworthy of allies. Having an alternative might help keep him honest.'

None of them argued. It was the cold, hard truth.

Liesel returned to her room. She sat on her bed, not even trying to sleep. Wisps of memory and fragments of conversation played through her mind. *I will protect you as if you were my own daughter,* Gavan had said on the day they met. That only made the pain feel worse.

You will survive this, Gavan had told her and Idris when they were captured. *You.* Not we. Had he known his fate?

Well, they'd done what he asked. They had steeled themselves. *You will survive this and be stronger for it,* he'd said.

'Am I any stronger?' Liesel whispered into the night.

She didn't feel like hardened steel. She felt brittle, as if one more blow would be enough for her to shatter into pieces.

SANC

KINGDOM OF MAGNIA, 675

King Edgar made the decision to leave Bidcote. The news that had come to court was dire.

First, travellers from the empire told the story of the killing of Emperor Coen. Sanc and Rimmon listened intently to the descriptions of Ezenachi's power. An army of thousands had been fixed, immobile, as Ezenachi had held their leader in the air before destroying him. Sanc felt like he had learned nothing about their enemy, except that he wielded incomprehensible power.

Second, the king received a warning of a building of pressure on his southern border. If Magnia was the next target, he had to act.

Queen Elfled and their children remained, with enough support to govern in Edgar's absence. Those reinforcements who left with him were grim-faced warriors, who looked like they were riding to their deaths.

Sanc and his companions went with them. Sanc felt no wiser about what they might do to stop the threat from Ezenachi. Rimmon's talk of travelling to other worlds kept returning to his thoughts. To seek some other god and bring them to Dalriya? And even if such a thing was possible, what if this other god was just as dangerous as Ezenachi?

As they rode, they questioned Herin. His physical recovery had been surprisingly fast. Now he was feeling better, there had to be more he could offer them about this enemy.

'You say you turned other people?' Rimmon asked him.

'Yes.' Herin spoke slowly, as if revisiting his memories caused him pain. 'I remember holding them down. Then, it was like—' he shivered, grimacing with some internal struggle. 'Like Ezenachi entered their minds through mine.'

Rimmon considered this. 'Here is my theory. Those like Herin, who Ezenachi turned himself, have the power to turn others. Those Herin turned, do not.'

'Makes sense,' Herin agreed.

'Which raises another question,' Rimmon continued. 'Why the need to create this middle class of the Turned? Ezenachi has intervened in conflicts, often decisively, then disappears again. Why, after killing Coen, did he not continue to subjugate the empire? Why, in all this time, has he not led an all-out attack on Magnia in person?'

'He has a weakness?' Sanc suggested, following Rimmon's question to its logical conclusion. 'When he uses his magic, it weakens him. Just like us.'

'Perhaps so,' Rimmon replied.

'Then think also of the gods we know of,' Jesper said, joining in. 'Madria and Diis. Both influenced events by residing inside their followers. Diis had Erkindrix, then Siavash. Madria had Elana, then Belwynn. Ezenachi lives inside the body of a Lipper.'

'Yes,' said Rimmon. 'He is confined in a vessel much weaker than himself. And the power he wields is so great, do you remember? The very air hummed with magic, like a river floods when it bursts its banks. This body he inhabits must need to recover afterwards.'

'Then now is the time to strike!' Herin said. 'We find him while he is weakened and finish him.'

'If only it were so simple,' Rimmon said. 'He will protect himself with his slaves. And even if we get to him, killing a god is harder than striking him down with a sword.'

'What if it isn't?' Herin demanded. 'What if you're over-complicating it, and we can end this right now?'

'What if I'm not,' said Rimmon, 'and I get us all killed? Then who's left to stop him?'

'A blade through the heart is enough to stop anyone,' Herin mumbled. But he didn't sound convinced by his own words, never mind persuading anyone else.

* * *

MAGNIA MET the land of the Lippers on an isthmus. A chain of ancient looking stone forts crossed the neck of land at its narrowest point, and this was where Edgar's southern army was garrisoned.

'These were Lipper forts,' the king explained to them as they approached one. He named it the Red Fort. It sat at the end of the road that had taken them south, close to the eastern shore of the isthmus. The red sandstone walls towered above them. The stone had been worked into a large but simply designed, square shaped fort.

'The Lippers built them to stop the advance of my Magnian ancestors. They worked very well—our histories suggest the Magnians soon accepted them as our southern border. Perhaps,' he added, waving one hand at the arid landscape, 'because of the infertile land hereabout, the Magnians later relinquished the entire region to the Lippers. When the attacks began, I counterattacked, pushing the Lippers back into their territory.

'We took every single fort, from Lantinen to Itainen. It seemed they hadn't anticipated such a move. Half of the forts lay completely empty. Anyway, ever since we have held this ground and kept them out. Never less than five thousand soldiers are stationed here throughout the year. Stonemasons and other craftsmen live here, too. A constant stream of supplies must be maintained to keep them all here. It's been no easy undertaking.' Edgar paused, looking like he would say more, then thought better of it. 'Come. There are few comforts here, but there is a warm fire and plenty to eat.'

Although army life was no longer a novelty for Sanc, he could still find the excitement amongst the hardship. Rimmon, Jesper, Herin and himself were allocated a space on the hard floor of the main hall, rolling their cloaks up to serve as seats. Rations were served—hard bread with a one-pot that seemed to be a mush of every ingredient they had in their stores.

'Different,' Jesper commented, spooning the food into his mouth with his fingers. He gave some to Rab, who went begging from one person to the next.

'May not compare so well with the cuisine of Valennes,' Herin said, 'but it's better than living off bugs and whatever else I've had for the last ten years.'

'Bugs?' Jesper asked.

'Aye. I have one very specific, very vivid memory. And if you think I'm sharing any of this,' he said to Rab, who'd come to try his luck, 'you've got another think coming.'

Rab seemed to understand and came over to gaze at Sanc's dinner, licking his lips.

Afterwards, they were all invited to a meeting with the king in his chambers. His bodyguard, Brictwin, stood impassively by the door. The only other person present was Edgar's steward, Wilchard. He looked a similar age to Edgar, with the same blond colouring as most Magnians, and they spoke to one another as friends.

'They've been testing the defences of all our forts,' Wilchard explained for their benefit, no doubt having shared all his news with Edgar privately. 'In greater numbers than we've seen for months. There are small numbers of Caladri with the Lippers. I've also had a report from our westernmost fort, on the Itainen. They claim a Caladri led an attack, and that she used magic.'

'Is that possible?' Edgar asked Rimmon.

'I have feared for some time that it is. Ezenachi's invasion of the Sea Caladri may have given him access to turned magic users.'

'That's all we need.' The king chewed on his lower lip, thinking. 'The easy option would be to hunker down here. But the invasion of

Cordence has changed things. Our eastern border is vulnerable. Why would they attack here and not there?'

'Any general who knew what they were doing would attack from both points,' Herin commented. 'It stretches your forces out.'

'The invasion of Cordence was carried out in surprise, with massive force,' Rimmon added. 'They know what they're doing.'

'Then there are the Caladri,' Edgar said. 'More precisely, their fleet. Our entire south coast is vulnerable.' He sighed, coming to a decision. 'Wilchard, I'll take over here. I'll send you with a company of our best to the east. Hold off any probing forces, but if they cross in massive numbers, you'll have to retreat here.'

'Understood,' Wilchard said. 'I'll not risk a defeat.' The steward looked at Rimmon, his eyes glancing at Sanc and back again. 'And long term? The king told me what this Ezenachi did in the empire. We can only hold them off for so long.'

'I wish I could say there was a clear route to victory,' Rimmon said. 'Ezenachi turned aside the army of the empire as if it was nothing.' The sorcerer put a hand to his chin. 'I have one idea.'

'Then you'd better think about putting it into practice,' the steward suggested. 'Before it's too late.'

* * *

THE MAGNIANS WERE busy over the next few days. Wilchard gathered his force and marched out for the border with Cordence. King Edgar left to tour the chain of forts that defended his kingdom. He planned to visit each one and encourage the warriors to hold fast.

Sanc and his friends remained in the Red Fort. For two days, there was no sign of the enemy. It was during the night of the third day that Sanc heard the warning cries, quickly followed by the blast of horns. Sanc and his friends slept close to one another. So it was that when he staggered to his feet, shaking off the sluggishness of sleep, Rimmon, Jesper, and Herin did the same. They moved as one, heading for the battlements of the fort.

The walkways were busy with soldiers. They seemed well drilled, taking up positions next to bins full of rocks, while archers stood by braziers. As he passed one group, Sanc could see they were busy coating their arrows in pitch. A rush of excitement passed through him. Despite the danger, Sanc had always imagined being on the walls of a besieged fortress, fending off an enemy attack. He recalled the tales of the great siege of Burkhard Castle in the empire. At least this enemy had no dragon to render the walls useless.

Sanc and his friends found a space for themselves and stood in a row, peering down into the darkness. Jesper and Herin strung bows and muttered to one another about range and the direction of the wind. The area around the fort was flattened, but still Sanc could see nothing. Then, the archers fired. Many arrows hit their target: great bundles of combustible material positioned thirty feet from the walls that the darkness had hidden until now. Several soon roared into life and their flickering light revealed the enemy.

There were not so many, and while they had brought siege equipment, it was basic stuff. Wheeled wooden walls to hide behind. Wooden ladders, tall enough to reach the battlements. They were all Lippers, from what Sanc could make out. He studied one of them, only lightly armoured, holding one side of a ladder. He had the same dead eyes as Herin once had.

The commander of the garrison ordered his archers to fire, and the Lippers came under a hail of arrows. Jesper and Herin joined in.

Sanc looked across to Rimmon, who shook his head.

'No need to alert the enemy to our presence,' he said.

'Got one!' Herin cried with enthusiasm.

Sanc looked at the man's eager smile. The fact that a few weeks ago, he would have been on the same side as the enemy didn't seem to bother him in the slightest.

The Lippers retreated into the night, dragging some of their equipment with them, leaving the rest behind.

The defenders waited. After a while, with no sign of a return, the commander barked out orders. The night watch would remain on duty, but everyone else was told to stand down.

Sanc and his friends returned to their spot in the hall. The space was alive with conversation. Few attempted to get back to sleep, with so much energy swirling through their bodies.

'What did you make of that?' Rimmon asked Herin.

'Possibly a probe of our defences,' the Magnian answered.

'Or?'

'They've drawn our forces down to the border. Now they'll keep us pinned here with attacks such as this. Then they'll attack on our flanks. From the sea, as Edgar suggested. There are miles of coastline. It's impossible to defend it all.'

They exchanged grim looks. Would Magnia fall, just like Cordence?

* * *

During the days, Sanc and Rimmon would leave the fort, trekking out into the arid landscape. Sometimes Jesper or Herin would join them. They acted as lookouts, in case the enemy should appear. Other times, Rab did the job. The dog took his work seriously, finding a high spot from which he silently scanned the surrounding terrain.

First, Rimmon would locate the other world he had found. Sanc had no idea how he did this, but he leant his teacher his power. They clasped hands, and Rimmon would close his eyes, concentrating, until he had done it. Then, his eyes still closed, he would search.

The more they did it, the faster Rimmon found the world. Then he began to get to the same location within the world more regularly, exploring the landscape.

'We have to go to a safe location,' he explained to Sanc. 'Somewhere remote, where no people might see. But not so remote that you'd have trouble negotiating the terrain or be threatened by wild beasts. Only when I have pinpointed the place and can get to it quickly can we risk going ahead.'

'How did you find this world?' Sanc asked. The whole thing sounded bizarre, even to his ears. He wondered what people without magic would make of it.

335

'It's hard to describe. The idea came first. Then I searched. I suppose you could call them visions, since I'm not actually there. But it's a place we can get to. I'm sure of it.'

After this, Rimmon taught Sanc teleportation.

'You've already done it,' he explained. 'You've moved objects, like stones and arrows. Teleportation is simply moving a person—yourself or someone else—to another location.'

This made sense. But it was strange. When it came to it, Sanc came against a barrier—something about it didn't come naturally. It was the first time magic hadn't come easily to him. Perhaps it was the stress of their situation, but Sanc struggled to find any success. He moved Rimmon from one location to another within his field of view. He moved Rab up and down. The dog simply went floppy, while keeping a straight face. Sanc wondered what he thought was happening.

But Sanc couldn't move himself at all. And the thought of tele-porting someone to a location he couldn't see just seemed impossible.

'Don't force it,' Rimmon advised. 'It will come of its own accord.'

But if there was one thing they knew, it was that they didn't have time to waste.

When they returned to the fort, it was to find there were new arrivals. Queen Elfled had come with a small band of warriors, led by her fierce looking bodyguard, Morlin.

'She's come to speak to you, Sanc,' Jesper told him.

Sanc found her standing in the fort's hall with Morlin by her side. She was still in her riding outfit. She looked out of place amongst the grime and stink, but she smiled pleasantly when she saw Sanc arrive. There was a touch of sadness to it, making him wonder why she had come to see him.

'May I speak with you in private, Sanc?' she asked.

'Of course.'

Morlin led them up to the royal chamber. It was a short walk, but long enough for Sanc to experience a growing feeling of dread. Morlin waited outside the room.

'Sit,' Elfled said, gesturing to her husband's bed. She sat next to him.

'I'm sorry to bring you sad news, Sanc. We received a messenger from Valennes. Your father has died.'

Sanc stared at her. He hadn't been expecting that. Maybe he should have? His father's injuries had been severe, after all. But he was not old. And Sanc had simply thought him too tough to die.

'He collapsed at dinner and didn't recover,' Elfled said into the silence. 'He passed away the next day. I'm sorry for your loss.'

'Thanks for coming to tell me,' Sanc said, unsure what else to say.

'I know you are here to help us,' Elfled said. 'And things are getting serious. But no one would begrudge you returning to Valennes to be with your family.'

Sanc nodded. He heard the words but was struggling to process them.

'There was other news,' Elfled added. 'Apparently, your sister married a few days before your father died.'

'What? Loysse?'

'To Duke Auberi of Famiens. So I've been told.'

Loysse had married the Duke of Famine? Part of him refused to believe it, but another part knew it to be true. At Arbeost, Loysse had told him she expected their father would soon see her married. And of course, he'd have chosen Auberi. Putting politics and the realm before the happiness of his children.

'Sanc?' Elfled said, looking at him with concern. 'Do you need to talk about it?'

He focused on the queen, aware he had been silent, deep in his own thoughts. 'I think I need some time alone,' he said, getting to his feet.

'Of course. Morlin,' she called.

The bodyguard opened the door and Sanc returned to the hall. Walking felt strange, and he knew he must be in shock.

Jesper and Rimmon were waiting for him in the hall. 'Everything alright?' asked the forester.

Jesper didn't know. And as much as Sanc just wanted to leave, he had a right to. 'It's my father. He's died.' Sanc told them what Elfled had said.

'I'm sorry, Sanc,' Jesper said. 'Do you want some company?'

'No. I need to be alone for a while. I'm going for a walk.'

Jesper looked uneasy. 'It's dangerous out there.'

'He can handle himself,' Rimmon said.

Jesper nodded. 'I know.'

Sanc gave them a small smile and left. Rab followed him, not understanding his desire to be by himself. But Rab didn't really count and Sanc allowed him to accompany him out of the fort.

They walked. Sanc struggled to understand how he felt about the loss of his father. He'd never known his mother and his father had been there all his life; yet, in a weird way, he still felt his mother's loss more. His father had protected him. But he'd never loved him. And Sanc didn't think his death hurt the way it was supposed to.

He thought instead of his siblings. Esterel would be made king. Sanc had always thought he would make a good king. Peyre would become even more influential in the kingdom. And then there was Loysse. He couldn't really imagine how she felt. If Bastien had died only a little sooner, maybe she wouldn't be married to Auberi. Because he couldn't imagine Esterel would have made such a match. But it was done now. He shook his head.

Queen Elfled had said no one would begrudge him if he returned home. But did his siblings need him? Not really. He'd had his uses when there was the war to win. But now? He knew most people at court hadn't trusted him; disliked and feared him, even. *I'd always be an outsider in Valennes.*

But if his siblings wanted him to return, maybe he should. *Did they even try to invite me to Loysse's wedding?* he suddenly wondered. Perhaps that was unfair. For Loysse to be married already, it must have all happened very quickly.

Do you want to return, Sanc? he asked himself. All things being equal, he would want to be at his father's funeral, if there was still time. But Magnia was under immediate threat. The whole of Dalriya was. He sighed. *The truth is, I belong here. With strange people, like Rimmon and Herin.* His magic hadn't been a choice, but it was something he was coming to accept. It brought responsibilities with it. He wouldn't hide from them.

He thought of the wizards from the stories Jesper told him. Pentas, with red eyes like his. Gustav the Hawk. Soren, the twin of Belwynn. Belwynn herself, he supposed. They hadn't lived easy lives. They'd all sacrificed themselves in the effort to win the war against the Isharites.

I'm one of them and my place is here, Sanc decided. He didn't resent it anymore. Didn't especially like it, either.

'It's just who I am,' he explained to Rab, ruffling the dog's head.

Rab seemed to understand the gravity of the moment and refrained from licking him.

EDGAR ARRIVED THAT NIGHT. He strode into the hall, clearly furious that Elfled had travelled into danger.

'What's she doing here?' he demanded of Morlin.

'Sorry, Your Majesty,' said the bodyguard. 'The Queen was insistent.'

'And I insisted that you not allow her to come.'

'Clearly, Morlin does what *I* tell him,' Elfled said.

'This is no laughing matter, Elfled.'

'I know. But I had to come and tell Sanc his news.'

'No, you didn't.'

Sanc felt embarrassed to be at the centre of the quarrel. He understood Edgar's anxiety. He was also grateful—and surprised—that Elfled had felt the need to travel here to deliver his news personally. He couldn't remember whether he'd even thanked her.

'Yes, I did. Sometimes there are things one must do, Edgar.'

Edgar fumed. 'You're leaving now.'

'It's pitch black. I'll leave first thing tomorrow,' Elfled said, trying to be conciliatory.

Edgar looked around the room, finding Rimmon. 'There was an assault on the fort west of here today. Full-scale. We arrived just in time. I saw the Caladri witch.' His face looked grave at the recollection. 'I fear things are coming to a head.'

* * *

EVERYONE in the hall woke early to cries of alarm. Sanc stumbled around, half-asleep. He put on his belt and scabbard, cloak, and shoes, then followed his friends to the steps that led to the battlements. No one was surprised there was another assault and the soldiers moved calmly.

Dawn had not long broken and night mist still clutched at the land. When Sanc reached the walkway, he discovered the attention of the soldiers was not directed south, toward the lands of the Lippers, but east. To the sea.

As if they all realised at once, Sanc, Rimmon, Jesper, and Herin rushed to the eastern battlements. They squeezed through the throng to get a look.

The mist extended out to sea, and it was not possible to see far. But they could see enough. Slim Caladri warships knifed silently through the waves, heading for the south coast of Magnia. They moved in and out of the mist like ghosts. Jesper pointed out a larger, flat-bottomed trader. But no one needed telling the Caladri weren't coming to trade. It would be rammed full of soldiers.

King Edgar's voice pulled Sanc away from the sight. He was demanding to meet his commanders and Sanc knew that included their group.

Down in the hall, they stood in a circle: the royal couple, the king's lieutenants and Sanc and his friends. Edgar had fear in his eyes. Everyone knew it was for the Queen. Sanc glanced at Elfled, who looked contrite that she had added to her husband's burdens.

'Morlin is taking Elfled north now. They won't stop until they reach Bidcote. Brictwin,' he said, gesturing at his bodyguard, 'will be going with them.'

Brictwin opened his mouth as if to protest, but Edgar raised a hand and the bodyguard kept quiet.

'Everyone else will stay here. These forts must hold. Those bastards won't venture into the heart of the kingdom with us still at their backs. At the least, we'll buy time for our people to flee north.

But we can't expect to defeat this menace alone. We need help. The Empire is leaderless and tamed. Guivergne is our only hope. The new king, Esterel, to be precise.' His eyes moved to Sanc, then Rimmon, a mute appeal in them. 'Elfled will have her hands full directing our people,' he added.

Did the king want Sanc to return to Valennes? Perhaps Rimmon could teleport him there. But wouldn't his magic be needed here, to defend the forts? He looked at Rimmon for guidance.

Rimmon was thinking, looking from one face to another. Finally, he spoke. 'Jesper, it must be you. Esterel trusts you and you can explain the severity of the situation. Sanc and I can't be spared or separated right now.'

Jesper looked pained. His instinct, Sanc knew, was to stay with him. He'd always been there for him, even if it was often unobtrusive, in the background. Even if, in recent years, Sanc could protect himself. The forester nodded his acquiescence. 'You're right, Rimmon. I feel a shame in leaving now, but it seems I am the obvious choice for the task.'

'There is no shame attached to any of you,' Edgar told the group of four. 'But you must go now. Those ships will soon make landfall and cut off any route out of here.'

'Wait,' Sanc said. 'Let me write a quick note to my brothers.'

'Be quick about it,' Edgar told him. He looked at Brictwin. 'Saddle up the six fastest horses and get going.' He turned to Elfled.

When Sanc saw tears come to the eyes of the king, he turned away, keen to give the couple a shred of privacy.

Rimmon helped him to find parchment, ink, and quill. Sanc scribbled down a few words, too rushed to do more. Esterel would understand.

He made his way to the yard at the north side of the fort, where Jesper waited. He gave his friend the note, and they embraced.

'Look after yourself,' Jesper told him. 'You're too important to get yourself killed.'

'I will,' Sanc promised.

Brictwin and Morlin arrived with the six horses, four for riding and two spares. Jesper and Elfled wasted no time in mounting up and the horses loped away, taking the road that would carry them north. None looked back, not even Elfled. She had said her last words to her husband, and they each had their tasks to fulfil.

'Toric protect her,' Sanc heard the king mutter.

PEYRE

VALENNES, KINGDOM OF GUIVERGNE, 675

'You need to speak,' Loysse told Peyre.

Auberi nodded his agreement.

They were in his sister and brother-in-law's rooms in The Bastion. Peyre felt a little sorry for them.

They had spent a couple of days in Famiens, before returning to Valennes for the royal funeral. They had stayed ever since. For there was a coronation to plan. Loysse had become the key organiser for the event, her rooms a centre of strategic planning where the great and the good mixed with entertainers, clergy, royal officials, chefs, and countless others who would play a role in the day. For, if Loysse's marriage had seemed grand, it would be dwarfed in scale by Esterel's coronation.

Their father's funeral had been a muted, sombre affair. Peyre couldn't help thinking it was preferable to the extravaganza Loysse was planning. He caught himself. *No, I will not turn into my father.*

'Alright, I will speak,' he conceded.

'Good,' said Loysse. 'Because Valennes still needs to get to know you, Peyre. The people must understand your role in things. You are the loyal younger brother. That's what they want. And at the coronation, you must be one of the leading actors. Otherwise, Esterel's friends will claim the limelight.'

'Huh,' Peyre grunted. That was accurate. Florent had returned from his short-lived stewardship of Morbaine. He, Sacha, and Miles of Corbenay were constantly in Esterel's company these days. Eating, drinking, sleeping together. Peyre wouldn't be surprised if the three of them stood around while Esterel took a crap. He smiled to himself. They'd probably congratulate him on how sweet it smelt.

He realised Loysse was looking at him with a raised eyebrow while he smiled to himself like a simpleton. 'I was just picturing—never mind.'

'I will write down some ideas for the speech,' she said, as if talking to a child. 'Maybe do a draft for you to look at.'

Ordinarily, Peyre would have taken offence. But he was perceptive enough to realise that Loysse needed all the work she was taking on. It kept her from dwelling on their father's death. And it gave her something to speak about with Auberi. Or, Peyre considered, maybe it was more than that. It allowed her to demonstrate to Auberi who she was—an able, intelligent woman. For his part, Peyre had noted, Auberi seemed completely smitten with his new wife. Peyre was warming a little to the Duke of Famine.

Peyre decided to be gracious and allow his sister to draft his speech. He could always add in a few jests and personal anecdotes to her version. Saying his farewells, he left them to it, aware their time alone would soon be interrupted by someone else.

Outside the door, Syele stood guard.

'Is it really necessary to have you posted out here?' he asked her.

'It's not for your sister's protection, Your Highness,' the Barissian answered. 'The Duke isn't well liked in Valennes. On account of his rebellion leading to the deaths of a few thousand people.'

And some important ones at that, Peyre said to himself. Sacha of Courion's father, for one. He'd never really liked Courion that well. Now, with his best friend about to become king, he was becoming insufferable. As if he owned the place. *I must stop that from happening. And not just for my own petty reasons.*

Peyre left Syele to it and went to find his brother. Finding Esterel's rooms empty, he tried Sacha's. Sure enough, there was the sound of laughter from inside. Entering, it was no surprise to find Esterel and his three companions, cups of wine in hand. Sacha's sister was there, too, along with some other ladies of the court. They, too, were drinking.

'Peyre!' Esterel cried. 'Come and join us!'

No point standing to attention like a fuddy-duddy, Peyre told himself. He grabbed a cup and turned to the nearest barrel.

'That one's empty,' Florent said. 'Try that one over there.'

Peyre managed to get himself a cup of wine and a seat, observing as he did so how many empty barrels there were. He could understand his brother's desire to party. In a few days' time, he would be king, with all the responsibilities that went with it. It must feel like he only had a few days of freedom left.

'We were just discussing what I should do with Guivergne once I am king,' Esterel said, his voice unreasonably loud. 'Miles, tell him what your plan was.'

'Esterel should build a new palace,' the Lord of Corbenay said, turning to Peyre. 'There should be a bathhouse, like they have in Persala, where only the prettiest maids may work.'

'And handsome young men, too,' Sacha's sister demanded.

'Hush your tongue, Coleta,' Miles demanded. 'This is my fantasy, not yours. As well as the usual baths, there will be one filled daily with wine.'

Peyre considered this. 'You would drink the wine in which everyone is swimming?'

'But think how easy it would make life,' Miles countered.

'Peyre makes a point,' Esterel admitted. 'I would have to establish rules. You must get completely clean first, before entering the wine pool.'

'And no pissing in it,' Sacha added.

One of the ladies giggled, hiccoughed, then sprayed wine from her nose with a cry of alarm. Peyre stared in astonishment, while Esterel and his friends rolled about laughing.

'Ignore these fools, Aizi,' Sacha's sister said. She helped her stand and led the ladies from the room, while Esterel cried with laughter.

'Oh gods, I think that was the funniest thing I have ever seen,' Esterel got out, clutching his chest in pain.

The gesture reminded Peyre so much of their father's collapse that it killed the humour of the moment. Although Esterel didn't notice, Peyre wasn't the only one who did.

'I suppose I had better go after them and check the lady is alright,' Sacha said. 'Otherwise, I'll get an earful from Coleta later.'

This was Peyre's moment. 'I had actually come to speak with you, Esterel, if you are also leaving?'

'I suppose so,' Esterel said, confused by the sudden end to the party.

Miles sighed, getting to his feet. 'I guess my wine bath idea is dead in the water after this.'

'Not to worry,' Florent said, patting him on the back. 'I will fill your bath with wine, and you can splash around in that for a bit. How does that sound?'

'Bloody amazing!'

Peyre walked with Esterel.

'A nap before dinner is called for,' Esterel said. He looked sideways at Peyre. 'You disapprove of the drinking, don't you?'

'No. Not really. I was thinking I would be doing exactly the same. You might be a little surprised by the matter I wanted to raise with you.'

'Oh yes?' Esterel said. 'Tell you what, let's go outside. Fresh air might do the trick.'

'Remember when you showed me The Bastion when I first arrived?' Peyre asked him.

'I do. Let's take another tour, for old times' sake.'

They exited the gatehouse, guards saluting them as they went. They began their walk around the walls of the fortress, the star-shaped projections creating sharp turns at regular intervals.

'It's about marriage,' Peyre began. 'You'll be king soon and you can do what you want. Who knows what father would have wanted. I fear you may sleepwalk into marrying Sacha's sister when there are better options.'

'Coleta, Peyre. I have told you her name several times now.'

'Sorry. Coleta.'

'And who are these better options?'

'I would argue for Liesel of Brasingia.'

Esterel looked at him askance. 'Remember that odd Kellish delegation who came to Arbeost? Nothing more was heard of that. And now you raise it again. Why Liesel? It was her brother who gave you that scar, after all. Not sure I want him for a brother-in-law. The Duke of Famine is bad enough.'

Peyre had gone over how to make the case to Esterel. Explaining that he and Walter wanted to rescue her from Essenberg wasn't an argument, even if that's where the impetus came from. 'She's beautiful and intelligent. She would make a great queen. And of course, she is as well born as they come. She brings you status. She would be a fitting match for you.'

'But Coleta is beautiful and intelligent. And I already know her. We get on. Most of the time. Why risk a match with someone I've never met?'

'But *I've* met her and I'm telling you.'

'What do you have against Coleta, Peyre? Is it Sacha's influence, because it wouldn't mean Sacha had any more power or anything like that.'

'It's not Coleta, Esterel. Please believe me. I don't know her. I'm sure she's lovely. I'm arguing for Liesel, not against anyone. This is a big decision to make. And I don't want to sound like father. Truly, I don't. But you are choosing the queen of Guivergne, as well as your wife.'

Esterel blew out a long breath. 'I'll think about it,' he said. 'I know it's a big decision, and I know you mean well.'

'Thank you,' said Peyre. 'That's all I can ask.'

I can ask, he told himself. *But I needed to convince, and I haven't done that.*

* * *

THE DAY of the coronation came and as Peyre wandered around The Bastion, down to breakfast, everyone wore a smile. He dropped into a chair next to Umbert. Opposite them, Loysse and Auberi were part way through their meal.

With a day of excitement ahead of them, there was a simple pleasure in sitting with his sister and talking quietly before the whirlwind began.

'I hadn't quite realised, until today, just how well loved Esterel is,' Loysse admitted to him. 'It seems there isn't a single person who dislikes him.'

Peyre glanced at Auberi and back to Loysse. He found it an odd thing to say, since her husband had fought to destroy their family. But perhaps that was how the pair dealt with their recent past. By pretending it hadn't happened.

'When I walk about the city these days,' he said to her, 'the thing I notice most is how much hope there is. After the dour reign of Nicolas and the divided reign of our father. People expect a golden age under Esterel. It is a powerful thing he has in his hands. But powerful things can be dangerous.'

'Then it's up to us to support him,' Loysse said.

Auberi nodded his agreement. Peyre wondered at the man's transformation. Sanc was the one with magic. But his sister seemed to have weaved a remarkable spell on their former enemy.

He thought of Liesel. She was never far from his thoughts. It made him believe the Duke of Famine's transformation might be real.

'NICE DAY FOR IT,' Umbert commented, as the procession left the gates of The Bastion.

'Of course, the sun comes out for Esterel,' Peyre said.

It was just as well, though. Loysse had convinced Esterel that his coronation should be a celebration for all the citizens of Valennes, and whoever else had travelled to the city.

The cathedral wasn't big enough for such an event. So instead, a huge outdoor platform had been built for the occasion. It was located in the open space to the north-west of the city, opposite The Bastion. Loysse had persuaded the Bishop of Valennes to conduct the service there. The nobility of Guivergne were guaranteed the best seats. But there was plenty of room for everyone else to witness the event.

As they approached, it looked like the entire city had already congregated there. Those with an eye for money making had set up for the day: food sellers, entertainers, and many shopkeepers had simply taken their wares to this new location. The soldiers at the front of the procession had to do a bit of good-humoured work to get the crowd to part and allow the notables up to the stage.

Peyre was shown to his seat at the top table, where he sat with the likes of Loysse, Auberi, the Duke of Martras, and the great officials of state, Lords Russell and Caisin. He thought it notable that not a single foreign dignitary attended the coronation. Of course, those to the south couldn't come. Even so, Guivergne seemed isolated. That was something Esterel should look to change.

Once everyone was in their proper place, the ceremony began. Esterel took to the stage with the Bishop of Valennes. The officials shouted for the crowd to quieten, with mixed results. Many of the people now congregated about the stage and watched in silence. On the outskirts, however, citizens continued their conversations, they drank and laughed, children played, sellers hawked their goods. Some in the crowd turned to shout at the offenders, which only added to the noise.

Peyre saw heads turning to Loysse, who looked mortified. What had seemed a great idea was turning into farce.

'Not to worry!' Esterel shouted so the people closest to the stage could hear him. 'Not everyone need hear every word!'

The bishop did his best, delivering the list of duties expected of a monarch. When he was done, Esterel responded, agreeing to serve the kingdom and its people; to rule with justice. But the end of his speech differed from Bastien's. Peyre remembered his father's final words—a promise to bring peace to the land. That, indeed, had been his overriding concern.

'I will bring glory and honour to Guivergne!' Esterel cried.

Peyre couldn't help smiling at the idea. It was so typical of his brother. Many of those present, especially of the younger generation, cheered loudly at these words. Peyre found himself grinning and joining in with the shouts. Miles of Corbenay stood from his seat, raising his hands aloft, and many others copied him.

Esterel tried to continue. Peyre heard him say something about a great nation. But the cheering had now spread out to the rest of the people who had gathered for the occasion. Peyre was sure most of them had no idea of the words they cheered; they simply understood that now was the moment they had come to witness.

Esterel gestured to the bishop that he was ready, and the man went to grab the crown, holding it aloft. Esterel had to bend his long legs to allow the prelate to get it on his head.

Then, it was pure theatre. Esterel paraded about the stage, lifting the crown up above his head, as if it were a prize he had won in a military contest. The crowd went ecstatic, the noise deafening. Like a fool, the new king pranced about from one end of the stage to the next, a stupid grin on his face, soaking up the admiration. Only Esterel could get away with it. The thing was, Peyre couldn't help the same stupid grin appearing on his own face. When he looked around, he saw that only a few guests could resist.

Loysse appeared at his side. She looked a little happier, Esterel having solved the problem of acoustics. 'There's no point even trying to do your speech,' she told him. 'Just go up on the stage with him.'

Peyre felt a weight of pressure he hadn't even known he had, suddenly lift.

Esterel had his own look of relief when he saw Peyre approach, perhaps having exhausted his antics on the stage. He took Peyre's hand, and they raised their arms in the air: a show of solidarity between brothers. Wild applause and more shouting greeted the gesture. It hit like a wave and Peyre laughed with joy at the reception. Adulation, he decided, would be easy to get used to.

Auberi and Domard of Martras came next. The four of them waved at the throng. The crowd was more subdued at this. Peyre heard some boos. That was to be expected. But the show of unity from the highest-ranking men in the realm wasn't the worst way to begin his brother's reign.

After this, the official part of the proceedings was over. Peyre, having avoided his speech, was now free to relax. He found Umbert, and they set off to peruse the beverages on sale. The first seller was keen to get his batch into their hands, giving them free mugs of dark brown ale.

'I could get used to this,' Peyre admitted to Umbert, taking a glug of foamy goodness.

'Why do the richest get free drinks?' Umbert wondered. 'Shouldn't it be the other way around?'

'Because,' said Peyre, 'a good word from me and many will visit his establishment.'

He watched his brother circulate amongst his new subjects. Behind him, a bevy of soldiers carried a chest, from which the king handed each citizen a freshly minted silver penny. The new coinage had Esterel's name and image on one side. They had been made by melting down the coins of their father. *How quickly,* Peyre thought, *the brief reign of King Bastien was consigned to history.*

But when he thought on it more, this was the day his father had been striving for all along. A peaceful succession. Their family secure. The potential, at least, for a long and prosperous reign. Peyre looked up to the heavens in acknowledgement of what his father had achieved.

Perhaps history will overlook you, father. An unsung king. But I will remember the lessons you gave me.

* * *

THE PARTY in The Bastion lasted the night. Like many others, Peyre saw little the day afterwards.

The next day, however, he was called for a meeting with the new king. He arrived at the council room, where Esterel seemed to have taken residence at one end of the table. It was not a council meeting, however. They were the only two in the room.

'Accounts?' Peyre asked, gesturing at the books and parchment laid out next to his brother.

'Yes. I felt the need to understand how everything works,' Esterel said, looking rueful.

'Well. Now the party's over, it's time to get to work?'

'Exactly,' Esterel said. He looked serious, and so Peyre took a seat, waiting for him to start.

'Peyre, I would offer you the duchy of Morbaine.'

'Oh! Thank you, Your Majesty.'

'You surely aren't surprised? And just call me Esterel when we are together. Please.'

Morbaine was the greatest dominion in the kingdom by far. Such a gift instantly made Peyre second only to Esterel in wealth and power.

'Well, yes, I am a little. There are no rules that it should stay in our family.'

'There aren't. But it should. I take it you accept?'

'Of course. I would be honoured to serve Morbaine.'

'Excellent,' said Esterel. 'My first appointment and probably the easiest. You will need to go to Morbaine and meet with the key figures there. Just like I did. But otherwise, I'm not expecting you to stay there. I hope you can still serve the realm on the Council?'

It was a lot to think about. Being duke of Morbaine but absent from the duchy seemed wrong, somehow. Esterel had done it, but everyone knew he wouldn't be duke forever. Still, it was his king asking him. 'I will do whatever you want, Esterel.'

'Good. I need you here. I know I have my friends, and they are full of themselves. I need other voices in Council for balance. Speaking of which.' Esterel gave a pained expression. 'I've decided to make Sacha royal steward. It's nothing against Lord Russell. It's just that Sacha knows me and I'm more comfortable with him.'

Peyre shrugged. 'It's your decision. I'm sure Russell will understand. He was father's confidante, not yours.'

'I'm sure you're right. But he's a good man. I just wondered if you might help me soften the blow. I was thinking, if you are going to be absent from Morbaine much of the time, would Lord Russell make a good steward for you? It's your decision, of course.'

Peyre thought about it. Lord Russell was experienced. He trusted him and would no doubt learn a thing or two as well. 'It makes sense to me. Russell and Umbert can accompany me south on my visit. It will give us a chance to see if the relationship works.'

Esterel looked relieved. 'I'm pleased. I will speak to him today.'

'Any other big changes I should know about?' Peyre asked.

'That's it, really. Caisin stays as Lord Chancellor. No one else comes close to his legal acumen. Though Florent has the brains for the post if he wishes to learn. Anyway, you'll need to make arrangements to travel. I thought I'd announce your appointment before dinner. There's been a lot of ceremony recently, but we need to mark it properly.'

'Yes,' Peyre said, 'of course.' He got to his feet.

Esterel joined him, and they embraced before Peyre left him to it.

It was only on the way to his rooms, his head full of his grand new title, that Liesel crossed his mind. *Damn. I've got nowhere with this marriage strategy. And I have tried.* Of course, he didn't want to see Liesel married to anyone else. Even Esterel. But most important was making her safe.

I'll get you out of there, Liesel. Just hold on a little while longer.

LIESEL

ESSENBERG, DUCHY OF KELLAND, 675

For the next few days, Liesel lived in a daze. Her mind kept returning to Idris's cell. It replayed the stilted conversation, focused on the red markings on his skin. Even worse, she couldn't stop herself from imagining how Idris had received his wounds, or Prince Gavan's final moments. Guilt hovered at her shoulder in her waking moments, and it disrupted her sleep.

Then, Tegyn came to court. The Atrabians had been informed of Gavan's death, and she had come with a small entourage to bring home his body.

At first, Liesel kept her distance, not daring to speak to her. She heard, second-hand, how Tegyn had made her request with dignity, containing the emotions which must have been there. Salvinus and Leopold both mocked her, but Liesel could sense the shame behind their words. Her brother acceded to Tegyn's request.

Liesel went to see Tegyn in the evening. She'd been given one of the worst-appointed suites in Essenberg Castle to stay in and Liesel fumed at the insult.

'You took your time,' Tegyn said to her as they took a seat together in her bedroom, the rest of her companions giving them some privacy.

'I've tried hard to convince people here that I'm no friend of Atrabia,' Liesel admitted. She looked at Tegyn's expression. 'Also, I feared speaking with you after what's happened.'

'I hope,' Tegyn said, 'given that we're close friends—practically sisters—that you don't think I blame you for any of this.'

Liesel felt a lump in her throat and waited to respond, knowing she would cry if she spoke too quickly. 'I blame myself, so it was easy to assume you did, too. I have done my best to persuade them that Idris may have his uses, whilst feigning that we are not too close. I pray it works.'

'Oh, Idris,' Tegyn said with a wave of her hand. 'He always lands on his feet.'

Liesel took her hand. 'Not this time, Tegyn. I—'

Tegyn politely but firmly withdrew her hand and returned Liesel's to her lap. 'Liesel, I've lost my father. I cannot think about my brother except to assume he will end up alright.'

'I understand.' Liesel felt obliged to change the subject. 'Are you and your mother being treated well in Atrabia?'

'Emlyn treats us with respect. The people would turn on him in a heartbeat if he did anything else, of course. Remember, this is Atrabia, not Kelland.'

Liesel nodded. 'I try to remember, though as each day passes here, I fear I'm losing all the goodness Atrabia gave me. One must be cold to survive here. I wish I had one friend I could trust a fraction as much as I trust you.'

Tegyn considered this. 'Then after my father's funeral, I must return here and help you.'

'I couldn't ask that. Your mother needs you—'

'My mother is safe and has many friends. You need me more.'

'How will we convince them to allow it? Convince Inge, I should say.'

'We must come up with a plan now,' Tegyn decided. 'We don't have long.'

* * *

TEGYN and the Atrabians left early the next morning, with Prince Gavan's wooden casket on the back of their cart.

Shortly afterwards, Liesel walked along a castle corridor towards Inge, as if by coincidence.

'Darling Liesel,' Inge said, looking her up and down. 'I heard you went to visit the Atrabian girl last night.'

Liesel made a face and nodded. 'She had something to ask me. She wants to come to Essenberg and be my court lady.' She said it as if she was not keen on the idea. Inge always seemed to favour the decisions that Liesel said she disliked.

Inge pursed her lips. 'She made the same request to me. You don't like the idea? Don't trust her?'

'I don't think it's to do with her brother or anything like that,' Liesel said. 'She's always been very keen to find a good marriage, and she thinks she will succeed if she comes to court.'

'I see,' said the witch. 'The girl has something about her, to come here and fetch her father. I'm of a mind to allow it. Just like her brother, she may have her uses. Don't you think, Liesel?'

'I suppose so,' Liesel answered, sounding reluctant.

Inge allowed herself one of her sly smiles. 'Then it's settled.'

MEANWHILE, the campaign to get Leopold the imperial title had been progressing well. All the dukes of Brasingia had agreed that Guslar should be the host city for the vote, scheduled for the end of summer. Leopold had been pleased with that, seeing it as a victory. He sent a diplomatic mission to Thesse, its role to put out feelers to Duke Friedrich about a potential marriage with Liesel.

She cringed every time she thought about it. What would Friedrich make of it? But Leopold and Inge believed she was trying to help Leopold become emperor, and in turn, they had forbidden Salvinus from going near her. He was rarely in Essenberg for long anyway, soon returning to Witmar from where he governed Luderia with Liesel's mother. At other times, he was sent here and there, cajoling or threatening wherever he went, building an alliance behind Leopold.

The diplomats came back with a cautiously warm response from Thesse. Even if Friedrich didn't back Leopold, there might be a way for him to join the family and integrate with the new order.

Then things took a turn for the worse. Spies came back with news of secret meetings between Walter and Friedrich. Victory looked less assured.

'It's Walter,' Leopold declared from his throne with a mix of anger and whining. He liked to sit there when he discussed the imperial vote. The chair seemed to give him confidence.

Only Inge and Liesel were there to advise him, and he often acted like a spoiled child when solely in their company.

'It's both of them,' Inge said. 'And the trouble is, Friedrich and Emmet will vote as a bloc. An alliance of three is dangerous.'

Liesel kept quiet. Inside, she was pleased to hear her uncle was moving against her brother. *These monsters can't be allowed to rule Brasingia.*

'You must kill him,' Leopold decided.

'You can't do that!' Liesel exclaimed.

Leopold struck the arm of the throne with his forearm. 'Why, by the gods? It would end the deadlock for good. I would inherit Barissia and be the only logical choice for emperor.'

'The Barissians wouldn't accept the murder of their duke. You'd start a civil war.'

'They'd accept it. Once I strung up a few dissenters. Most men are craven, Liesel,' he said, as if imparting some great wisdom. 'They'll fall into line once it's clear who's in charge.'

'That would be the last resort,' Inge said, putting a hand to her head. 'Though I'm not ruling it out. Better if we can assure ourselves of getting to four votes. That means firstly, ensuring Emlyn of Atrabia stays true. Salvinus regularly visits with him and doesn't waste a chance to remind him that what we did to Gavan, we can do to him. I doubt he'll switch allegiance. That just leaves Jeremias.'

'Well, Jeremias will elect me!' Leopold said with confidence. Then he frowned, looking at Inge's response. 'Won't he? He's my brother-in-law, for Gerhold's sake!'

'I think he will,' said Inge. 'But it wouldn't harm to remind him of his loyalty to us.' The witch looked at Liesel. 'How your father and the Kellish saved Rotelegen from the Isharites. How Leopold gave him his sister in marriage. How he and Katrina have two beautiful children. How lost they would be, if what happened to Gavan happened to their father.'

Liesel frowned. 'You want me to go to Guslar and speak with Jeremias?'

'Yes,' said the witch.

'And threaten him?'

'Don't be stupid, Liesel,' Inge said.

Inge rarely spoke with such hostility in her voice and Liesel tensed, fearful she'd made a bad mistake.

'You don't threaten him directly. You just make sure he knows what happened to Gavan here. What might happen to Gavan's son. You say how terrible Salvinus is, how powerful I am. You tell him what you saw in Thesse—how close the empire came to obliteration.

'Jeremias isn't the brightest man in Brasingia, but he knows all these things already. You remind him of these things to ensure he doesn't get ideas about discarding his alliance with us. Then you repeat it all to your sister. You're a clever girl when you put your mind to it, Liesel. I'm sure you are capable.'

'Of course I can do it,' said Liesel, pretending to be offended.

* * *

LIESEL WAS GIVEN a guard of three men and three women. She knew their role was to prevent her from escaping as much as it was to protect her. Not that escape was her plan. The last thing she wanted was to inflict herself on anyone else.

Every step of the journey from Essenberg to Guslar was taken on the Great Road, and it only required one night's stop. In the town of Herdorf, she stayed in a house owned by Leopold. From her bedroom window, she could see the hulking form of Burkhard Castle: two giant karst rocks that loomed over the surrounding territory.

It was where her father had staved off the hordes of Drobax and their Isharite masters. Until it was taken, prompting a hasty but successful retreat. She'd heard that no attempt had been made to restore the damaged fortress. Stone walls lay broken where they'd fallen and the bridge that had once linked the two crags had not been replaced. No one had the will to see it done.

She doubted that Leopold ever would. Her brother thought only of himself, not the realm. He even seemed disinterested in Ezenachi and the threat the creature posed. He'd welcomed the death of Coen, not seeming to worry that if he took the imperial title, he might be next.

She sighed, making herself look away. She felt lonely and couldn't wait to see her sister.

BY LATE AFTERNOON the next day, their little party had made it to Guslar. The Rotelegen capital was a Persaleian city by design, built to a plan: straight roads everywhere, leading to the central square. Here lay the ducal castle, a Brasingian stone monstrosity amid the elegance of its surroundings. Guslar was a distinctive, proud city, on the up since it had been deserted during the Isharite invasion. In pure size, though, Liesel could tell, it held only a fraction of the population of Essenberg.

Her brother-in-law's officials were quick to welcome her and get her settled in a pleasant guest room. After refreshing herself from the journey, she was taken down to the main hall.

'Liesel!' cried Katrina.

There was her sister, two little children in tow. The only thing that stopped Liesel from running over while screaming was that it might scare her niece and nephew. She walked sedately, like the daughter of an emperor was supposed to. After embracing her sister, both trying not to cry, she knelt down and took the hand of her niece.

'I'm so pleased to meet you, Hilde. You look just like your mother.'

The girl looked up at her mother doubtfully.

'Say hello to your auntie, Hilde.'

'Hello Auntie Liesel,' the girl said, and Liesel fell in love.

She stood to get a peek at her nephew, wrapped in blankets and held tight in his mother's arms. 'And Stefan looks like his father,' Liesel observed.

'Yes,' Katrina agreed. 'I've just got him to go to sleep. But you can hold him later.'

They left the hall and walked through the gardens. After a while, Hilde held Liesel's hand, and she thought she was in heaven.

'Your children are adorable, Katrina.'

'I wondered when you would get a chance to see them. When I heard what happened, that you'd been taken back to Essenberg, I feared the worst. Yet here you are! How did you manage that?'

Liesel's mind returned her to the visit to Idris's cell. But her sister didn't need to know those details. 'I've convinced Inge I'm a changed woman. Loyal and trustworthy. It was actually her idea to send me here.'

'She trusts you that much?'

'Not really. I have guards with me. It's a gamble on her part, I suppose. She wants me to speak to you and Jeremias.'

'Oh. I see,' said Katrina, a nervous look coming to her face. 'Still, a few guards couldn't stop us spiriting you away somewhere.'

Liesel shrugged. 'I don't know where to go that would be safe. For the people who took me in more so than myself. I'm in no immediate danger.' *But Idris would be if I betrayed Leopold a second time.* 'Inge has agreed that my friend from Atrabia can come and stay with me. I'm alright.'

'That's such a relief to hear. It gives us time. Uncle Walter has spoken to us about you. You know what he's like. He wants to get you away from them again. But with everything going on right now—'

'I understand. And you? I need you to tell me everything I've missed.'

'Honestly, apart from worrying about you, the last few years have been bliss. I have these two little ones now. And I know it sounds awful to say it, but when Jeremias's mother passed away, it made my life so much happier.'

'Katrina!' Liesel gasped, nodding at her niece. Hilde shouldn't hear such words.

'I know. But she was an old hag. And the people here were so used to doing what she told them they didn't seem able to stop. At last, I feel like I am the duchess of Rotelegen, not her. It's like a dark cloud over Guslar has gone. I've given Jeremias and the people an heir and, well…I feel loved. And blessed.'

'I'm so happy for you,' Liesel said.

'Thank you. And really, the last thing I want is to see what I have here threatened.'

It was an ominous statement. Liesel could understand her sister's point of view. She swallowed her response, rather than saying it out loud. *Good luck with that, sister.*

IN THE EVENING, Liesel dined with Jeremias and Katrina in their main hall. They were alone at the top table—their children elsewhere, occupied by their nursemaid.

'So, Inge sent you?' Jeremias asked.

'She and Leopold have become worried about the election. They're convinced Uncle Walter has come to an agreement with Friedrich of Thesse. If true, it means they need to make sure they have your vote.'

Jeremias and Katrina gave one another a long look.

'It's true,' Jeremias said at last. 'Walter has made contact. He says Barissia, Thesse and Gotbeck are ready to make me emperor.'

Liesel's jaw dropped. A plan to make Jeremias emperor? She was quick to see her uncle's thinking; quick to admire it. Jeremias might be reluctant to risk his alliance with Kelland. But an offer of the imperial title itself could persuade him like nothing else. And Jeremias was infinitely preferable to Leopold.

'And what have you said?' she asked.

'That I'd consider it.'

'You must say yes,' Liesel said.

'Why must he?' Katrina demanded. 'Why risk everything we have here and earn the wrath of Inge?'

'Because Jeremias would become emperor. You would be empress, Katrina.'

'I don't care about that,' her sister said. She exchanged another look with Jeremias. 'And it's naïve to think Inge would accept such an outcome. It's the lives of our children we would risk as well as our own.'

Liesel frowned. 'I don't think even Inge would take it out on your children.'

'Stefan is Leopold's heir right now,' Katrina said. 'I know Leopold. He would see him as a threat.'

Katrina's words had more than a hint of paranoia to them. But Liesel knew she was right about one thing. Inge and Leopold weren't likely to shrug and accept the outcome if Jeremias was elected. But there was more to this.

'What's the alternative?' Liesel asked her sister. 'Allow Leopold to become emperor? Bad enough in itself. But I was there in Thesse, Katrina. I saw Ezenachi and what he did. The empire's facing a threat not so different from the one our father had to deal with. You think Leopold is the person to handle it?'

'You want my husband to take Ezenachi on?' Katrina asked. 'Besides,' she added, sharing another look with Jeremias. 'Father wasn't always the hero you make him out to be.'

'I know,' Liesel admitted. For a moment, she was transported back to the chapel in Essenberg Castle. Inge whispering in her ear about her relationship with their father. Something else she would spare her sister. Or did the look she had shared with her husband mean Katrina already knew about it? 'But Brasingia needs to do something. If Leopold is elected, it could be the end for all of us. Rotelegen will not be immune if the empire disintegrates.'

'Or it could all just blow over,' Katrina said. 'We keep ourselves to ourselves and survive. What's the point in making enemies of these forces and drawing them down on us?'

Liesel studied Jeremias. She could tell he was in two minds. He was, more than anything else, a survivor. His father and brothers slain when he was a child, his duchy taken from him. He'd regained his birth right against the odds. Now he faced an unenviable choice. Whichever path he took might lead to his destruction.

She pushed her food around her trencher. An unpleasant thought had come to her. What if all the choices and paths they had before them ended with the same result? She shook her head. Surely the gods could not be so cruel?

SANC

KINGDOM OF MAGNIA, 675

King Edgar sent messengers to the other forts in the chain, warning them of the new threat from the north. The Caladri ships would have made landfall by now. Ezenachi's enslaved warriors would be marching on Magnian soil.

Time seemed to drag. It was excruciating, simply waiting for the enemy to arrive. But Edgar's strategy was defence, and he didn't have the numbers to confront the enemy out in the open. The day wore on and there was no enemy to be seen.

The king came to speak with them as the sun set. 'What if they ignore us and march deeper into Magnia?' he asked Herin.

Herin had commanded armies, and Edgar valued his opinion. Or perhaps, Sanc realised, he could talk to Herin as an equal, instead of having to have all the answers. Leadership looked like a lonely place.

'The Caladri will have landed men on the south coast and secured the area,' Herin suggested. 'The Cordentines will have crossed into Magnia, with the goal of meeting up with the Caladri. I would place serious money on them coming here. Taking these forts will allow the Lippers to join with them, head north unimpeded and bring supplies overland.'

Edgar nodded. 'Maybe I should have marched north when we saw the ships. Abandoned these forts.'

Herin shrugged. 'Depends. You wanted to buy your kingdom some time. Ask for aid. This is the best way to do that.'

'Yes,' Edgar agreed. 'That's what I wanted.'

The king wished them good night and left them to it.

Sanc sat, pulling his cloak about him. He didn't feel like sleep. A fire burned at one end of the hall, but otherwise it was pitch black. Rimmon and Herin were a presence nearby, even if he couldn't make them out in the darkness. He felt the absence of Jesper by his side.

'I fear we must make provision for a worst-case scenario,' came Rimmon's voice, to one side of Sanc. He said it quietly, not wanting the Magnians to overhear.

'Go on,' said Herin. He was in front of them, lying down.

'I can teleport a few of us out of here should the fort fall to the enemy. There would be risks involved, and I would have to leave myself enough spare power to do it. If Ezenachi comes, he could stop me. I have escaped him in the past, and he may have learned from it.'

'Ezenachi might come?' Sanc asked. Their situation was terrifying enough without that thought.

'He might,' Herin said. 'If you two frustrate his plans enough. There's no way I'm letting myself be captured again, by the way.'

'I can't let him capture me, either,' Rimmon said. 'He would use me against the nations of Dalriya. But it's Sanc that matters the most. He's the one who has the potential to save us. By travelling to another world and finding a power that can match Ezenachi. If Sanc is lost, we all are.'

There was a silence as Rimmon's words sank in. Sanc found himself grateful for the darkness, so they could not see the fear in his eyes.

'So, what are you saying?' Herin asked.

'I'm saying we must be ready to leave. Ready to leave the people we fight with behind. That will not be easy.'

* * *

THE NIGHT PASSED WITHOUT INCIDENT. The first warriors to arrive came from neither north nor south, but from the west. Magnians, bringing hard news for their king. The westernmost fort in the chain had been lost in a night-time attack, led by the Caladri sorcerer.

Sanc could feel the noose tightening on them, and he went up to the battlements. It felt better to look out across the terrain and watch for the enemy's approach than wait inside.

He was one of the first to see the cavalry force coming down the coast road towards them. The warriors on duty shouted a warning and soon King Edgar appeared, his lieutenants with him.

'It's Wilchard!' someone cried.

Indeed, Sanc could make out the royal steward. He rode with other Magnians, perhaps as many as two hundred, easily distinguished from the nations who served Ezenachi.

'Thank Toric they escaped,' Edgar said, some good humour entering his voice for the first time in days. 'Let's get the gate open for them.'

'Wait,' Sanc said. His eyes trained on Wilchard, he noticed the familiar dead eyes he had observed in Herin. 'He's turned. They all are.'

'It's true,' confirmed a warrior with eyesight as keen as Sanc's.

Edgar looked from Sanc to Wilchard. 'No. It can't be.' He looked at Sanc with a mute appeal in his eyes, as if it would change Sanc's mind.

Sanc didn't know what to say and returned his gaze to Wilchard's Magnians. They stopped close to the gatehouse, looking up silently at the battlements.

One of Edgar's lieutenants drew their attention to a second force on the road behind the cavalry. This was a much larger host, arriving on foot. As they neared, Sanc could see it comprised both Cordentines and Caladri. They kept coming, hundreds becoming thousands. It was exactly as Herin had predicted: they had come to clear the forts.

Rimmon and Herin arrived on the scene. They looked out grimly at the new arrivals.

'Expect a force from the south,' Herin said, gesturing to the other side of the fort.

With reluctance, Edgar drew his gaze from his lost friend. 'Defend the walls!' he ordered. Then he pointed at Sanc and his friends. 'I must speak with you.'

The king strode over to them. He looked around, assuring himself there were no eavesdroppers. 'I need you to rescue Wilchard,' he said. 'Bring him back, like you did with Herin.'

Rimmon gave the king a sharp look. 'That is near impossible. How can we capture him when he is surrounded by an army?'

'With magic, of course,' Edgar hissed. 'You would do it for someone you valued. Well, I need Wilchard. He is my most trusted adviser. And my best friend.' Grief and anger played out on the king's face, threatening to overwhelm him.

'We will do what we can,' Rimmon said reluctantly. 'But getting ourselves killed in a half-baked rescue attempt will only make the situation more hopeless.'

Edgar closed his eyes, breathing deeply. When he opened them, a measure of control had returned. 'I know I already owe you much, Rimmon. Just—if it's possible. Please do it.'

'I understand,' Rimmon said, placing a hand on the man's shoulder. 'But focus your mind on the people who still fight for you now. We have work to do.'

HERIN WAS PROVED correct once more. The Lippers arrived from the south in numbers that equalled those to the north, led by the Caladri sorcerer. It was impossible to know whether the other forts still stood, or if the Red Fort was the last. It seemed the attackers to the north had been waiting for their allies, because now Wilchard raised a hand and the Cordentines and Caladri moved closer, surrounding the fort on all sides. Some carried long wooden ladders, which they readied for the assault.

'Look here,' Herin called from the gatehouse wall. Sanc and Rimmon joined him. The Lippers had ladders as well, but Herin pointed to a large battering ram being wheeled towards the gates. A canopy of animal hides protected the engine's operators. It was soon prickled with arrows, but even fire arrows got nowhere, failing to spread their flames to the contraption.

Rimmon looked at Sanc. 'Let's see what we can do.'

They both held a hand out towards the siege engine and released their magic. The weight of it resisted them at first, but then it rose. Another burst of power and it toppled over to one side. The Magnian archers fired at the Lippers inside, revealed like insects under a rock.

A blast of magic came at Sanc's position, but Rimmon blocked it.

Sanc looked for its source. The Caladri wizard looked at them with a blank stare. She was blonde haired, slim, of indeterminate age. She looked no different to the other Caladri he could see, and she was a wisp of a thing, really. But looks can be deceptive.

When Sanc sent a volley of magic at her, she negated it as if it was nothing. Rimmon had told him, plenty of times, that defence was the easiest of spells, and Sanc declined to waste more energy on the enemy sorcerer. If they continued to target the Lipper siege engines, the enemy would still struggle to breach the walls.

Frantic shouts came from the north walls and, with a grudging look at one another, Sanc, Rimmon, and Herin left their position and made their way to the source. As they reached the north walls, Sanc got a shock. Turned Cordentines—men and women of all ages—had somehow climbed the walls and were on the battlements. A swathe of Magnian fighters lay dead in their wake, and they were threatening to overrun the battlements completely.

As he ran towards them, Sanc sent blasts of magic at those he could see. Rimmon joined in and Herin let off an arrow before discarding his bow and drawing his sword. Seeing this, Sanc did the same.

'Careful!' Rimmon warned him.

But Sanc was keen to see action. Whilst Herin wielded his sword two-handed, Sanc combined his sword with his magic. He exulted in the power he had. He had never been a great fighter, but the combination of the two was exhilarating. His magic could defend him while he swung his blade—so much more versatile than a shield, it could protect him from head to toe. Then, in an instant, he could switch his approach, using his magic as an offensive weapon, his sword becoming a blocking tool. Hacking one enemy down, blasting away the next, he cut his way through to the source of the Cordentine offensive, Herin fighting at his side.

The problem was obvious. A ladder, propped up over the top of the fort's battlements, had a magical aura around it, preventing the Magnian defenders from getting close. With Herin protecting him, he built up his power, then blasted the ladder. The top part of the ladder exploded into splinters.

He peered down, searching. Rimmon joined him.

'There,' Sanc said, pointing out a Caladri figure who was looking up at them from the centre of a unit of Caladri fighters, hand outstretched.

Rimmon sent an arc of fire at the Caladri sorcerer, who placed a disc of defensive magic above himself until the fire burned out. Revealed to the defenders, the Caladri was then forced to defend himself from a hail of arrows.

Rimmon pulled Sanc away from the edge of the battlements. 'So, they have two magi, one on each side,' he said. 'Both are well protected by warriors. We could try to take one out, but that's a mighty risk. And it would give the other the chance to breach the fort's defences.'

'What do you think we should do?' Sanc asked.

'The safer option is for us to split up. We each defend one wall. Keep an eye on the west and east walls as best we can. They'll struggle to repeat their success if one of us is trained on them all the time.'

Sanc nodded. It sounded more sensible. There were so many Turned down there—so many more of them than the Magnians had—that Sanc was sure the walls were their only chance of survival. If they made a breach, it would all be over very quickly.

'Stay with him, Herin,' Rimmon said, before returning to the other side of the fort.

Sanc looked at his blood-stained weapon as the people he had killed were tossed over the side of the battlements onto the attackers below. Men and women who had been turned by Ezenachi—innocent, since they had no control over what they did—he had slain. Of course, they would have killed the Magnian defenders. Even so, he felt sick at what he had done—at the exultation he had felt while he did it.

Herin noticed and took his sword from him, cleaning it of gore. 'It's not as easy as in the stories, eh?' the warrior said. 'Here,' he said, returning the weapon. 'You can sheathe it now.'

Sanc did as Herin suggested and took up position on the northern battlements. What proceeded was a test of focus against a Turned Caladri sorcerer. The Cordentines approached the walls, pushing their long ladders up against them. The Magnians used poles to push them away and axes to break off the top sections.

Sanc's opponent would protect the ladder and the attackers who climbed it; Sanc would smash through the protection. The Caladri would send a blast of magic, which Sanc had to defend. Occasionally, he was targeted by Caladri archers from down below. His opponent was targeted just as frequently.

The contest continued and Sanc lost grip of time. It wasn't possible for either of them to win, since they negated each other's power. More likely to swing the outcome would be a lapse of concentration. Sanc worried about it. The Caladri was a puppet of Ezenachi —mindless, he would keep going forever. Sanc was inexperienced. He started to wonder whether an attack on the sorcerer might have been the better option. That said, the enemy were prepared for that, too. Surrounded by armed Caladri, a direct attack on the sorcerer looked almost suicidal.

Sanc was slow to notice the new power that joined the siege, concentrating as he was on his contest with his Caladri opponent. A fizz and dryness in the mouth. Then a shaking, as if the Red Fort moved back and forth.

The voice he heard screaming sounded familiar. He turned, searching for the origin. He saw Rimmon, wild-eyed with terror. Sanc knew what it must be before Rimmon got his words out.

'He comes!' Rimmon cried. 'We must leave!' The sorcerer didn't wait for a response, hurtling down the stone steps into the depths of the fort.

The warriors of Magnia had stopped. They looked from the departing sorcerer to Sanc. Herin looked at him. Edgar looked at him.

'What of my followers?' asked the king, his voice sombre.

'Everyone get to the hall,' Sanc shouted. 'Now!'

He followed Rimmon down the steps, knowing there was no time to debate it. Either they followed or they didn't.

They followed. Almost every warrior left in the fort, it seemed, packing into the hall. Hundreds of them, Edgar and Herin among them.

'I can't get this many out,' Rimmon said to him. Frustration vied with panic on his face.

'I can,' Sanc said, trying to lend him some calm.

'We've been casting magic for hours,' Rimmon argued. 'We don't have the reserves left to bring this many.'

'Use mine,' Sanc assured him. 'If we don't make it, at least we died trying to save people.'

Rimmon let out a breath. Sanc's words seemed to work, as if leaving it to fate removed his doubts. 'Link hands,' he commanded those assembled, grabbing Sanc's.

Herin grabbed hold of Rab before taking Sanc's other hand.

'Use my power, Rimmon.' Sanc said.

Rimmon looked at him with a strange expression. As if reminding himself who Sanc was. 'I'll have to choose a closer location if we're to stand a chance of this working.'

'So be it.'

Rimmon closed his eyes.

Sanc fed him his magic and Rimmon took it, greedy for his power. It left him in waves, and he cried out in pain. He felt the fort shake again. Dust and rubble fell from the ceiling. The sound of a wall collapsing.

'He's here,' Rimmon hissed through clenched teeth.

Fear clutched at Sanc. Then he felt his stomach swim with the sensation of moving. His sight left him, though he felt it when they exploded through the stone wall of the hall. Then his hearing went. He could still feel the hands he clutched in his. One was Rimmon's, still feeding on Sanc's power. It was impossible to put a time on how long they travelled like this.

They stopped. Sanc opened his eyes, then shut them again when dizziness hit him so hard, he thought he would faint. He realised he was gulping in air; could feel his chest panting with the exertion. He slowed his breathing and felt his body gradually relax.

He opened his eyes once more. He saw his hands. His fingers had dug through the turf he knelt on, into the soil underneath. The smell of vomit assailed him.

He staggered to his feet, looking around. Everyone had made it. But many were stretched out or doubled over, losing the contents of their stomachs.

Then, close by, he saw Herin knelt beside Rimmon. His teacher was pale and lifeless, blood tricking from his nose. Sanc lurched over.

'He's alright, lad. Well, he's breathing, at least.'

Sanc looked at Rimmon, worried. The Haskan had told him plenty of times: if a sorcerer overuses their magic, they can lose it. Forever. Had he pushed Rimmon too hard by insisting they all leave? How would he live with himself?

'Don't worry, Sanc,' Herin said, sensing his concern. 'You did a brave thing. No one could fault you for it.'

'Agreed,' Edgar declared, walking over. 'I thought I would never see my wife again.' He gestured at his warriors. 'I wasn't the only one. Now we have a chance.'

He offered his hand. Sanc took it, and the king embraced him.

'Well,' Herin said, looking about them. They had travelled to a hillock. Open country surrounded them. 'I know where we are. May I suggest we get moving?'

'What about Rimmon?' Sanc asked.

'Help me get him up. I can carry him.'

As they began moving him, Rimmon woke. He looked about wildly, before realising where he was. Herin helped him to his feet. He stood, legs wobbling. 'We did it,' he said to Sanc, evidently surprised.

'Are you alright?' Sanc asked him. 'Your magic?'

'Yes. I can sense it. I did as you asked and used whatever you could offer. You are fine, too?'

'I feel drained,' Sanc admitted. 'Nauseous.'

'I'm surprised you don't feel worse. You used a lot of power. Not to mention the teleportation itself. That's enough to mess with anyone.'

'Thank you for getting us out,' Edgar said to the sorcerer as Rimmon took in some deep breaths.

'You're welcome, Your Majesty. May I suggest you get your people moving? We are not so very far from the Red Fort. And if it's not already apparent, Sanc and I have no reserves left to get us out of further trouble.'

The Magnians wasted no time in moving. Nervous looks were cast behind them. Nervous looks were cast ahead, too, since they couldn't be sure that the invaders hadn't already passed this way. But without a single horse between them, there wasn't much anyone could do except put one foot in front of the other.

At first, they looked a sorry lot, but the exercise and fresh air gradually removed the effects of the teleportation and Sanc was impressed with the pace they were able to set. Rimmon suffered with it the most. But the sorcerer's fear propelled him on. He didn't once ask for a rest.

It had been a long day, but they pushed until the light faded. Then came a discussion about whether to walk through the night. Perhaps, if they hadn't survived a siege that day, they would have. But many were dead on their feet and a night march would doubtless see some fall behind, get lost, or even injured.

When the outskirts of a village came into view, the debate was settled. They would sleep, and with any luck, find food and drink.

The village would also offer the first clue as to the situation in Magnia. As they walked past the first buildings, it soon became clear it was deserted.

'No signs of a struggle,' Herin commented. 'I don't think the enemy has got this far.'

They waited as Edgar sent his men into houses. They were all empty. Some scraps of food were found, but most things of value had been taken. A group of soldiers came back from their investigations with an older man.

'Your Majesty,' one of them said to Edgar, presenting the man. 'He says they were all told to leave. On Queen Elfled's orders.'

Sanc saw the visible relief on the king's face—his wife had made it out. Of course, that meant Jesper had, too. It was the news they had all needed to hear.

'You didn't follow my queen's orders?' Edgar asked the villager.

'Your Majesty,' the man said with a bow. 'I told them I trusted that you and our fine boys would hold the pass against the Lippers. No need for everyone to overreact and leave.'

'We didn't hold the pass,' Edgar said sternly. 'Barely escaped with our lives. And the enemy has come through the Cordentine border, anyway. You're lucky it was I who came through here first, not those killers.' He paused, eyeing the man, who looked suitably chastened. 'You'll leave with us in the morning.'

'Yes, Your Majesty.'

Edgar set up a watch around the village. It didn't involve Sanc or Rimmon, who were both desperately tired by this point. They lay down in one of the empty houses, on empty stomachs. Herin sat by the door with Rab, peering outside. His presence helped Sanc to feel secure, and he soon gave in to sleep.

PEYRE

DUCHY OF MORBAINE, 675

Peyre left Valennes with a score of companions. There was his good friend Umbert, and Umbert's father, Lord Russell. They would help him with the government of Morbaine. Elger led the Barissian Guard who had served Peyre ever since he had left Colde-berg for Valennes two years ago. They had no loyalty to any other lord in Guivergne. They owed their positions to him alone, and he had rewarded them generously. Such things were important in Peyre's mind. Almost all the original group had stayed with him. The only noteworthy absentee was Syele, and she now served Loysse in Famiens, at his request.

They took the roads south through Guivergne. Then, through the newly conquered lands of the Midder Steppe, now as much a part of Guivergne as any other. Peyre had been there for the conquest; had been sent into exile in Brasingia at the end of it. It was strange to recall those moments. His uncle, the king, at loggerheads with his father, the duke of Morbaine. Who would have thought both brothers would be gone so soon? *Now it is Esterel and I who hold those titles. I hope we don't make the same mistakes they did.*

Once they crossed into Morbaine, Lord Russell manoeuvred his mount next to Peyre. 'Where would you like to start?' he asked. 'It is usual to stop at half a dozen towns to meet with the nobility of each region.'

'Would it be wrong to go to Arbeost?' Peyre asked him. 'I'm being sentimental, I suppose.'

'Not at all. That is one advantage of being duke. You get to decide. And after all, your father ruled from there.'

'Then let's spend a night or two at the Chateau and plan a route around Morbaine.'

You get to decide. *Of course I do,* Peyre reprimanded himself. *I will have to get used to it. After all, Esterel slipped into the role of king easily enough.*

Umbert rode ahead to warn the Chateau of their arrival. Finding an extra twenty mouths to feed would doubtless take a bit of preparation. Not to mention finding somewhere for them all to sleep.

When they reached the village, it looked just the same. At the Chateau, he took his father's rooms to live in. *You are the duke now,* he reminded himself. It was as he sat alone and looked about the room his father had slept in that it finally sank in. *He's not coming back,* he told himself. *You are in charge, Peyre.*

The steward of The Chateau fed them in the hall. All twenty of them sat together at a long table. Peyre hadn't met the man before—an appointment of Florent, Esterel's friend, apparently. Indeed, there were few faces he *did* recognise. He couldn't help finding it a little sad. The people who mattered to him didn't live in Arbeost any longer, so what was the place to him now?

'Any old memories returning?' Umbert asked him. 'Like sneaking food from the kitchen and riding off for the day.'

Peyre had to smile at that. 'Aye. Carefree days, weren't they?'

'I never did find out what the pair of you got up to on those expeditions,' Lord Russell said.

Peyre shared a look with Umbert.

'I am sworn to secrecy, father,' Umbert informed him.

'I see. It's like that, is it?'

The steward approached the table. 'A man by the name of Jesper is requesting an audience, Your Grace,' he said to Peyre. 'He insists it's of the utmost urgency.'

'Of course. Let him in.'

Jesper was soon striding towards them. Peyre could tell from his demeanour he had serious news to impart; and from his mud-stained riding clothes and fatigued appearance, that he had been riding hard.

'Come,' said Umbert, clearly reaching the same conclusion as he got to his feet. 'Let's find Jesper space at the table.' He grabbed a chair and placed it opposite Peyre.

When Peyre gestured for Jesper to take it, he sank down with gratitude. The forester took a cup of watered wine, downing it quickly with a shaking hand.

'News about Sanc?' Peyre asked him, fearful for his brother.

'About Sanc and about Magnia, Your Highness. When I heard you were come into Morbaine, I came here as fast as I could.'

'Your Grace,' Lord Russell said, correcting him.

When Jesper frowned, Peyre felt the need to explain. 'Esterel has made me duke of Morbaine. That's why I'm here.'

'Ah,' Jesper acknowledged. 'Please accept my apologies. My condolences for the loss of your father, the king. So much has happened it slipped my mind.'

'Of course, Jesper,' Peyre said. 'Please tell us.'

The light of hope found its way to a face that had looked so grim, as Jesper considered Peyre anew. 'We travelled south with King Edgar, to the chain of forts the Magnians hold against the Lippers. There were renewed attacks on these that we had to fight off. Then, one morning, we saw Caladri ships. Heading for the south coast of Magnia. The king and his advisers thought it inevitable the enemy would also come from the border with Cordence. The king stayed in his fort with Sanc and Rimmon. Their plan was to delay the enemy and give his people time to escape.'

Peyre didn't know where to start first. Sanc trapped in a fort while Ezenachi's army surrounded them from all sides? And then there were his new responsibilities. 'So Ezenachi's conquests continue,' he said. 'And if Magnia falls, this creature will get as far as the border with Morbaine?'

'Precisely,' Jesper said. 'I left the fort in the company of Queen Elfled of Magnia, to seek help. When I left her, she was making plans for the evacuation of her people north. I can't say what has happened to Sanc and the king, or how much territory the Magnians have conceded.

'But King Edgar and Rimmon made it clear they needed the help of Guivergne. That you are here in Morbaine may be great fortune, Peyre. You could raise an army and head south far quicker than if I had to travel on to Valennes.' The forester looked from Peyre's face to Lord Russell's and back again. 'I know it's a lot that I ask. But this is the message I was asked to bring. Speaking of which, Sanc asked me to deliver this,' he said, taking a folded piece of parchment from inside his tunic and handing it to Peyre.

'Even if His Grace felt able to act without the consent of the king,' Lord Russell said, 'it would be with the army of Morbaine only. I sympathise with the plight of the Magnians. But I would advise it would be far wiser to defend our own border and wait for King Esterel to hear this news.'

Peyre nodded, looking up after reading his brother's scrawl. 'Either way, an army must be raised immediately and taken south. We must inform the king as soon as possible. Though regarding my right to act, I am the duke, and such a title brings certain advantages.' He allowed himself a slight smile as he looked at Lord Russell. 'I get to decide.'

* * *

JESPER WAS CLEARLY EXHAUSTED, and so Peyre made the hard decision to send Umbert and Elger back to Valennes with a message for Esterel. They were the men he trusted most, and with the best horses and a spare each, he was sure at least one of them would make it to Valennes within a week.

Everyone else left Arbeost for their tour of Morbaine. Peyre's visit to his duchy had taken on a new importance. He was grateful for Lord Russell's skills of organisation and diplomacy as they spoke with each group of noblemen and asked for their help.

As for the warriors they recruited, they were easy to convince. Peyre knew most of them from the campaigns in Guivergne. There was a bond of shared experience that made the task much easier. Peyre received the sympathy of the men who had fought under his father and helped put Bastien on the throne.

Then there were the newcomers, mostly younger men, who seemed keen to serve. The veterans of the campaign in Guivergne had returned home with tales of victory and purses full of coin. Enthusiasm to fight for Peyre was high. He didn't mention they would face a very different enemy, with little chance of enrichment. But privately, he worried what he was leading these people into and felt a weight of responsibility for them he had never experienced before.

When all was done, four thousand warriors congregated in the south-east corner of the duchy. The locals had no information that added to what Jesper had already delivered. Rumours of war had come to Morbaine, but that was all.

'I see little point in sitting here,' Peyre said to his council of noble leaders. 'Even if Esterel were to do everything in his power to join us, his army would still be two weeks away.'

He got nods of agreement from some; looks of concern from others. Their willingness to venture into Magnia varied considerably from one man to the next. Peyre knew his job wasn't to convince them all. If he gave a clear order, they would come because he'd told them to. Their private thoughts, they would keep to themselves, or at least to some hushed conversations with those they knew agreed with them.

More of a concern was the logistical support. Peyre knew very well that his father worked for days if not weeks before a campaign, on getting the right supplies in place. For all Lord Russell's help with this, they'd simply not had the time. Four thousand was a lot of mouths to feed. Any intervention in Magnia would, from necessity, need to be brief.

'I will take three thousand into Magnia with me,' he told them. 'Lord Russell will oversee the rest here. They will be busy fortifying the border.'

Ideally, Peyre would have taken Lord Russell with him. But he had one eye on the worst of outcomes. What if his force were defeated, and he was killed? At least he wouldn't be leaving his duchy completely undefended.

Once the division was organised, Peyre wasted no time in leading his force into Magnia. He was aware the Magnian army might be desperate for help and the difference of a day or even a few hours could be the difference between success and failure. He travelled at the front of the column, while behind him, most of his warriors marched on foot. Jesper led mounted scouts ahead of the army. It wasn't just a matter of looking out for enemies. The local Magnians needed reassurance about the army that passed through their lands.

It took a full day's march until Peyre was able to get a better grip on the task he faced. Jesper directed the army to head south-west to the town of Radstock. The town burghers were welcoming and helped them pitch camp in the fields outside town. There was no room inside because Radstock was already full of Magnian refugees from the south.

When Peyre met with the burghers, they did their best to help in other ways, sending some food for his hungry soldiers. Clearly, though, they were already stretched. But they had been in communication with Queen Elfled.

'What warriors she has are occupying the castles on the old border between North and South Magnia,' one of them explained. 'If you can take your army there, it will make a huge difference,' he added.

'The queen doesn't have a large army?' Peyre asked.

The man made a face. 'She doesn't really have an army at all. Most fighting men were stationed on the border with the Lippers.'

'Any news of them?'

'No. Only that there are Cordentines, Caladri and Lippers heading north as they please through Magnia. We just hope the king hasn't fallen.'

Peyre nodded. *As I hope the same for my brother.*

SANC

KINGDOM OF MAGNIA, 675

Edgar roused his troops before sunrise. Sanc struggled to wake. His body craved more sleep. His magic was far from replenished. Some harsh words from Herin got him to his feet, however. Then they were all walking again, still in darkness. At least they now had a road to follow north, leading them into the rich heartland of Magnia.

'The enemy front cannot be that far behind us,' Herin mused, as a band of orange spread on the eastern horizon and pinks and purples appeared in the sky above. 'I wonder what Ezenachi's plan is.'

'How do you mean?' Sanc asked, not understanding what he was getting at.

'This invasion follows on closely from the conquest of Cordence. Is his goal Magnia only? Does he intend to press on further?'

Further north meant Morbaine, and a protective feeling for his homeland came over Sanc. For the first time in a while, he thought of his family, dealing with the loss of their father.

'Because for all that they're winning,' Herin continued, 'his numbers are not overwhelming.'

They seemed overwhelming to Sanc. But then, he thought,

suppose Guivergne and Brasingia raised great armies against Ezenachi. Would they not then have the advantage in numbers?

'He does not yet have the numbers,' Rimmon agreed.

'But he stopped the entire Brasingian army,' Sanc said. 'So what difference do numbers make, anyway?' With a shudder, he recalled the sensation as the god approached the Red Fort. The fantasy he had allowed himself in his most private thoughts—that he would be the hero who would defeat Ezenachi—had vanished in an instant.

'That's the point, Sanc,' Rimmon said. 'It is still Ezenachi himself who makes the difference in battle. That is why there is hope—kill him and Dalriya survives. Ezenachi is not all powerful. If he was, he would have taken the forts himself and wiped us out. He didn't. He only came to the Red Fort when we were holding off his forces. Perhaps attracted by our use of magic, as well. Think of how we feel today after our expenditure yesterday. Then think how much Ezenachi expended to immobilise an imperial army thousands strong. It costs him Sanc, like it would cost any magic user. He cannot do it day after day. But the longer this goes on—the more realms he destroys—the more the balance tips in his favour.'

Sanc nodded his understanding. 'So, it comes back to your plan to find help from some other world?'

'Yes. It always comes back to that.'

They walked all morning, passing through villages and towns, all emptied of people. Just after midday, they saw the horseman. He was some distance away, on a high rocky ridge, looking in their direction.

'He must be a scout,' Herin said, some relief in his voice.

The Magnian soldiers waved at the rider. Edgar told them to stop when some started shouting.

The horseman left his position, and the Magnians kept walking, with more of a spring in their step than before.

The next sighting came mid-afternoon. A score of riders heading straight for them. King Edgar called a halt, and the Magnians peered ahead, trying to gain clues about who it might be. As they neared, Sanc noticed half a dozen of the horses were riderless. A little closer, and Edgar recognised one of the figures.

'Brictwin,' he said, pleased.

The king's long march was over. Sanc, Rimmon and Herin's too, since they were each given a mount. A few of the riders were ordered to stay with the rest of the Magnians, who still had a long way to walk. For Brictwin informed them the closest occupied settlement was Bidcote.

The riders wasted no time in departing north, leaving the hundreds of Magnians who remained on foot to jeer them—mostly in a good-natured way—as they left.

'Queen Elfled ordered that everywhere south of Bidcote should be evacuated and no protection given,' Brictwin told them as they rode. He looked at his king awkwardly. 'We had to work on the basis that you were lost, Your Majesty,' he said guiltily.

'Of course you did,' Edgar agreed. He glanced at Sanc. 'We almost were. Where is Elfled now?'

'She has withdrawn most of our forces to the castles that lie on the old border between North and South. It was agreed that was the best place to make a stand. Should we need to.'

Edgar raised an eyebrow at this. 'Seems the kingdom functions perfectly well in my absence.'

They reached Bidcote in the twilight. As he lay in bed, finally fed, Sanc considered the changes that had come to the king's estate. It was sparsely settled. People, animals, machines—even crops—had been taken north. It was some undertaking, but at what cost? Giving up so much land threatened to cause a famine.

Sanc considered the outcomes Elfled had been forced to weigh up. Arguably, hungry Magnians were a lesser evil than Magnians turned to do Ezenachi's bidding. Surely, their enemy had invaded the kingdom to win himself more slaves? So far, they had denied him the numbers he would have anticipated.

* * *

NEXT DAY they made the final leg of their journey north, through land not yet abandoned to the enemy. By mid-afternoon, they came upon the Magnian castles.

Brictwin led them to one of the largest of these, called Granstow. It was impressive, with stone walls, and towers in each corner. But it was no Red Fort. These castles were homes as well as fortresses—each one manned by a Magnian nobleman, with his family and servants. Their strength was in their number. If the Lippers and their allies got this far, they would find them everywhere, halting their progress in each town, each crossing of river or road, each high place.

They passed under the raised portcullis of the barbican and entered the lower bailey. A small group waited for them. Queen Elfled stood with her son, Ida; her bodyguard, Morlin, close by.

With a cry, Edgar leapt from his horse and ran to her, holding her to him. He grabbed his son next. It was an affecting scene. Sanc knew it would be played out many times over when the poor Magnian warriors from the Red Fort finished their long march.

Everyone else followed Edgar's lead and dismounted.

'I'll take your horse, Your Highness,' Brictwin told Sanc and took the reins from him.

'Come,' Elfled said to Sanc and his friends, 'get refreshments and tell me about your remarkable escape.'

'Aye,' Edgar said. 'Though we have much else to discuss and plan.'

'We must still find time to celebrate,' Elfled said, and Edgar didn't argue, beaming at his wife.

THEY STOOD in the hall of Granstow Castle as Edgar told the story of the assault on the Red Fort—the pain of seeing his friend Wilchard; the fear engendered by the arrival of Ezenachi; how Sanc and Rimmon had spirited them to safety. Elfled found the energy to react to each part of her husband's tale. But talk had to turn to their current predicament.

'I can't argue with your strategy,' he told his wife. 'A stand here, in the centre of the kingdom, makes the most sense. Though it almost broke my heart to travel through South Magnia emptied of people. They are being cared for?'

'Those who can't fight I sent north. It has been beyond my resources to organise their support, but I trust that the North Magnians will give them shelter.'

'What of Jesper,' Edgar asked, 'and his mission to Guivergne?'

'He wasted no time in continuing his journey northward. I have heard nothing from him since.'

Edgar nodded. 'We must prepare as if no help is coming. Hold these defences if we are able. If we cannot hold, I am lost as to what can be done. A retreat north, perhaps. Maybe our two wizards could repeat their heroics from the Red Fort?'

'I fear not, Your Majesty,' Rimmon said. 'Sanc and I have arrived at a hard decision. He must be sent away to fetch help for Dalriya.'

'But he is needed here!' Edgar declared.

'You think he can stop Ezenachi?'

'Maybe not. But we are in more trouble without him.'

'Sanc will always be needed,' Rimmon said. 'If Magnia falls, he will be needed to defend the next realm Ezenachi attacks. There will never be a good time to do this. Then, there is the other danger. Should Ezenachi capture and turn Sanc, it will give him a powerful tool to complete his conquests. You saw yourself how the Caladri magi he turned have given him new possibilities—to lead attacks even when he is not present.'

Edgar looked sorrowful. 'I understand what you say. Gods, I had hoped I would pass a strong kingdom onto my son. This is an inheritance of ash and blood.'

'Don't lose hope, Edgar,' Elfled murmured. 'You won't be going with him, Rimmon?'

'I will stay here. To coordinate the resistance as best I can. Our role is to give Sanc the time he needs to bring help.'

'If he can't?' Edgar asked.

'Then at least he escapes this.' Rimmon sighed. 'There is much I cannot see, I admit. Maybe I'm sending Sanc on a useless, dangerous quest. Maybe he'll be better off wherever he goes than here. But the basic truth is this: Ezenachi is too powerful for us. If we really want to save Dalriya, we need some other god who can match him.'

The small group looked at one another, the gravity of what they faced weighing on them.

You are happy with this, Sanc?' Edgar asked him.

'I see no other option,' Sanc admitted.

'You're sending him alone?' Elfled asked.

'He must be sent far away, Elfled,' Rimmon explained. 'An extra person is more cost. I am not even sure our magic can do it, though I am more confident than I was after what we managed a few days ago.'

'Try sending me,' Herin suggested.

'If I did,' Rimmon told his friend, 'Sanc would be the priority. I would sacrifice you if need be.'

'I'm dispensable,' Herin said. 'I know that. But a companion would be useful.'

'It would. If you are willing to risk your life, then so be it.'

'There's no need,' Sanc told Herin. 'I can look after myself.'

Herin grunted. 'You saved my life. That's how I see it. So we'd only be even.'

'Very well,' Rimmon said. 'Then there's no time like the present.'

'Now?' Sanc blurted. He needed time. Time to ready himself.

'There will never be a good time,' the sorcerer said.

'For goodness' sake,' Elfled said sharply. 'Let me get them a pack of supplies each first, at least!'

SANC WAITED with Rimmon and Herin on the grassy area outside the castle for the queen to bring them their provisions. Sanc sat on the ground, as the reality of what he was about to do threatened to unnerve him. He stroked Rab, which gave him a little comfort. If they were alone, he would have spoken to him, explained why he was leaving. But he didn't think the great heroes had stupid, one-sided conversations with animals.

He couldn't help feeling like he was running away, leaving these people to face catastrophe without him. He had got used to the idea of being a sorcerer—accepted, to a degree, that his powers were a blessing as well as a curse. But what was the point if he couldn't even protect those he loved from Ezenachi?

'You'll explain it to my brothers and sister?' he asked Rimmon.

'Of course. You trust me?' he asked, looking at both Sanc and Herin.

'As much as anyone, I suppose,' Herin said.

'You know, I once served Diis,' Rimmon reminded them, but he looked at Sanc. 'A god who came close to taking Dalriya for himself. I decided, with Herin, to turn on him. At the last minute, some might say. But I'd have rather died than helped him to enslave our world. I would do anything to stop Ezenachi. This, I believe, is the best chance we have.'

'Don't worry,' Sanc heard himself say. 'We've got this.'

Rimmon allowed himself a smile.

Elfled and Edgar returned with Morlin, who handed them each a pack.

Herin gave his a sniff.

'Meat, eggs, cheese, bread, wine,' Elfled told him. 'Blankets.'

'Not bad,' he acknowledged.

'Good luck,' Edgar told them.

Rimmon, Sanc, and Herin gripped each other's hands, forming a triangle. Sanc could feel his teacher begin the teleportation.

Rab whined.

'Don't worry, boy,' Sanc said to him, feeling himself choke up. 'It'll be alright.'

Sanc felt that nauseous sensation and began to move.

The dog ran at him and leapt.

Sanc let go of Herin's hand and caught Rab, pulling him into his chest.

His vision blurred until he lost it completely. Time seemed to disappear. His hearing left him. He felt the sensation of movement, of air rushing past his face. He could feel his grip on Rimmon's hand, his teacher drawing on his powers to help with the magic. He could feel Rab tucked into his chest. A dizziness pressed on him. He fought against it. Then the last of Sanc's senses deserted him.

PEYRE

KINGDOM OF MAGNIA, 675

It was a two-day march to the central belt of Magnia, where the castles built by earlier generations to fight one another were now being used to defend themselves from an external menace. The road south would take them to one such, Granstow, where it was said Queen Elfled had established her court.

The light was already disappearing when they came upon the first castle. It was located near the southern border of the old North Magnia. The family who owned it had done their best to make it ready, relying on only a few warriors, and the people who lived on their estate. They had been instructed to look south, either for allies to give shelter to or enemies to keep out. Beyond that, they knew little, except they had heard that King Edgar had joined his queen at Granstow. Peyre was not surprised they hadn't heard of one Sanc of Guivergne, but it still gave him some hope that his brother had escaped from the overwhelmed southern border.

He decided to keep the march going, driving his force on to reach Granstow. The sun left the sky and still they marched, content to know all they had to do was stick to the road they were on. When Jesper returned with his scouts to say that Granstow was up ahead, a cheer rose from the ranks, and Peyre breathed a sigh of relief.

A small group of riders appeared, some holding torches, as Peyre's army approached the castle walls that loomed in the darkness. He recognised the figure of Rimmon the sorcerer, the torches shedding enough light to illuminate his long, orange locks. He didn't realise King Edgar himself had come to meet him until Rimmon was introducing them to each other.

'Peyre is duke of Morbaine now,' Jesper offered, correcting his friend.

'I am sorry to hear of your father's death, Your Grace,' Edgar told Peyre. 'He was a good man.'

'Thank you, Your Majesty. Is Sanc here?' Peyre asked.

A shadow fell across Rimmon's face then. Was there guilt, too? 'He is not. There is much to explain. May I suggest we get you into the castle and get your warriors settled? Then we can explain all that has happened since we left Valennes.'

'Is he dead?' Peyre demanded.

'No. As far as I know, he lives.'

What weasel words were these?

'Come,' said the king, perhaps sensing Peyre's dissatisfaction. He looked at the warriors behind Peyre with some unease before gesturing to his castle. 'It is a complicated story. There is no way I can thank you enough for heeding our call for help in our darkest hour. But at least let me get you a bed and some supper. I promise I will tell you everything I know before I go to my own bed.'

'Very well,' Peyre said. Part of him had marched all this way to save Sanc, even if defending Morbaine was the reason he had given. Now, it sounded like the chances of even seeing him were small. But Edgar's look had been one he recognised well enough. There was magic to be discussed, and it seemed Edgar, just like Peyre's father, preferred to do that with as few people listening in as possible.

* * *

PEYRE WOKE in a bed in Granstow Castle. It would have been rude to turn the offer down and return to his troops. He had been ready to do it last night—full of anger at the story he'd been told about Sanc. Now, he wasn't sure what to think.

Sanc had saved the lives of King Edgar and many of his warriors. His reward? Sent to some far-off land, alone—well, with a dog and a Magnian for company—on a vague, madcap quest. But Peyre's outrage of last night had dissipated. Sanc wasn't a boy anymore. He had the right to make his own decisions. And it was debatable whether he'd have been any safer here.

Ezenachi's army was expected today. If Sanc were here, he'd have been in the thick of the fighting.

Sanc was a sorcerer. That was the reality Peyre had to accept. *My brother's life will never be safe or natural.*

He met with the inner circle of the Magnian defence: the king and queen, Rimmon, and Jesper. It was noticeable that no other Magnians were there. But Edgar had told him about the fate of his friend and steward, Wilchard—turned by Ezenachi's followers into an enemy. It seemed this man had been a key cog in the kingdom's government and Peyre equated it to if his father had lost Lord Russell.

'The nearest enemy is three hours march from Granstow,' Jesper informed them. 'They do not make camp like a regular army, but lie on the ground wherever they have stopped for the night.'

'Their threat is in their numbers and complete obedience to their orders,' said Edgar. 'We have never seen them show fear or any emotion, but they do make intelligent decisions. They retreat when they are beaten and coordinate attacks. Still, they are not the best trained army. Our plan had been to hold them off in our castles—keep them from breaking through into the northern half of Magnia. But duke Peyre's army gives us another option. I can bring three thousand warriors into the field to match his. Take the fight to the enemy, rather than wait in our strongholds to be overwhelmed.'

'I would agree,' Peyre said. 'My army would be best used in such a way. We are not here to garrison your castles. I can't keep them in the field for more than a few days on our own supplies.'

'Agreed,' said Rimmon. 'Before you leave to give your orders and set the plan in motion, I have some things that need to be said should the worst happen. I will use my magic to aid you. But should Ezenachi come, I must escape. The last thing I want is to become one of his slaves.'

It's the last thing any of us want, Peyre said to himself. Though he understood how a turned sorcerer like Rimmon would be a problem for them.

'If I fall today,' Rimmon continued, 'there is a task that must be carried out. I would pass it to you. For Sanc to carry out his quest and bring aid, our own task must be to hold off Ezenachi until he returns. The people of Dalriya need to unite as they did against the Isharites. But also, in that war, the seven weapons of Madria came together. None of us have the power to kill Ezenachi with them. But that doesn't mean they can't be of use.'

'Of course,' King Edgar said, 'they would be of great help. But where are they?'

Rimmon grimaced. 'I have no special knowledge about their locations. All I can do is summarise what is known. Oisin, King of the Giants, returned with his Spear to Halvia.'

'I know Oisin,' said Jesper. 'Perhaps I can get passage across the Lantinen and find him. But the last I heard, he and the Vismarians were still at war with the Drobax.'

Rimmon nodded. 'You are the best man for that task, Jesper. The champion who wielded Bolivar's Sword—Maragin—is still a Krykker chieftain. It might be possible for a party from Guivergne to meet with her,' he said, looking at Peyre.

Peyre shrugged. He knew the stories of the seven weapons of Madria. They had filled his childhood. Was he now expected to search for them? The sorcerer presumed too much if he thought Peyre would become his lackey.

'Gyrmund returned the Jalakh Bow to Khan Gansukh, as he had promised. It is said the Khan used it himself to destroy the remnants of the Isharites and their Drobax monsters. The chances of him relinquishing the weapon seem slim. I assume Moneva kept Toric's Dagger. But neither Gyrmund nor Moneva have been seen for nearly twenty years.'

'The one person who might know where Gyrmund went is Farred,' said King Edgar.

'I know Farred,' Peyre said reluctantly.

'Perhaps he can help us,' Rimmon said. 'After that, I am unsure what happened to the weapons of the fallen champions. The cloak of the Queen of the Asrai. Was it returned to their mysterious isle? The Shield of Persala that Herin's brother, Clarin, wielded. Finally, Onella's Staff, used by Soren. Maybe the other champions can shed light on their whereabouts. Maybe the Kalinthians know, since the champions fell in their capital, Heractus.' The sorcerer held his hands out, indicating he was done.

'We understand what needs to be done, Rimmon,' Queen Elfled said. 'But you will lead the search for the weapons, I am sure.'

'Indeed,' said Edgar. 'Now, I must send orders out to the castles asking for their soldiers. When we are ready, it will be an honour to fight with the warriors of Morbaine, Duke Peyre.'

Peyre nodded to the king at the compliment.

'We have taken a battering and suffered loss,' Edgar continued. 'Now it's time for revenge.'

＊ ＊ ＊

EDGAR GOT WHAT HE WANTED—A force as large as Peyre's with which to face the invaders of his kingdom. Rimmon was somewhere in the Magnian force, positioned to the right of Peyre's Morbainais. Edgar himself stood in the shield wall, stretched along a rise. The Magnians had barely any cavalry, their horses lost during the invasion of the south.

'We must beware of the Caladri wizards,' Jesper warned Peyre as they watched the enemy drawing close. Peyre had positioned his units on the same rise that looked down on the approaching army. The enemy's force comprised Lippers, Cordentines, Caladri, and any Magnians they had turned. It was larger, perhaps ten thousand to their six. But battles weren't won by numbers alone. Peyre's Morbainais were well drilled, with victories in Guivergne to draw on.

'What can we do about them?' Peyre asked. That was the problem, he knew. In Guivergne, they had Sanc and Rimmon to support them. Now, they had Rimmon only, against two Caladri sorcerers.

Jesper patted his bow. 'It's not the Jalakh Bow, but it might serve us. Taking them out seems to be our best chance. Even Sanc struggled to penetrate their magical defences.'

Peyre's anger threatened to resurface. *Why send Sanc away now, when they needed him?* But anger would get them nowhere. He knew what his father would say. *Work with what you've got, Peyre.* Wishing for more was a waste of energy and focus.

The enemy slowed, organising themselves into rows of fighters. Not a shield wall, though. The shield wall was all about discipline—warriors working together to defend and counter. But their enemies were too irregular for such a tactic. Some carried shields, but their neighbours didn't. Lippers stood next to Caladri—different sizes and different fighting styles. It was a mishmash of peoples, united only because they were under Ezenachi's control.

A few rode horses. Wilchard, Edgar's friend, was among them, according to Jesper. *We have the best cavalry on the field*, Peyre told himself, keen to find the positives as the moment of truth neared.

The enemy came. Uphill. Unhurried. Peyre tried not to dwell on the most distinctive thing about them. Not a single one spoke. It was unnerving to hear the marching feet, the clink of armour and weapons, but not even one voice.

In contrast, the Morbainais shouted, sang, and jeered at the enemy. Some took surreptitious looks behind them at Peyre. Mounted on a huge stallion in full armour, he hoped he gave them courage. For the time fast approached.

Doubts crept through Peyre's mind. Why risk his people's lives in Magnia? Why not wait for Esterel? Why was he fighting without his most steadfast supporters, like Umbert and Lord Russell? Had he gone to war without preparing properly? He imagined Esterel, sat on his throne in Valennes, being given the news of his brother's death, and the destruction of the army of Morbaine. Well. Too late to change his mind now. People would judge his decisions on what happened next.

The time had come.

He rode around the flank of his troops. They cheered his passage, and he drew on it, feeling his confidence rise. By the time he stopped before the front rank of the Morbainais infantry, it seemed every warrior shouted his name. When he scraped his sword from its scabbard and raised it aloft, they howled like mad things.

Men of all ages, some women amongst them, bared their teeth and roared. Weapons cracked against shields sounded like thunder. He had thought to say a few words, but like Esterel's coronation, there was no way he would be heard beyond the experienced men of the first rank—and they didn't need his advice. Instead, he pointed his sword towards the enemy who came for them. The challenge his warriors sent would have frozen the blood of any other army. But Peyre supposed it didn't even register with Ezenachi's Turned.

He kicked his horse and rode aside, returning to his place with his cavalry. Jesper was gone now, inserting himself within the ranks of the Morbainais. There was no one else to talk to. Not his father or Lord Russell; not Brancat or Esterel; not even Umbert, Gosse, Elger, or Syele. *You are in charge now, Peyre.*

He nodded to his trumpeters. They blew their buisines, giving the order to advance. His infantrymen moved forward in clean lines. The gap between the two armies closed rapidly as both sides marched against one another. Peyre looked across at the Magnians. They followed his lead, marching down the rise.

A crack rang out across the battlefield as the Morbainais shield wall met the enemy. The Turned didn't speak, but Peyre heard them grunt, roar, and scream in pain. They were uncomfortable noises to hear, reminding him of hunting animals more than battling men. These had been ordinary people—some of them, mere days ago. Did they deserve to get hacked to pieces on this rise? No. But they had to be stopped.

His first ranks were tearing through them. Their shields blocked and shoved, spears skewered, swords found gaps. The Turned were being pushed back under the onslaught, the bodies that fell soon stepped over by the advancing Morbainais. A different kind of opponent would have turned and run at this point, but Peyre knew the Turned wouldn't. His warriors were moving so fast that Peyre now worried about the flanks of the enemy. Longer than his lines, they could come around his infantry and attack from the side and rear, encircling them.

He watched until he could wait no longer. 'Ready! Line!' he shouted to his cavalry.

Feet were placed inside stirrups and helmets placed on heads. Pages came with lances and the Morbainais knights gathered together, their long spears pointing to the sky. Peyre's trumpeters put the mouthpieces of their buisines to their lips.

Peyre looked at the men beside and behind, waiting until he was satisfied with their positioning. 'Trot!' he shouted, and they moved off, the trumpeters repeating his command.

To lead a band of cavalry into battle has to be one of the finest things in life, Peyre thought. The weight of his armour carried by his mount; the bounce of the beast's legs across the turf; it's excitement, so keen to be unleashed; the thud of the other riders who were with him, so that together they formed a mighty, mobile hammer that could hit anywhere on the battlefield. Esterel had taken all the glory of leading the cavalry in the campaigns in Guivergne. *Now it's my turn.*

'Gallop!'

They crossed the field towards the fighting, the ground flying past. Peyre swung them out wide, then back, facing the Turned who were moving in behind his infantry. He exulted at his timing. The enemy had moved around, concentrating on the Morbainais infantry who were carving their way through their opponents. They had their backs to Peyre's cavalry. He knew the Turned wouldn't break at the sight and sound of his horsemen—they lacked the sensible fear of normal men. But with their backs to him, they wouldn't have the time to stop his advance.

'Charge!' he yelled when they got within distance.

He gave his stallion its head, and it leapt towards the enemy. The speed was exhilarating now. He lowered his lance, tucking it under his armpit to secure the weight. Even so, it took a bit of adjusting to get his grip just right. Few of the other horses had kept pace with his, but he could feel the pounding of his companions behind him. Those in the rear would fan out to the sides so they would hit in the shape of an arrow head, sharp enough to punch a hole in the enemy's defence.

The enemy heard them coming at the last moment, but there was nothing they could do—nowhere for them to run. Peyre aimed the point of his lance at a Lipper and the impact drove the weapon into its chest. As soon as he felt it stick, he released without even thinking about it, Brancat's training kicking in.

Peyre's mount buffeted a Caladri, knocking it to the ground. He drew his sword and as the creature got to its feet, he chopped into its neck, sending it back down. He heard a scream behind him and turned to see a horse had been speared by a Lipper. A group of Turned dragged at the rider. Peyre drove his stallion towards them. It reared up, kicking out at the nearest assailant, who went down like a sack of grain. As he fought to control the animal, more knights appeared with lance or sword. It was carnage, as the enemy was hacked to pieces until the rider was freed from his horse and standing on two feet.

Peyre looked around him. The ground was littered with the dead, slick with blood and innards. The enemy who had survived the charge had backed away from them, returning to the safety of their main force, which itself was still being pushed back by the Morbainais infantry. He looked across at the other side of the battle-field. The Magnians were having a tougher time of it, not progressing nearly as much. Edgar and Rimmon had talked of Caladri sorcerers and Peyre wondered if one or both were on the opposite side of the field. Perhaps they had need of his cavalry over there.

He dismounted. 'Pick up lances,' he shouted.

His cavalry was free to re-arm, and the idea of crossing to the other side of the battlefield grew in his mind—another successful charge, and they might claim a victory.

Peyre readied his force. Some held reclaimed lances, some swords, or other close-fighting weapons. Placing himself in the front row again, Peyre turned to inspect his riders before issuing the order to advance.

He took them towards the front line of the Magnian army. 'Gallop!' he shouted. But he hadn't gone far when he saw the enemy cavalry force heading their way. *They mean to hinder us.*

'Charge!' he shouted, nudging his stallion towards the threat. He could see they were Magnians. They held short weapons rather than lances and were not so well armoured as his unit. They rode in a line, not in a wedge.

As the two forces met, Peyre's confidence soared. His lance strike didn't connect cleanly, but he thought he'd done enough to knock his target from his horse. His stallion barged past the enemy horse as he drew his sword. He took a blow on the arm, but it scuffed off his armour. Then he was through the enemy. He turned his mount about, returning to the fray as the main body of his cavalry hit the enemy. He came in from behind, laying about with his sword. The space soon resembled a butcher's yard as the Turned Magnians were put to the slaughter. With only a few of them left to be mopped up, Peyre turned back towards his destination, trotting towards the Magnian lines once more.

As he did so, a wave of dizziness came over him, and he struggled to stay in the saddle. As he righted himself, he saw two of his riders had slipped from their mounts. The dizziness was affecting his whole unit. A few moments of confusion followed, before Peyre realised what the cause must be. Ezenachi had come.

'Beware!' he shouted. It came out unclear—his mouth struggling to form the word.

A ripple of energy spread across the battlefield. His horse whinnied and skipped back and forth, unsettled.

'Line!' Peyre called. He understood what was happening. Ezenachi always seemed to interfere when his army was facing a setback. *I can't allow him to turn the tables,* Peyre told himself. *Let's see what he can do against us.*

He called the trot early, knowing his cavalry weren't lined up perfectly. But he couldn't afford to wait. Catching Ezenachi by surprise was his best chance. He could see the enemy withdrawing from the Magnians as he called the gallop. As they neared the space where the two sides had fought one another, he felt the magic get stronger. His throat constricted and there was a fizzing sensation on his tongue and gums.

Suddenly, a patch of ground ahead of him seethed and churned. Peyre was forced to pull his mount up sharply. His entire unit was stopped, desperately trying to avoid clattering into one another.

Ahead, the lines of Turned parted and a single figure walked between them. One hand was pointed in Peyre's direction, the other straight ahead, which was where he looked.

'You cannot escape me this time,' it said, the voice larger than its body—dry like parched earth, echoing like some vast cavern. Ezenachi made a series of brisk, pulling gestures with his arm, as if winding in a fishing line.

From the ranks of the Magnians, Rimmon staggered towards him, caught on Ezenachi's invisible line. He raised a hand and let rip a ball of burning fire.

Ezenachi flicked his other wrist and negated the attack as if it was nothing. 'You have done it more than once. And I was wary of your young ally. A presence I have observed for a while now. Growing in power. But I sense them no longer. They are gone?'

Peyre dismounted. He drew his sword and strode towards Ezenachi, hoping that an attack might give Rimmon a chance to escape.

The creature—who looked no different to any other Lipper warrior—swivelled his head towards Peyre and made a fist.

Peyre was immobilised. What was more, he could feel his heart under pressure—it thumped alarmingly, as if threatening to explode.

'Move again, and I will finish you,' Ezenachi said, anger pouring off him. 'I asked you a question!' he shouted, turning to Rimmon, who screamed in agony at some invisible torture.

Peyre turned his head slowly to look at the Magnians. They were held in place, many on their knees. It was the same as the stories of what Ezenachi had done to the army of Brasingia. But seeing it in the flesh was a different thing entirely.

'He is dead,' Rimmon got out, face still crumpled in pain.

Ezenachi gave the sorcerer a look of disdain. 'I will get the truth from you when you become my follower.' He turned around, putting his back to the Magnians, and began to walk away.

'No!' Rimmon screamed, his face full of terror, as he was dragged behind.

Instinctively, Peyre moved to help him, but he was still restrained, and he felt his heart shudder as he tried to move. He stopped, weeping tears of frustration.

Then he saw movement from the corner of his eye. Jesper had left the infantry and crossed the battlefield, getting as far as Peyre had done. Down on one knee, he released an arrow. Peyre watched it arc high, and then come down at a frightening pace. It was close to its target. He saw Rimmon lurch at the last moment. The arrow took him in the eye. His body convulsed once, and then went still.

How did the sorcerer do that? Peyre asked himself, aghast. Move *into* the flight of the arrow? He couldn't imagine having the will to do such a thing.

Ezenachi continued to walk. When he stopped, he turned to see he was dragging a corpse behind him. He emitted a chilling roar of frustration. Peyre saw a snarl of menace appear on the god's face. 'You will pay for that.'

He shot his hand towards the Magnians.

He doesn't know who shot the arrow, Peyre realised.

As Ezenachi's hand rose, a figure ascended into the air from the ranks of the Magnians. Edgar.

The Magnians gave a desperate moan as the king was held, unmoving.

They know as well as I how this ends.

Edgar looked down at Ezenachi, brave and defiant. Then he exploded, the shattered body parts falling onto his people.

'Your king was a thorn in my side for many years,' Ezenachi told the Magnians. 'I give him credit for that. Even at the last, he surprised me, coming to fight here.' The Lipper turned to Peyre and gestured at him.

The pressure on Peyre ended. He sucked in a deep breath. *It's my turn now,* he realised.

'You turned the tide here,' he said, looking Peyre up and down. 'You are from Guivergne?'

'I am Peyre, Duke of Morbaine,' he stated, determined not to show fear. 'My king will arrive soon to drive your forces from Magnia.'

Ezenachi seemed to study him for a moment. 'Nobly said, duke.' Peyre thought his time had come but Ezenachi turned back to the Magnians.

'It was high time the Lippers took this land. It is theirs from times past, and they have waited patiently to regain it. But the Magnians have shown themselves to be brave and resourceful. So, I offer your kingdom this. Where we stand now will be the new border between our realms. The Lippers will not go beyond it. Magnians may live in peace. But if any of your people cross this border, it will be seen as an act of war. The truce will end. I will destroy Magnia and Guivergne. Their people will become my followers, just like the people of Cordence.'

Ezenachi turned from them one last time, not waiting for a response. He walked away. His entire army followed him.

At one point, Peyre had thought they would win. He didn't know what to call this outcome. He shuddered at what he had witnessed. He looked around, making eye contact with Jesper, his cavalrymen, the Magnian warriors.

Haunted faces looked back.

Peyre didn't know Queen Elfled. He was surprised to find her so strong. He had expected inconsolable wailing—her husband had been killed, after all, in a most brutal fashion. She insisted on hearing all the details. Then it was she who raised the spirits of those who had gathered in the hall of Granstow Castle.

'You defended Magnia, and most of you came back alive. That is the outcome Edgar hoped for, so don't despair that he has gone.'

The Magnian noblemen mumbled an acknowledgement. One of them, the warrior named Brictwin, who had been Edgar's bodyguard, said nothing. He seemed devoid of speech. Instead, he wore a blank look of utter loss that was hard to look at.

There was one other who looked as bad. Peyre glanced at Jesper. The forester stared at the floor, a disturbing look in his eyes. He had killed Rimmon. He had lost Sanc and his other friend, Herin, to some other world. He'd even lost Rab. He was the one who looked more alone, more vulnerable, than Elfled. She continued to speak.

'What you must do now is serve our son, Ida, as you have served Edgar so well. You must have faith in him, as I do, that he will lead us out of this nightmare.'

Peyre wondered at that. The boy was only Sanc's age. *But then, look how much faith and hope people have placed in my little brother.*

When Elfled was done, she took Peyre aside. They left the hall and walked outside together, saying nothing for a while.

'I am sorry for your loss,' Peyre said at last.

'I am broken by it,' she admitted in a quiet voice.

He looked at her. It was strange that someone who admitted such a thing could also be so beautiful.

'But there is too much for me to do now to give in to that,' Elfled added. 'Thank you again for your help. You saved us.'

Peyre felt himself go red. 'Hardly,' he said.

'I understand you must return to Morbaine now. But I trust you will tell your brother of our situation?'

'Yes, of course. I will tell him we must continue to support Magnia.'

'Thank you. Rimmon told us what our priority must be now,' she said. 'Find as many of Madria's weapons as we can. Unite the people of Dalriya.'

Peyre nodded. He wasn't going to disagree with a grieving widow.

They said their farewells. Elfled had to speak to her children. Peyre did not know how someone would go about having that conversation, but something told him the queen would cope.

Alone, Peyre stared across the fields surrounding the castle. He gazed to the northeast. To Essenberg. *I have had enough of gods and sorcerers and talk of magic weapons. I've had my fill of titles, crowns, and armies, of war and bloodshed. There is only one thing that truly matters to me anymore. I have delayed too long already.*

Hold on a while longer, Liesel. I will free you from that nest of vipers.

* * *

THIS IS the end of Book One of Heirs of War. Sanc, Peyre, and Liesel will return in Book Two.

Can't wait to find out where Sanc ends up? Continue to read Chapter One of the sequel.

ABOUT

Thank you for taking the time to read *An Inheritance of Ash and Blood*. If you enjoyed it, please consider telling your friends or posting a short review. Word of mouth is an author's best friend and much appreciated. Thank you, again. Jamie

Sign up to Jamie's newsletter and get a free digital copy of his short story collection, *Mercs & Magi*
subscribe.jamieedmundson.com

facebook.com/JamieEdmundsonWriter
twitter.com/jamie_edmundson
bookbub.com/authors/jamie-edmundson
goodreads.com/Jamie_Edmundson
amazon.com/Jamie-Edmundson/e/B06ZY1WDPH

A CRUCIBLE OF FIRE AND STEEL

BOOK TWO OF HEIRS OF WAR: A PREVIEW

Find out where Sanc ends up in the first chapter of the sequel to *An Inheritance of Ash and Blood.*

SANC

UNKNOWN LANDS, 675

Sanc was woken by a dog licking his face.

'Get off, Rab,' he croaked, pushing him away.

He sat up, feeling groggy. He looked around to get his bearings. The sun was high in the sky, suggesting it was the middle of the day. He was on a grassy slope that looked like pasture land. He and Rab were alone. He had no idea how long he'd been there. The effect of the teleportation, combined with the amount of magic used to power it had clearly left him out cold.

'Where's Herin?' he mumbled. He recalled, as Rimmon's spell had begun to teleport him away, Rab had jumped at him. He'd grabbed the dog, letting go of Herin as he did so. Did that mean Herin hadn't been transported?

He got to his feet, looking around. Standing made him dizzy. He tried walking it off, but almost fainted and sat back down. If, as Rimmon had planned, he had indeed travelled to another world, it was no surprise his body suffered for it.

Rab seemed alright, if a little confused by Sanc. But he was a good boy and lay next to his master, assuming that Sanc was going to sleep again.

'I'm sorry, boy,' Sanc said, patting him.

The area seemed uninhabited, which made him feel safe for now. He tried to think. Was it possible that Herin had come with him and decided to explore alone while Sanc slept? It would have been strange. Surely, he would have tried to wake Sanc? Sanc looked about. There was no other depression in the grass or signs of footsteps. No object had been left to let Sanc know Herin was here.

'Looks like we're on our own, Rab,' he said. 'In a strange world. I wish you hadn't done that. I could have done with Herin's help.'

But he couldn't be angry. After allowing himself some more rest, he tried walking again. It was better the second time. Taking it easy, he walked up the slope, thinking he might get to a view of the surrounding area. As he walked, the enormity of the task he faced threatened to overwhelm him. Alone in an unknown land, he had to find someone to help him defeat Ezenachi. The more he considered it, the more it sounded like madness.

He reached the top. It afforded him a good view of the area. In the direction he had walked, he could see hilly land, probably given over to pasture like the one he stood on. Back in the direction he had come from, the land was flatter.

He could see a vast lake, its far end somewhere beyond the horizon. There were settlements along its shore. He looked back and forth, weighing up the options. He might hide safely in the empty, undulating lands. But he was here to find help, so what was the point of that? The settled area by the lake might have people who could help him. He carried provisions in his pack, but they wouldn't last forever. On the other hand, a stranger from another land, who didn't speak their language, would likely be met with hostility.

Think, Sanc, he urged himself.

The language. That was the first barrier. He remembered how he had entered the mind of the Lipper prisoner in Magnia. That connection had allowed him to understand the Lipper's thoughts. Once he had, he'd discovered the Lipper didn't want to be rescued, like Herin had. He'd been loyal to Ezenachi.

Still, it was the principle that mattered. He must try to do the same with the people who lived here. Once he could communicate with them, his quest would become slightly easier.

'I will wait until night,' he said.

Rab tilted his head at the words, as if trying to understand Sanc's plan.

'I can see the light of every mind as it sleeps. That will allow me to approach someone without the risk of alarming them.'

Content that he had a plan of sorts, Sanc made his way back down the slope towards the lake. He moved into a wooded area. It allowed him to approach the outskirts of one of the lake settlements without being seen. The wooden houses were attractive and spaced out. It seemed a nice place to live.

He decided to retreat a safer distance into the woods and wait for nightfall. He settled down by a fallen white oak. He knew he should ration the food Queen Elfled had provided in his pack. But eating a little of it relieved the boredom. He had to give some to Rab, anyway. He worried if he wasn't fed, Rab might go off to hunt and get himself in trouble.

At last, the sun began to set. Sanc looked at the sky. It was no different from the sky over Dalriya. Was he really in another world? Or had he simply travelled a huge distance, somewhere beyond the sea? He didn't know how to find the answer. Occasionally, voices drifted to him from the nearby settlement, but not loud enough to hear what was being said. He waited until twilight. Only then did he close his eyes and search for the sources of light. There were a few, all of them located towards the lake area. But it was still too early. Most people must still be awake.

He waited for dusk. As it came, he was surprised to hear voices again, but this time coming from behind him. He peered through the darkness, listening. What he heard put him on edge. The heavy footsteps and male voices put him in mind of soldiers. He couldn't tell how close they were, but he was sure they were getting nearer. *It would be foolish to take risks,* he told himself. Gathering Rab to him, he cast his magic.

As the soldiers neared, they were persuaded Sanc wasn't there, crouching by the oak, hand on the hilt of his sword. The magic told them they couldn't hear Rab's nervous growling as they passed by, on their way to the lake, perhaps forty of them in all. They were warriors, alright. They seemed well armed, but looked dirty, bedraggled, and unshaven. Sanc knew that look. Men who were at war—who had been away from the comforts of home for some time.

Sanc heard them talking to one another. At least one question was resolved. He couldn't understand a thing they were saying. They were whispering, and it sounded like some of them were giving orders to the others. He let out a sigh of relief as they passed by without seeing him.

Paranoia hit him then. Could it be coincidence they had arrived at his precise location? Surely it had to be? Yet sorcerers were capable of detecting one another, especially when they used magic. There was no doubt he and Rimmon had expended a serious amount of magic to get Sanc here. Might a native magic user have detected the source and sent the warriors out to find him? The idea that a sorcerer might be out there in the darkness put him even more on edge.

Then the screaming started.

Sanc hadn't appreciated that the troop of warriors might attack the settlement on the lake. It struck home, even further, how completely ignorant he was of the land he had travelled to. He didn't know who the lake dwellers were or who their enemies were. Didn't know who was in the wrong and who was in the right. But the screams of women and children unsettled him. He doubted they had done anything to deserve punishment. He got to his feet and stood irresolute. The sensible thing was to stay out of it, surely.

No. I can't.

'Wait,' he instructed Rab.

He drew his sword and walked after the warriors. Turning, he saw Rab was following him. *He's not going to wait while I walk into danger,* Sanc realised.

'I can't treat you like a baby,' he told the dog. 'If you're coming, you must look after yourself.'

Sanc continued towards the sound of fighting and screaming.

Firelight cast flickering shadows on the scene before him. Some houses had been set alight. It was still impossible to tell what the objective of the attackers was. As he reached the first houses, two warriors came to meet him.

Their leather mail looked bulky, suggesting they had a second layer of protection underneath. Both carried spear and shield and had short swords at their belts. It made Sanc wish he had a shield with him. He patted the knife at his belt: the bone-handled weapon had been a gift from his father. Then he thought better of it. A spare hand was more useful to him than a shield or knife.

One of the men peered at him, as if trying to work out who he was. He shouted something that sounded like a challenge. Rab growled back.

Sanc kept on walking. He was committed now. He needed to find out what was happening. If it was a massacre, he had to stop it.

The warrior gave up on talking. Sanc saw him balance his weight and draw his arm backwards. He knew what was coming. The spear shot towards him.

Anger, frustration, and fear spurred Sanc on. He raised a hand, catching the spear in his magic. He turned it around in mid-air, sending it back to his enemy with interest.

The man's eyes shot wide open, but his training kicked in. He raised his shield to block the returning spear. At the last moment, Sanc tugged the man's arm to the side. The spear slammed into his chest. The blade sliced through his armour, and he was sent flying backwards by the impact.

His comrade turned and ran.

Sanc reacted quickly, desperate to stop the man from giving a warning. Sanc used his magic to hold him in place as he ran for the warrior. The man fought Sanc's restraints, pushing to free himself, and it took concentration for Sanc to hold him and move at the same time. As Sanc neared, the man gave up and turned to face him. They came together. The warrior led with his shield, trying to clatter into Sanc.

Holding his hand up, Sanc stopped his enemy's shield-arm short.

The warrior thrust with his spear. Sanc moved to one side. Just as he had been taught to do by Brancat, he raked his sword blade along the length of the pole. He caught the man's gloved hand, disarming him. His opponent tried to move, but Sanc still held his shield-arm immobile. Sanc launched an overhead swing. Seeing it, the warrior raised his free arm up to catch the blow. Changing course, Sanc shifted to the side. As he did so, he swung his sword around at shoulder height. It bit into the back of the warrior's neck, nearly severing it off. His body sank to the ground.

Sanc looked at his kills. It wasn't how he had been taught to fight, and if Brancat or anyone from Arbeost had been watching, they'd have called it dishonourable. He felt the same. But he hadn't come to this place to seek honour. He'd come to save all those people back home.

Wasting no more time, he made his way through the settlement. There was a central green that faced the lake, where a dock was full of boats. It occurred to Sanc these vessels might be a prize worth taking in time of war. There seemed little else of value.

Twenty or so warriors had gathered in this area. Kneeling or sitting on the ground, weapons pointed their way, was a large group of residents. So, it seemed the warriors weren't killing everyone. Not yet, at least. He witnessed this group of captives added to, as four warriors arrived with a woman and her two children. Once their catch was deposited, they left again. Presumably to find more.

Sanc and Rab padded away, leaving this scene for now. Better to find smaller numbers of the enemy first. He heard a struggle coming from one house. Wasting no time, he entered through the open door. Inside the open plan home, a woman and children cowered in one corner, while three warriors beat at a bloodied man. The warriors didn't know what him them. Sanc took one from behind while holding another still. Rab bit into the ankle of the other. He screamed in fright before raising his weapon to strike at the dog. Sanc thrust again, into the man's armpit. His blade sunk deep as the man cried in agony. He twisted away, crashing to the floor, taking Sanc's sword with him. Sanc let Rab deal with him for the moment. He took his knife and slit the throat of the man he was holding.

The man on the floor shouted at him as he approached, probably pleading for his life. But that wasn't possible. Sanc stamped down when he tried to move and then knelt on him. They struggled for a few moments before Sanc's knife opened another neck. He stood carefully. The floor of the house was slippery now. He was covered in blood, and worse; stunk of it. But it couldn't be helped. The man of the house had positioned himself in front of his family, perhaps trying to protect them from Sanc. Sanc pointed outside. It would be best if they left and hid in the woods until it was all over.

He'd killed five now. But that wasn't enough. Sanc wasn't ready to approach the main force on the green yet. Instead, he walked between the houses of the settlement, using the darkness as cover. He used his magic, too. He was sure the illusion of invisibility was broken if he was spotted moving about. But in these conditions, he thought it might give him an extra layer of protection.

Rab was his shadow. He understood they were hunting and stayed silent as they tracked their prey.

Five became eight, became twelve, became fifteen. By that point, the warriors knew something was up—had probably discovered some of their fallen. Sanc studied them from behind a garden wall. There were still about twenty of them. He didn't think he was rating his magic too highly to believe he could probably defeat all twenty.

But something could easily go wrong—it would just take one unseen archer, hiding somewhere, to kill him. He also had to consider the consequences. A massive display of magic like that could get him into trouble. The people who witnessed it would talk. It would be better to keep his abilities secret.

Meanwhile, the enemy seemed unsure what to do. There were plenty of raised voices, but Sanc couldn't work out what was going on. *Maybe I should do it?* he asked himself. *After all, they could have reinforcements coming for all I know. Now might be the best time.*

Then another thought hit him as if from nowhere. There was another thing he could hide if he so chose. His eyes. They had done nothing but cause him trouble his entire life. They could be the death of him here. He cast another illusion. This time, anyone who looked at him would convince themselves he had brown eyes. He had no way to test it. *If it doesn't work, so be it. I have nothing to lose.* He readied himself to leave his hiding place and face the enemy.

Just as he was convincing himself to move, the warriors acted. Whoever was in charge divided them into three groups. Two groups left the green, walking in different directions through the settlement. *Looking for me.* The third stayed with their prisoners. Only eight of them guarding around four times that number.

Sanc put a hand on Rab as one of the search groups passed nearby. Again, he used his magic to suppress sight and sound. When they were gone, he knew it was time to act. He wouldn't get a better chance.

He walked towards the group guarding the prisoners with purpose, sword in hand, limiting their time to think. They shouted at him. One put a blade at a girl's throat. Sanc ignored it all.

One of their number stepped towards him. He was large, muscular; metal rings circled his huge arms and decorated his beard, while his face was red with anger. He held a war axe two-handed. It was a fearsome looking weapon, no doubt capable of splitting Sanc in two. When his comrades came with him, he gave a curt command. He would take Sanc alone.

Sanc supposed he understood the man's confidence. Sanc wasn't much to look at compared to this warrior—a one-handed sword the only perceivable threat. He could only guess what else prompted the single challenge—perhaps if he was the leader, honour demanded he take Sanc out himself. But it played straight into Sanc's hands. If he could defeat these warriors without alerting anyone to his powers, he would feel a lot better.

'Wait,' Sanc commanded Rab.

Rab growled at the man but did as he was told.

Not giving the leader a chance to change his mind, Sanc dashed towards him. With a grin that showed his yellowed teeth, the warrior bounded towards him. He barely drew back his axe before swinging it towards Sanc. But that was as far as he got. Taking no risks, Sanc held him in place. He didn't slow his own movement and, with time to be accurate, sank his sword blade point first through his opponent's neck. Releasing his magical hold, he gripped the hilt tight with both hands. His sword came free as the man sank to the ground.

The killing may have looked odd, but Sanc was satisfied there had been nothing obvious to mark him out as a sorcerer. As the leader's men now came to avenge him, Sanc rushed towards them. Years of training, combined with his growing powers, now kicked in. As the nearest spear-wielding warrior came within range, an invisible blast of magic sent the man immediately behind him tumbling to the ground. Rab, unable to hold back any longer, was onto him, locking his jaw on a hand.

Sanc held the first warrior in the middle of his spear thrust and used all his strength to slash his sword into the man's face. As he released his hold on the warrior, two thrown axes came for him. Sanc sent them wide and ran, stabbing down at the grounded man before he could get up.

He made for the axe throwers, who were desperately drawing their swords as he came for them. Behind them, he saw another throwing axe hurtling towards him. He made sure it hit the back of the head of one axe thrower, while he ran through the other.

He'd killed five warriors in a matter of moments. As he drew breath, the fight resolved itself. A sixth warrior was bundled to the ground by a group of captives, while the remaining two turned and ran.

The people of the settlement—a few men among women and children—gaped at him. Sanc understood they didn't know what to make of him. 'Pick up the weapons,' he said, pointing at the swords and axes of the men he had killed.

They didn't understand his words, but the gesture was clear enough, and once one woman grabbed a sword, others wasted no time in arming themselves. One man, who had claimed the two-handed axe, tried speaking to Sanc. Sanc could only shrug. The man gestured at his town. Some buildings were still aflame, but with access to so much water, Sanc didn't think they would have a problem putting them out.

He gestured in the same direction. 'I will come with you to fight the other warriors,' he said, assuming that would be the man's main concern. He walked towards the buildings, and everyone came with him.

With growing confidence that Sanc was an ally, they led him through the settlement, scouring for the enemy. They found none living. The family Sanc had rescued appeared, the father's face still bloody from his beating. He pointed towards the woodland Sanc had hidden in, talking fast. He pointed at Sanc briefly. The man who had claimed the axe looked that way too, talking quietly. Sanc guessed the warriors had retreated into the trees.

The axeman organised things. He gestured at Sanc to follow him. Half a dozen of them walked towards the wooded area, then stopped, peering into the trees. Gradually, the plan became clear to Sanc. They stood guard while the rest of the people put out the fires. Sanc had to tell Rab to stay put, since the dog seemed keen to enter the woods. After a while, when the fires were out and there had been no more sign of the attackers, the man led them back into the settlement. The bodies of the dead had been collected. The people stood around for a while. The shock of the attack turned to grief as children cried and women wailed.

Now the immediate threat was over, Sanc took a moment to study these people. They looked different from the attackers. The lakesiders were mostly short and slim in stature, with brown eyes and hair. Their attackers were much larger, with long hair of varying shades. *I'm still completely ignorant of who they are and what has gone on here,* he complained to himself bitterly.

The axeman spoke to Sanc. He looked as frustrated as Sanc felt at their inability to communicate. Sanc put the palm of his hand to his own chest then pointed to the man, who seemed to be a leader here, before gesturing towards a house. Seeming to understand, the man gave out some orders to those around him before leading Sanc to the house.

They entered. It was an open plan design like the others Sanc had been in, with a central fire. Sanc sat down by the fire, placing his sword on the ground. The man did the same, depositing his axe while he muttered some words.

Holding his hands up, Sanc leaned forward, then slowly moved his arms. The man looked at him questioningly, his round eyes hesitant about whether to trust this strange newcomer.

'It's alright,' Sanc said, knowing the man didn't understand the words, but might be reassured by the tone. 'I just need to learn your damned language.'

The man let Sanc place his hands on each side of his head. Sanc closed his eyes and searched for the connection to the man's mind. It was there, glowing with a faint light. Just as before, the process of trying to speak to him telepathically led Sanc to the part of his mind that controlled language. Once he identified it, he found he could draw the information he needed.

Sanc gasped as he withdrew his hands. He felt woozy now. He'd drawn on the last of his reserves. He'd hardly been careful with the amount of magic he had used today. Rimmon had warned him countless times about this. *I must learn to be more disciplined,* he told himself. *Work within my limits. I could have tried this task tomorrow, after a night's sleep. What if more warriors come?*

He opened his eyes, focusing on the man before him. He frowned as he concentrated on what to say. Understanding a language did not mean it was easy to speak it. 'Can you understand my words now?' he asked.

The man's eyes shot open in surprise. He spoke quickly, excitedly, and Sanc couldn't follow what he said.

'Slower.'

Now it was the other man's turn to frown in concentration as he chose what to say. 'Thank you for saving us.'

'You are welcome.'

'Did the king send you to help us?'

So, there is a king somewhere. Sanc had so many questions, but he had to be wary of revealing too much. If these people realised how little he knew—that he had come here from some other world—they might become scared of him. At the same time, lying might cause problems later.

'No. I sent myself.'

The man frowned. Sanc didn't think he'd said that last bit very well. But being vague about himself wasn't a bad thing right now.

'My name is Sanc,' he offered.

That was a better place to start. The man put a hand to his chest. 'Cleph. You will stay in this house tonight.'

'Thank you,' Sanc said.

Cleph smiled. Then his face became serious again. 'First. Will you help us bury our dead?'